CAPTURED BY THE ALIEN

ALIEN WARRIOR MATES I - THE COMPLETE COLLECTION

GRACE KENSINGTON

1

The hairs on the back of my neck stood. It happened every time my boss was near. He gave me the creeps and on more than one occasion I had to politely remind him to keep his filthy hands to himself. Ever since I turned down his advances he made up his mind to give me the worst cases and projects. I lifted my tired eyes to see him standing in front of my desk with a smirk. I knew that look. It meant he had something planned—and I wasn't going to like it.

"Ms. Baines, I have a new assignment for you."

Leaning back in my chair I nodded giving him permission to sit in the chair and waited for him to spit it out.

"You're going on a trip."

"Where to?"

"Uoria."

I gulped. Out of all the places he could have sent me and it was to the planet full of the most temperamental species humans had ever studied. "What for?"

"We need to learn more about them, what's in their blood."

I gasped. "You know that's against the rules, Ryan." Everyone knew that the King and Queen made the rules. They still allowed us to do testing, but never of their blood. And I knew what happened to those who tried getting the blood of a Denynso. They never came back that's what.

He shrugged. "You're sneaky enough and no one pays much attention to you. We need to know what makes them so powerful."

His eyes lit up and I shuddered. I knew exactly why he wanted a sample of their blood. It was the same reason every other scientist wanted it, and it was exactly why they had all failed.

"Oh, and preferably the blood from their strongest warrior is what you need to get. You've heard of him, right?"

Of course, I had. Everyone in my line of work had heard of the monstrous Denynso called Pyra. He was one mean son of a bitch and no one wanted near him. Well, besides all the women that vied for a place in his bed. But there was nothing scientific about that.

"You know I won't do that."

He shrugged. "Then your job and reputation are as good as gone. You'll never work again. Not in this field!" He spun on his heel and looked over his shoulder. "Might as well practice saying, "Do you want fries with that?" because that's the only work you'll ever get. You know how much we need this information."

"Wait," I said and sighed. I couldn't lose my job. It was all I had, my livelihood. I'd have to find a way to convince the leaders to let me have a sample and test it. Maybe fudge the results or something. I would find a way. "I'll do it!" I prayed I lived long enough to explain why I was asking for the one thing they'd refused since we learned of their species.

His smile widened as if he had won the biggest prize. He knew I wouldn't be coming back and that was his plan all along. They'd kill me before I got close enough to the warrior, and if I managed to sneak by, he'd break my neck with two fingers. I shuddered. This wasn't going to be a fun vacation. I needed to form a plan and offer the Denynso something they couldn't resist, but I didn't have anything—not really. I only hoped I could get them on the off chance that they wouldn't want me to lose my job. Maybe they'd feel sorry for me, throw me a bone or something. No matter how small it was, I'd take it.

"Good, I knew you'd see it my way. You need to be ready at four a.m."

Then he left me stewing knowing he'd given me an impossible task. If I was going down, I was taking that piece of shit down with me. I smiled evilly. They were an angry species. It shouldn't be too hard to piss them off and let them know it was all Ryan's idea.

After he left me alone, I did what I was best at. I hacked the system and copied the surveillance from my office. Right there I'd be able to prove what was going on to the Denynso, if I could play it. I already knew there wasn't electricity, but I'd charge my laptop for that purpose alone. Proof my boss was a scumbag and it was his idea to send me there to specifically break their rules. Maybe I'd have a chance to survive my stay there, but coming back home wouldn't be so great.

I was ready to go and waited for my boss well before four. I hadn't slept at all. All night I planned how I would handle the situation my boss had put me in. I knew they would be expecting another scientist. I'd have to meet with them before I step foot on their compound. From what I had learned it was a very secure planet. Warriors scoured the land to keep watch over the humans, and were on the lookout for an attack from their enemies.

I shuddered and thought about what I'd heard about their enemies. There were several horror stories of the attacks on Uoria. The Klimnu were disgusting beasts. Luckily, they hadn't managed to make it to Earth yet or humans would be in big trouble.

Ryan strolled up to me at four on the dot and smiled handing over my paperwork.

"Here's all the stuff you'll need when you get there. I have you down as routine testing for plant and animal life. You're there for up to six months. That should be plenty of time to get what I need." He gave me a look and I didn't miss the tone.

I nodded, but inside I was fuming. He was trying to get me killed. I was his competition, and the one that turned his ass down. He didn't take rejection well, and now I was paying for it. But I was smarter than him and would come out on top.

"All right, well you know how to get in contact if you need anything, but I'm sure you won't."

I kept my mouth shut because this was all a fucking set up. I couldn't believe he'd stoop so low, but maybe it had something to do with the fact that I was up for the promotion he wanted. Luckily, I'd learned to control my Irish temper. My mother always told me one day it would come in handy to have self-control, and now I was learning.

Without a word, I picked up my bags and boarded the ship. I was nervous as hell. This was the first time I was traveling to another planet, and I wasn't too sure about it. I wasn't the type of person who wanted to experience new things. I'd much rather stay in the lab by myself. I felt Ryan's eyes burning into my back and straightened without turning back. He wouldn't get a rise out of me. As soon as the metal door clanged closed I let out the breath I'd been holding and muttered, "stupid ass mother fucker." He would get his.

The very human pilot chuckled. Apparently I spoke a little louder than I thought. Oh well. Everyone knew how I felt about Ryan so it wouldn't be a surprise that I'd be cursing him. They also knew I had a temper and I held a grudge like no other. I glared at the man and he shrugged before getting ready to take off.

The ship shook and my stomach dropped. Leaning back in my seat I held my breath and closed my eyes. My hands gripped the arm rests and I clenched my teeth as I was lifted into the air at an unknown speed. My stomach rose back up into my throat and I nearly lost what little I had eaten. As soon as the ship leveled some I was able to relax but the speed hadn't slowed and I kept my eyes shut hoping the medication I had taken would kick in soon knocking my ass out.

I woke up to the pilot shaking me. I swung my fist and smiled when I heard the satisfying crunch of the bone in his nose breaking. I didn't like being touched especially without permission.

"Shit!" he shrieked. "What the hell, I was only waking you up. I've been trying for nearly an hour. These warriors are starting to get antsy."

I shot up and grimaced. "Sorry," I replied sheepishly. Now I felt bad. "Sorry about your nose."

"It fucking hurts. No wonder everyone is scared of you." His eyes watered and he'd lifted his shirt to catch the blood.

I smirked. "Yeah, well next time refrain from touching me. Use a blow horn if you have to, but keep your damn hands to yourself."

He nodded and winced. "You got it, but please get the hell of my ship."

I stood and stretched knowing I'd just slept for probably five days. My body wasn't ready to stand and I wobbled but caught myself before I fell. "Give me five."

He didn't respond so I took it as an okay and paced the small area while the rest of my body woke up. I needed to be alert when I met the King and Queen. My insides fluttered like butterflies. I wasn't the biggest socialite and meeting people, human or not, wasn't my thing. After the given five minutes I walked behind the pilot and laid a hand on his shoulder. He jumped and looked at me in fear.

"Thank you for the ride, and again, I'm sorry about your nose."

He nodded curtly. The bleeding had stopped but his right eye was almost swollen shut. "I'll remember the blow horn next time."

I chuckled. At least he was able to find humor in getting his ass kicked by a woman.

I stepped off the ship and gasped. It was so familiar, yet not. Everything was so alive. The grass waved in wind, and the sky was almost violet with pinks and oranges. It was breathtaking. I stood taking in the surroundings. The ship rumbled to life vibrating the ground. I didn't even bother looking back. I was stuck here for the next six months. Life was about to get a whole hell of a lot more interesting.

My view was blocked by the largest body I had ever seen. Even I felt tiny compared to the beast in front of me, and instinctively I balled my hands into fists. I had to be in front of the warrior everyone spoke about.

"You're the new one?" he asked in a gruff voice that vibrated along my skin. The sound shot right through my body.

I gulped and looked up, and then up some more before nodding. "Yes, I'm Eden Baines."

He smirked down at me. "Come, you must meet the King and Queen." His voice was a bit tenser, and I wondered why. Must have been that temper I had heard about.

3

Pyra wanted to roar. The moment she spoke, something inside of him came to life. As a heat so intense filled him, he was barely able to hold back his gasp. It wasn't acceptable. This measly human was not his mate. She was tiny. There was no way she'd be able to handle all seven feet, and three inches of him.

He wasn't ready to be shackled down by the all-consuming love he'd feel for her. His body was already going through the change, and they hadn't even touched. He'd had this feeling for days. He was edgier than normal, though for him that wasn't saying much. Now he understood why he had flown off the handle more than once and fought five of his brethren.

He stalked to the main house, not looking back. He couldn't look at her, not yet. He wasn't sure he'd be able to keep his hands to himself if he really *saw* her. From what he'd seen she was perfect. Fairly tall for a human woman, pale skin, fiery red hair, that he knew would match the glint in her bright green eyes. He noticed every tiny freckle that dusted her skin. He hadn't missed the slight gap between her two front teeth when she spoke. He also didn't miss the way she averted her eyes or didn't offer her hand like most of the others did. She didn't want to be there, he could tell right off.

She did well to keep up with him. She kept space between them, and it was only her heavy breathing that let him know that his pace was too fast. His mind automatically went to helping his mate and he slowed—too much so, because she slammed right into him and flew back from the force of hitting him.

She yelped and skidded on the soft grass. "Hey fucker," she yelled.

He spun around surprised by the vulgar word coming from her sweet looking lips.

"You nearly killed me!" She stood and wiped her hands on her jeans. Her face was flushed from anger. When she realized all the warriors nearby stopped, her flush deepened and she looked at the ground nibbling her lip.

Pyra wanted to brush her hair from her face, wanted to suck that lip, but instead he bowed his head. "I apologize."

She glared up at him as if she thought he wasn't serious, but she nodded and started walking again. He turned back around and turned toward the path to the Great House.

He could hear the loud thump of her heart but kept his eyes forward. She was a spitfire, but now she was embarrassed. He could sense it. "You know, you sound much like us when we get pissed. You have a formidable temper." he called over his shoulder.

"So I've heard," she grumbled and he chuckled.

"Here that's normal, don't feel embarrassed by your outburst. My brothers were all just surprised to see a human act like us so much."

"I usually have better control."

"I doubt it. I think you react without thinking 90 percent of the time."

"If that was the case I'd have lost my job the first time my boss touched my ass. So no, I think I'm good with control."

He liked her snarky attitude, but what she said pissed him the hell off. He spun and again she ran into him apparently not paying attention and this time before she flew back he gripped her shoulders and held her up. She gasped and looked at him with wide eyes. She felt it too. The touch of the mate, he closed his eyes and bit his lips trying to gain control. All it took was the one touch and he wanted to throw her on the ground and ravage her until she knew who she belonged to. He rubbed his thumbs in circles on each shoulder and then the pain hit.

The little woman brought her knee up a second time when the first wasn't enough. She kneed him hard and shoved him back. Dammit she was tough. He buckled over and groaned. When he lifted his eyes he knew there was fire in them because she backed away fearfully.

"That fuckin' hurt!"

"Well don't touch me asshole!"

Oh yes, she was his. As much as his nuts hurt, his dick was still harder. Her hands were fisted in defense and her chest heaved. More strands of her hair fell from the tie and surrounded her face. Her pouty lips puckered up and her nose scrunched adorably.

When he could stand normally again, because he wasn't lying, it had hurt like a bitch. She was one tough human. "You are amazing," he breathed.

She froze and he could see her body shaking in rage. Someone had hurt her because she learned very quickly that she did *not* like to be touched.

She stood tall and waited, for what he wasn't sure, but he knew she wasn't going to be easy. His mate would challenge him. He smiled thinking his life just got a hell of a lot more interesting. "I won't touch you, but this time I was trying to keep you from getting hurt."

She glared. "Fine, but let's get a move on please. I need to talk to your King and Queen."

"Very well." He wasn't happy that she didn't seem to like him; not even a little bit. He was the type that grew on others over time. Yeah that was it. He led the way and met his parents. They'd heard the commotion and were about to send his brothers for him. He shook his head.

"It's okay she doesn't like being touched." He told them with a shrug. She was behind him so she didn't see the look that passed between him and his parents. His father smirked and his mother, though leery, smiled wide. That was all they needed to know, and no harm would come of her. Ever.

She stood beside him after she had composed herself and gasped. His parents made quite an impression. Father with his foot-tall Mohawk, much like his own, and his pure orange eyes signifying his mating. He was even taller than Pyra at seven and a half feet tall. He had jagged scars from the battles he had survived. They were a badge of honor for their kind. His mother had knee length white hair and her eyes were also orange but lighter. She was tall, thin, and at nearly seven feet her frame was willowy.

"Dr. Baines meet Queen Thiea and King Creia."

She bowed and stepped in front of him. "It's very nice to meet you. Sorry about the—commotion."

His father chuckled. "That's nothing dear. It's common for stifles here. You are Eden correct? I do not like all these—formalities you humans use."

"Yes, I'm Eden."

"Very well, come in dear."

She seemed surprised by how accepting their kind could be. As long as the humans followed their damn rules, and there weren't many. Don't hurt any of them. Don't lie to them, and don't try to steal their blood. Simple, yet so many humans broke those rules. Pyra hoped his human would be the exception. He'd hate to have to protect someone he didn't trust.

4

———

I followed the King, who looked very much like the warrior following behind me and gasped. No wonder he was so well known. He had a temper, was a cocky son of a bitch, and he was the King and Queen's son. It all made sense now. There was no way in hell I'd get a sample of his blood. Ryan was out of his god damn mind if he thought I'd even try. The man was huge, and I had a feeling it wouldn't be hard for him to snap me in two.

I felt the warrior behind me. My back stayed tense as he stared at me. He kept a good distance between us, but the heat coming from him was outrageous. I looked over my shoulder to see a strange flicker of orange in his eyes. It looked like the King's but it didn't last before they shifted back to blue. I blinked and faced forward so I didn't keep making an ass out of myself. There was something about the giant that brought out the worst in me. I didn't like how my heart raced or my pulse fluttered deep inside.

The King led me into a huge room with a huge table. It was filled with all sorts of food I had never seen before and my stomach dropped. Trying new things wasn't really my thing. I had brought food for myself that would last a year so I wouldn't starve. Pyra seemed to sense my discomfort and he huddled close behind me.

"It's okay. The food is actually a lot better than it looks," he whispered.

He was too close. I could smell his scent. It was a bit spicy and my mouth watered. Suddenly I was hungry for something other than food. "I'm not hungry." I was going to be stubborn as hell. No way would I admit anything going on inside of me right now. I couldn't allow it to happen. It didn't matter that he was the sexiest man I'd ever met, or that I couldn't remember the last time I'd been with a man. No part of his body would touch any part of mine. I was here to study their land. Maybe I would be able to convince myself of that eventually.

He chuckled and I felt his breath whisper across the back of my neck. I clenched my teeth holding back my building anger. Anger was good. I could deal with being pissed. That was normal.

"Please get out of my space," I hissed.

He didn't move back. Instead he placed one of his giant fucking hands on my hip. If I didn't want to look like a complete asshole I had to deal with it, but he would pay. I smiled at the thought of kneeing him in his groin again. This time I wouldn't go easy on him. "If you want to keep that hand, I suggest you remove it from my body," I whispered sweetly.

He leaned into my space even more. Damn he was

arrogant. It didn't seem to matter what the species was, apparently males were all alike.

"Make me.", he taunted. He wanted me to lose my temper. I couldn't—no I wouldn't give him the satisfaction.

"You're gonna regret this, warrior." I officially hated him. I couldn't see why the women all wanted him. Sure, I bet his body was unbelievable, but his attitude sucked. I didn't appreciate men who thought they were god's gift to women. He didn't respect boundaries and that was a big thing for me. I couldn't stand someone who thought they didn't have to stay out of my personal space.

"Oh yeah?" He rubbed his finger across my hip bone, slow and intimate, too intimately. I was going to murder him. "I look forward to anything you dish out, angel."

I chuckled. No one had ever accused me of that before. "We'll see."

Every word that slipped from my lips was met with a touch that threatened to bring me to my knees. I wouldn't let him win. It was physical, that was it.

The King cleared his throat and his smirk in my direction was unsettling. It was as though he was waiting us out.

"Sit please dear."

I gulped and pulled away from the hulking man behind me, but he stepped around me and pulled out the chair. My eyes widened in surprise. I didn't think he had a gentle bone in his body.

He shrugged. "What? My mother raised me too."

I nodded and sat down waiting for the King to tell me the rules. I knew he'd tell me, and I had planned to talk to him about my boss, but I didn't want to do it in front of the warrior.

"I'm sure you know that we are graceful in letting humans invade our lands to run tests, and learn more about our species..."

I nodded.

"There are a few things we do not allow however, and under no circumstances are those rules to be broken. The paper you signed gives us the right to punish you within our laws if you break them in any way."

Again I nodded. I hadn't known that, but then again I should have read the fine print. *If* I made it home I was going to make Ryan sing soprano. He was going to wish he was dead by the time I was done with him.

The King's eyes slanted. "Do you speak, Eden?"

I shrugged. "I'm not much of a talker, or a socialite for that matter. I speak when I have something important to add to the conversation."

"I see," he replied. He was curious about me.

"So, I assume you won't be causing problems. Other than the temper I've already witnessed." With that he smiled.

I blushed. "I do have a temper. Usually it's easier to control."

"Ah, Pyra brings out the worst in you then, or maybe the best yes?"

I laughed I couldn't help it. "I highly doubt my temper is to be considered my best, no offense."

Pyra stiffened and when I glanced at him, he was looking at me strangely. I wasn't sure what he was thinking but he was focused on something. I looked down to see if I had gotten something on my clothes but there wasn't anything there so I shrugged. He was strange. The fact that I was so aware of the giant man sitting silently at the table didn't sit well with me. I didn't like it, not even a little bit.

5

———

Eden's emotions were so strong that Pyra could nearly taste her nerves. He wasn't sure what triggered it, but he noticed her eyes widened and the scent of her fear coated his skin. He watched her, waiting for another sign as to what could have scared her but she was tough and almost as fast as he felt it, it disappeared. Her posture was still stiff and her jaw was clenched tight.

"Is there anything you would like to ask?" his father asked.

Pyra didn't miss her gaze shift to his uneasily then back to his father.

"I'd like to talk to you," she said and licked her lips. "I'd like for him to leave the room first if you don't mind."

The King's brows rose as did his. He didn't want to be away from her, but at his father's nod he fumed. "Very well," he said to her. He gestured for Pyra to leave. What the hell?

"But—"

His father shook his head warning him with a flare to his orange eyes. "No, it's fine. You may wait for her outside so you can take her to her home while she is here."

He growled and need surged through him. He didn't want her anywhere but with him or with anyone but him. It was outrageous how he was feeling. "Fine," he replied and then he shoved the chair knocking it back. Before leaving he leaned against the back of Eden's chair. His face was right next to hers and he smiled when she shuddered. She wasn't as unaffected as she appeared. "I'll be waiting for you, and then we will talk." It was a promise as much as it was a threat. She'd better not try to sneak off without him.

He could feel her glare. "Don't hold your breath."

He loved her temper. Their relationship was going to be volatile, but for some reason he had a feeling she was going to temper him down. Already he was feeling softer, gentler. He wasn't sure if that was a good thing or not, hopefully it didn't interfere with anything outside of the home. With her he could be different, but with everything else in his life, his temper and rage was a necessity.

He chuckled and took a chance kissing her cheek. He knew she'd hold it together in front of his father. Her body went rigid and he felt her breath stopped for a second before she breathed heavily. Pyra groaned as soon as his lips met her flesh. Her skin was so soft and her scent was so sweet. He couldn't wait to have her. His cock hardened thinking about how soft she'd feel when she submitted to him. He could imagine her sprawled out on his bed and kissed her cheek once more before tearing himself away from her. His eyes shifted to orange and in a rough voice he said, "I'll be outside waiting for you."

She didn't even look at him, but he could feel her rage. She wanted to hit him—badly. He'd be prepared for her anger, but hopefully talking with his father would give her time to cool down. He'd pay for kissing her—twice, but with a smile he realized he didn't care. It was worth it.

He glanced at his father and frowned. His dad was watching her body language. He noticed something Pyra didn't and that meant he needed to talk to his dad.

"Pyra if you would please step out while Eden and I speak, and then and I'd like to have a word with you afterwards." His tone was low and brooked no argument. She wouldn't have noticed the tenseness, but a lump formed in his throat. Something was off with his mate, it was the only explanation.

He nodded and strode outside wondering what his father sensed that he hadn't.

6

———

As soon as the door shut and Pyra was away from me my body relaxed. His touch and taunts were going to drive me mad. I hated them, but worst of all it was because I hated how much I enjoyed his banter, enjoyed his touch. I'd never liked a man's touch before, and that was the worst part of this. My own personal demons would try to suck me in and I'd fall into the nightmare that used to be my life.

Things I hated to think about normally bubbled to the surface, invading all thoughts and feelings, but with him, my past was almost a distant memory. Only my body instinctively reacted as if I was reliving every horrid thing that happened back then. I shuddered. I would never be normal.

"My dear, you look as though you've seen a ghost." He leaned back in his chair and his kind eyes calmed me. There was something about this male that put me at ease. I didn't get it.

"Are you unwell? I know my son can be overwhelming, and I would apologize for his behavior, but I can't because I understand it."

If that wasn't vague or anything.

I didn't understand his son's behavior. It wasn't appropriate, but who was I to tell the King his son needed a lesson in human boundaries. "I'm fine." Leaning forward in my chair and resting my hands on the table I took a deep breath. "My boss sent me here to do the testing."

"Yes, I'm aware of Dr. Austin. I find him to be quite —disturbed."

I chuckled. "That's an understatement, but I'm not here to tell you how much of a creep he is. I need to come clean before you found out somehow—most likely by him."

Now the King straightened in his seat. Not as relaxed as he was. "Come clean? For what?"

I licked my lip and smiled. "He didn't send me here to study plant and animal life."

"Go on."

"He sent me here to try to sneak the blood of your most powerful warrior." I gulped. "I didn't plan to come, and in fact I refused at first, but Ryan hates me. He threatened me so I agreed, but I swear I have no intention of trying to steal any of your blood. I'm an honest person, and I generally don't let others control me, but my work is the only thing I have. If he fired me, I would be ruined. I needed to get him off my back long enough to go over his head. If I get transferred to another company during the time I'm here, then I won't have to worry about him any longer."

The whole time the King watched me as if assessing me for any signs of a lie. "And why would he do such a drastic thing to you, knowing the possibility of you being killed?"

I shuddered. "Two reasons. The first is because I'm up for the same promotion he wants. I'll probably get it because unlike him I have morals and I'm more qualified. And two, he's been trying to get me to date him for years and has sexually harassed me on more than one occasion. I've rejected him more times than I can count."

I hoped that my honesty paid off. I didn't tell people my personal issues, and Ryan's persistence was quite the problem.

"Do you have proof?" I didn't miss the strange look in his eye.

I sighed. "I have surveillance video, but on the video, it shows me agreeing to do it, but I swear I won't go anywhere near your warriors, especially the one Ryan requested the blood from. I'll stick to animals and plants like I originally planned."

He nodded and his frown deepened. "Don't make a promise you can't keep, my dear. Staying away from that particular warrior isn't' going to be an easy task."

"It will if he leaves me alone. If he won't then I promise not to go near him with a needle."

He chuckled and nodded. "Very well, I believe you. I don't sense any lies, but I still want to see this surveillance you speak of. I don't like knowing that someone is actively trying to steal our blood. I think he isn't much of a man to send you to do the dirty work and that angers me very much. We won't be working with this Dr. Austin again. If you're telling the truth, you can stay as long as you'd like to complete your tests of our lands."

I nodded and my shoulders fell. A weight had been lifted. "I need my bag."

"Very well, I will also need my son to see this video. He needs to be briefed in case Dr. Austin sends someone else when he realizes you won't do his dirty work."

I gulped, but shrugged. "Okay my bag is outside."

"Wait here."

I sat back as the King disappeared to get his son. That man was going to be the end of my self-control. I could feel my temper as it mixed with desire. Dammit I needed to cool the hell down, and I certainly didn't need a man to help me in any way.

PYRA CAME BACK with the King carrying my bags. He smiled at me, and I nearly lost my breath. It was such an unrefined looked. All of the tough, 'I am man, hear me roar' persona was gone. It was the most real I'd seen him, and I wasn't sure how I felt about seeing his 'human' side. I didn't want to like him. As long as he pissed me off I would be okay.

He handed me my bag and sat in the same chair he had vacated and leaned back in a relaxed position, but I wasn't fooled. He was tensed back like a Cobra waiting to strike. I'd be lying if I didn't find it completely and utterly sexy.

"So, we have a stupid doctor on our hands, yeah?"

The king must have filled him in. I didn't miss the anger in his tone. I knew it was horrible to learn because they'd been working with Ryan for several years now, and I was taking that trust away. I pulled my laptop bag onto the table and slipped my small notebook out. I booted it up and tapped my fingers on the table. "I don't know how well it will work here, or how long my battery will last."

"As long as we see what you told me about."

I looked at him with serious eyes. "You will."

I went back to work and signed in. The file opened easily, and I turned the screen to the king and prayed he would believe me when I told him I had no intention of following through. I really didn't want to endure the kind of punishments they had in mind, and for some reason I really wanted him to trust me, to like me. It wasn't often I cared what someone believed of me, but I found myself caring very much what the King of Uoria thought of me.

The video played and the King watched in fascination as the whole scene played out—just as I had told him.

"What a fucking bastard!"

I jumped when the King slammed his fists on the table and then shoved his chair back. It crashed against the wall and shattered. I had a feeling I was about to see exactly how deadly this species was. He sped from the room, but I barely saw him move. It was unreal. One minute he was there and then poof he was gone. Pyra looked as shocked as I felt.

"Whatever you told him—must have been verified and bad. I haven't seen him this pissed off in ages." Pyra's voice sounded numb to my ears.

"I told the truth before someone else did."

"I'm almost afraid to watch because if he reacted that way, I can't imagine how I'd react."

I sat back and sighed. "Is he coming back?"

"Yes, when he calms down."

I leaned back and closed my eyes wondering if I was going to be punished for my part even though I would never betray them. I'd only be on Uoria for a short time, but I felt— almost at home. When I opened my eyes again he stood there staring at my laptop.

Pyra must not have been able to ignore his curiosity. He stood where his father's chair had been and played the video. The further the video went the more his posture changed, his eyes flared, his body tensed and his jaw was tight. I could hear his teeth grinding together, but he was so calm when he closed the lid to my laptop.

"My father already told me some of why you agreed, but I need to know. I need to hear it from you that you swear you won't try to steal anyone's blood, especially mine."

I gulped. I didn't' get what was so special about their blood but it wasn't my place. I never intended to step where I wasn't allowed. I was a rule follower. "I swear. I only said I would so he wouldn't take my life away from me. Without being a scientist, I'm nothing. It's all I have in the world. I would never break the rules like that, and Ryan knows that, but he didn't expect me to come clean and show you proof of what he is trying to do. He wants me punished."

Pyra's eyes bored into mine. "Why though? Why would he risk your life?"

"He hates me."

"Why?" he asked in a whisper and stepped closer to me.

I could feel his rage, see his body shaking and instead of scaring me, it aroused me. I knew he wouldn't hurt me, but I didn't know why or how I knew it. I just did.

"We are up for the same promotion. He really wants it."

Now he stood in front on me and I looked up. "It's more than that yeah?"

I gulped. "I don't know."

"Don't lie to me; I know what you told my dad."

Of course he told him about the other stuff. I'd hoped he hadn't and now he was testing me. It didn't feel good. "I rejected him."

"Why did you reject him?"

I chuckled. "Because I hate him."

"No other reason?"

"I don't like to be touched, and he has a problem keeping his hands to himself. I've broken his nose and his wrist."

He nodded and moved closer. Our bodies were almost touching, but not quite. I couldn't breathe. His body heat was suffocating. He was a man in every sense of the word, and I was drowning in his want, his need.

"He didn't leave me alone," I whispered.

"I'll kill him."

I gasped and shook my head. "No."

He leaned in and his lips were so close I could taste him. As soon as I shut my eyes and was about to close the distance the king came back in a whoosh and cleared his throat. I jumped back from Pyra and shook my head. I glared at him and he stepped back. I was pissed at myself. I almost caved, and if not for his father I would have felt his lips on mine. I wasn't sure what was worst; the fact that I yearned for the touch and it was interrupted or that he had the balls to try it in the first place.

7

The King came back into the room interrupting the almost kiss. I was grateful because I didn't want to cave. No matter how much my body disagreed with my mind. It didn't matter that he was attractive and that there was a huge part of me that wanted to jump him. I didn't know what was going on, but I couldn't allow it to happen. His growl of frustration sent a thrill down my spine.

His father sat back down considerably more calm, but the rage was right below the surface, simmering. "Dear, I wanted to say thank you for coming forth with this video and being honest right away. Not many of you would do that, and I know that I've had to send many humans back home because I'd caught them doing unfavorable things. I wish there were more people like you from your world. After speaking to my wife, we have decided to discuss a compromise. I will get back with you when we decide exactly what it will be. Until then, please explore as much as you'd like, but keep the rules in mind, and do not under any circumstances, contact your boss. If you do, you'll be sent home, and you'll never be allowed to come back."

I sighed in relief. "Thank you for trusting me, and I have no intention of contacting Ryan. I look forward to studying the plant and animal life."

He stared me down with gentle eyes. "I don't know why I trust you, but please don't abuse it. I do hold grudges once the faith is broken."

I held out my hand, the first initiation of physical contact. He looked at my hand then back at my face as he pulled my hand into his. They were warm and soft and instead of shaking it he grasped it between both of his hands. Heat engulfed me and there was a strange zing, almost like magic before a slight bit of pain, and when he pulled back there was a small symbol on my hand. I gasped and studied it. It was small and the black lines swirled and twisted nicely together. It was intricate, but when I looked harder I noticed the lines were letters.

"It's a mark. Letting others know you are one of us now. It's means, 'sister of our brethren' in our language."

I knew they didn't do this often—if at all, and I was honored. Tears filled my eyes and I sniffled. "Thank you. I promise you won't regret it!"

He smiled. "And you don't have to worry about your problem back home anymore."

"I didn't tell you what he did to have you fix it. I was dealing with it."

He rolled his eyes and I swear he looked just like his son. "I know which is why I did it." He smiled and rubbed the mark. "And how exactly have you handled it? By ignoring his advances and threatening him. You're tough, but apparently it didn't work or he wouldn't have sent you here to break our most sacred rule."

I slumped in my seat. "I didn't know what to do."

"You can stay here." Pyra said and I looked at him. I'd forgotten he was even in the room.

"Uh, I don't know if I'd fit in here too well. Besides you never let humans stay for more than six months, though I'll stay the whole allotted time if that's all right. The longer I'm away from home the better right now."

"There are exceptions to every rule," he said but he watched his father as if waiting for him to chime in.

The king nodded and smiled kindly at me. As much as Pyra drove me wild with anger and the harder it was getting to fight his advances, I felt the exact opposite about his father. I felt at ease with him. I'd never had a dad, but if I could imagine one, King Creia would be the perfect image.

"You may stay. When my mate and I decide on what we plan to do we will have lunch, but for now you must get settled. Pyra will take you to your cabin."

I nodded and stood. "Thank you, I'm exhausted." And I was. I'd 'slept' the whole way, but it wasn't really sleeping. I was basically unconscious the whole time.

Pyra stood and walked over to his father. They hugged and I heard faint whispers, but I was too tired to care. I picked up my laptop and slid it back into my bag.

He took the strap from me. "I've got it."

Normally I would have fought him, but every part of me hurt. I don't know why it took so long to kick in, but I wasn't sure if I'd make it much longer before crashing. "Thanks," I muttered.

He nodded and I followed behind him leaving the

house. He jogged down the stairs and I sighed. My legs were heavy, and it felt like I wasn't moving at all. Pyra stopped and studied me.

"I could carry you if you want." I didn't miss the tone. He was messing with me. I thought.

That was all it took to wake my body up enough to get moving. "In your dreams warrior," I sneered at him.

He laughed and spun walking down a path. I followed as fast as I could. I would not give him the satisfaction of knowing I really wanted to drop to the ground and sleep for a week.

8

He'd been so close to tasting those suckable lips, and then his father had to come back and ruin it all. She was so beautiful, perfect really. He loved that she was honest. The video had made him want to rip the man to shreds, but it was what his father had told him about the scumbag that really pushed him over the edge. Sexually harassing his mate, now that was grounds for killing.

There was so much to her. She clearly had a problem with others touching her. He wanted to know what had happened. Why the thought of being touched turned her into a quivering mess or a ball of rage. Something happened to her, but he had no clue what it could have been. Humans were strange creatures. He'd find out everything one way or another.

He turned and saw her standing on the porch. Exhaustion filled her eyes, but she was stubborn and wouldn't admit how tired she was. Not to him at least, but she told his father. Pyra loved it. As soon as it looked like she was done all he had to do was taunt her, and she was back to being the independent woman he was becoming accustomed to. He'd noticed it right from the start.

He shook his head when he saw the mark of his kind on her hand. She was the first in years. He couldn't have been more shocked when his father marked her with their sign. He knew it wasn't because she was his mate. The king wouldn't honor someone with that status if he or she wasn't worthy, and being his mate didn't make her worthy, even if it made her family. She had already earned his respect and that was tough as shit to do.

He led her to the newest cabin. It was the closest to his home. If he had his way she'd be in his home, and in his bed, but he knew that wouldn't happen. Not until he got her to cave. She had to admit that she liked him at least a little bit, and right now by the way he felt her emotions and the fact she was glaring daggers at his back, he knew that wouldn't be happening—today. He couldn't help but laugh. She wasn't going to make it easy and as frustrating as it was not to be able to pull her into his arms anytime he wanted, he was proud to have a mate that didn't cave. He loved a challenge, and he always got what he wanted. And he wanted Eden.

At first, the thought of having a human mate wasn't appealing at all, but the more he was around her the more he wanted her, and it wasn't just physical. That's what shocked him the most. He was a sexual being and proved it time and time again with the females. None of them were anything more than gratification, and they knew that, but with her, he could imagine lying with her, holding her. He shook his head. His brothers would bust his nuts if they knew the soft thoughts running through his head. He never thought he'd be that way, but his father told him it would be the best and worst feeling in the world. Falling in love was everything to his kind.

The path narrowed and dipped deeper behind the trees. She'd have all the privacy she wanted. The cabin was the most updated and he was glad he picked it. She followed behind him breathing heavily.

"We're almost there."

"I'm fine," she replied.

He sped up and jogged up the stairs. Pulling out her key, he unlocked the door and went inside. He put her bags down. He was back outside and sitting on the steps before she made it.

"You could have waited for me."

He shrugged. "You're too slow."

She stomped a foot and cringed. "My legs are shorter than yours, you jerk."

He laughed. She was too tired to put any heat behind her voice. "Uh-huh, has nothing to do with how tired you are?"

She jutted out her lip. "Nope, I'm fine."

"Okay well let's go in. I'll show you around your new home."

Her eyes widened and she licked her lips.

Interesting.

His eyes tracked the movement and he wanted to trace the path her tongue made.

"You don't need to show me around. I'm sure I can figure it out."

His eyes shot back to hers. "You need to know how to work everything. There is no electricity here."

"I know."

"So I'll help you get set up and then I promise I'll leave you alone."

"Fine, let's get it over with." She said and pushed past him to climb the stairs.

He watched the sway of her hips and it took all his will power to keep his hands to himself. He went in behind her and shut the door. He sighed in relief knowing he was alone with her. That's all he wanted. If she would get to know him, the real him, maybe just maybe things would be different and she wouldn't hate him so badly. He hoped she'd throw him a bone. His fingers itched to touch her skin, but he knew that one touch would lead to so much more, and she wouldn't let that happen.

9

———

The door clicked shut and I froze. I was too tired and that was worrisome. I wasn't sure I'd be able to stop myself from falling into his arms. Not when my body seemed to crave the giant beast. I didn't know what it was about him, but each time he was near me, my heart galloped and my core clenched in need.

I smiled. If it was only physical attraction, if I caved maybe the need would go away? My time here would run smoother if I didn't constantly feel aroused, and from what I'd heard about his reputation, once he got what he wanted he'd leave me alone. It was a win-win, only my heart jumped at the thought of being just another woman he bedded.

I took a deep breath and turned towards him. In the cabin, he was even more imposing. He prowled toward me, with desire in his eyes. "I need to take a shower."

"Water runs well here. I'll wait."

I glared. "Or you can leave and come back after I'm done so I can have some privacy."

"There's a door."

I knew he wouldn't give more than that. "Fine, but stay out of the room."

He held up his hands and smiled wide. "I'll be on my best behavior."

I laughed. "Somehow I don't think I should be reassured by that."

"Guess you'll find out, yeah?" He started down the hall with my bags and I followed behind him. His shirt was so tight I could see each one of his muscles flex with every move he made.

He pushed open the door and placed my bags by a large bed. "This is your room, and the bathroom is right over there. We may not have electricity, but we use solar power to work our heating system. You'll get approximately ten minutes before the water turns cold."

"Okay, thanks." I replied and waited for him to leave. He stood and stared for several seconds. "I think I can take it from here."

"Are you sure? I could help."

He chuckled but it sounded like he was struggling. He wasn't messing with me like he had since I stepped foot on Uoria. I'd have to get better at controlling myself. Or maybe I needed to loosen up. Here was sexy man in my room who obviously wanted me. The lust bubbled over with how he devoured my body. I wanted see how far he'd go.

He stood facing me and I smiled. It was a real smile and I stepped in his direction. He flinched but didn't move back. I shrugged and before he knew it I pulled my shirt off over my head. All thoughts left me. At that moment the only thing that mattered was him touching me.

He groaned and his eyes widened. The orangish color I'd seen a few times was back. I cocked my head to the side watching him, waiting, but he was frozen.

I reached behind my back and undid the clasp to my bra and slid it to the floor. His giant body shook and it looked like he was using every ounce of his self-control to keep his feet planted on the floor. He was surprisingly in control. It was impressive, but I wanted him to break. I wanted to feel the heat I saw behind the depths of his strange colored eyes that did strange things to me. They called to me, said I needed to submit to him. I was his for the taking. Instead of getting pissed I moaned and my eyes fluttered shut long enough to let the feelings of his desire wash over me.

When I opened my eyes, he was still watching me. His chest heaved and his lips parted when I slid my hand underneath the waist band of my jeans. I wiggled my hips and pushed them down my legs taking my panties with them. In a matter of minutes I stood naked in front of a man I really couldn't stand, but one I wanted desperately.

"Oh goddess, you're perfect," he whispered.

I hadn't expected him to say something so perfect and his reverence shot to my core. I nibbled my lip waiting for him to take control, but he was still frozen in his spot.

"Are you going to stand there and stare at me, or are you going to move your ass over here?" My snarky attitude shook him out of his daze and he growled.

He strode to me in two giant steps and crushed my

body to his. His mouth slammed down on mine and I lost my breath. There was so much power behind his kiss, and when his tongue entered my mouth I was done for. I gasped and wrapped my arms around him. He lifted me from the floor and tightened his hold. My body lit on fire.

When he pulled back he was panting for breath. "I thought you didn't like me," he said.

"I don't."

"Sure," he replied with a small smile and kissed me again.

My shower was forgotten when he tossed me on the bed. I watched as his clothes were shredded from his body. The pile on the floor built and then he climbed on the bed hovering over me. I wanted to warn him, but it was too late. He slid into me with a speed unknown to man. I screamed and my muscles clenched. He froze and stared down at me.

"You were an innocent?"

I glared. "Not exactly, but it's been a long time, like years, and that fucking hurt." Tears slid down my cheeks.

"I'm so sorry Eden." And for the first time I saw real regret in his eyes.

My heart clenched I didn't like him upset. "Hey, it's okay, but be gentle with me."

I wasn't sure if he was capable of gentle, but he proved me wrong. He took his time making love to my body. Each thrust was slow and steady. I caught on to his movements and lifted my hips meeting each new thrust. My body stretched and it no longer hurt. It was as if I was made for him. He fit me perfectly and when he twisted his hips the tip of his erection hit with such a force I climaxed without warning. My body bowed and my muscles tensed around him, holding him in place. I felt him come and we stayed locked together until both of our bodies came down from release.

10

___

I lay looking at the ceiling wondering what the hell I just did. My body ached, but mostly I felt more relaxed than I ever had. Pyra was next to me, and even though I could feel his eyes on me I didn't look at him.

"You weren't ready."

My eyes filled with tears. No I most certainly was not ready. No matter how much I enjoyed it at the moment, now—now I felt dirty. I shook my head doing my best to hold the tears back.

"I'm not sorry we made love, but I am sorry it was too soon for you."

I looked at him to see how his eyes glowed orange at me. I don't think they ever turned back to his normal blue since I had stripped. "I need to go for a walk."

He nodded and got out of bed. "I'll go with you."

I rolled out of bed and flinched. "No, I want to go alone."

"Okay, I'll walk you out then at least. I have to go meet

with my brothers. It's time for my scheduled patrol anyway." His voice was low and there was none of his playful banter.

"That's fine, I'll get dressed." I stood and gasped. Every muscle in my body was sore. I knew he hadn't meant to hurt me, but oh how I hurt.

He growled and I looked over at him. He frowned and looked disheartened. "I hurt you."

"I know you didn't on purpose."

"I should have known. It didn't have to be painful for you. If I wasn't such a jack ass you'd be fine right now."

"Hey, didn't I tell you it had been a very long time. That's not your fault."

He turned away and picked up his clothes. They weren't torn at all. He got dressed without looking my way. I dressed in the same clothes I had been wearing and put my shoes on. I needed out. The scent of sex filled the air and it was too much.

Pyra walked in front of me and I followed stiffly behind him. Shutting the door, I took a deep breath of the air. It was clean and fresh, so much better than home. I followed him down the stairs and tipped my head back. The sun was no longer up here, and stars filled the sky. They were huge and so much easier to spot than at home. It was amazing how much Uoria was like home, but it was fresher. The Denynso took care of their lands. They didn't take anything for granted.

Out of nowhere I was lifted in the air and thrown. I screamed and my eyes widened. The thing that threw me sped into my direction and wrapped a clawed hand around my throat stopping me midair. My body jerked forward like whiplash. My heart thudded rapidly in my chest, and I lost my breath.

I'd never seen anything so vile as the creature before me. His eyes were red and his sharp teeth dripped spit. He ran his tongue along the tips and leaned in toward me. I tried to scream again, but I'd lost my voice. Kicking out I landed a blow to his lower body. He roared and dropped me. I fell to the ground with a thud. My back burned and the scent of copper filled my nose. It was blood—and it was mine. The monster rushed down toward me, and even as I tried to lift my hands he fell on top on me holding me down. His claws bit into my wrists.

"You smell sweet." The thing said and then his teeth were in my neck.

My voice was gone. I cried and sobbed, but each move I made only seemed to make the creature more excited. He sucked harder on my neck taking more of my blood. His grunts and groans did nothing to ease my fear. I felt myself fading away. I'd only been on Uoria for a day and I was already going to die. I smiled. At least I'd never have to go back home again.

The thing's body was ripped from mine and I saw orange eyes staring down at me. I lifted my shaky hand up hoping he'd end it for me. Everything hurt, and I didn't want to suffer.

Instead he bent down lifted me carefully into his arms. The feel of his warmth surrounding me was a comforting blanket. He moved so fast, but I was fading faster. There was nothing to do but wait.

TBC

(To be continued in Part II...)

SAVED BY THE ALIEN

GRACE KENSINGTON
SAVED BY THE
ALIEN
ALIEN WARRIOR MATES I | BOOK 2

1
______

Pyra raced to the infirmary carrying a limp Eden in his arms. Her eyes were closed and her lips were pale with a bluish hue. Her body was cold and the wounds on her neck hadn't stopped bleeding. The Klimnu had torn into her, and no one knew how their bite affected humans. She was the first human to be attacked—that they knew of.

He shoved the door opened roughly not willing to set her down to use his hands. "Ciyrs!" he yelled and his voice echoed in the building rattling the glass cabinets.

His friend came running looking pissed like he wanted to rip him apart until he saw Eden's lifeless body in his arms. The words died on his lips and he ran over to them with wide eyes.

"Shit, what the hell happened to her?"

"Klimnu attack."

Ciyrs paled. "Here lay her down. I need to get some things."

"Hurry up brother she is fading and too fucking fast!"

He rushed around the room doing who knew what and Pyra was starting to lose his patience. Finally, his brother, and the healer of the Denynso, sat on a rolling chair and slid toward the gurney that Eden lay on. She didn't move, and he could barely see her breathing. If it weren't for their newly formed link he would think she was already dead, but she was alive. His mate was a fighter.

Brushing her hair from her forehead he prayed she'd be okay.

Ciyrs went to lay his hand on her but before even the tip of his finger touched her; Pyra roared and shoved him off the chair and across the room with a growl. He slammed back against the hard wall shaking the building with the force of his body and fell to the ground.

Luckily Ciyrs was the calm one of them. Instead of blowing a gasket he stood and shook it off only shooting Pyra a 'fuck you' glare. "I have to touch her to heal her."

Pyra shook his head. "I'm sorry it was instinct and she's injured, plus the bond is brand fucking new.

"I know I sense it. I won't touch her inappropriately."

He sighed. "I know, but I can't watch." He spun around and leaned his back against the gurney hoping his body heat and closeness would help her fight and heal.

He knew the moment Ciyrs touched her. The room heated exponentially and he felt his inner magic immerse into her body. He turned just as her torso lifted into the air and she took in a large breath. Her eyes shot open and then she screamed. The piercing wail hurt his ears and glass shattered. The whole compound would hear her pain. He couldn't take it. It was blinding inde-scribable pain and he wanted to kill.

Pyra roared, but news travelled fast, and when he would have slammed Ciyrs into a wall he was restrained by not only his brother warriors and his brother, but his father laid a hand on him trying to soothe him. He hadn't even realized they were there until strong arms held him back.

"He's helping her."

He shook his head and tears slid down his cheeks. "It's hurting her."

"No son, it's not—not the way you think it is. She was dead. He's bringing her back to life."

Pyra froze. No way. She couldn't have been dead. But when he looked, really looked at Eden he saw the signs. The blue on her lips was still present.

Ciyrs's hands laid flat. One was over her heart and the other on her head. His eyes were shut tight in concentration and sweat poured from him. His face was pale and his hands began to shake. He realized what his brother was going through to save his mate. He'd never be able to repay him and owed him a great debt.

He wondered what it would do to her. Ciyrs hadn't ever brought a human back to life. He knew with another Denynso it would mean a link was formed between the healer and the saved. He didn't like the thought of them having a link.

"It will be like a brother and sister relationship, son. Nothing more."

"How'd you know what I was thinking?"

He shrugged. "Because that would be my first thought

as well. The most important thing is that he saved her, and she will live because of his gift."

"I know, I'll never be able to repay him."

Finally, Ciyrs removed his hands from her body and opened his eyes. Pyra physically watched as the magical link formed between them. Her eyes widened and so did his brother's. It was like something inside them recognized each other and when he bent to kiss her, Pyra tried to move, but again he was held back.

"It can ruin the healing magic. They have to bond."

He growled. "I know, but we just bonded before her attack. It's too fresh."

The king placed his hand on his son's shoulder. "You'll survive. Ciyrs is your brother."

So he watched as his good friend kissed his mate. Only he didn't kiss her lips, he kissed her forehead and caressed her cheek. "My sister," he whispered and every voice in the room went silent waiting to see what happened. No one dared to even breathe. She was the first human to be healed, hell to be brought back to life in their long history.

She smiled when he helped her sit up. Her neck wound healed right before their eyes and hers latched on to Pyra's. She smiled at him and then looked at Ciyrs. "I can never thank you enough. If you ever need anything, don't hesitate to ask."

Ciyrs nodded and helped her stand, and she wrapped her arms around him hugging him close. He made it brief before unlatching her arms from around him. "Go see your mate before he rips my head off."

She nodded and turned to him. She blushed and walked over to him. She was quiet and docile, and he wondered if she would regain her temper. He sure as hell hoped she did. It was part of her charm.

When she walked right into his arms he was thrilled and curious. "I'm so sorry," she whispered.

He was confused. "What are you sorry about?"

"Scaring you, I felt it. It was strange. The whole time you held me, I felt your pain and suffering. It nearly suffocated me, and I tried to wake up, but I couldn't."

"It's okay Eden. You're alive now."

He looked over her head and saw Ciyrs watching them. His eyes shined, but there was something else in his expression, protectiveness.

He led her over to him and pulled him into a hug. "Never am I more appreciative than I am right now, brother. Thank you."

He nodded and smiled. "It's surreal, I didn't think it was going to work. I also don't know what the affects will be so I need to keep an eye on her and keep notes for future reference just in case, not that I plan to have to do that again. I'm utterly and totally drained. I need to freakin' sleep for a week."

"Rest and I'll keep track of any strangeness. First, it seems her temper is gone."

Ciyrs laughed. "It will probably come back. Her body went through a horrible ordeal, and she was technically dead."

Those words made him shudder; he didn't want to think of what would have happened had Ciyrs not been able to save her.

2

———

I felt different. I knew I had died, and Ciyrs brought me back to life. Shit. There were so many mixed feeling inside of me. I wasn't sure I'd ever feel like *me* again. How I felt about the man in front of me now was different than it was before that monster attacked me. I couldn't even remember why I fought against our bond. Now it felt like second nature. The bond with the healer was a different story.

It was a good bond, and I could feel a part of him inside me. It soothed me and made me feel safe, like nothing would ever happen to me again.

'You're my sister now', his voice echoed in my mind and my eyes widened. It was strange hearing voices in my head, but I knew his words were true. It felt like I had known him forever.

Pyra smiled at me, but the worry in his eyes still lingered. I could feel his suffering. He hated himself, blamed himself for the attack. How was he supposed to know there was going to be an attack at that very moment? I didn't blame him.

I wrapped my arms around his waist and hugged his giant body. I tipped my head back staring at him willing his sadness away. "Stop blaming yourself."

His eyes watered but he shook his head. "That's not going to happen, Eden." Then he brushed my hair away from my face. The touch sent a million sensations through my body.

"Can we go home now?" he asked holding me close.

Home? I didn't have one really. That cabin was nice, but if I was going to be honest, I was a little afraid to be left alone after what happened. Pyra sensed my fear.

"There is no way I am letting you out of my sight."

I nodded and a fire tried to come to life. My temper would be back, and when it was, when I didn't feel so damn serene, I'd kick his ass. I turned and waved at Ciyrs. It was strange, but I almost felt like a little girl looking up to her big brother. I wasn't sure how I felt about that bond. That feeling of anger kept growing, and I would bide my time and wait patiently. My anger was my crutch. It's how I survived so long.

He tipped his chin and I was led out of the building. Pyra tensed and his hand tightened on mine.

"Can I just pick you up and run. This is bringing too much back."

It was the fact that he asked and how vulnerable he sounded that made me agree.

"This one time, but don't get used to carting me around." Yes. I was starting to feel slightly normal again. He lifted me in his arms and ran. It felt like the wind was whipping in my face, and before I could ask, we were standing on the porch to a different place.

"Welcome home," he said with a smile and placed me gently on my feet. I raised a brow. There was no more arrogance in his voice. It seemed both of us were going through a change, and I wondered if his normal cockiness would come back like my temper was.

I refrained from saying anything mean because he was seriously upset. I followed behind him and gasped. His home was not what one would expect. Most men, human ones anyways, were known to be slobs. But his home was sparkling clean. I was afraid to walk across the floor.

"Well come on, I'm not going to bite and my house isn't going to attack you."

I sighed and kicked my shoes off before setting them nicely against the wall.

Pyra laughed. "You didn't have to do that."

"Oh, yes I did. Your place is super clean."

He sat on the couch and patted the spot next to him. I eyed the spot and sighed. My head was full of so much and all I wanted to do was rest.

'Come sit with me, love.'

I reeled back. "What the hell is that?"

"It's part of our bond, a link was formed and we have the ability to speak through the mind."

'Are you fucking kidding me?'

His chuckle reverberated in my mind, and I felt his relief.

'Your temper is coming back, I was worried.'

"Talk out loud it feels like you're yelling in my head."

"Until you get used to it, that's how it will feel. It's normal from what I've been told."

"You knew this was going to happen?"

"Yes," he replied.

Fire burned inside. "You didn't think that might have been important to mention before we fucked?"

His mouth dropped open, and I saw the hurt in his eyes.

"Is that what you think we did?"

I wanted to scream, to yell, and to say yes, that is what I think it was, but I couldn't and I lowered my head shaking it. "No."

He sped towards me and lifted my chin. "We made love Eden, and whether you like it or not things between us changed the moment I came inside of you. You're mine and I'm yours. I do hope you will love me someday."

He leaned in and kissed me. All it took was one touch and I was gone, melted into a puddle of growing messy love. He was right.

I moaned and wrapped my arms around him urging him to lift me in the air. I had almost died. Certainly that meant something needed to change. Life was too short to be so pissed off all the time.

His body shook and he carried me to the couch. When he sat down he situated me on his lap and I straddled him without breaking our kiss. I pushed my lower body against him and his hands gripped me tighter as if he was afraid to let go.

When I pulled back his eyes glowed and I was breathless.

"Well, does that mean you're okay with our bond now?"

I shrugged. "You're growing on me. I won't promise not to get mad or freak out, but I'll try not to be a complete bitch."

He nodded. "I can live with that, and you're not a bitch. You've had bad things happen to you."

I tensed and eyed him. "How do you know?"

"Your memories."

"You've seen them?"

"Only a few, but it just happened during the bond. It opened you up to me, allowed me to get to know you on a closer level."

I went to pull away but he gripped my hips.

"Hey it's part of the bond, Eden. I didn't invade your mind on purpose. Your mind opened up to me."

I sighed not liking that he'd seen some of the darker things in my life. Tears fell from my eyes before I could stop them. I was not a crier, but I guess dying kind of changes a person.

"Oh love, it's going to be okay. I don't judge you, and if I ever make a trip to Earth, I'll hunt him down and kill him." Pyra was pissed, and somehow that made it better.

It was in that moment I couldn't ignore how I felt. The growing love was taking over all the hate that I held buried inside of me. He knew of my darkest secrets and still wanted me. And I knew that he wasn't just throwing out words to make me feel better. If I ever took him back with me, he would hunt my stepfather down and kill him. Should I have been scared? *Hell yes.* Was I? *Not even a little bit.*

3

Pyra carried Eden to bed when she fell asleep with her head on his shoulder. He saw the moment she decided to stop fighting the bond. After that the silence stretched between them, but it was no longer uncomfortable.

He never thought the day would come that he felt calm and at peace. It wouldn't last, but it was nice for the time being. Stripping off his clothes he got into bed and pulled Eden next to him. He wouldn't be able to be away from her, at least not for a while. His brothers already knew he was going to be spending more time away.

As far as he could tell, so far, she was fine and functioning well after her attack. She hadn't really seemed too chatty, but he didn't think that was really anything new.

She squirmed and her elbow nearly landed in his face but he deftly dodged it. She kicked and cried trying to get away. He let her go and she thrashed around on the bed. Her body broke out in a sweat, and she ripped the blanket from her body. It was then the scent of her arousal hit him and he gritted his teeth. Of course.

"Touch me," she said and let her legs fall open. He watched her and waited to see if she was going to wake up.

When he touched her skin it was a hot as lava, much like his felt when he was over emotional. Her back arched off the bed, and he realized she was actually hurting. He didn't know if she'd be pissed, but he sat up and leaned over her before he yanked her bottoms off. She didn't even open her eyes, and when saw how wet she was he nearly lost it. Whatever was going on was real, but she wasn't aware of what her body was feeling.

She shivered and moaned when the cool air kissed her burning skin. He slid her legs flat and kept them apart. When he slid his hand up her thigh she groaned.

He ran his finger over her slit and her hips jerked and she sobbed. Tears slid down her cheeks. "It hurts, please make it stop."

He didn't know what was going on, but she was in a major state of arousal and he couldn't figure out why it hadn't woken her up. He rubbed her clit with the tip of his index finger and her mouth fell open on a drawn-out moan.

"Wake up love," he said hoping she'd open her eyes. He felt wrong touching her without her permission, but it seemed to be helping.

She stuck out her lip when he stopped his movements.

"EDEN!"

Her body jerked and her eyes fluttered but still she didn't wake up. He sat and watched her without touching her. Not even five minutes later she was crying again. Sobbing about the pain, and he'd had enough. She could kick his ass later.

He climbed on top of her bearing all his weight. "Wake up, Eden." Then he slid inside of her.

Her eyes shot open and she gasped. "What the hell do you think you're doing?"

"You were hurting love, I tried waking you, but even yelling at you, you didn't even try to open your eyes. Do you still hurt?" he asked and twisted his hips. He slid in deep hitting her g-spot and she screamed.

When her eyes focused, she glared. "Why am I so fucking turned on right now? Did you do this on purpose?"

His eyes flared. "No, I just explained to you what happened. You didn't wake up until I was buried deep inside of you, love."

She eyed him but then nodded confused when she realized he was telling the truth.

'I would never do anything without your permission unless it was an emergency.'

He felt her anger disappear and she kissed him, sliding her tongue into his mouth and pressed her lips against his with a force he wasn't used to.

When she pulled back he could have sworn he saw orange, but that was impossible, wasn't it?

"Fuck me," she said and her voice ended on a growl.

"Shit, you're so fucking hot." Then he plowed into her hard. He'd worry about her changes later; right now he needed her more than he needed his breath. She moaned and groaned crying out and scratching his back. She went wild.

When she wrapped her legs tightly around his waist pulling him deeper inside of her he gasped. She felt different and he knew exactly what she felt like. She had changed, and it was because Ciyrs saved her. He had to tell him, but now he rode his mate hard. Her whimpers and pleas were driving him into a lust he couldn't manage, and his eyes glazed over. His inner beast took over fucking her, and she loved every damn minute of it. She met each movement and her breathy pleas drove him over the edge.

The bed creaked and groaned, and she screamed when the mattress collapsed beneath them. He rolled quick and kept her from getting hurt.

"What the hell?"

He grunted when his back landed against the wooden frame, but he smiled so she didn't notice, but she did.

"Why did you do that? You can't let yourself get hurt."

"I can and I'll always do my best to keep you safe no matter what, love."

"Do you?"

"Hmm?" he asked and grunted when he tried to move. A sharp pain shot up his spine and he mentally cursed. "Do I what?"

She blushed and looked down. "Love me?"

He was shocked by her question. Couldn't she feel it? Humans were strange. "Of course I do. Do you feel it?"

She shrugged and pulled off of his body and stood holding out her hand to help him up. "No, not really; I mean I know you care for me, but—"

"Eden, I've loved you since the first touch. I didn't think you were ready to hear it. Hell, you just started to be able to tolerate me."

The tips of her ears turned red and she nibbled her lip. "Oh, well that makes sense."

He stood slowly and his back cried in protest. He moaned and sucked in a breath. He didn't want to worry her, but she saw his pain and spun him to look at his back. She gasped and placed her hand on the place where the wood splintered in his back.

Her hand caught fire and he felt magic. It was similar to Ciyrs's and then the pain in his back started to disappear. He turned his head to the side and watched as her hand glowed green. She was fucking healing him.

He was stunned speechless as he stood still. When she yanked her hand back the glow disappeared, and he felt no pain.

"How—how did I do that?" She stared at her hand holding it away from her. "Did he give me his gift?"

Pyra didn't know the answer. "Love, I've got no fucking clue how you did that. He brought you back; maybe it's some residual power?" He didn't believe that for a minute, but he could see she was on the verge of panic. Her eyes were round and wide and she was pale. Her body began to shake, and then she fell to the ground and convulsed.

"Shit," he yelled and grabbed a large shirt and put it over her head and slid her panties and shorts back on. The shaking got worse and he scooped her into his arms forgetting he was butt ass naked, but at that point he didn't care. Her body lit up like a human Christmas tree. She turned green. It was dark and all the Denynso gawked at them as he sped by. Most couldn't make out much because he moved fast, and again he slammed into the infirmary.

Ciyrs froze and his eyes went from sleepy to panic in two seconds flat.

"How do you explain this brother?"

"Why is she glowing, and why is she having a damn seizure?"

"She fucking healed me!"

Thankfully Ciyrs didn't bother asking why he needed the healing.

"That isn't possible." He grabbed her hand and Pyra watched as his brother went from disbelief to calm. As soon as she touched his friend she stopped convulsing and her body laid flat in his arms in a relaxed state. The glow slowly dissipated from her body.

Pyra was stunned. "Can I get some shorts?"

Ciyrs pointed. "You go get them, I can't leave her right now."

Pyra's jealousy reared its ugly head. "SHE'S MINE!"

There was no response from the other man as he brushed hair from Eden's face. She opened her eyes and groaned. She looked at Ciyrs and smiled. "Hey, you again."

"Yes, well this time it seems we have a different issue, sweetheart."

She frowned. "What happened?

"You don't remember?"

"No, the last thing I remember is—" she blushed. "Is waking up to that beast over there. Enough said."

Ciyrs laughed. "Okay so you and Pyra were intimate, then what?"

"I don't know." She narrowed her eyes in concentration, but she really didn't remember. Pyra could tell.

"We broke the bed, your eyes glowed."

She shook her head. "I remember hurting and being really aroused."

"Yes, she was in pain and thrashing around. I tried waking her but she wouldn't wake up so I decided to make love to her. As soon as I was in her she woke up and boom we were fucking like animals. The bed broke, and I spun us so she wouldn't get hurt, but I did instead. She panicked, and as soon as she laid her hand on me, she healed me. Then she fell into convulsions."

Ciyrs smiled when she covered her face with her free hand.

"Hey it's nothing to be embarrassed about. We're all sexual creatures and you've just bonded. It's natural. Though it's concerning about how he explained everything. I want to run tests on you okay?"

"Sure, if it'll help."

Pyra curbed his anger and watched them interact. He knew it wasn't anything more than platonic with them, but the way she leaned into him and relied on him when he could tell she was hurting pissed him right the hell off. She was his mate, and Ciyrs wasn't much help. He was actually babying her. He'd never seen anything like it. Their bond was strange, and he wasn't sure how well he'd handle it, or if he'd get used to it—anytime soon.

4

———

I sat on the table—again and held my arm still while Ciyrs took another tube of blood. He was as confused as I was about these strange things going on inside of me. I felt strange and my body felt sick. I was weak and tired. I wanted to sleep but he told Pyra to keep me awake. Only Pyra was mad at me. I could feel it. Even as he sat in the chair as far away as I'd allow and talked to me, there was distrust in his voice and my heart clenched.

I didn't like it and when I tried to hold his hand he pulled away. I didn't think I had done anything wrong, but I was having memory problems. Maybe I had. He would barely look at me. I tried to catch his eye and when I finally did, I pleaded with him. If I could feel his anger, then he should be able to feel my sorrow.

He sighed and shook his head standing. "Are you okay with her Ciyrs?"

Her new bondee smiled and nodded. "Sure thing man, you go do what you need. She'll be safe here."

Her mate spun on his heel and stormed out. He'd

finally gotten shorts, but his chest was bare and she watched him go and her heart ached for him.

"He can't handle the bond sweetie. It will take time."

"How do you know?"

"The same way you can feel his anger, I can feel your confusion and the hurt by his disregard. I know him though, he's got a lot of things in his head, and he doesn't handle strong emotion well."

"I don't like that he's mad at me."

"Oh baby girl, he isn't mad at you. He's mad at himself, and maybe even me, but not you. He doesn't like sharing you and because of our new special bond your attachment here isn't only to him. We all crave the day we'll find our mate, and he was no different, no matter how he acted. And imagine he finds you, you complete the bond, and then technically you die. How would you feel?"

"Protective, I wouldn't want to leave his side."

Ciyrs shook his head. "Males are different. He wants you to need him, but right now he feels you need me more."

"Oh," I said and frowned.

"Be patient with him," Ciyrs said and brushed the tear away from my cheek.

I nodded. Males were unique in their own right, but add in a whole different species and it was a whole different ball park. I didn't expect for it to matter so much that he was upset with me. I had never really cared one way or another if a man was angry with me, but now—it was different.

. . .

HE BLEW through the woods running at speed no one would be able to see, not the warriors or even his father. He was fast especially when he was pissed. This was different. He wasn't even really angry. He was jealous of another person. Never before had that happened, especially not over a woman, but Eden was his. They hadn't even mated for long enough for the bond to nestle in his soul.

Everything was unstable. He could feel how upset she was, and at that moment he had to walk away. Now that he had blown off some steam he felt like an asshole. She'd just had a seizure and recently been brought back to life. He could have been a lot more supportive, but he didn't know how to be. She went from hating him to acceptance of their connection in what felt like a split second.

He plopped on the ground and looked over at the horizon. The rising sun usually soothed him, but the ache was too deep. He craved Eden, wanted to be right there with her, but he couldn't trust himself now. Not to react in the right way. He worried his temper would eventually take its toll and she would end up hating him.

He heard a rustle from behind him but he didn't bother moving. He sensed Ciyrs before he saw him. "Why aren't you with Eden?"

He sighed and sat next to him stretching out. "Your dad is with her. She's doing better if you care."

Pyra growled not liking his tone. "I fucking care."

Ciyrs shrugged. "She doesn't understand what's going on, hell neither do I. I didn't know how deep it would go, brother. I wouldn't ever do anything, but I won't lie. A part of my heart aches for her, but it isn't in the way you think." He groaned. "I'm explaining this all wrong. It's almost like she is the female version of me. The softer side. It's weird as hell, but I'll always want to protect her, wipe away her tears, and beat the shit out her mate when he hurts her, and right now if you don't get back to her and apologize for being an ass, I'll do it."

Pyra laughed. "Right, you don't even have a fucking temper, not like the rest of us."

"I have a temper, but I also have control," he seethed.

"Try me, I could use a punching bag right now, and you're the perfect target since you're the issue." He stood and narrowed his eyes. He needed to kick his ass, then it would all be good.

Ciyrs stood. "You have no idea, do you?" He shook his head and then swung.

Pyra didn't have time to duck and with the force of the hit, he was thrown into the tree. The bark scraped down his back and he gasped as the pain hit before he fell to the ground. "Holy shit that fucking hurt!"

Ciyrs stood looking unaffected. "Good." There was nothing in his eyes, not even anger, but he felt the protectiveness radiating off him. "She's like the baby sister I lost you dumb shit. Get over it." Then he ran and was gone.

Pyra stared at the spot his friend had stood and couldn't hide his shock. No one ever saw the violent side of their healer. And then he felt even worse. If he would punch the living shit out of him for being an ass to Eden, then he certainly had some apologizing to do. He rubbed his cheek and cringed. It hurt like a bitch, and he would never underestimate his less tempered brother.

5

I lay on the cot moping. I listened to the King explain Pyra the same way Ciyrs had. Now I was pissed. I understood it was hard to go through this. Hell, I was the one who was attacked by a damn rabid beast, died, healed, and now I had a damn seizure. I'd only been on Uoria for a short time, but it felt like a lifetime.

I was beginning to think that I should go home. I wasn't having much luck and my supposed mate vanished. I wanted to be by myself even if it was only for a little bit, but right now no one would leave me alone. If it wasn't one Denynso it was another. I was grateful they cared, but damn could a girl get some privacy? I needed a good cry, and I sure as hell wouldn't do it in front of anyone.

I stood and stretched feeling a dull ache spread through my body. There was something seriously wrong. I wasn't equipped for this. I was probably still dying or something. Shaking my head, I paced the room slowly, but even that wore me out. Light danced before me and I swayed on my feet. Shit I was about to pass out—again. I closed my eyes and stood still hoping the feeling would go away. Instead I looked up into the King's gentle orange eyes. I felt him lift me like I was weightless and was placed on the cot. Closing my eyes, I decided passing out was better than falling over every damn time I moved.

3 months later

I woke up to see a whole slew of faces staring at me. All of them had various levels of concern in their eyes. I groaned and tried to sit up, but nothing worked. I tried to speak but my mouth was dry and it tasted like something died. A straw was placed between my lips and I sucked the water down. It tasted funny but I wasn't about to complain. I tried to think but my head was cloudy.

The others were still staring at me, and it was making me nervous. I spit the straw out. "What?" I asked and the sound of my voice wasn't mine. It was deep and raspy. What the hell?

"You scared the shit out of us sweetie," Ciyrs said and knelt by me.

"Why? Did I pass out again?"

He laughed but I saw his tears. When I reached out to wipe it away my arm wouldn't move. "Why the hell can't I move?"

"You were in a coma."

"I see. For how long?"

"Three months."

I gasped. "Oh, well that might explain it, what happened?"

"My healing did a lot more than we knew. I'll explain it once you have some time. Gyyx went to get Pyra."

"He's not here?"

He chuckled. "He hasn't left your side for more than a few hours sweetie. His dad sent him home to rest. He was in bad shape."

"Oh, okay." I closed my eyes, but then I felt the gentle touch from Ciyrs and peeked.

"Just checking to make sure you weren't going to fall back into your coma."

"I think I'm good. I feel better than before."

"You should."

The door slammed open and warriors were shoved to the side when Pyra came in with wide eyes. Ciyrs moved without having to be shoved out of the way and Pyra dropped to his knees. Everyone else scattered to give us privacy.

He stared into my eyes with tears in his own and picked up my hands gently in his. "I am so sorry. God, I am such an asshole."

He sounded devastated, and I wanted so badly to comfort him. "Help me sit up."

He brought my hands to his lips and kissed my cold fingers and nodded. He lifted me like I was a fragile piece of glass. Then he sat down and I leaned against his warm body. Instantly my heart picked up and his heat warmed me. I shivered and he wrapped his arm around me pulling me onto his lap. He kissed my cheek and I felt the wetness of his tears. When I tried to lift my hand this time I was able to and I wiped his tear.

"I'm okay."

He shook his head and sobbed holding me. I never imagined such a strong man like Pyra would be sobbing like a child, but he was. "Hey, it's okay."

"Are you sure?"

"I don't feel sick or anything."

His body shook. "Did you before, that night?"

He was referring to our last night, apparently three long fucking months ago. The night I was broken hearted for the first time over a man. Knowing I'd been out that long and knowing how much he must have suffered I couldn't even bring myself to be angry. I thought about his question. "Yeah, I felt weak and really sick like I could fall over at any moment." I sighed. "And apparently that's what happened. I vaguely remember your dad catching me."

"Yeah he did, and then you wouldn't wake up. Nothing worked, and Ciyrs thought you wouldn't ever wake up. All the tests showed there was nothing wrong. He's been a wreck. He blames himself, and he made it his mission to figure out what was wrong and save you."

"It's no one's fault. I guess I needed a vacation from me."

"That's not funny."

"I'm sorry Pyra. I'm sorry you were mad at me, and I don't even understand why. I'm sorry about the bond between me and Ciyrs too."

"Don't. None of it matters. I am the asshole—"

"Let's just move on then."

"You'll forgive me that easily?"

I raised a brow. "Don't you think the last few months have been punishment enough?"

He gulped and nodded. "It was the worst hell I've ever been in. They made me leave you every couple of days to shower and sleep. Otherwise I sat by you trying to find a way to wake you."

I leaned into him and he wrapped both his arms around me. "Do you need anything?"

I shook my head. "Just you. I'm so cold, and I've missed you."

He let out a breath. "God, I've missed you too, love. Don't ever do that again."

He kissed my hair and I shuddered. "I'm probably pretty gross, but I doubt I can take a shower."

"If you don't mind Mom helping you she offered knowing you'd probably want to get cleaned up. She's been here every other day or so giving you a sponge bath."

I blushed. "Oh man, that's so horrible." I knew my hair was disgusting. "I would like that. That's what I want, and I think the water will warm me up. My bones ache from being cold."

"I'll go get her."

He lifted me back on the couch to where I could lean in the corner and not fall over and went outside. A few seconds later his mother came in smiling.

"It's so good to see you're awake. We were all pretty terrified."

I nodded. I hadn't had a chance to get to know her, but she was basically my mother in law. "Thank you for taking care of me."

"Of course honey. You're family, and I wouldn't trust any of the men to do this right. They wouldn't know what to do." She laughed and I smiled.

She helped me to my feet and I wobbled. "How long is this going to last?"

"It could be a few days."

My shoulders slumped as I was led to the bathroom. I moved like an old woman and when I looked in the mirror I gasped in horror. I looked horrible.

6

———

Pyra waited for Eden to get cleaned up and paced around. He didn't want to be away from her any longer than he had to be. There was too much lost time, and he was a wreck. He'd gone home and taken a shower while his mother was with her.

His mother helped her out and she smiled at him. "She's all good to go. I told her to just holler if she needed me."

He jumped up and kissed her cheek. "Thank you." He took over and guided Eden to the couch. He hated how weak she was. She was rail thin and didn't look well, but to him she was the most beautiful woman in the world.

"I feel like an old woman. Get me a walker so I don't need help," she said tensely.

He chuckled. His mate didn't like to be taken care of, or needing help.

"Do you want to go home instead of staying here? Ciyrs can do the tests later."

"I want it over with. I want to know if I'm still going to freaking glow and heal like I did."

"I doubt it. He thinks that is what caused this, but since no healer in all of history has ever brought a human back to life we have no fucking clue."

"I still feel different, only less sick."

He went into panic and sat her down and rushed away without waiting for her to say anything else. Ciyrs came rushing in behind him.

"He says you still feel off?"

I glared. "I didn't mean to go get the doctor. I meant the changes I felt before, I still feel them, but I don't feel like I'm going to pass out or anything. I don't feel like me though."

Both men visibly relaxed and she laughed. "Geez calm down."

"Eden, you have no idea what it was like for us."

"I know, I wasn't aware of anything."

"Well we were."

"Fine, do your tests if you have to."

Ciyrs took another few vials of blood and Pyra took her home. She wouldn't be leaving his sight, and if he had to be somewhere someone would be with her. Last time he left her she went into a three-month long coma.

I LAY in Pyra's bed and sipped broth from a coffee mug. It had been three weeks since I woke up and I was still too weak and everything else I ate came back up. From Pyra's worried expression, he was about to cart me back home and have human doctors do some tests. Ciyrs still hadn't found anything and no one would listen to me. I was fine—mostly. He hadn't touched me sexually since that last night and I needed a release. He was so worried about hurting me, but I worried it was because I was so ugly. I couldn't even stand to look at myself. I was a skeleton. It didn't matter how much I tried to eat. Something in my life was missing, only I didn't know what it was.

He came in and smiled. "How are you feeling, love."

"The same. Come sit with me."

He nodded and sat next to me. I was getting stronger. I climbed on his lap and laid my head on his chest. It was my favorite place to be. I felt his heart thump, and he wrapped his arms around me holding me close. I tipped my head back and looked at him.

"Kiss me."

"It's too soon."

I glared. "I've been awake for over three weeks. When isn't it going to be too soon for you? Have you wondered if maybe that's what I need?"

"If that could heal you baby I would fuck you into the next universe."

I gasped at his words and my eyes dilated.

It was then his eyes widened. "Your eyes—they're orange."

I felt him harden for the first time and moaned. "Kiss me, please I need you."

I felt his resolve chipping away. "I don't want to hurt you."

"You won't."

He closed his eyes, and I took the opportunity to press my lips on his. He stayed still while I kissed him. I kept the pressure light and slid my tongue along his bottom lip. His hands tightened, and I smiled against his mouth. He would give me what I wanted.

I pressed my body against his and rubbed against him. "Please, please take this ache away."

His eyes shot open. "You're hurting?"

I sighed and gripped his hand and shoved it between my legs. I knew he'd feel the heat and wetness through my shorts. "For you. Do you not want me?"

He growled. "Of course I do."

"Then prove it."

His eyes flared and he set me on the bed and stood stripping. I smiled. Finally, my core throbbed. I didn't know what the hell was wrong, but something inside of me knew if he would give me what I needed I'd start getting better.

I lifted my shirt off and wrapped my arms around myself. I didn't like my body, but when he eyes brightened I knew he still found me desirable.

"They're still orange. I don't know how this is fucking possible, but you're one of us now, or at least you've adopted some characteristics."

He was stunned, and at the moment I didn't care what the hell color my eyes were. I wanted him in me, over me, and under me.

He walked towards the bed. His eyes were feral and a wave of lust washed over me. "Hurry."

"Lay down. I've got to do this right, gently. I refuse to hurt you."

I nodded and laid down spreading my legs wide for him. He could see the proof of my arousal.

"Oh shit." His control broke and he was on me, but when I felt his fear I rubbed his back.

"You won't hurt me," I whispered.

"Never." He slid inside me so agonizingly slow I cried out in frustration and went to lift my hips but he growled. "No, we do this my way."

I whimpered when he slid out and then slowly eased back in.

My body wanted him so badly. "I can't wait, seriously I need you inside of me now." Then before he realized what I was doing I wrapped my legs around him and that pushed the rest of him inside me.

I moaned and clenched tightly around him holding his cock inside of me. "See I'm fine. Actually, I am better than fine. Oh god, you feel so good."

His eyes widened. "You feel—different, familiar."

I knew what he wasn't saying. I suddenly knew what happened. Why I was so sick. Somehow Ciyrs changed me. I was now a female Denynso. I wasn't sure how much so but enough that my eyes were orange, and apparently my pussy felt like a female Denynso.

"I've changed."

He nodded and thrust in and out of me with ease. When I showed no discomfort, he calmed and sped up. It was still slow and sensual, and I held on to him tightly as he rocked into my body. My senses heightened, and I could smell his arousal and mine mixed. I moaned and cried out when I climaxed. When my pussy tightened around him he grunted and I felt him come inside of me.

He clenched his teeth and sped up to finish releasing his seed inside of me. I grabbed his face and kissed him with love. For the first time I felt it, I felt how he felt for me when we met. It all made sense. He was mine and I was his—forever. I would never let him go.

News traveled fast. Pyra was still coming to terms with the fact that Ciyrs had turned his mate into one of them. They still weren't sure how much of their genetics she had, but it was enough that her eyes were orange and her reproductive system was like the Denynso females.

Turned out she did need him to make love to her. She was going through the mating heat as he did. It's why she craved him and ached. Once they completed the bond for a second time, she seemed fine.

She was able to eat and was putting on some weight and almost had all of her normal energy back.

Eden spun in a circle out in the grass. Ciyrs released her from bed rest but made her promise to lie down if she felt weak and tell Pyra right away. So far, her symptoms were gone.

"It's about time. I'm out of lock down."

He chuckled. She could be so dramatic, but he fucking loved her, and he was ready to tell her, and he knew she loved him too, but she had yet to even hint at feeling that way.

"Come here, love."

She spun and danced toward him. He'd never seen her so girly. It was amusing and sexy all at the same time. Her cheeks were flushed and she glowed. "Come get me," she teased and ran.

He loved the chase and narrowed his eyes until she sped faster than ever before. Then he ran and caught up to her wrapping his arm around her waist and lifting her off the ground. "Damn, do you realize how fast you were going?

She laughed. "No why?"

"You've picked up another characteristic."

She grinned.

He kissed her and when she pulled back he saw tears in her eyes.

"What's wrong love?"

She shook her head. "I love you."

He froze and glared. "That's what I was about to say. You just stole my thunder woman." But then he spun her around in his arms. "I love you too."

I WAS CHANGING MORE each day and growing stronger too. I was starting to throw up again however and that was concerning considering I had been sick for too long. I didn't want to go backwards.

Ciyrs met us at the field. "Hey can I borrow you for a little bit, sweetie?"

I looked to Pyra first. I learned quickly that he came

first and my bond with Ciyrs came second. It was a delicate balance.

He nodded. "Don't keep her too long, I have plans tonight."

I laughed and spun and ran into his arms kissing his lips before running to my brother because that's what he was, though technically he was my maker. I wrapped my arms around him and he kissed my hair.

"Let's go before you piss your mate off."

He let go of me, but I looped my arm with his. Pyra was more bark than bite, and he'd really learned that there was nothing more than family love between me and Ciyrs. It didn't surprise me when we went back to the infirmary.

"I want to try something," he said and held open the door for me.

I went inside and saw one of the warriors sitting on the table shaking. He was pale and blood seeped out of a wound on his stomach.

"What happened to you?" I asked and instinct pushed me to him. My need to help took over and I lifted his shirt and gasped.

"Fight."

"With who?"

"Klimnu."

I froze.

He grinned. "It's all good Eden baby, just a scratch, but it hurts like a bitch. I was hoping Mr. Healer here could help me out."

The man in question stood back and crossed him arms. "I think Eden's going to heal you."

I laughed. "That's funny, I haven't shown any signs since my coma."

"You're changing more each day. Try again. It's a small wound so focus and heal him. That will tell us what we need to know."

I shrugged. "Okay but don't say I didn't warn you. I'm probably useless to this poor guy here."

He smirked. "I highly doubt you're useless to anyone."

Ciyrs growled. "Shut it, Ero."

I grabbed a warm rag and cleaned the blood from his wound. He flinched but didn't make a sound. I was gentle, and once the blood was gone I could see it was really just a scratch, but it was deep. I cupped my hand over it and closed my eyes focusing just like I had seen Ciyrs do. I felt my hand warm and Ero groaned. I opened my eyes and his head fell back and his lips were parted. I watched as my hand glowed green like it had before, and then his skin knit itself back together. When Ero moaned, I pulled back.

"You're all good." I blushed when I noticed the affect the healing had on him. He blushed too and looked away covering his lap.

"Shit Eden, I'm sorry."

Ciyrs chuckled. "It's normal to get aroused by the healer's touch."

I laughed. "Pyra will hate this even more now."

"How do you feel? Sick?"

I shrugged. "I'm fine right now."

He nodded and Ero hopped off the table and bolted from the room.

"He won't come near me again for a while, will he?"

"If he knows what's good for him no."

"It wasn't his fault though."

"Doesn't matter, you're Pyra's."

I glared and cocked a brow. "And you're point is?"

"Hey it would be no different if he aroused another woman, right?"

My eyes flared, and I growled stalking toward him. I wrapped my hand around his throat lifting him from the ground. "Don't even say that."

Then just as quickly as I felt it, the anger was gone and I let go stepping back in a panic. "Oh my god, I'm so sorry."

His eyes were wide. I'd never shown any kind of temper toward him, and our relationship was the happy go lucky type. He was pretty much the only one who saw that side of me.

"What the hell was that?" He rubbed his neck.

Tears spilled down my cheek. "I don't know."

Then I ran to the bathroom and emptied the contents in my stomach. For the next hour, I lay with my face against the tile and growled anytime Ciyrs tried to help me. I'd hurt him, and I was literally sick over it. What was I turning into?

8

———

Pyra pounded on the door, but she ignored him. He knew she was okay because he heard her sobbing and that actually scared him more. "Love, open this damn door now!"

"Go away!" she yelled back.

He sighed and went to talk to Ciyrs. His friend was shaken up. When Ciyrs called for him he ran in a panic thinking something horrible had happened. Every time he was away from her he feared she would slip back into a coma. When he found out that she freaked out about a comment Ciyrs had said, he couldn't help but chuckle. A female, especially his female who already had a temper, didn't mess around when it came to their mates. He'd found that out when he made a comment about how he used to sleep around. His nuts still ached anytime he thought about her reaction.

"You shouldn't have teased her."

"Yeah well, she's never been violent towards me, and

she's still sick. I want to test her blood again. What if this is her way of rejecting the change?"

Pyra paled. He hadn't thought of that. "I'll get her." He stormed down the hall and slammed the door open. What he saw stopped him in his tracks. She was asleep on the cold, hard floor. Without thinking he scooped her up and carried her shivering body out of the bathroom. She reeked of vomit, but he didn't care. He laid her on the table. "I'll be back."

Then he disappeared. He went to the main house and found his mother. "Mother."

She looked up from her breakfast and her smile fell from her face as soon as she saw him.

"Is she okay?"

He ran his hands over his Mohawk. "She healed one of the other warriors today. Ciyrs said something triggering her temper and she nearly choked him out. After she realized she hurt him, she freaked out and was in the bathroom throwing up again."

He didn't notice his mother's eyes light up. She wiped her face and pushed her plate up and stood. She was always so poised. "Go back and wait for me."

He nodded knowing not to question her.

When he came back, Eden was awake and her puffy eyes shined with tears. "I'm horrible. How could I have hurt him?"

"It's okay love, I'm sure he's over it by now."

"I know you didn't mean it, sweetie," he said and kissed her forehead.

She sniffled. "I'm so fucking emotional, it's ridiculous. I'm never like this, and I never have been."

"That's because you are carrying my son's child—my

grandchild," his mother said as she walked into the infirmary. Silence followed his mother's announcement.

Ciyrs smacked his head. "Why the hell didn't I think of that?"

"Simply because you're not a woman."

He hurried away to use some of the blood to test her for pregnancy.

"That's why I'm so sick—and mean?"

His mother laughed. "Honey I hate to say this but you're usually mean. It's the teary, sappy emotions that are new."

Eden laughed and shook her head. "Thanks for that."

"Anytime. You fit in well here. You were made to be one of us. We simply didn't know it was possible, and who knows maybe it isn't."

"So, I'm probably a fluke?"

"It's quite possible you are. But we are blessed and thrilled to have you here with us. You're a wonderful daughter."

Eden burst into tears again and Pyra cringed. He didn't know what to do with tears. Anger, sure was easy, but her being upset riled him up. Made him want to hit something to fix it, but it wouldn't work with the sad stuff.

They waited impatiently for the test to be done. A pregnancy test by blood took a bit longer, but when Ciyrs came back he beamed. "By god we got it. Congratulations, you're going to be parents."

Eden paled. "Of what though?"

"Who knows, but Denynso is apparently quite dominant, and since you're one of us now, I would assume your baby will take after our genes. We won't know until birth though."

Eden looked towards the Queen, "What's pregnancy like for you?"

"Much like yours really. Only seven months instead of nearly ten."

"That could be a blessing," Eden replied and rubbed her belly. He stared at her hand and she froze. "Are you okay?"

He shook his head and gazed at his mate. She was carrying his child, and she was more Denynso than human now. He never imagined his life would turn out like this, and now he was going to be a dad. Was he ready to take on a baby that could very possibly be more temperamental than the both of them combined? Probably not, but he sure as hell wouldn't change it. She smiled at him and his heart melted further, she was perfect.

"I'm good love," He lifted her hand and laced their fingers. "Let's go home."

She nodded and yawned. "I am tired."

Instead of waiting for her to stand he lifted her and carried her out of the infirmary.

When he got home she walked in and stopped looking around. "I've finally begun to think of this place as home. I don't know if I would ever want to go back to Earth now. I wasn't happy there, and even though I loved my job, I hated my boss. I didn't have any friends, and my family left much to be desired. I'm more at home here than I ever have been anywhere. I think it was fate."

He stood behind the love of his life and wrapped his arms around her. He thought so too. Things were about to change, and he needed to work with the others to secure their compound. In seven short months, the start of the new Denynso generation would be born. He didn't want his child living the way he and his brothers did. It was time for a change, and he was going to make sure it happened or he would die trying. Nothing else mattered now. Just his new family.

WANTED BY THE ALIEN

COVER

GRACE KENSINGTON
WANTED BY THE
ALIEN
ALIEN WARRIOR MATES I | BOOK 3

1

———

He swung his fist against the bag and it broke apart. The sand spilled to the ground in a cloudy pile of dust. He bent at the knees and braced his hands on his knees breathing heavily. For the past several days he felt like he was going crazy. Never before had his emotions been so palpable, and he found he didn't like it.

He always gave the brothers a hard time about their temper and had prided himself on being in control of his own. Now though, he felt no better than Pyra when he was pissed that Eden spent time with him. Hell, he understood how hard it was for him, but it wasn't something he could control.

Now Pyra was even more protective. Eden was carrying his child and no one really knew what that entailed. She was the first human turned Denynso, and she was also about ten weeks pregnant now. He had been running tests, and so far, everything seemed normal. He refused to lose her. She was his sister. It was almost like she was the other half of his soul, like a twin, only closer.

He spun and slammed his fist into the other bag and that's all it took for the seams to split. Sweat poured from his skin and his palms were sweaty. Violence wasn't his thing.

"Ciyrs, what the hell brother?" Pyra asked and looked at him curiously.

His body shook and for a second he swore he saw everything in orange, but that was impossible, none of the females here were his mate. Shaking his head his vision went back to normal and he focused on his friend's words.

"I felt angry."

Pyra laughed and looked between both ruined bags. "I'd fucking say you did. What happened? You never get mad." Then his eyes widened and he panicked. "Is everything okay with Eden?"

"Yeah, she's not why I'm pissed. In fact, she's doing great, though be careful she's getting emotional."

"Why?"

"Pregnancy hormones I guess. Our kind only gets mean. Apparently, humans cry—a lot."

He chuckled. "Eden doesn't cry."

Ciyrs cringed. "She does now. Seriously be careful. Don't be mean or too sweet. She'll cry."

Pyra shook his head still not believing him. "Okay so if it isn't Eden, why the hell are you so emotional?"

"I don't know. I've been having strange dreams, and then I'm not really sleeping. I've been on edge all week, and I don't know why. I do know I don't like it. I'm not a warrior, I'm a healer. It's important I stay centered. But my power is on the fritz too. Ero, of course came in today after another fight with a Klimnu and I healed him, but then my temper flared, and here I am."

Pyra smiled. "And it feels like you want to kill everything?"

Ciyrs frowned. "Yes."

"Your mate is either here or coming. I swear that's how I felt before Eden showed up. For a few days before, and then when she was here I got a hard on that wouldn't go away, no matter what I fucking did. That's how you'll know she's here brother, and it sucks now. The built-up anger rages uncontrollably. You remember all the fights I got into? Even it scared me, and I'm probably the most temperamental of us all."

He shook his head. "That's not real reassuring Pyra, but I don't think I'm feeling the same thing you did. I don't know if I will have a mate, ever."

"Why not?"

"I don't know how my connection to Eden has changed that either. I thought it was maybe because of our bond, but I don't get angry after seeing her. I actually feel a lot more at peace."

"You'll figure it out. You're the brains around here."

"I hope so and soon; I can't keep doing this. I don't like how it makes me feel afterwards."

"Well let me know when you start feeling the way I did. And I guess my work out is pointless now. You've ruined my favorite equipment." He chuckled and sped from the room leaving Ciyrs alone.

Ciyrs left the gym and sped to the infirmary. It was

basically his home, and he'd been spending more and more time there trying to figure out how he had turned Eden. The baby she carried would be his godchild, and he wanted to make sure she was alright. And, that there wouldn't be any more surprises.

After calming down, he decided to call it a night and go home for a change. It had been nearly a week since he last saw his own bed. The Klimnu attacks were getting more violent. They were more organized, and the warriors were doing their best to keep them at bay, and kept getting injured in the process. No one could figure out how they were getting onto the compound.

There had to be an access point somewhere they weren't seeing, but King Creia wasn't having any luck with the others of their kind. Ciyrs knew there were other clans of Denynso, different races so to speak, but they had always stayed segregated from each other. They were all very territorial, and there were boundaries no one would cross. The leaders were talking about alliances but nothing had been set in stone. Apparently, it was only his compound that had been breached so far, and the others didn't want to take the chance of the Klimnu finding their compounds. It was understandable, but still didn't make sense for them not to work together.

Ciyrs sighed and rubbed his tired eyes. Suddenly his eyes flared orange and he hardened painfully. He gasped and instinctively gripped his cock and sucked in a breath. He hadn't had an erection like this for—longer than he liked to think about. He gripped himself and moaned. Yep he was definitely going home. But Pyra's words ran through his mind. If his warrior friend was right, he'd stay this way until he mated.

For the first time in weeks Ciyrs smiled. If Pyra was right, he'd be meeting his mate. He'd finally have the one thing he craved more than anything in the world.

2

———

I sat with my shoulders hunched over. As much as I wanted to do my articles, meeting the famous Denynso was still nerve wracking. I'd heard so much about them, and now I was going to their home... Uoria. On a normal basis, I was the type of woman who stayed to myself. I had firm control over all of my emotions and wasn't a people person, unless it was for the job.

I rode the ship and my knee bounced nervously. I couldn't shake the feeling that something bad was going to happen. I sighed and pushed my hair from my face and adjusted my glasses. Soon I'd meet the King and Queen of the compound.

The pilot came back and smiled. "It's about landing time Miss Eliana."

"Thanks," I replied keeping my eyes lowered. Then I held on tight to the arm rests as the ship descended to the ground faster than I would have liked. My heart raced and I felt it in my throat. The flying part was okay, the landing not so much. I broke out in a sweat and swore.

When the ship hit the ground softly and shuddered to a stop I let out the breath I had been holding.

I stood and braced my hand on the chair as I regained my equilibrium. My latest email let me know I would be escorted by the warrior named Pyra. Everyone back home had heard of him. He was sort of legendary everywhere. I knew he was huge, and that he was newly mated to a scientist named Eden.

I jumped when the ship door slid open and chuckled. I clearly needed to get my nerves under control. Taking a deep breath, I stepped down carrying my travel bags. It was dark and the sky was an amazing shade of blue with a mix of violet. Stars filled the sky and the scent of fresh grass filled my senses. The air was so clean, not like back at home where every corner carried a different stench.

Naturally, I wasn't paying attention and ran into a hard wall of muscle. I looked up and up some more until my head tilted back painfully. Orange eyes stared down at me with a smirk. "Crap you're freakin' huge," I said without thinking.

The man's mouth crooked up into a smirk. "And you're tiny as can be, woman. You must be Eliana?"

I would have been offended, but I couldn't deny how small I looked. Compared to him I was like an infant. "Yeah, and you must be the famous Pyra."

"Famous?"

"Yep, you're a legend back home."

He shrugged. "Well, I guess that's a compliment then. The King and Queen have been anxious about your arrival. You're doing a story about us? To make us more appealing to your kind?"

I giggled. "A series of stories, articles about what it's like here. Your King and Queen seem very determined to mix our species and about helping each other out. It's a win-win really. I am a damn good writer so this will be a success."

"Well let's go." He gripped my bags and smiled. "My mate has been complaining I'm not a gentleman. If only she could see me now."

"I'll be sure to tell her." I said deadpanned. Here was this big giant of a man and he was worried about what a woman thought of him. It surprised me. I'd heard of his reputation, and it wasn't how he seemed to me. He seemed like a happy man who wanted his mate's approval.

"Thanks, it's important that she knows I'm sweet right now. She's carrying my child." He beamed and I was taken back. This was the first I'd heard of a pregnancy.

"Whoa, that's—uh great. Congratulations."

He frowned. "I shouldn't have told a complete stranger that. I'm just happy, and you're a reporter no less. Shit."

"I won't tell, and let's just say that was off the record until you want to go public Earth-bound?" I smiled trying to reassure him.

"Promise?"

Something in his eyes pleaded with me. "Yes, my lips are sealed."

He nodded and led me down a long path to a giant house. It was beautiful and grand. Better than any house I'd ever seen in my life. I'd grown up in the ghetto and now lived in a crummy apartment. Journalism didn't pay well, not yet anyway. I had no regrets though. I would starve just to be able to write every day of my life.

Suddenly my escort was thrown back and another man tackled him slamming his fist into Pyra's face. Pyra didn't stay down long and he held the other man close with his arm around his neck.

"Ciyrs, what the fuck?"

His eyes glowed orange, but only for a second as he locked gazes with me. I gasped and felt my panties dampen. What the hell?

The man literally growled. "Mine," he roared and tried to break free.

Pyra laughed and held him tighter. "Calm the fuck down. Do you even need to freak out right now? Think of Eden you douchebag."

The other man named Ciyrs, instantly calmed and nodded, his eyes changed from orange to a color I couldn't make out in the dark.

"Sorry," he muttered and then he looked away from me. Pyra let him go and he sped off, so fast I didn't really see him go. He was nothing but an amazingly fast blur.

Pyra rubbed his jaw and frowned. "Well that was unnecessary, but fucking funny. I called it."

I stared at him confused and he shook his head. "You'll understand soon. Very soon indeed."

He continued walking to the house slowly. As he said that, the other man came back looking a lot calmer than he was and glared at Pyra. "Go back to Eden, I got this."

Pyra smiled and nodded. "It's nice to meet you shorty, and remember your lips are sealed." His smiled widened when the other man's eyes flared with anger and he fisted his hands. "See ya around."

"Thanks," I replied and cocked my head to the side to look at the heaving chest of the other man.

His hand gripped my chin tipping it back to meet my eyes. His touch was electrifying and I shivered.

"Your lips are sealed for what?"

I figured he knew so I shrugged. "The new generation. He slipped. I promised I wouldn't write about it."

"I see." He stared at me with such intensity I gasped. There was something about him. He was perfect. His voice vibrated along my skin, sending shivers down my spine to the front of my body and settling in the space between my legs.

3

———

So, the fucker was right. Ciyrs was on his way home when he passed Pyra walking with the smallest woman he'd ever laid eyes on. She was at least a foot and a half shorter than him, and his eyes flared orange and a rage so deep and strong, one he'd never felt before took over when he heard her speak. She was with Pyra and even though rationally he knew Pyra was with Eden, a beast inside of him snapped. She wasn't supposed to be around any other males.

Before he knew what he was doing he attacked the cocky warrior and slammed him to the ground, but even in a rage Pyra still out maneuvered him.

He kept his finger on her chin but she still couldn't meet his eyes. "What's your name beautiful?"

Her eyes widened and she licked her lips. His eyes followed the movement and he raged harder wanting her so badly.

"Eliana."

Her voice came out as a mere whisper, and she stared at him in confusion.

He rubbed his thumb gently along her jaw before letting go. "I'm Ciyrs, and I apologize about that. I'm usually not so—violent."

She laughed. "Isn't that kind of a Denynso trait?"

"I have more control." He let go of her chin and scrubbed his hand down his face and sighed. "Normally."

"I see, so what's changed?"

"We need to take you to see the leaders. They are watching right now—with amusement I might add." He changed the subject. It wasn't the right time to tell her. She had just gotten here, and he wanted to give her a moment to get used to the changes.

She glanced around him and her eyes widened. "Are you all giants?"

"Yes."

"Well, I'm not going to fit in well then."

He scanned her body. She was tiny, thin, and short. Her breasts were perfect and so was she. "You'll fit in fine."

He led her to the house and climbed the stairs not bothering to hide his apparent erection. He was in too much pain to care.

"What happened to Pyra?" the king asked.

"I sent him home to Eden."

"I see."

"Sorry about my—display."

Creia laughed and clapped him on the back. "We've been there, son. It's fine. Let's meet our newest family member shall we."

She didn't say anything as she stood staring at them.

She followed him inside and he felt her gaze burning into his back. All he wanted to do was strip the clothes from her body and make love to her. This was out of control. He had control. Losing it was unacceptable.

He pulled out a chair and gestured to Eliana to sit and she smiled timidly at him. Without a word, she sat in the chair. He could already sense her. He could hear her heart race as if it was his own. He refrained from touching her and sat in the other free chair. The king and queen stared at him and then his lovely queen smiled. "I see."

That's all she needed to say. Everyone knew, and now maybe he wouldn't have to be so apologetic. It was fucking unreal how much he wanted to hurt someone.

"It's nice to meet you Mrs. Conner."

She cleared her throat. "Oh, it's Miss actually, I'm not married, but I would prefer no formalities. I'm Eliana."

"Very well, you may call me Creia if you wish. This is my mate Thiea."

"It's nice to meet you both. It's an honor to be here really. I can't wait to learn about your culture."

"You know there are some things that must be left out correct?"

"Yes, every article will come to you first before I send it back. I won't print anything without your approval."

"Very good. Now you've met my son and our residential healer." He gestured toward Ciyrs. There are many more, but you must be careful, and I'd like to assign you a guard. We've had some—security issues."

"I'll do it." Ciyrs said.

"You're not a warrior."

He clenched his teeth. "But I can protect her. I have something the others don't."

She didn't say a word, but her eyes stayed on his.

"If that is satisfactory to Eliana, then fine, but she will be assigned a warrior as well."

He growled and slammed his hands on the table. "I don't need anyone to fucking guard her."

The king smirked and he paled.

"Oh dammit, I'm so sorry. This is getting out of control."

"On a normal basis, I would have thrown your ass to the ground Ciyrs, but because I understand what you are going through that's your one and only free pass. Do not let it happen again."

He nodded and licked his lips. "Yes sir, I apologize."

"Very well. Take Eliana to her cabin so she can get settled." He turned to her and smiled. "If you leave the cabin, you have to be accompanied until we fix our issue. I apologize for not giving you a fair warning throughout our emails, but I was afraid you'd change your mind about coming."

She smiled. "I understand and I have no problem with being guarded by Ciyrs."

He nearly groaned with how she spoke his name. He couldn't wait to hear her scream it.

"Even though he isn't trained like the warriors?"

She shrugged. "He seems very capable of protecting me, and for some reason I trust him. So, I'm good."

The king leaned back satisfied, and Ciyrs wanted to beat his chest. She trusted him already. He smiled and nodded at her. "I won't let anything happen to you."

"I know," she replied.

In that moment time stood still and the air thickened with her scent. She smelled sweet and spicy all at once. He could also sense her need to be accepted. She was like him. She held back too. His mate was strong and controlled.

4

My breath caught and time stood still. His eyes glowed orange again, and I found myself lost in the depths. There was something so powerful about the way he looked at me. I felt something in my heart. It was trying to tell me something. But I looked away. The thing I craved so badly would never happen. My whole life I knew a life alone would be inevitable. I was destined to live solo. That's what my mom told me right before she left me.

I looked away and took a deep breath stopping the tears before they filled my eyes. I wasn't weak, and I certainly wasn't going to cry in front of them. I plastered a smile on my face.

"I'm actually really tired if you don't mind."

The king stood and laughed. "Of course, we really have no idea what the trip is like."

"Long," I said and kept my smile.

"Okay well, meet with me when you are feeling better, and you can give me a run down on what your plans are."

"Sounds great, thank you."

Ciyrs led me from the house with his giant hand on my lower back. His heat burned my skin. He kept quiet as he led me down a dirt path. We passed others and all of them stopped to stare, but then their eyes widened and they moved on. It didn't take long for me to figure out what was going on.

He was protective of me for some reason. It almost seemed like he was possessive. That didn't make sense though. I'd just met him.

"You'll love it here," he said and smiled. "There's a lot you'll be able to write about."

I nodded and stepped closer to him to see what he'd do. He wrapped his free arm around my waist and his fingers dug into my hip. I didn't have a lot of meat on my bones and I gasped.

He let go and sighed. "Sorry, I have to remember you're small."

"Is that bad?"

"No, you're delicate and need to be handled with care. I like that—a lot."

I lowered my eyes nervously, but I couldn't ignore the bulge in his pants. He was big everywhere. I'd never been with a man, ever. I couldn't imagine being able to handle someone like Ciyrs, but oh I would love to try. He did funny things to me.

He gripped my hip again, but this time kept his fingers loose. We didn't talk. The silence was comfortable as he led me down a different path.

"The cabin up here is empty. It was Eden's when she first came, but she didn't stay long before she mated with Pyra."

"It happens fast for your species then? Mating I mean?"

"I guess so, besides the king and queen, Pyra was the first to mate. It's new for us really. We're all envious of Pyra and hope that by combining our kinds, more of us will find our loves. It's the most important thing in our lives, especially now that we know it's possible to mate with humans. Though Eden isn't anymore."

"She isn't what?"

He stopped. "I shouldn't have said that."

I grabbed his hand. "I won't tell."

"She got attacked and died, I tried to heal her, but instead I had to bring her back to life. Apparently doing that turned her into one of us, and she and I are connected too, but only like brother and sister. She's able to heal now as well."

I felt an anger I'd never felt before. I didn't like hearing about him having a connection with another woman. Jealousy clouded my features, and I found my heart pounding and my hands clenched. "Oh." I didn't know why I was so pissed, but it was the first time in a long time I'd been angry. He felt me tense up and rubbed my hip.

"What's wrong?"

I shook my head shutting the anger off. "Nothing. So, you can turn humans then?"

"I don't know. It's the first time it ever happened, and we don't know if it was a fluke or something I'll always be able to do."

"You're pretty powerful then."

"I don't see it that way. I saved her because my friend was desperate. I always feel like I'm less because I choose not to be a warrior. I don't like violence believe it or not." He said and chuckled.

"You're not less."

"Thank you for saying that."

I shrugged. "You've got a good heart. I can tell."

"Are you going to tell me what pissed you off now?"

I thought he'd let it go, but I was wrong. "No."

"You were upset after I talked about Eden and my connection to her."

My cheeks heated and I nibbled my lip. "I don't know why. I didn't like you talking about her."

For a minute, he didn't talk. He sped up to the cabin dragging me behind him. He led me up the path and I gasped. It was big and beautiful. I climbed the stairs behind him, and when I went inside I nearly cried. The living area was bigger than my apartment back home, and it smelled clean. If I was honest this cabin was nicer than anything I had ever lived in. I felt ashamed. I didn't come from wealth or whatever it was the Denynso came from. I was at the bottom of the chain. From the wrong side of the tracks so to speak. Each day was a struggle for me, and I wouldn't admit the truth to anyone. No one knew my main reason for taking the assignment. I wouldn't tell them.

"This is it. There are two rooms and a bathroom. The kitchen has been fully stocked, and when you need more food, it can be delivered to you."

I stood in the middle of the room and the tears came. I couldn't stop them. I didn't know what was going on, but I felt overwhelmed and undeserving. I was basically here to use them, and even though they wanted me to write about them it felt wrong. Humans were selfish and feared the unknown. Would I actually be helping? I vowed I would do my best though.

"What's wrong?"

I turned away and my shoulders shook.

"Are you crying?" he asked, and I heard torment in his voice.

He came behind me and wrapped his arms around me. I was small so his forearms covered my chest. He was warm and comforting. Around him I didn't have to hide or pretend. I felt I could be me.

5

———

She was crying, and he didn't know what to do. The females never cried, or at least they never allowed the males to see it. He spun her to face him and became frustrated when she was able to avoid eye contact. He growled and lifted her in his arms and plopped down on the couch holding her on his lap.

She gasped and scrambled to get off of him, but he didn't let go.

"What wrong beautiful?"

"It's—" she shook her head and pressed her lips together.

He felt her resistance. "You can talk to me, always."

"Right, like I haven't heard that a million times in my life. I'm 28 years old, and I'm alone. No friends, no family. I'm on my own, always have been." Her eyes widened as if she told him something she hadn't planned to share.

"Well, you're not anymore. Do you want to know why you have those strange feelings?"

She nodded, and Ciyrs sighed. He didn't want to freak her out so soon, but he realized his mate had some baggage and some major trust issues.

"You're my mate. It's why I went crazy on Pyra for talking to you. It's why I shockingly yelled at my leader when he thought about assigning a warrior to you instead of me. It's why my eyes shift to orange, and it's why you feel how hard my body is beneath yours."

Her lips parted on a gasp and her emerald eyes rounded in surprise. She didn't speak and he gripped her small hand in his. She blinked and the surprise was gone. "Your mate? You've just met me, you can't possibly know that."

"That's how it works; you can ask Pyra and the king if you don't believe me. Instant soul wrenching attraction. You feel it too. Though humans see it as lust correct?"

She nodded. "I've never—"

She blushed and he gripped her fingers. "Never what?"

"I'm a virgin," she said quickly. "I know I'm a little too old, but I've never found anyone that deserved to take that away from me."

Now it was Ciyrs's turn to be surprised. Eden had told him about human women. Sex was something that was used for many things for humans as well as for them. It was a past time; a time to enjoy and being intimate with another person brings closeness. Knowing his mate had never had a man inside of her had him nearly panting. She tried to cover her face in shame, but he pulled her hands back.

"That is nothing to be ashamed of. I—wow, I think I'm the luckiest man alive. I'll be your first and your last."

She glared through the last of her tears. "What makes you think that?"

"We're mates."

"How do I know that isn't some line to get in my pants?"

He growled but then shook his head. She was trying to get to him. "You'll see. You feel it, and soon you won't be able to fight your feelings. You'll see they are real and that I'm not just messing with you to use you. I would never—"

She shook her head and pressed her finger against his lips quieting him. "Don't make promises you can't keep. I've had enough broken promises in my life. I couldn't stand to have another one, not from you."

Eliana stood from his lap and paced. "I'd like to be alone now. I need to sleep."

He thought about arguing, but the look on her face held him back. She pleaded to be left alone, and he knew it had been too soon. She had just arrived and he'd already upset her. He shook his head. "I'm sorry. I'll be outside."

"You don't need to right? Only if I needed to leave the cabin."

"I don't want to leave you alone."

She sighed. "Fine, but I'm going to bed."

Watching her walk away was hard, but letting her walk away upset was devastating. He needed to talk to Eden. She'd be able to help. He closed his eyes and thought of her. They'd formed their telepathic link. It was something Pyra was still pissed about, but it actually had come in handy so he shut up about it even if he hated it.

'What's wrong Ciyrs?'

'She's mad already. Can you talk?'

'Pyra says we're on our way.'

'Thank you, baby doll.'

In a few minutes Pyra and Eden were standing in front of him. The lights were out inside and he looked at his feet. "I think I messed up already."

Eden sat next to him and wrapped her arm around him. "Tell me what happened."

"When we got inside she started to cry. I'm not used to it. You're the first female I've ever seen cry and that sucked, but seeing her tears was devastating."

Pyra sat on his other side sporting a bruised jaw. "Did she tell you why?"

"Not really. I told her we were mates, she told me she was a virgin, and then I told her how happy that made me—"

Eden laughed. "Are you stupid? She was probably embarrassed as hell. She's older than me?"

"28."

"Then there's a reason she's held so tightly to her v-card. What else?"

"She stopped me from telling her she was no longer alone. Apparently, she doesn't have family or anything. She cut me off telling me not to make promises I couldn't keep. That she couldn't handle it."

Eden nodded and teared up. Her hormones kicked in. "Oh my. She's had a bad life. She doesn't trust, and she's been disappointed too much. I totally get it. You'll have to be gentle with her heart Ciyrs. She isn't going to know how to take you or accept your loyalty to her. If it's as bad as I'm thinking, she'll be scared shitless of you now."

"Why?" He panicked inside. She'd already been able to shut down and kicked him out. "I didn't mean to upset her. I didn't want to tell her about her being my mate just yet, but she freaked out when I talked about you and didn't understand why, so I explained it to her. I don't want there to be lies between us, and after what happened with you and Pyra at the beginning there can't be miscommunication; not with the Klimnu getting through to our lands. I need her aware and with me, not pissed at me."

Pyra stood and laid his hands on Ciyrs's shoulders. "Calm down, just go in there and take charge. She'll be nervous, but if you let her shut you out, she'll think you don't care. You saw what happened with me and Eden, don't make the same mistakes I did."

He nodded. Pyra had been miserable especially when she was in her coma and hadn't been able to be there for her. He thought she was going to die mad at him. They'd been lucky though. "You're right. Thanks, and sorry for dragging you out this late."

Eden nodded pulling him into a hug. "Get your mate. Convince her you mean business."

Then they sped away in the dark. It was pitch black out now, and in a few hours the sun would rise. He climbed the stairs and quietly walked inside shutting and locking the door. He walked down the hall and pushed her door open. She was lying on her bed looking at the ceiling and her eyes were open.

"Can I come in?"

She jumped, but nodded.

He slipped his boots off and went to the other side of

her bed. Above the covers, he lay next to her with his heart beating wildly in his chest. When she reached for his hand he sighed in relief just by her touch. She didn't say anything and neither did he. Instead he listened as her breathing evened out letting him know she had fallen asleep.

6

———

It wasn't possible to feel like this so quickly, but I did. I turned to face the man who called me his and smiled. After my outburst, I felt like an idiot and wished I could take it back. He didn't seem to mind, and when his eyes zeroed in on my lips I licked them inviting him to kiss me. I wasn't only a virgin. I'd never been kissed either. A few times someone had tried and gotten my cheek, but I'd never been *kissed*. Not in the way that I read about in stories. Oh, how I wished he would.

His eyes changed and I gasped. It was amazing. They went from a deep ocean blue to a glowing orange. This time they didn't change back.

"Are you scared?"

I nodded. "Not for the reason you are thinking though."

"Do you know what I'm thinking?"

"Your eyes."

"They don't scare you?"

"Not even a little bit."

He leaned in, and then his lips were on mine softly, then demanding, and it was the most amazing feeling I had ever had. His tongue licked my bottom lip and instinctively I knew what he was asking, and I parted my lips slowly letting him in. His tongue found mine and heat rushed throughout my body.

He moaned and pulled my body against him. I felt the hardness beneath the fabric of his pants. My body quaked with pleasure, and I whimpered when he pulled back.

His eyes were wide and his face was flushed. Strands of white hair hung in his face and he blew them out of his way. His eyes glowed brighter and his body shook.

"You're beautiful," I said and he was. I'd never seen anyone like him before.

"That's my line, Eliana. And you are beautiful," he replied and groaned when I felt a bit braver and slid my leg over his hip bringing us closer together.

I kissed him again liking the closeness. He was so big, and I felt tiny and safe with his arms wrapped around me. He slid his hand up the back of my shirt and ran his fingers down my spine. I arched pressing my breasts into him. My core ached with need and I fidgeted against him. I might have been a virgin, but I knew exactly what was going on with my body. I was educated.

"I don't want to rush you, love," he said and I smiled.

"I have this ache." My voice was low, and I almost didn't recognize it.

Then I felt his finger slip between my legs. I was only wearing thin shorts and the heat from his finger burned. I gasped when he slid his finger beneath the fabric meeting my bare flesh. He froze when he felt the wetness and his body tensed.

"Good god, you're burning up," he said and massaged me.

I threw my head back, and then his lips were on my throat. My body jerked against his hand when he sped up his motions. It was fantastic. I withered and cried out. He kept going and I squirmed. "It's too much," I cried out and when he kissed me, and then I felt him slide his finger inside of me. I moaned into his mouth and rode against him. Nothing felt so strange and amazing at the same time. It was unreal. I wanted—no I needed more, and then the feeling inside of me boiled over as my body tensed and I released for the first time. My eyes were like saucers, and I pulled back from his kiss and let out a guttural groan. I rocked against his hand and then my body slowed down as my climax eased into the tiny waves of aftershocks.

My heart raced, and I shook with a feeling I wasn't sure what to make of. He smiled and kissed the corner of my mouth almost as if he couldn't resist.

"Wow," I said and let my head fall back. He removed his hand from my shorts and from the corner of my eye I watched him lick his finger. I thought I would be repulsed but it only made me clench inside.

"That was amazing."

He nodded watching me. "You know, now you're mine."

His voice had turned deep and taken on a possessive edge. I nodded and laid my hand over his heart. "Yours," I whispered. Never before had one word meant so much to me, and even though I wasn't sure exactly what it meant for him, I knew he was mine too.

I HEARD a noise and tiptoed through my new home carrying the first thing I could use as a weapon, a small wood log. Who knew I'd feel secure with the hard wood between my fingers, but I did. The sun peaked through the curtains as I made my way to the front door. Since I was short, I had the advantage. On the other side of the door I saw the top of a head with a white Mohawk and sighed in relief. It had to be Pyra.

I stepped close and opened the door holding the wood close. When I opened the door, I quickly realized my mistake. I found it wasn't him. In the giant warrior's place stood a grotesques thing; I wasn't sure what it was, but I knew it was time to be terrified. It smiled at me with needle sharp teeth and bright red eyes. It tilted its head to the side and cackled. Every hair on my body stood, and I went to slam the door, but it reached out with razor sharp claws and pulled me outside. The sting of its claw digging into my skin brought tears to my eyes, and I whimpered in pain. I didn't even have a chance to fight.

"Shut up!" And everything inside of me went silent. I tried to scream, but I couldn't. My voice was gone and my eyes were wide as tears streamed down them. I had a feeling this thing was what they talked about. This thing was their breech in security.

He lifted me over his shoulder gripping my tiny frame tightly, and then we disappeared. There was nothing but inky darkness, and then I was thrown on something smelly and damp. I cringed and screamed. This time my voice worked, and I heard the evil cackle again before I heard the sound of a lock sliding into place. I couldn't see anything, and I wrapped my arms around my knees and rocked. Something had taken me that easily. It was smart and somehow tricked me. I was alone and my body shook from more than the freezing bitter cold. I'd never felt fear like this before.

7

───────

Ciyrs woke up and felt the bed beside him. The sheet was cold, and he jumped up in a panic. She was gone. He stormed through the cabin and roared. The windows shook and pictures crashed to the floor shattering the glass. The front door was open and he glared out into the sun. There was a strange silence as if the land was scared.

He raced to the Great House and pounded on the door without stopping. The king opened the door and the smile he had on his face fell immediately.

"No!"

"She's gone. I don't know how. I stayed with her all night. But she's fucking gone, and I'm terrified."

The King closed his eyes and sent a message. He was able to call to the warriors. In a matter of a few minutes, every warrior was climbing the stairs. Pyra and Eden attached by each other's side came to him. Eden threw her arms around him. She felt his pain and he sobbed into her hair. "She's gone baby doll. I failed."

He pulled back and looked at his feet. "You were right. She needed a warrior, not some useless healer like me." He couldn't take it, and when the king went to speak he shook his head and he was gone. It was his fault. His stupid possessiveness put her in danger, and now he didn't know what to do. He wasn't a warrior. He was just a healer. He had magic, but it wasn't enough to bring her back.

He went into the infirmary where he belonged and fell to the floor sobbing like he never had before. It was bad enough he always felt this way, but now his own uselessness had been reaffirmed. He would never be strong. Not like his brothers.

It wasn't long before the doors opened and every warrior and the king filed into his space. The infirmary was his.

It was the king who approached him. He wrapped Ciyrs in his arms and held him.

"You are not useless, and if we have in any way made you feel inferior then we apologize."

The rest of the warriors all agreed with loud voices. When Creia pulled back he saw the others waiting expectantly.

Eden was the only woman, but she was who he needed. She stepped around Pyra and took his hand. "You can find her. You're connected, I can feel it. The bond has started and your eyes are still orange."

He nodded. They'd begun the bond all right.

"Then focus, just like you taught me when healing. Focus on her. Her scent, the feel of her skin, the sound of her heart. Listen to your heart; it will lead you to her."

He nodded again and closed his eyes.

It was so dark, so cold. I shivered and tears soaked my skin and shirt. It wasn't him. "I feel her."

"Go back Ciyrs, find your mate."

The sound of the lock made me shake in fear. They were back and he was going to touch me again. Get inside my head. He'd tricked me before, and now I didn't know what was real and what wasn't. This time when he came he looked like—ME

Ciyrs's eyes shot open and he gasped. "Illusions. Those fuckers have her!"

The room erupted in loud shouts and promises of retribution. "The Klimnu are stronger than we knew. Those things can take on our appearances. It's why they can walk through the compound without much notice. How the hell do they do that?"

Eden sobbed. "She's so scared."

"You feel her?"

"Yes, she—she doesn't understand. She thought it was Pyra at the door, she let him in."

Pyra froze. "I didn't fucking go to her cabin."

"No, but one of them knew she would trust you. How are they getting so much information on us?"

"They're here somewhere we haven't searched. They have to be," Pyra replied and he growled anger taking over.

It wasn't going to be good if all the warriors lost it right now. They needed to be calm and work together to find Eliana.

Eden stomped her foot and yelled. "STOP!" the whole building shook with her rage and her eyes glowed with anger. She fisted her hands and tears streamed down her cheeks. "Focus, Ciyrs's mate is in the hands of one of those slimy bastards. We can't let them do to her what they did to me. I feel her. She's terrified. I don't know why I feel her, maybe it's because of our bond, but I literally feel like my heart is being ripped from my chest. So buck up Warriors you're going on a mission. Get our fucking mate back!"

The men were all stunned to silence. She was commanding, and no one wanted to cross her. They all shut up and the king smirked, "Well, if I need to get them in line again I know who to call. But now Eden you need to focus too, between you and Ciyrs you should be able to find her."

She nodded and grabbed his hands and closed her eyes. He let his eyes close too. The feel of her hands in his reassured him, but there was only darkness, and in the distance he thought he heard whimpering.

'Tell me girl!'

'I don't know. I've only been there one day.'

He cackled and she cringed. 'How are you so close to the healer then?'

She shook her head refusing to speak.

Pain tore through her shoulders as his claws dug into her skin, sinking into her flesh, ripping, tearing. She screamed a blood curdling scream, but it did no good.

Eden gasped and yanked her hands away from him. His body shook. "They're hurting her. Trying to get information. She refused."

Eden paled, and then she vomited all over the floor. He caught her before she fell to the floor. He carried her to the table.

"I felt it."

"No more, you can't take the stress. We have to think of the baby."

"I need to help find her."

"No, we can't risk you baby doll. I'll have to focus harder on my own."

Despair filled him. He'd felt her pain too. They were going to torture his mate, and there wasn't a damn thing he could do about it. It seemed like the damned Klimnu were always one step ahead of them.

8

They left me alone again. It was better than having them close. At least I could handle the darkness. The damp cold wasn't any worse than his touch. He came and looked like Ciyrs and laughed when he saw the hope in my eyes. The hope that Ciyrs hadn't broken his promise. That he wouldn't let anything happen to me. But then the figure morphed back into his monstrous self. I cringed as the beady red eyes looked at me as if he could read my soul.

"Are you ready to tell me what I want to know?"

I glared at him. I didn't care how badly they hurt me, I was a fighter. I had never once given up in my terrible life, and I wouldn't start now. Not when I finally had something to live for. I knew Ciyrs was looking for me. I felt his pain. The only problem was I couldn't figure out how to tell him where I was. I didn't fucking know where I was.

My shoulders and arms throbbed in pain. The blood had finally dried, but anytime I moved the scabs would break open, and it would start all over again. So I sat as still as possible and tried to figure out what to do.

The thing crowded me and then his vile tongue licked my face. I gagged and I would have thrown up if there was anything left in my stomach. His breath was like death and decay. "You taste good."

I shuddered. It wasn't the first time he'd said that, and this thing liked to lick. He wrapped his bony fingers around my throat and I gasped. He squeezed tighter and licked the tears the leaked from my eyes. I tried to breathe slow and not panic, but my eyes widened and my pulse fluttered. The fear was back full force. The tips of his claws dug into my neck and I felt the warm red liquid slide down my neck. He panted and lifted me to my feet. He pressed his bony body against mine and I felt his arousal. My body shook with the mixture of fear and revulsion.

"I need to know. How did you get so close so fast? We've been studying them for a long time, and even our illusions haven't gotten us far. We need their king. He is the key to our freedom."

I choked and gripped skin and bone trying to dig my nails into his skin. I felt my body losing its life right before he removed his hand and I fell to the ground. I held my throat and gasped for breath. Coughing I looked into his eyes. "I don't know anything I swear," I said gasping. My throat burned, and I felt the tiny holes from his claws. If this didn't stop I wouldn't last much longer. I'd already lost a lot of blood. I wasn't even sure how long they had me.

"What are you?"

He made his strange cackling sound and licked his thin bluish lips. "I am Klimnu, and we are the more superior race. Your little warriors haven't caught us yet, and each day we get stronger. The longer we're here, the more we feed off of their tempers, and the stronger we become."

"They'll figure it out," I said. I wanted to make him mad. Making him mad made him go away.

"No they won't, not from you. I'm bored with you already." He sighed as if it pained him to say.

"Go ahead and kill me. I've got nothing to offer you." I hope he didn't really kill me. I didn't have anything, but I hoped he would think otherwise. I needed to stall long enough to find a way to communicate with Ciyrs. It shouldn't be so damn hard. I was his fucking mate.

CIYRS' eyes shot open. She taunted them, and he'd never been so scared in his life. What the hell was she doing? He needed her to cooperate. He burned with a rage so deep. He couldn't wait to get a hold of the slimy bastard that touched her. He was going to tear him apart with his bare hands. His body shook with the urge to kill, something his healing soul didn't normally feel. He needed to find her and he needed to get revenge. His body came to life and for the first time he felt like he was one of his brothers. He didn't feel weak or useless.

The magic soared through his body and he gasped when his hands glowed, but instead of being the normal white, his power burned red. His body lit up and he cried out when the heat became too much. That was new, but he didn't fear it, he wanted to use it because inside he knew it did the opposite of his healing. He wasn't sure how it happened but he somehow became much more useful.

9

———

The next morning, they were still no closer to finding her. She'd now been in the hands of the Klimnu for nearly two days. He could feel her, but she was fading. He no longer felt her fear, or her will to fight. He didn't know what they'd done to her, she'd somehow shut him out, but he knew it was bad. She wasn't the same anymore. He knew he hadn't gotten to know her well before she was taken, but he knew. Eliana wasn't Eliana any longer.

He paced the room and Ero came in holding his stomach. He was bleeding pretty badly, but Ciyrs didn't care. He had pretty much lost all hope of ever finding her, and if she died a part of him would too. He wouldn't be good for anything.

"Hey, uh, I know it may not be a good time, but can you?" Ero walked over to him slowly. Everyone was leery about Ciyrs. No one knew how he was going to react at any given moment. He wasn't stable.

"Sit."

Ero nodded and sat on the table.

Ciyrs laid him back and closed his eyes. He felt both parts of him. The one no one knew about and his healing side. He was tempted to test his new power, but deep inside he couldn't. It didn't matter how lost he was. He would not hurt one of his brothers. He called to his good half and healed him. It felt good on his fingertips. The heat from his power flowed into Ero.

Ero's eyes fluttered shut and he moaned. Ciyrs was used to this. His power had that effect on them all. It was why it was so private. He knew his warrior brothers would be embarrassed if someone saw their raging hard on after he patched them up. It was why Pyra hated it when Eden healed.

He felt Ero's hand reach for his and he let him grip his fingers as the healing finished. Sometimes he thought the warrior did it on purpose. He was hurt more times than not, and the thoughts of him having feelings for him had crossed his mind more than once, but he shook it off.

He just wanted someone to care. Ero wasn't like them all. He wasn't as big or as strong. He was an orphan and the king and queen basically adopted him when he was a kid. For all intents, he was Pyra's brother, but he was a jack ass most of the time. Like he had to make up for what he lacked in size.

"Enough," he said and Ero opened his eyes blushing.

"Sorry, you would think it wouldn't do that to me anymore."

Ciyrs sighed. "It's normal, but I need to be alone please."

"Still no luck in finding her?"

"No and she's giving up."

Ero shrugged. "A real mate wouldn't."

It was the wrong thing to say. Ciyrs glared at him and in one swift move held him in the air by his throat.

"You stupid fucker. You need to learn to keep your damn mouth shut. She is my fucking mate. How dare you!"

Ero struggled in his grasp but Ciyrs was gone. All the control he held over the years broke. His hand heated up and his warrior friend screamed.

He wasn't aware of anything after. He blacked out and when he opened his eyes he tugged at his arms. He was restrained to a bed. "What the hell?"

Pyra came into view, then Eden. Her face was streaked with tears. "What's wrong baby doll?"

"You don't remember?"

"Uh—help me out here, because I so obviously don't know what's going on. Why the hell am I being restrained?"

"Ciyrs you injured Ero badly."

He shook his head. "No I wouldn't do that. He can be an ass, but we all know why."

"You did. I had to heal his wounds. I don't know what you did, but his flesh around his neck was burned, like he was in a fire."

Realization dawned on his then. He didn't remember but he remembered the feelings. "Oh fuck."

"Where is he? I have to apologize. He just made me snap, I know that much. I healed him, and then he made a comment about Eliana not being a real mate and I lost it."

"Fucking shit, he knows better by now. No wonder you lost it, but how the hell did you burn him?"

"I seem to have gotten a new power. One I'm not sure will be good until I get a handle on my temper."

Eden tensed. "What kind of power?"

"Not the good kind baby doll. At least if it's used on friends." Ciyrs shook his head. "I am two different people now. A part of me heals and the other part of me destroys. I'm torn between good and bad and I have no fucking idea what to do. I need Eliana, I need my fucking mate." Then he broke down and sobbed. Eden climbed on the bed and wrapped her arms around him pulling him close.

"Shh, we'll find her. I don't know how but we will."

"It's no use. I don't feel her anymore."

Eden pulled back and her brows knitted together. "I do."

"What?" He felt a bit of hope.

"Yeah she isn't doing well, but she's still alive."

"Don't fuck with me baby doll."

"Hey don't!" Pyra growled.

"Oh calm down he's just excited." She brushed his tears away. "She's alive. I bet she shut you out. Probably not on purpose either. I think it's time I reached out again."

He shook his head. "But the baby. I can't ask you to do that."

"You're not. But I'm doing it. We need her back. I won't be able to go on feeling your suffering on a daily basis Ciyrs. Your pain is my pain."

He nodded understanding because she understood what he went through. Her pain was his too.

He looked at Pyra who growled. "Like I have a choice. She won't listen to me."

Ciyrs had to bite back a smile. Eden was a stubborn woman, and he knew she was the key to finding Eliana, or so he hoped.

10

———

"It's no use. They won't find you. I told you we're smarter than them. We can block them."

I sighed and let my head fall back. I had been trying to get a message out. But it was like there was a block. My messages weren't getting out. "Why? I don't have the answers you're looking for. Can't you just let me go?"

He laughed and his eyes burned brighter. "We've already established that I'm not stupid and you want me to send you back?"

"It's not like I'd be able to tell them where I was. I've seen nothing but your freaky eyes and darkness for days."

He backhanded me and I tasted blood, but I was done playing his fucking game. I stood on wobbly feet and fisted my hands. I felt the end was near, and I wasn't going down without one hell of a fight. If I didn't get to live to see my mate again I was going to make this Klimnu bastard pay.

He stood back relaxed and amused by the look of his

smile. I focused on Ciyrs and his love for me. I knew he loved me. It didn't matter how little time we'd known one another. It was true, and it was as real as the beat of my heart. His orange eyes stared back at me and I gasped. It was that damned illusion again.

"You could never be him."

"Oh, but I can," he said and gripped my hips and ground his creepy ass erection against my stomach.

I shuddered and spit on his face. "You're not even a fourth of the man as Ciyrs and you make me sick you creepy bastard."

He wiped the spit from his cheek and let me go laughing. "You think that's going to upset me?" I stared as he licked my spit from his bony fingers. EW. I shook my head and shuddered.

I was losing my damned mind. My body shook with a rage I had never felt before and my arms to the tips of my fingers heated and when I lifted my arm they glowed red. "Holy shit!"

The Klimnu stared frozen in shock for a few seconds before he stepped back. "What are you?" He tilted his head seemingly entranced by the glow of my body.

"I'm nothing." But at that moment I certainly was something. I focused more and the heat burned stronger. I broke out in a sweat and stalked towards the monster who figured out he might have been in a little bit of trouble. I narrowed my eyes and wrapped my small hand around his tiny throat. His eyes widened and his mouth opened and he let out a wail that shot straight to my head. It pierced my ears and I couldn't stop the pain reverberating through my body. I screamed too and tightened my hold on the monster who stole me away from my new home. I would not give up.

The smell of burning flesh filled my nose and my eyes watered. His body struggled helplessly against me. His body lost its strength as I sucked his life away. That's what I was doing, I was taking his life.

After his eyes rolled back into his skull I dropped his bones to the ground. They shattered into a pile of dust and I looked at my hand. It no longer glowed, but his ash covered my hands. I wiped them on my jeans and took a deep breath.

"What the hell happened?" I asked, but there was no one there to answer me.

I bent and dug through the pile of ash and found the keys he used to lock me inside. Feeling around for the door I gripped the cool metal of the door and sighed. Pulling it open, I waited for others to come, but it was silent, and I tiptoed down a dimly lit hall. The light was bright to my eyes. When I made it to the end of the hall I looked both ways wondering which way was right. I shook my head and went left hoping for the best. I needed to get out of this place, and I needed my mate. I needed Ciyrs.

HEALED BY THE ALIEN

COVER

GRACE KENSINGTON
HEALED BY THE ALIEN
ALIEN WARRIOR MATES I | BOOK 4

1

———

Ciyrs shot up from bed. After days, the king had forced him to rest. He finally fell asleep until the dream. He blinked his eyes and looked around his room. The sun had risen and peaked around the corners of his curtains. After Eden had tried and failed to reach out to Eliana, he had all but given up. If he couldn't sense her, he couldn't find her. The warriors were out searching for her, but so far nothing.

He jumped up when he heard a loud banging on the door. "Ciyrs you fucker get up!"

He groaned when he heard Gyyx yelling outside and he ran to the door wondering if something had happened. He pulled open the door and frowned. Gyyx stood on his porch heaving and his eyes were orange. "Your mate—I think I might have found her—the general area she is in anyways."

He stared at Pyra's younger brother and couldn't get over how much they looked alike. The long white Mohawk, the blue eyes that were orange at the moment.

He was huge but not as big as his older brother. *Wait did he just say he might have found her?* In a moment, too quick to stop, his hand gripped the shirt Gyyx wore and he lifted him off the ground.

"Where?"

"What the hell Ciyrs? Put me down you asshole."

"Shit, sorry. I seem to be changing."

Gyyx chuckled and smoothed his shirt out. "Apparently. But anyways, for the past day and a half, some of us have been searching further out looking for your lady. And now I'm reacting just like my brother. My eyes shift, and I'm hard as shit. Basically, I am pretty sure she's my mate too—"

Ciyrs roared. "No way. She's mine. You're mistaken."

"Why the hell am I freaking out then?"

Ciyrs's eyes widened. "Maybe your mate is here. These Klimnu seem to be pretty good at getting on our land. What's to say they haven't intercepted visitors?"

Gyyx's jaw clenched. "So what you're saying is—my mate could have already been taken by those slimy bastards, and I'm just now figuring it out?"

"Yeah sounds plausible."

"Shit, I'm already a terrible mate. She's gonna hate me."

"Don't be so hard on yourself. I didn't know what was going on until Pyra laughed at my temper."

"But shouldn't I have sensed her?"

"Not if she hasn't been here long. She's got to be close."

"And I have a feeling where we find your Elaina, I'll find my mate. Unless Elaina is meant for both of us."

Ciyrs's hand glowed red and he held back from killing

the man before him. He had to remember he was a friend. "No, she's only meant to be mine."

Gyyx backed away with his hands up in surrender. "So fucker lets go find our women. You are connected to your mate already I'm not. We need to find them and then figure out how the hell the Klimnu are taking our women."

"Let's go," Ciyrs replied. The sooner he found Elaina the sooner he could really sleep, and next time he wouldn't let go of her. She wasn't leaving his sight—ever again.

Gyyx led the way slowing to a normal speed so Ciyrs could keep up. He was grateful because even though he learned he had warrior abilities he still wasn't a warrior, he was a healer.

"Where did you get a sense that—" Ciyrs said and froze when a vision of Eliana slammed into him.

She ran frantically through the maze of halls. Her feet were dirty, and she ignored the rocks beneath her soles. The pain of something sharp imbedded into her foot and she sucked in a breath but kept moving. She had to get away. She shoved her hair out of her face and bit her lip tasting the copper of her blood. She hurt everywhere, but she couldn't stop moving. She didn't know when more would come. She didn't know how she turned the one to ash. She was a freak. Tears slid down her cheeks, but still she kept moving.

The sound of sobbing startled her and Eliana froze looking wildly into the darkness. Her eyes had finally adjusted and she could make out a shaking figure. Red flags rose and she was about to keep moving until she heard the mere whisper, "help me."

Eliana was scared, but she edged her way closer to the

figure. When she stood over the prone woman she gasped. The woman was rail thin and pale. She had bite marks all over her body and she wore only a bra and panties. Her ribs poked out of her side and the stench filled her nose. She did her best not to gag, but this woman had been there for a while.

"You're not one of them?"

The woman didn't speak but she saw the slight shake to her head.

"You better not be," she grumbled and bent to lift the woman.

She shrieked and her body shook before she stopped moving all together. Eliana felt for a pulse and sighed when she realized the woman was unconscious. Lifting her from the ground the best she could, she half carried and half dragged the woman from the small prison. Taking a deep breath, she sent out a prayer that she would find the damn exit.

"I found her; she has a woman with her."

Gyyx froze and spun to look at him. "A woman?" his eyes shifted to orange.

"Yeah, she's unconscious, sick, injured, but alive. Eliana is bringing her out. They're at the old warehouse. The one that was supposed to be torn down. How the hell did we miss it?"

They ran using their speed. For the first time Ciyrs used all the things he locked up inside. He had no idea what they would come across on the way, but right now there were two women who needed him. One needed some major healing and the other—well she just needed him.

She was getting heavy, and I was tiring out, but I couldn't stop. Not until I found my way out. Everything hurt. I'd never been more tired, but my will to survive was stronger than my need to rest. I pushed through, but ran into another dead in. I screamed in frustration and tried to keep my tears locked up tight, but I was slowly falling apart. Who the hell created a maze like this?

I sobbed and fell to the ground with my arms wrapped around the strange woman. I let out all of my fears and allowed myself time to cry. Then I'd pick myself back up and find my way out. I rocked back and forth holding tight to the only other person around—and she wasn't even conscious.

I screamed when hands wrapped around my arm pulling me up from the ground. I kicked and tried to get away but the arms tightened holding me against a hard, warm body. I couldn't be taken—not again. I wouldn't survive it again.

"Baby, calm down, it's me."

I froze and opened my eyes. Looking back at me were orange eyes ringed in dark circles. "Ciyrs?"

"Fucking hell baby, I'm so sorry!" Then he buried his face into my neck.

I didn't have any fear it wasn't him. His touch was right. I relaxed my body into his and then pulled back remembering the woman I'd found. "The woman, she's hurt."

Ciyrs looked down at the prone woman to see Gyyx pull her into his arms. His eyes were orange and a tear slid down his cheek.

"She's mine. You were right."

I slid down Ciyrs's body ignoring his protest and fell to the floor. "She's been out the whole time. Except at first. I don't know what happened. I guess the shock finally wore off."

Gyyx looked at me with his eye shining. "Thank you for taking her with you. Most people wouldn't do that."

I laid my hand on his and in a split-second I was whipped away. Ciyrs growled. "You can't touch him right now baby. I'm already going crazy."

"He's hurting. Look at him."

"He'll be fine as soon as we get back and I work on his mate. Better yet Eden will. He won't want to rip her head off. I probably can't get near her."

"I know you won't do anything Ciyrs, let's get the hell out of here. We'll tell the others to patrol here until we can burn this fucking building to the ground."

I wrapped my arms around Ciyrs and shut my eyes as he sped from my own personal hell. I'd make sure this building burned. No one would suffer in those cells again. I looked at Gyyx and the woman I had found. She probably knew better than anyone else what is was like to be in their hands. It looked like she had been there for a while. The poor woman was rail thin and sickly looking. But I could tell by the look in the Denynso's eyes that she was the most beautiful creature to him. It was the way Ciyrs looked at me.

With my head on his shoulder, I felt the cool rush of air as the wind whipped around us. He ran fast and I was grateful when I opened my eyes to find myself in his house. He kissed me and held me close while I sobbed. There were so many things to talk about, but all I wanted to do was fall apart and clean the Klimnu off of me.

"I tried finding you, and I failed. Eden tried to use her connection to help. She felt you but couldn't figure out where you were. The warriors have been searching nonstop. I'm so sorry I failed you." Ciyrs fell to his knees in front of me.

I placed my hand on his head. He had his arms wrapped tightly around my waist and he sobbed. I did my best to comfort him. "Oh Ciyrs, you didn't fail me."

He tipped his head up looking at me. I wiped his tears. "It's not your fault I was taken."

"I should have known. We're mates. Our bond was formed."

"Newly mated. Who knows how long it takes for it to really click. I don't blame you."

He nodded, but I could tell he wasn't convinced. "I need to get cleaned up."

Reluctantly he pulled away and gripped my hand like

a life line as he led me to his bathroom. Without a word, he turned on the shower and then he pulled off my clothes. I shivered when I was naked and didn't miss the way his eyes glowed.

"Can I help?"

I nodded and nibbled my lip. I needed his closeness. No matter how dirty I felt.

He stripped off his clothes and led me into the shower. The warmth of the water eased the aches and pains and washed away the dirt, but it didn't wash away the memory of the touch. I closed my eyes and Ciyrs spun me around. In a few moments, I felt his hands in my hair lathering in some shampoo and then he tipped my head back rinsing my hair. I let him take care of me. I knew he needed it. He was a care giver. It's what he did. He healed, and when his large hands stroked my body gently with the sudsy cloth he healed a part of me. I knew his touch. I knew he would never hurt me.

After all that had happened, I felt the ache between my legs. I couldn't control the desire building and I turned facing him. He tensed when he scented my arousal and shook his head.

"I'd love to but I need to take care of you first."

"But that is taking care of me." I picked up his hand and brought it between my legs spreading them, allowing him to feel the wetness. "I need you. And I know you need me."

His erection sprung to life and I wrapped my small hand around it. "See, you want me."

He groaned when I slid my slick hand down and ran my thumb over the tip. "Of course I do Eliana. I've missed you like hell. I've nearly gone insane without you."

I licked my lip. "Then show me."

I needed to get my mind off of it all, and there was no better way than to lose myself in the man I loved—loved, that was the first time I admitted it to myself. I loved Ciyrs.

3

———

She was trying to kill him. Ciyrs watched her eyes dilate and scented the musky scent of her arousal. He was trying to behave and take care of her before sinking into her. He didn't want to push her if she wasn't ready, but apparently she was. He felt her wetness, saw it in her eyes, and when she touched him he knew he was a goner.

In a rough move, he lifted her and shoved her against the tiled wall. "Wrap your legs around me."

She did and then he slid inside of her in one swift movement. She cried out and tightened her legs around him. He groaned when it pushed him deeper inside. She was hot, wet, and her muscles clenched around his cock. His body spasmed and then she kissed him like a starving woman. Her tongue touched his and he held her against the wall making love to her. He went slowly even when his body raged to mark her again. Let the world know she was his. He needed to reestablish his bond with her, but he held back afraid to scare her. Hell, he scared himself.

His new power wasn't the only new change. There was more to him now. He was more than the loveable healer. He had a dark side now, and Ciyrs wasn't sure what to do about it. Should he embrace it or run?

"I love you Ciyrs," she said and moaned when the shock of her words had him driving into her rougher.

He watched her eyes and knew she was serious. "I love you too Eliana."

This time when he kissed her, he let the wild in him out. His body heated and she gasped into his mouth. He pulled back to make sure she was okay.

"Your skin is so hot."

"We have a lot to talk about—after."

Then he drove into her taking what was his. She was his and he held her tight against him. She withered and moaned squirming against him and the wall. The more she struggled to move the more aroused he became. "God please don't fucking stop."

Her skin was slick with water and sweat as the shower still poured over them. He rocked into her, and when she screamed his name and yanked his hair pulling his head back he roared as he came inside of her. She quivered and held on to him as he rode out his climax.

He stood holding her against the wall breathing heavily. His skin had gone back to normal, and she gripped his jaw and kissed him lightly on the lips. "I never knew I could miss someone so much."

"Oh baby, I missed you too. Ask anyone; I was sort of nuts knowing you were out there somewhere hurting."

She shivered and he pulled out settling her on her feet. Instead of getting out he took the rag and lathered up more soap. With gentle circles, he cleaned her body before his own. "Let's look you over. You were running barefoot. They probably need healed. Then we need to check on Gyyx's mate."

"I want to see if she's awake."

He pulled her out of the shower and wrapped a towel around her body before grabbing his own and wrapping it around his waist.

He was still aroused, and the need to make love to her all week came to mind, but he had other responsibilities. Gyyx needed him and he owed him a great debt. If it weren't for the royal warrior, he might not have found Eliana.

She rushed to the room and found her bags. He stood back and watched as she pulled out a pair of yoga pants and a tight T-shirt. He went to get dressed himself. By the time he was dressed she was done and groaned when she lifted her arms and stretched. The smooth pale skin peaked out from her shirt.

"Let's go check on them. You can have me again later," she said and smirked.

"Sorry. I've been told the mating fever is fierce. I think it's even worse since it got interrupted and you were taken."

She looped her arm through his and smiled up at him. "I understand. I've never felt like this before. We do need to talk though. There are some things that happened. Something I don't understand."

"I know baby. We will."

He led her outside and by the time they made it to the infirmary the news had spread and everyone offered their support and asked if she needed anything. Eliana was family now. It was their way. The moment he knew she was his, he knew everyone would accept her. She was one of them now.

Eden smiled as soon as she saw them. "Thank god he found you."

Eliana recoiled from Eden and her eyes widened. "Why do I love her?" she asked in a whisper.

"That's Eden. Apparently you have a connection to her through me. What you feel is all of our emotions."

"Oh."

"She was the one who was able to tell me you were alive. You'd shut me out and I panicked."

"How's the woman I found?" She asked, but by the look of sorrow on Gyyx's face it wasn't good.

Eden sighed. "I've healed her body the best I can. She had some nasty bites and such. I don't know, I don't think I'm as strong as Ciyrs, and with the baby I don't have as much energy." She rubbed her belly smiling.

Gyyx looked at him pleading. "Please help her."

"Just don't try to rip my arms off when I touch her."

"I won't. I want her to wake up."

He kept his hand wrapped around Eliana's and stood next to Eden. She backed away giving him space, and he took a deep breath before letting go of his mate's hand. With cautious movements he lowered his hands to the unconscious woman. As soon as his hands made contact an electric shock tore through him. He was thrown back against the wall and landed with a large thump.

Eliana ran to him and helped him to his feet. "What the hell was that?"

Gyyx looked at him with wide eyes. "I didn't touch you I swear."

"I know, but she certainly didn't want me touching her. Eden, did you get shocked?"

"No, but I'm also not as strong as you."

Ciyrs rubbed his head and eyed the new stranger. She was certainly alive. They had no idea who she was, or how long she was with the Klimnu. He could sense she was human so he knew she wasn't actually one of their enemies. It was strange. It was almost as if she knew he wasn't her mate. She didn't want his touch.

"Touch her Gyyx," he said trying to test his theory.

"What?"

He sighed. "Work with me here. Touch her."

Gyyx ran his finger over the bare skin of her arm. He wasn't slammed around and in the silence they heard a small gasp. She didn't wake up, but there was movement behind her closed lids.

"She knows you. Somehow she knows you're the one meant to touch her. Now I'm going to touch her again and see what happens."

Clenching his jaw, he did the same thing Gyyx did and before he finished his move pain tore through his body and he was again thrown back. This time it felt like the electric shock had been powered up a notch. "Holy fucking shit, that hurt."

"I think your theory is correct, Ciyrs, please stop the pain hurts me too," said Eden and her face was pale.

He rushed to her side. "Oh baby doll, I'm sorry. I just wanted to see if this woman was aware. Part of her is." He pulled her into a hug and froze when he heard a gasp.

He pulled away from Eden only to turn to see his mate running out of the infirmary. Shit. He winced and ran after her. He couldn't leave her alone. Not so soon after getting her back, but he had a feeling he was in trouble.

4

———

I couldn't take it. I knew they had a bond, but his cute little pet name for her, and the way they hugged. Something inside of me snapped and I had to get out. Rationally I knew I had nothing to worry about. She was mated to Pyra, and my bond with Ciyrs was growing stronger by the hour. I'd never felt this type of jealously before, and I didn't like it.

I grew up alone, always being second best. I wouldn't do it again. I was either his number one or nothing. Too many years of being shoved off had hardened my heart. The part of me that craved love also feared it as much.

I ran faster than I ever had before, and when I came to a rock that looked over a huge lake I sat down. The sun glistened on the water and it sparkled. It was beautiful, and I found myself falling in love with the land even more.

I felt a presence and tensed. It was Pyra—last time I saw him I was kidnapped. I opened my mouth to scream, but there was something real about him. I eyed him weary ready to defend myself.

"It's really you, right?"

"Yes, I'm so sorry that you were kidnapped. I hate that it was my face they stole. Those fuckers are going to pay —one day. As soon as we can figure out how to get the upper hand."

His temper, yep it was certainly Pyra. "They feed off of your temper."

"How do you know?"

"The one who took me, he told me. He also said they need the king. Something about his power is important to their kind. But you guys are good. Those nasty pricks haven't been able to get to him."

Pyra paced. "They will not take my father. I'll kill them all first." He eyed me curiously. "So why are you out here alone after you just got back?"

I shook my head feeling stupid. He was right. I shouldn't have been running off alone. Tears spilled before I could stop them. "Their bond, how do you deal with it?"

He nodded in understanding and sat on the ground. "Ah, the bond between my mate and yours. It sucks, I won't lie. They have a connection that is unbreakable, and it's annoying as shit. No matter how much I love my brother, I don't like that he knows things I don't, or before I do. Eden keeps us in line. It's not easy, but I promise you'll adjust. It's just something you live with for the other. You love Ciyrs?"

I nodded.

"Then you love Eden?"

"Apparently so, meeting her was strange. I'd never

had such feelings for a woman before. It was quite off putting especially because I didn't understand it. He said they had a bond, but I didn't realize it would affect me too. I guess I'm just jealous and scared all at once."

"It will get better with time. Soon it will be like a bee buzzing in your ear. You swat it away, but it keeps coming back for more until eventually you just ignore it and let it buzz in your ear. I'll admit I've destroyed a lot of things dealing with it."

"Maybe I need to. No offense against your mate, but I don't feel comfortable with it at all. I don't want to be second. I've spent my whole life that way. Always the second choice. Always the second in line. I promised myself to be first even if I had to spend my life alone to achieve it."

"You'll always be first baby." I hadn't heard Ciyrs and I cringed knowing he'd heard my little break down.

I didn't turn towards him, and I smiled down at Pyra when he patted my leg before leaving us alone.

"I'm sorry I didn't think to explain things better. I also shouldn't have put my hands on her in front of you. Not this soon after fully completing the bond again. I just— it's so hard to explain."

"I understand," I said, but I didn't. Maybe one day I would, but until then I wouldn't ever be okay with his emotions for her. "I feel your love for her. It's not something I'm okay with, but I suppose I don't have a choice. No matter how much I want you to myself, it will never happen."

I stood and faced him but I couldn't meet his eye. Seemed fate hated me just as I always thought.

"It's not even like that, sweetheart. I love her like a

sister. Denynso are close by nature anyways. We love strong, but the love I feel for her is certainly different than the love I feel for you. You're always going to be my number one, but she will always be important to me."

I nodded. It wasn't rational, but I wanted to be alone, away from them all. I wouldn't lie, I felt like throwing a tantrum like a child, but I was almost 30, I was an adult, even if I didn't want to be at the moment. "Please take me somewhere so I can be alone."

He sighed and tried to grab my hand. I yanked it back and did my best to ignore the hurt.

"I can't, not right now okay. Please I just need to find a way to deal with this in my own way."

He nodded and walked in front of me keeping his pace slow. I felt the tension and I felt how upset he was, but I couldn't do anything about it when I couldn't even deal with myself. "It's not your fault I know. It's going to take some adjusting." I kept my voice low, but I knew he heard me. He didn't turn around or respond, and I felt my heartbreak. It was my own damn fault. I'd hurt him, but things inside of me were different now. After being locked away in a cage I realized something. I deserved to have everything I ever wanted. All the loathing and self-hate that was ingrained into me my whole life suddenly hadn't mattered.

I fought to take my life back, and this was just another step. If he knew me he'd understand. One day I'd tell him. Until then things were going to be tense.

He led me to the huge house I had started in and the queen opened the door. She smiled at him but then her smile fell when she saw the distance between us. My face was streaked with tears.

"Oh my dears, what's wrong?"

Ciyrs went rigid. "Can she stay with you guys for a while? She needs some time." His tone was low and controlled, but I heard the catch.

"Time? For what?"

"She realized the depth of the bond between me and Eden. She's struggling." Then he ran away. There was no goodbye or anything. He didn't even look at me.

The tears came in a flood and I fell to the ground sobbing. I felt the queen's arm around me as she lifted me from the ground. "Oh my dear, Shh. It will be okay. One day you'll understand. Eden isn't a threat to your bond. She's your sister."

I nodded as she led me inside. "I know that, but it's hard. He doesn't understand what my life was like. People like me weren't loved. We were chosen when what the person wanted wasn't available. My past is haunting me."

Before I knew it, I was sitting at a table with food in front of me.

"Eat, and talk. I'm here to listen."

And I did. For the first time in my life I talked about all the things I held locked up inside. All the things that haunted my dreams. All the things that made me who I was. She listened patiently asking questions here and there, but mostly she listened. I'd never talked about any of this. By the time I had finished eating, a heavy weight had been lifted off of my shoulder. I was free from all the demons of my past.

5

———

Ciyrs sat on the porch only feeling slightly guilty for eavesdropping. He didn't get it. He felt her shut down completely. When she pulled back from his touch, he nearly fell apart. She'd been gone for a week, and that whole time he went crazy. He just got her back, and already she was pushing him away.

Now though after hearing her story he understood. The bond with Eden was strong, but for his mate he would do anything. If he needed to put some space between them he would. But he wouldn't leave Eliana alone again. She needed him to show her that she was important. He could do that.

Wiping away the tears he stood and took a deep breath before going inside. She seemed to know he was there because her body tensed. He saw her back go rigid.

"I'm so sorry baby," he said and then he knelt beside her chair.

"It's not your fault. I shouldn't have run and I should

have talked to you, it's just hard." She wiped her eyes. "I'm guessing you heard."

"You're nuts if you thought I was actually going to leave you alone. We're stubborn."

The queen laughed. "That we are. It's in our nature to love and stay close to one another. We're one giant family. One you're now a part of. Get used to everyone being in your business now dear." Then she nodded at Ciyrs and left them alone.

As soon as they were alone, he pulled her into his arms and hugged her close. "Please stop being angry with me. I can't control my bond, but I'll do whatever it takes to prove to you that I'm utterly in love with you—only."

"I know that, and I'm sorry I acted like a spoiled child. It's just really hard knowing you have such a close bond with another woman. I've never been this jealous in my life. I don't like what it does to me."

"It's understandable. Now can we go back because I really want to figure out how to get that damn woman to wake up? I have a feeling Gyyx is going to be the next one of us to fall apart if we don't figure out what's wrong."

"I sort of had an idea about that, so let's go."

"What idea?"

"You'll hear it when the others do. It's my own theory."

He nodded and stood bringing her to her feet. "Well let's go see if we can figure out if you're right or not."

"Then we can go home right?"

"Home?"

She nodded. "Anywhere with you is home."

He smiled and picked up his pace to get back to the infirmary. When they went inside Eden nodded. She'd felt everything between them, and understood. When she came over to Elaina she pulled her hand from mine and laid it on her heart. "I love Ciyrs and I love you, but not the way I love Pyra. You never have to worry. There isn't anything between us."

"I know," she whispered. "It's just tough, try being in our shoes sometime though. I understand what Pyra feels."

Eden's eyes flared. "I understand that, but every time you hurt him, you hurt me. I feel it all. I feel your distrust and that hurts me."

Eliana pulled her hand back. "I'm sorry, but where I come from trust is earned. No offense."

"Fair enough," Eden said and walked away.

Ciyrs felt her emotions brewing and took a deep breath. She was upset that Eliana didn't automatically trust her word. She wasn't used to it.

He led her over to where the woman and Gyyx were. "She has an idea."

Gyyx looked at her with such pleading hope. "I'm all ears. I'm willing to do anything."

"Good because this might come off as a little strange." She ran her hand over Gyyx's hand that was wrapped around the woman's. "She knows you. There is something that allows her subconscious to enjoy your touch. We all witnessed what happened. I can touch her, and she is calm, probably because I'm not only a woman, but I'm the one who found her. She was awake when we met." She fidgeted. "You're her mate, right?"

"Yes."

"Then do to her what you would do if she were awake."

His eyes widened. "You mean?"

Eliana blushed. "Yes, if anything can save her, it's the intimate touch of her mate. I think if you were to give her an orgasm, well let's just say it may save her life. The sooner she wakes up the better."

Gyyx didn't look convinced. "I don't think it would be appropriate to touch my mate when she isn't aware."

Eden stepped up. "Pyra did. Remember? It was his touch that brought me out of whatever happened. Remember I healed him after."

"Yeah but you were also in the midst of turning Eden, this is different. She's been tortured, what if they've—hell I can't even say it." Gyyx was tortured.

Eliana smiled. "Normally I'd agree with you. I've been on the streets for a lot of my life. You don't just touch an unconscious woman, but this is different. I'm not saying have sex with her. Just touch her. I'm sure you know how to make a woman climax."

"Well yeah."

Ciyrs liked her idea. It would let them know. "I think she's right. She's already proven to like your touch. Just don't go overboard, and be sure to keep your balls safe when she wakes up freaking out because you're touching her. Have an explanation ready."

Eliana elbowed him. "She'll certainly be surprised. But obviously she senses you and is fine. She's probably aware and we don't even know it. She might understand everything we're saying right now."

Gyyx ran his hand over her stomach. They watched as her eyes fluttered.

"See she wants your touch. Why don't you take her into a private area? We'll leave you alone."

Ciyrs was amazed. All it took was the smallest intimate touch and the woman reacted. Not enough to wake up, but enough to let them know she was in there somewhere. She was the key to finding out how to get rid of the Klimnu for good. By the looks of it, she had been with them for a while and he had a feeling she'd have a score to settle. The sooner she woke up the better it was for everyone. Not just Gyyx, who looked as tortured as he had before finding Eliana.

6

<hr>

I tugged on Ciyrs's hand. "Let's leave them alone. I know I'm right. I want to go home."

She loved his smile, and his face lit up when she said home. "Okay baby." Then he turned to his friend. "I'll be back to check on her later."

"We're going to be fine," Gyyx replied. "Now take your woman home."

When they stepped out onto the grass he scooped me up in his arms and ran. My giggle echoed through the wind.

When he put me on my feet I had my own idea. I wanted to do something for him. Something I had never done before. All the time he searched for me, and then all the crap with my stupid emotions. I spun and ran to the bedroom knowing he'd follow. I slid out of my pants when he walked in the room. When he would have touched me I shook my head and held out my hand stopping him in place.

I stood naked and smiled. "Strip."

He raised a brow but there was no hesitance in following my order.

I watched him strip and licked my lips. He was gorgeous and his muscles enticed me. I wanted to lick him everywhere, and that's what I was going to do. I was going to take care of him. When he stood naked I pointed to the bed. "Lay down, on your back."

Again, he listened and I felt the stirring of his emotions. He was aroused and curious all at once. He wanted to see what I was going to do. I crawled on the bed in between his legs pushing them apart so I could settle comfortably. His eyes widened when I licked my lips.

"Baby, you don't—"

"Shh."

His mouth shut.

"Put your hands behind your head. You're not allowed to move."

His eyes flared and he moved slowly, but he relaxed his hands behind his head and smirked at me. "Whatever you want baby."

I ran my hands up his legs and thighs, close to his large erection. The tip leaked and I bent to lick it off. As soon as my tongue touched the head his hips bucked.

I shook my head. "No moving."

He began to realize the situation. I was going to be in charge. I sucked his head into my mouth and swirled my tongue around it eliciting a loud groan from his lips. It was all I needed to build my confidence.

I used one hand to cup his balls and opened my mouth wider taking more of him into my mouth. Flattening my tongue against the underside, I pushed him further into my mouth. The tip hit the back of my throat and my eyes watered, but I didn't gag. Bobbing my head up and down, I let my saliva cover his cock. His body was tense and when I looked up I saw him staring down at me.

Keeping eye contact I picked up my pace arousing him further. His eyes glowed and his chest heaved, but still he let me suck and lick him the way I wanted.

I let his cock fall from my lips and ran my tongue on his silky smoothness. Using my hand I worked him up further and sucked him back into my mouth. Fast, slow, swirl, repeat. Over and over I completed the steps until his body shook beneath mine. I felt the difference, and knew he was about to come. I wanted him inside of me. I pulled back and smiled licking my lips. He watched me with such lust I nearly came. Instead, I climbed on his lap and lifted myself over him.

Without warning I slammed down on him taking him all in one deep thrust.

He yelled and gripped my hips. "Fuck," he said and growled.

I laughed and leaned in to kiss him. Our tongues tangled and I rode him slowly. Rocking against him I worked him up again. This time I'd let him finish.

Ciyrs flipped me on my back without breaking our connection. He drove into me with such force I lost my breath. It wasn't long before I was screaming his name and milking his orgasm. I shook beneath him and my hips rose to meet his over and over again. The sound of our bodies slapping filled the air. The scent of our sex mixed arousing me further. I sobbed incoherently and let him take me. He owned me in every way. Digging my short nails into his back only proved to push him over the edge and he fucked me. The bed creaked and groaned, as the headboard slammed against the wall.

He came a second time and my body tightened around him. I never knew it was possible to climax more than once. When he slowed to a stop the ache already began. My body was new to sex, and sex like that was bound to cause some discomfort. When he pulled out I cringed and gasped.

Ciyrs noticed and shook his head. "Dammit, I'm sorry. You just drove me crazy."

"It's okay. I expected some pain. It was amazing though."

"Hell yeah it was, but that still doesn't mean I should hurt you."

I kissed his chest and smiled. "I'll be fine I promise."

He grumbled something but pulled me into his body. I lay my head on his chest and sighed. "It's weird."

"What is baby?"

"My whole life sucked, but then it led up to this one moment, and it's almost like none of it ever mattered."

"You were meant to come here. You were meant to find me. I didn't really live until now. I spent time healing and taking care of my brothers, and now—now I feel like I belong more. There's more to me than my gift. I didn't believe that before."

"Ciyrs, you're definitely so much more than your gift."

I couldn't believe he ever thought anything less. There was so much to him, and I loved everything about him. No matter my insecurities about his creepy bond with the other woman, and whatever that fiery power was. It didn't matter; he was mine.

ial mente

7

She was simply amazing. He'd never felt as alive as he did with Eliana. The things she went through were different than his life, but in the end the only thing that really mattered is how much they connected with their own personal thoughts. They had so many things in common that it mixed with their differences creating a good balance. They took the rest of the night and talked.

In the early morning, the pounding on the door started. Ciyrs sighed and climbed out of his bed. He didn't want to leave her, but she was sleeping.

He opened the door to see the king at the door. "They need you son."

"Is she all right?"

The king shook his head. "She isn't awake. Gyyx can't bring himself to do what your mate suggested. It's time to burn that building to the ground. All of us are going. You and Eliana too. It's time."

"Who is going to watch the woman?"

"Gyyx won't leave her."

"I should have figured. Okay let me wake her. I know she wants that building to be gone. She dreamed of it, and is terrified of it."

"Good, so meet us there. Pyra and Eden are there scoping it out. Theia is there and so are nearly all the warriors."

"Okay we'll be there soon."

The king nodded and left. Ciyrs wasn't sure if it was a good idea to have everyone there. Gyyx would want him there. He would probably want Eliana there too. He walked back in the room and smiled at his mate. Her eyes were on him.

"What's going on?"

"We're burning the building to the ground. Everyone is going except for Gyyx."

She sat up and smiled. "I want to go."

"I know. I told the king we would be there shortly. Are you sure you're ready to be so close to the place you were imprisoned?"

"Yes, I want to know for sure the building is gone."

He understood. He felt the same. "Okay well move your ass then. The others are waiting for us. I want to check in on Gyyx first too."

She climbed out of bed and went straight to her bags.

After checking on Gyyx and his mate and seeing no change he told him he had to try it. His touch had to be the key. He let him know everyone was going to be at the Wasteland so he had the whole compound to himself. It was the perfect time to bring his mate back to life.

Gyyx nodded and smiled. "Make sure it burns good brother."

"Will do."

Eliana had hugged him and kissed his cheek. She whispered something he didn't hear, but whatever it was seemed to light up his brother's eyes. He held back his jealously knowing she was his. It was still hard to see her make another man smile. Even if said man could really use the happiness.

He tugged her away and they locked the doors securing the two inside of the infirmary which was the safest place on the compound.

By the time they got to the Wasteland the others were all separated. He found Eden and Pyra and held Eliana close.

"So here's how it's going to work. We're going to burn this mother fucker to the ground. If those bastards attack, we are going to fight. Ciyrs, you need to get the women out of here and back to the infirmary with Gyyx—"

Eliana spoke up. "No, he needs to fight. I know what he can do. His new gift is what saved me. I somehow tapped into it. It burnt the Klimnu to a crisp. I think Eden and the queen are more than capable of taking care of themselves. We can get back ourselves."

"Hell no woman. Fine if Ciyrs needs to stay to kick some Klimnu ass then Ero can take you all back."

Ero stepped up and nodded. Though Ciyrs could see he wasn't happy about it. "Let me be back up just in case."

"Fine Ero and Ullie will take the women to safety if they attack. Otherwise we get to watch the horror of our history turn to ash. No one will ever be locked inside of that building ever again."

Pyra was a great leader. He knew just what to say to pump everyone up. Ciyrs was too, but he was worried. He'd never fought with the warriors before. He always did damage control, and healing afterwards.

Eliana kissed him. "You've got this."

"Did you really use my new power to kill?"

She nodded. "It was kill or be killed. Sometimes you have no choice." The she grabbed his face. "Use it wisely."

"I'm afraid that it will darken my soul."

"Is my soul dark?"

"No of course not baby."

"Then yours won't be either. It's a gift, not a curse. You were given another way to help protect your people—to protect me."

When she put it like that he couldn't begrudge his new power. It just meant he needed to practice with it. Just as he had with the healing, only this time he needed the enemies. No one was sure that they would even attack. His heart raced with adrenaline, and he wondered if this was how the warriors felt on a daily basis. It would explain their temper and aggression.

The first group of warriors eased their way from out of the woods and made their way to the building. Everyone else watched in silence as fire balls were thrown at the building.

No one moved. Hell, he wasn't even sure if he breathed. Smoke filled the air as the flames erupted catching fire from all the dust and debris. The cloud of smoke filled the air and he watched in awe as glass from the barred windows shattered into the air exploding with a loud crack. It was then he tensed. The first Klimnu appeared.

Its red eyes narrowed on the group. It was time. He kissed Eliana and said. "I love you, now go get your ass with the others. I need you to be safe."

She was frozen as her eyes stayed glued to the monster going towards Pyra. He wasn't sure why, but she seemed to have formed a special relationship with him. Maybe it was because they both had to deal with his and Eden's bond.

"Baby, go. Ero and Ullie will take you to safety."

He shook her and she looked at him licking her lips. "I—I don't know if I can leave you."

"It's all good, sweetheart. I have something they don't but I won't be able to focus until I know you're safe. So please for my sanity, go."

It was then a strong hand wrapped around her arm yanking her away. She looked over her shoulder to see the fire spreading, but the Klimnu were coming in droves. All the warriors were fighting. He gave her one last look before joining the fray of the fight. He'd never felt so exhilarated before. The women were gone, and now he could focus.

A Klimnu snuck up on him. It cackled and scraped its claws down his cheek. "Why would they let you stay around? You're nothing but the useless healer." it said with a voice full of hatred.

He glared and didn't even bother wiping the blood from his face. "You just made your last mistake underestimating me."

His hand lit up and the heat surrounded him. His

hand burned with a flame that begged to come free. In a movement too fast for the Klimnu, Ciyrs snapped. He wrapped his hand around its bony neck and incinerated him. The scent of burning flesh filled the air and then he disappeared into a pile of ash. "Holy Fuck," he said and ran towards the king. There were three on him and Ciyrs heard Eliana's conversation with Pyra. They wanted him. But he wouldn't let them have his king.

He charged the one who jumped on Creia's back. The instant his hand touched the Klimnu the beast erupted into flames and ran around shrieking in pain until he disappeared into a pile. Seemed Ciyrs was pretty fucking powerful. The heat from his hand traveled down his body until it felt like he was surrounded by a wall of flames. Only the flames weren't there. He felt them bubbling beneath the surface.

8

———

I hated leaving Ciyrs, but I had complete faith he could take care of himself. Eden held my hand digging her nails into the flesh of my palm. I felt her nerves as if they were my own. She was scared. No scratch that, she was fucking terrified.

"Hey, it will be okay."

She looked at me pleading.

"Seriously Eden, you've mated to the legendary Denynso who has the fiercest reputation where I come from. Plus, you're carrying his child. He won't let anything happen to anyone. Plus, Ciyrs has his new gift, and I can tell you right now, it will come in handy."

"You really believe it?"

"Of course I do. I have faith in them all, and you should too. You know your mate and mine."

She nodded and a small smile curled her lip up. "Thanks. Sorry I'm not usually this much of a pussy. It's the hormones I swear. Makes me crazy. I've never cried so much in my god damn life."

"It's okay to cry. I'm scared for them too, but I can't focus on that. What we need to focus on is getting Gyyx to listen to me and freaking pleasure his unconscious mate. I know it sounds terrible, but I think his touch is the key. Every time he touches her more intimately her body reacts. So, he just needs to shock her awake."

Eden nodded. "I know, but he feels it's wrong. I can appreciate that, but he's more stubborn than Pyra."

"I can see that."

"Ladies how about less talking and more moving faster," Ero grumbled and then a Klimnu appeared.

"You," it said looking right at me. "You killed him you stupid cunt."

I gasped. This must have been the other one. Ero moved in front of us, and the Klimnu backhanded him sending him flying backwards. He landed against the tree shaking it to the roots before falling to the ground— unconscious. Of course.

Ullie stared at the Klimnu, but I saw something was off. He didn't look scared, nor did he look like he cared one way or another about us. It was up to me. I had to save them. Eden, though I didn't know her well enough was important. She was pregnant and important to my mate, so therefore she was important to me. "Now would be a good time to use your fancy connection," I whispered.

She shook and I felt her fear. The Klimnu laughed.

Its cackle sounded just like the one who kept torturing me. The anger rose and I pushed the queen and Eden behind me. It cackled again.

"You measly human, you are no match against me,

and your warrior here—well he isn't who he seems. He's a traitor and won't be a help to you."

The queen gasped, but I didn't react. It didn't surprise me. I hadn't seen him around much. He didn't say anything. He paled knowing he was ousted, and if we managed to make it out of this he was screwed. The others would tear him apart.

I held up my hand when I felt the burn. Seemed Ciyrs was always going to be able to sense when I needed his help. That must have been our special connection. Apparently we didn't all get telepathy. Again, I was able to tap into his power. My hand shot out and wrapped around the Klimnu's throat. "Die you mother fucker!"

The scent, the feel felt the same as before. Only this time I got dizzy. Hands held me up as I killed my second Klimnu. Ash covered my hands, and I wiped them on my jeans. It was Deja vu. All over again I found myself locked in that damn building trying to find my way out. The panic took over until I felt a sting across my cheek. I shook my head and brought my hand to my face. "That freakin' hurt."

Eden blushed. "Sorry you just seemed to be lost there for a minute. We really need to go before more come. You just killed that thing and I don't want to stick around for more."

"We have to get Ero," I said.

I backtracked and found him on the ground. He wasn't as big as the others so it wasn't as hard to help him up. The queen and Eden both came to help and working as one with the queen's hidden speed we made it back to the infirmary without any more attacks. Ullie was gone. Eden banged on the door, and I pushed her aside pulling the keys from my pocket. Ciyrs slipped them to me before I was pulled away.

I unlocked the door and we dragged Ero inside. Gyyx was sitting by his mate's side and his eyes widened. He jumped up and pulled the doors shut locking them.

"What the fuck happened?" He wrapped his arms around his mother and held her close.

"Klimnu attacked. Ciyrs sent us with Ero and Ullie, and now we're here," I said and shrugged before dropping into the chair. Gyyx carried Ero's body to the empty cot.

"Yes, but how did you get away if Ero is out. Where's Ullie?"

"He is a traitor to our kind," the queen said sadly.

"What do you mean mother?"

She sighed. "He is working with the enemy, and he got away."

His eyes flared with anger but then he seemed confused. "Then how did you manage to get back?"

"Ciyrs's mate... She's a badass who tapped into his new gift and saved us!" Eden replied and for the first time since meeting her I didn't see her as a threat, and I felt like I fit a little better.

He chuckled and planted himself back in his chair next to the woman who was the biggest mystery to us all.

We waited and waited nervously for the men to come back. None of us wanted to see our mates hurt or any of the other warriors, for that matter. I nibbled my lip praying everyone would come back safely.

∽

THE FEEL of his hands woke me up. I smiled and jumped up into his arms. "You're back!"

"Of course I am baby. How are you holding up?"

I looked around and saw the room was full of warriors. All of them seemed to be all right. "No one is dead?"

The room went silent and then everyone laughed.

"No baby, we're all good. Some bruising and shit, but those bastards are gone. At least for now. We kicked ass, and the Wasteland building is gone. Burnt to the ground."

I nodded as my eyes filled with tears. "Good. How's Ero?"

"He's fine," Ero said and smirked. "I heard you were pretty badass while I was out?"

I shrugged. "Someone had to do it," I replied and smiled.

He shoved me and then paced across the room. Everyone was fine. The Wasteland was filled with Klimnu ashes, and I was home. I pulled Ciyrs down for a kiss and swore I'd appreciate him every day. He was the perfect mate for me—flawlessly perfect.

Ciyrs pulled me to the side and we sat against the wall. Everyone was hyped up over the fight and talked about his power. I knew he was awesome, and I knew how the power felt. It was addictive, and I had only used it twice. From the conversations, he had killed over twenty Klimnu on his own. I was proud of him. Seemed he was finally getting the recognition he should have always had, but he smiled and leaned back with me.

"I don't feel my soul darkening baby."

"I told you."

"I'm not so afraid of it now."

"Good, because again it saved my life. Because of you I'm okay and so are Eden and the queen."

He nodded and kissed my head. The silence was nice. We were in our own little world. No one could enter it. I felt his love shatter the rest of the chill that had once surrounded my heart. I was finally free from my past and all the things I had always feared didn't matter anymore.

9

Ciyrs felt a change. Eliana was less tense, more relaxed, and more affectionate. It felt like she wasn't worried about anything anymore. It matched how he felt. There was still the issue of Ullie, and the idea that the Klimnu would come back. They weren't going to give up just because they lost some of their kind.

They were fighters, and they were violent bastards. They got off on other people's pain and suffering. Now that they knew where they were coming from the security would raise. Everyone would be on the lookout for Ullie, and King Creia would be the one to decide what happens to him. He personally wanted to rip his head off. They had sent him to protect the women, but instead he let the Klimnu attack, and it could have gone a completely different way. That was the problem.

Pyra was aching to go kill him too. Eden could have died. He could have lost his whole family in one short period. Ciyrs figured the warriors would be keeping their eyes open even more than usual.

He stood and stretched bringing Eliana to her feet. "Can we go home now?"

"I want to check on our mystery woman first. Gyyx needs to stop being so damn stubborn, and he was probably going to, but we came banging on the door before he had more than an hour alone with her."

They walked over to his lost brother. "Hey dude, sorry things didn't go as planned."

"I'll do it, but not here. I won't make this medical. I want to take her home with me. I want to clean her up. I want so much," he said softly.

"Then do that. She will be okay with you. I have a feeling she'd probably rather have that kind of privacy anyways."

"You really think so?"

"I do. I don't know why. I can't explain it, but it's this feeling I get. I learned a long time ago to follow my gut. I think you should take her home. Make it more personal rather than medical. This place is too sterile."

"Hey it's supposed to be," Ciyrs said freighting offense.

Gyyx chuckled. "Okay but if something bad happens, you'll come right?"

"Of course."

"Thank you." Gyyx picked her up in his arms and Eliana made sure her body was covered fully.

"He'll be okay and so will she. I hate seeing him so sad. His eyes match the sorrow I saw in hers before she went unconscious."

Ciyrs didn't want to think of anything sad. He wanted to take his mate home and make love to her all-night long. He wanted to celebrate his new gift. He wanted to celebrate life. He figured the Klimnu would need to regroup and maybe they'd get a break from attacks; at least for a while.

But what does that mean for later? Are they gone for good or just regrouping to bring a massive force the next time around?

BONDED BY THE ALIEN PRINCE

COVER

GRACE KENSINGTON
BONDED BY THE
ALIEN
PRINCE
ALIEN WARRIOR MATES I | BOOK 5

1

———

Gyyx knew it was time to test out Eliana's theory. Hell, everyone told him it was a good idea. Eden, Pyra, and Ciyrs watched him in torment as he held back from touching her in any way other than loving. He wanted her to wake up. What if the only way to wake her was to violate her? Then she would never forgive him or trust him. That was his fear. But the worst of it all: what if his touch wasn't enough? What if she never woke up?

He thought about all those things each day sitting by her side. He had taken her home—to his home three days before, and instead of touching her he spent the majority of his time sitting by her side or down in his basement training room. He didn't answer the door when anyone knocked either. He needed to be alone, and after the first day everyone seemed to get that.

Gyyx stepped out of the shower and took a deep breath. He sighed as he shaved off his scruff . He couldn't take it anymore. It was time to listen to everyone else. Dropping his towel, he slipped on some very light shorts and made his way to his room where his mate lay. She hadn't moved at all since he laid her there, yet she looked so peaceful, like she was only sleeping.

She was so tiny. Every part of her was small, and he worried about that when she woke up, because she would fucking wake up. He couldn't give up hope on that. Her hair was long and black with some sort of funky cut. He didn't know her eye color or anything else about her. He just knew he would have to be very gentle with her.

He lay on the bed next to her and kissed her cheek. Her small nose twitched, and he watched hoping her eyes would open on their own, but nothing happened. He slid his arm over her waist and held her. "I really hope you won't be pissed at me sweetheart. I've waited hoping you'd come back to me on your own." As he spoke he slid the tip of his finger down her thin arm. She was pale and nearly skin and bone.

Gyyx was stubborn. For hours he lay holding her willing her to wake up, but it was no use. He knew she needed more help.

The next time he heard the knock he knew it was his father and he couldn't ignore him anymore. He kissed her on the mouth and sighed. "I'll be back, sweetheart."

He went to his door and let his dad in.

"She isn't awake yet?"

"No, I can't bring myself to touch her. Not without her consent. It's wrong."

His dad nodded. "Now son, normally I would agree with you, but she has been out for what a week now?"

"Yes."

"Ciyrs and Eden have tried everything they can think of?"

Again, he nodded. "Yes."

"Maybe it's time to be unconventional. I know you wouldn't do anything to hurt her, and if Ciyrs is right and she is aware and unable to wake up, she can hear your hesitance. If you can get her to wake up and if she is angry you can explain it to her."

"If she doesn't run the opposite way. Dad, could you have done that?" He didn't like thinking about his parents, but he needed to know.

"I would have probably been stubborn like you, but in the end yes, if it saved her and brought her back to me. I know it's hard, but look at your mate. What if she cannot wake up without you? Could you forgive yourself if she never wakes up because you can't let go of your morals for something important?"

Gyyx shook his head. "I guess not. I know I need to at least try. It's just hard to... you know?"

"Maybe come to dinner and get—"

"No I won't leave her."

"Very well, but soon you're going to have to. Your mother is worried and wants to make sure you're okay."

"Of course, I'm not okay."

"Son, don't be so stubborn. Either go now and see your mom or you're coming over tomorrow. I won't take her being upset anymore."

Gyyx sighed. "I don't mean to upset her. I'll go tomorrow, but I need someone here with my mate."

"I'll stay while you have a lunch with your mom."

"Okay, then I'll see you tomorrow." He rushed to get his dad out of his house. He didn't like talking to anyone.

He didn't want to be told what to do, and he felt horrible he had upset his mother, but he couldn't bring himself to leave the beautiful and vulnerable woman in his bed.

His dad got the hint and smiled pulling him into a hug. "Just do it son, you don't have to have sex with her, use your damn fingers."

He choked and pulled back. "Damn dad, that doesn't make me want to do anything now. I don't need you to tell me the same thing everyone has, and I mean everyone. I get it. I need to freaking give my woman, who is unconscious, an orgasm. Yay for me I get to be a fuckin' pervert."

"Oh Gyyx you're so far from that, but I get it. I know it's difficult, but hell we want her awake nearly as much as you. She's family after all. We all want to know what happened. How those slimy bastards got her, and of course we want to figure out what she knows."

Gyyx glared. "You won't be questioning her as soon as she wakes up. She's going to need time. I won't allow it, and I don't care what you do to me." His eyes flared orange and his body shook with rage. No one would bombard his mate.

His dad held up his hands. "I didn't mean right away, son. I'll let your tone go only because you're my son and you're under a lot of pressure right now, but don't think for a minute you tell me what to do. I'm not only your father, I am the king and you will do as I say, when I say."

Gyyx paled. It wasn't often he was on the other end of his dad's power and he found he didn't like it. "Yes, sir," he said through clenched teeth.

His dad nodded and he didn't miss his smirk before he spun and left Gyyx alone.

2

———

I t was time to grow a pair and bring his mate back, and if that meant touching her in ways he only allowed himself to dream of then so be it. No one would leave him alone about it, and he knew deep down they were right. There was nothing in any of her tests that showed something was wrong. She was 100 percent healthy except for the fact she wouldn't fucking wake up. Ciyrs had tried everything, done every test he could think of and so had Eden.

He locked his door yet again and made his way back to his room where she lay peacefully. This time he slid under the blanket and pulled her close. She was definitely warm. Her skin was smooth. He felt like a giant compared to her. She was small, and she was perfect. He would treat her like a delicate flower if she so desired. She was already his everything, and he didn't even know her. He didn't have to. All he needed to know was that she was his.

He took a deep breath and nuzzled her neck as he

lifted the shirt Eliana had put on her. Running his fingers over her smooth skin he closed his eyes and took in her scent. She felt warm and good lying next to him. He yearned for her touch. Sliding his hand up he ran his finger over her bare nipple and swore he heard her gasp, but when he pulled back there was nothing.

Now he watched her and continued massaging her small breasts. He loved how soft her skin was and after taking it slow he slid his hand back down her torso. He dipped his hand beneath her panties and gasped. She was wet. He locked his eyes on her face as he ran his finger over her in slow circles.

At first nothing changed, but then her body began to shake. He kept his eyes on her for any sign of discomfort or waking up. Her eyes fluttered behind her closed lids and he leaned forward and kissed her lips. They were warm and a bit dry but he didn't care. Then he slid a finger inside of her rocking it into her like he would if he were making love to her. It wasn't long before he felt her body tighten up.

Her body jerked, and he felt the rush of her orgasm right before she screamed. Gyyx held her body as she shook with her climax before he slid his finger out. When he looked at his mate her eyes were open and the most beautiful brown eyes stared back at him. Her lips were parted, and she let out a moan to rival the goddesses.

"Thank fuck you're awake!" Gyyx lifted her into his arms and held her close. She lay limply until he started to sob. For the first time in a very long time he let go of all the emotions he had held back.

She was slow to move, but her thin arm wrapped around his neck and her fingers ran through his flattened

Mohawk. He vibrated from her touch, and when she pulled his head back he looked at her with tear filled eyes.

She shook her head and he wasn't sure if she could talk, but then she pressed her lips against his lightly. "Thank you," she whispered.

He smiled. "Anytime, sweetheart. Let me get you something to drink."

She nodded and he slid her off his lap and onto the mattress before springing out of bed to go get her a drink. He came back with a cold glass filled to the brim with ice and water. He stuck a straw in the glass to make it easier.

He held the glass as she sipped her water watching him with what looked like curiosity.

When she spit the straw out he set the glass on the table next to his bed. "What's your name?"

"Leia and you're Gyyx?" She pushed her stringy hair from her face and blushed. "I said it right?"

She did and he nodded. "So, you were aware while you were—sleeping?"

"Yes, I tried to wake up, but it felt like I was being chained down. I couldn't wake up no matter how much I tried. I listened. You shouldn't have been upset. It wasn't your fault I wasn't waking up."

"I thought by doing what I just did, it would be violating you. I couldn't bear to do it without your permission."

"Thank you for that. It's very sweet that you struggled so badly to touch me that way."

"So, you heard everything huh?"

She nodded and gave him a small smile. "I did."

"Shit."

She chuckled but it turned into a cough, and he quickly grabbed her water so she could get a drink. "I'm still so tired. I didn't exactly sleep during those days. I was constantly trying to break out of whatever held me back. It was strange, I was in my own head, it was like sleep paralysis but more intense and let's just say I never want to experience anything like that again."

"Then you need to rest."

Her eyes lit up and she gasped. "Where's the girl who saved me? I want to thank her. She could have left me instead of dragging me out of that hell."

"She's here still. After you rest and stuff, everyone will want to meet you. You're my mate."

She blushed. "I gathered, from what everyone said. I soaked in a lot of information while I was out." She reached out and grazed his cheek. "It's why your eyes are orange right?"

"Yes," he whispered.

She tilted her head to the side. "So, because I'm your mate, touching me—intimately was able to pull me out of whatever was going on with me?"

He shrugged. "I guess so. It was Eliana's idea. I fought it for several days, but after my father came today, well I needed to just try. I hope you aren't angry with me."

She shook her head. "No, I'm not. Right now I'd like for you to lay with me and sleep. You didn't really sleep much either, and I think we could both use some rest."

He yawned and nodded. "I was afraid to sleep."

"Shh. It's all right I get it." The she laid down pulling him down too. She held his hand, and he buried his face into her hair breathing her in.

"Don't stay asleep this time."

"I won't," she muttered and then her breathing evened out.

Gyyx listened to her soft snores until he too fell asleep. She was home and everything was okay in his world.

3

____

When I woke up everything was surreal. For months I had been locked away in the darkness, and now I lay next to a man who I knew grieved for me, even though he didn't even know me. I felt his growing affection and worry over me the whole time I was out.

He smiled in his sleep and pulled me closer. I lay still hoping to let him sleep for a bit before I needed to get up. I'd been in bed too long.

He was handsome and sweet. More loyal than anyone I had ever met. I knew instinctively that he would never do me wrong.

I covered his hand with mine and ran my finger along his knuckles and he shivered. His giant body crowded against me and his face nuzzled my neck. I felt the goosebumps from his breath before his lips touched the skin.

He didn't say anything as he kissed my neck with slow pecks as his large hand slid up to cup my breast. He groaned when I pushed back against him. I loved his touch. There was something so—mesmerizing about it. He moved slowly, but he knew what he was doing, and there was no doubt he would please me.

"You're so perfect," he whispered.

I chuckled because that was so far from the truth. I lay on my back and gave him better access to my body. I'd never craved anyone like I craved him, and even though I didn't really know him, I felt this strange connection. I felt him when I was out. I heard him and listened to everyone else talk about him. I'd learned a lot about him.

When his hand slid down my body I tensed waiting for him to touch me where I craved him the most. But he didn't. Instead he flattened his hand across my abdomen holding his trembling hand in place.

I looked over to see bright orange eyes staring at me. Instead of saying anything I licked my lips and pushed his hand lower and pleaded with my eyes. His flared brighter when he felt my heat. I wore only panties.

"Are you sure?" he asked in a low voice.

I nodded. "Please, I think I need you." Then I lifted my hips pushing into his hand to prove my point.

He leaned in and kissed me before sitting up. At first I wasn't aware of what he was doing until he slid me into the middle of the bed and then in a surprising move he ripped the panties from my body. I gasped when I felt myself dampen more and spread my legs for him.

Instead of doing what I wanted though, he lifted me and pulled the shirt over my head leaving me naked. I shivered from the chill, but the way he looked at me heated me back up really quick.

"You're so small, I'm afraid to hurt you."

I laughed. "I'm made of sturdy stuff."

He raised a brow.

"I'm tougher than I look."

He nodded and in a slow move ran his finger along my slit. I bit my lip and lifted my hips. I needed more than light touches. For days I lay unconscious waiting to see how long it would take him to do what all the others told him he needed to do. Every time he touched me it was so sweet and loving. I wanted something more passionate.

"Stop holding back."

"I have to or I'll lose control." He sounded so pained.

I took a deep breath and sat up. I cupped his jaw and peering into his orange eyes. "I want you to fucking touch me the way you would any other woman. Don't look at how small I am. Show me how much you want me." I kissed him and when he would have pulled back I pressed my naked body against him. He groaned and his hand gripped my ass holding me against his growing erection. I gasped and squirmed trying to get closer. That was what I wanted—needed.

When I sucked his tongue in my mouth he yanked his mouth back with wide eyes and slammed me down on the bed. I gasped and laughed until I felt his cock poised to enter me. Then I moaned when he rubbed the tip against my clit.

"I won't be able to make love to you the way I want to."

I shook my head near tears because I wanted him inside of me so badly. I'd never felt such arousal over something as small as manhandling me. "I don't care. We have the rest of our lives, right?"

He nodded licking his lips. "If I hurt you in any way you have to tell me okay?"

"I will I promise. Now fuck me dammit!"

That must have been the last straw as he slammed into me. I screamed in both pain and pleasure as the tip of his cock hit the back of my inner walls. I gasped for breath from the force and kept my eyes locked on his. He pulled back and in the same move he slammed into me again. This time it was a bit lighter.

"Don't stop," I begged.

He growled and kissed me demanding I open for him so I did. His tongue fought mine for control and I submitted. I let him have me the way he needed. I didn't know how I knew it but there was something that told me he needed me to just let him do what he wanted. I had no problem submitting to him. He was my mate after all. I felt a stirring of my climax coming and pressed my hips against him before I pulled back from his kiss. Panting I smiled and rubbed his cheek. "Take me Gyyx, I'm yours."

And wham, he rocked into me and each thrust was faster and deeper than the last. He held my body tightly against his. Sweat coated his skin and mine and our bodies were slick against each other. From his brow, the drops dripped to my chest. He kept his pace fast and hard and my body loved it. It didn't matter that I was small because I was made for this warrior prince.

When his thrusts became uneven and more erratic I wrapped my legs around his waist and tilted my pelvis to give him the best access as he drove into me. I felt a rush right before I yelled.

"Oh Gyyx, please." I couldn't hold back and the rest of what I said came out as a jumbled incoherent mess.

He moaned and then his finger slid between our bodies and he pinched my clit. I screamed and came hard. Moaning, sobbing, and crying I came apart around him. My inner muscles clinched around his cock bringing him with me. He yelled out in surprised and rocked into me until every bit of his seed was inside of me. I felt the connection.

When he slowed to a stop both of us were panting and shaking from our release. We stuck together in a sweaty, sticky mess and I laughed. I couldn't help it. I'd never been with someone so amazing before, and I was pretty sure this was the beginning of what love felt like.

He might have been rough, but I felt every emotion with every thrust. It was not just sex. It was more.

4

Never before had Gyyx felt anything like being with Leia. She was everything he ever desired in one tiny package. She wasn't as fragile as she appeared, and she definitely didn't want to be treated as such. He lost it and let go. Now he felt like an asshole when she slid out of bed slowly.

She looked over her shoulder and smiled at him. "I'd love to have a shower."

"Of course. I'll make you something to eat then."

"You don't have to take care of me."

He frowned. "It's my job to take care of you. I'm your mate."

Leia chuckled. "Okay but remember I'm capable of doing things too."

"When you're better. You were unconscious for a week."

"Fair enough. Now point me in the right direction, and I need clothes."

"Of course."

She nodded and followed his finger. She wanted to be left alone, he could tell, and it was hard to leave her after just mating with her. He felt the bond growing slowly and being away from her wasn't reassuring at all, but he knew she had gone through a lot, and he didn't want to push her before she was ready.

Before she went into the bathroom she stood in front of him and kissed his cheek. "Thank you."

"Anytime, sweetheart."

Gyyx left Leia to clean up and took that time to run to his brother's as Eden was closer to Leia's size than Elaina was. He knocked on the door impatiently.

Eden opened the door and her eyes widened. "She's awake."

"Yes, but she isn't ready for people yet. I just need some clothes for her."

"Of course, come in."

He followed her inside and smiled. His little niece or nephew was growing inside of her. "How are you feeling?"

Eden smiled and rubbed her growing belly. "Eh, some days are better than others." She left him standing in the living room and walked down the hallway.

He stood shifting on his feet nervous about leaving her alone. When Eden came back she had a huge bag. "From the women. They should all fit her, and there are all the things she'll need that you have no idea about." Eden laughed and handed him the bag.

"Thank you so much. I'll see you all tomorrow. I figure she'll want to get out tomorrow, but today she is mine."

"Understandable."

"Thanks Eden."

"Bye Gyyx."

He left and shut the door. Then he ran home to his mate. Hopefully the girls really knew what they were doing. She'd probably be more comfortable if the things she had fit her. She was pretty tiny compared to both of the others.

He went inside his cabin and went straight to his room. He heard sobbing and dropped the bag on the bed. He shoved the door opened and pulled the shower curtain open without even bothering to announce himself. He wasn't quite so she didn't freak out. Instead he saw his mate curled up on the floor of the shower sobbing.

He didn't care about getting wet as he crowded inside of the stall and wrapped his arms around her holding her. She shook and shivered. Her body was freezing.

"Sweetheart what's wrong?"

She shook her head frantically. "I'm not ready to talk about it."

He knew better than to push so he let it go for the time being. "That's fine but whenever you are I'm all ears, okay?"

She sniffed and nodded before putting on a fake smile. He wiped beneath her eyes and kissed her cheek.

"No need to pretend with me. I can feel your pain."

She paled. "Sorry, it's just hard ya know. I lived every day in fear, and when I realized you left, it freaked me out."

Gyyx growled. "I knew I shouldn't have left you alone."

"No, it's all right. You needed to get me stuff to wear,

and I know you weren't gone long. It's just—next time I have to go with you."

"Of course you can go with me next time, Leia. I won't leave you alone again. Until you feel comfortable. I'm sorry."

Gyyx scooped her into his arms and stepped out dripping water everywhere but he didn't care as he yanked the towel she'd picked out and covered her shaking body.

"The girls went sort of crazy. I hope everything fits you, and that you have everything you needed. Eden said they got everything."

"Thank you," she whispered. "I'm sure it's perfect."

He set her on her feet and brushed her cheek. "I'm just going to figure out what to feed you while you're getting dressed and stuff."

Her eyes widened in panic and her small hand clutched his arm. "Not leaving though?"

"No, not leaving."

She relaxed, and he left her next to her bag and went to the kitchen to get her some food. He knew she had to be starving.

He chose fruit and cheeses and poured two glasses of ice water. He placed everything on the tray and carried it to his room. Leia had slipped into a light sleeveless dress that dipped low revealing her small perky breasts. She was standing in front of the mirror with frown.

"What's wrong sweetheart? You look beautiful."

"I'm too skinny."

"No, you're perfect."

She spun around and faced him. "I'm not, but thank you for thinking so."

Just then her stomach rumbled and she blushed

before going back to sit on the bed. He could see how hungry she was.

When Gyyx set the tray in front of her she went to grab the food. He grabbed her hand in his. "Don't eat too fast or you'll make yourself sick."

"I won't."

He sat next to her watching her eat. She didn't seem to mind him staring, and she devoured the plate. Even eating slowly everything disappeared quickly. When she shoved the tray away Gyyx ate what was left. He was happy to see her smile.

"Thank you. Now we can go meet everyone?"

"I was hoping to talk first. I know you're not ready to talk about your imprisonment, but tell me about you."

She settled back against the pillows and nodded. "Okay sure. There isn't much about me. Not anything exciting or anything. Actually, my life is probably quite boring compared to yours."

"I doubt I will find anything about you boring Leia."

It was true; he found her fascinating even over the smallest things. Like how she took a cube of cheese and broke it in half again with her fingers before eating it. Or how she rolled her eyes every time he gave her a compliment, and in the next breath she would blush and thank him. She had so many layers and he wanted to peel each and every one of them back to see who Leia was inside and out.

5

———

I wasn't used to people being interested in me. I was the girl that always got overlooked. He was so sweet and attractive, and I was just me. I didn't think I was ugly or anything, but I had a past I wasn't proud of, and one that probably wasn't very deserving of the warrior's love. He sat on the bed waiting for me to give him anything, but I was afraid. So instead of opening up I decided distraction was the best bet. I would tell him soon, but I wanted to enjoy him before I told him the truth and saw the look of disgust on his face. I wasn't ready for that. Not from him. I think I would probably break when he knew who I was.

I knelt and went in front of him. Right away his huge hands gripped my hips and when I leaned in to kiss him his eyes shut. My lips covered his, and I kissed him with everything I had. I wanted to distract him. I was good at the intimate aspects; it was the talking and the getting to know each other that I wasn't so good at.

He groaned into my mouth when I ran my tongue

over his in a slow enticing way. I showed him how much I cared without words. When he pulled me closer I straddled his lap and one of his hands slid up my thigh under the dress. My legs were already spread for him, and when his finger grazed me he ripped his mouth from mine and stared at me with bright orange eyes.

"No fucking panties?"

I blushed and shrugged. "Not here, with you."

"My god."

I brushed my lips over his and smirked. "That's a good thing right. This way you can take me anytime you want without having that tiny fabric in the way."

I felt his intake of breath and in the next his slid his finger inside of me. "I like that sweetheart, but you are never allowed to leave here without your panties, got it?"

I moaned and bit my lip before I nodded. "Yes, Gyyx." I didn't even recognize my own voice. Something about him ordering me around while thrusting his finger inside of me like he would be doing with his cock turned me on more than I thought possible. He sped up and I rode his finger, then there was two stretching me for him. I gasped and kept moving.

"Good girl." Then his lips were on mine, demanding and hard. They punished me in an oh so pleasant way. I whimpered when I climaxed and grinded against him as my body shook with such force I nearly toppled. I felt his breathing pick up when my inner muscles clenched around him. He pulled his fingers out and pulled back from kissing me. They glistened with proof of my release and he growled as his eyes glowed brighter than I'd seen them.

He sucked one finger, then the next into his mouth,

the whole time keeping his eyes locked with mine. I pulled one of his fingers toward me and licked it too. He smirked and slammed me against the bed. My dress was shoved up above my waist, and then I felt the wet tip of his erection poised to enter me.

"Make love to me, Gyyx," I said.

His eyes still bright softened and his smile went from seductive to sweet. "Whatever you want sweetheart," he said and slid into me. It was agonizingly slow and I felt every inch of him take me.

When he reached the hilt and held sill caging me with his arms I wriggled my body until the tip hit that one special spot and I whimpered. He watched me and when he realized what I was doing he took over hitting my g-spot over and over again making me shatter before he even began.

I came with a scream that could be heard for miles and held on to him. "Now Gyyx."

He nodded and kissed me before slamming into me. He rode me hard again, just like before, but something was different about it. He seemed to be in complete control this time, and I realized he was the type of man who liked to play rough...

Well I was a woman who played rough. Making love didn't have to be soft. I liked feeling the pressure of him inside of me. I loved feeling every ridge of his cock rubbing against my inner walls. I loved the sound of flesh slapping flesh and the scent of passionate sex in the air and my head banging against the headboard because of the force of our love making. It was raw, passionate, and real.

My eyes rolled back, and I anchored my legs around

him holding on for dear life as he rammed into me. It was so good that the sounds coming from my lips were unintelligible. I muttered and gasped and yelled digging my nails roughly into the flesh of his arms. He grunted when I drew blood but that did nothing more but turn him on more.

He rocked into me, and when I squeezed his erection with my inner walls forcing his climax he buried his face into my neck and bit me—hard. I yelped and had my third orgasm as he spilled his seed inside of me.

His body rocked unstable against mine and he shook. His body was slick with sweat and so was mine. I wrapped my arms around him, holding him close as he slowed to a stop. His breathing was heavy and he didn't move for a few minutes as I rubbed his back.

When he pulled his head away he looked confused. "Who are you?"

I tried to smile and shrugged. "I'm your mate."

He chuckled. "You're fucking amazing."

Again, I blushed. He probably wouldn't think so once he knew of my past. I'd managed to dodge the questions I knew were coming—for now.

"Are you hurting though? I was a little too rough again."

I kissed his lips softly. "I love it. I'm not hurting, and you weren't too rough. It was just right. I love the rawness in you Gyyx, it's so sexy." It really was. I'd never liked sissy men, and getting a mate like Gyyx was perfect. He was the perfect amount of sweet and hard. He treated me like a princess and in the bedroom...well I definitely wasn't a princess.

6
———

She certainly knew how to dodge talking. Gyyx had never met a woman who liked to play the way he did. He didn't expect his tiny little mate to be able to handle him that way, but she proved a second time that she not only could handle it, but she seemed to prefer it. He loved how her body reacted to his, and even though she was small she could certainly take a lot.

He loved everything about her, but he had a feeling the reason why she distracted him from talking was because there was something about her past she wasn't proud of, but he didn't care about that. He would never judge her based on things she had already done. To him past mistakes were what made the person. Everyone made mistakes; it was how those mistakes affected their lives afterward that mattered.

He lay next to her slowing his breathing. Her small hand rubbed his chest, and he picked it up and brought it to his lips kissing her knuckles.

"I know what you did Leia, and it's okay. You're not ready to talk yet."

He looked at her as she paled. "I'm sorry. There are some things in my past I'm not proud of. I'm not ready to see your shame."

He tensed when he saw a tear slide down her cheek.

"Oh sweetheart, I would never be ashamed of you. No matter what you think you did that was so horrible, that is in your past. Everyone has to make mistakes in their life to grow. There are a lot of things I've done, that I'm not too proud of myself. Everyone does it."

She wiped at her eyes and nodded. "My past wasn't too long ago though. Before I was taken it was still a part of who I was. In a way those things that took me, saved me from myself."

Gyyx growled. He hated knowing that she was ever taken. "How long did they have you?"

She closed her eyes and licked her lips. "57 days. One of them had a thing about counting the days." She shrugged. "I didn't care after a while. It was my punishment. That's what they told me. It was like they knew all of my secrets. I had gone numb."

"Oh sweetheart, nothing you ever did could have deserved being kidnapped by those slimy monsters." He hated how down she was. There was something that happened she wasn't proud of; he would prove to her he didn't care as soon as she told him what it was she thought was so bad. In the meantime, he didn't pry. "The Klimnu are smart bastards. We have been struggling with their attacks for years. They are always ahead of us. We got lucky to burn that prison in the Wastelands down. My brothers have been patrolling more. We aren't letting them take any more of our women. They attacked Eden, took Eliana, and now you. It's getting ridiculous."

She nodded and laid her head on his chest. "I did things to survive, but that's no excuse for liking what I did."

He kept his mouth shut and ran his fingers though strands of her hair hoping she would keep talking. She did and it killed him not to interrupt and wipe away the tears he felt drip on his bare chest.

"My father kicked me out when I was 17. Mom had just passed away and he couldn't cope. He got drunk and he got mean. More times than not he used his fists instead of his words to show me just how angry he was. I left and was on the streets. I wasn't dressed provocatively or anything, but I was walking in a bad part of town. It was where the hookers did their thing. One of the men stopped me and offered me a place to stay and warmth. I only had to do everything he said. At that point it was freezing cold so I agreed without even realizing what I was getting myself into. Or maybe I did.

"For months he used me and my body in any way he chose. In reward he pampered me, and at first I hadn't realized he'd been drugging me. It was when I told him I was too tired that the withdrawals came. It was then I knew he was using drugs to keep me. I had no idea I was an addict until he took them away. I went crazy, and he kicked me to the curb. I was used and abused.

The story could go on forever. I was with several different men who did the same thing, but it seemed to be something I couldn't get away from. The last man though he hurt me physically, and I ran away. It was then I met an elder woman who ran the bakery. She gave me food and gave me a place to stay. She is the one who helped me get clean and off the streets. That was right before I was taken." She sobbed. "She probably thinks I went back, but I was enrolled in college, working at her bakery. I was really getting my life together."

"That's why I was coming here actually. I'm an artist, and I was supposed to be the first student here. I don't know if you know about the program, your dad arranged with our college to send one student every semester to study the lands and learn about your culture. I was the first, but I got intercepted."

Gyyx was tense. All the things she had just laid on him confused him. Why would anyone give their body away to people who hurt them? He didn't think lower of her, it just surprised him. He didn't understand women from Earth. They were so different than Denynso women. They were more emotional and reactive. He licked his lips. "Yeah, we thought the college changed their mind since no one showed up. We haven't been able to get in contact with the administrator or anything."

She sat up and watched him weary as if she were waiting for him to say something horrible about her not so recent past. He wouldn't. She made decisions to survive. He had no idea what living on Earth was like. He didn't know what it was like to be shoved to the street by someone who was supposed to love him. "I don't think any differently about you sweetheart."

Her eyes widened and she sobbed covering her face with her tiny hands. It was the most heartbreaking thing

he had ever seen. She was so ashamed of herself. He
could feel her self-hate, and he wanted to wash it all away.
He would too. He would love her the way she deserved,
and he would help her love herself as well as love him.

7

Didn't he hear a word I said? It was strange; I could feel his love and affection grow. He didn't look at me with disgust. He did look sad, but not because of the choices I made. Maybe it was more because of the choices that I thought I had to make. I needed to survive, and then once I realized how stupid I was, it was too late. I was sucked into the life on the street. I lived it and breathed it. I'd learned a lot, and I had suffered a lot. After nearly five years it was hard to go straight and narrow. I'd been clean for a couple of months before I was picked to be a foreign exchange student as part of the Uoria Program.

"I thought maybe getting away from all the problems for three months would help me heal. I thought I would save me from myself."

"It was smart, but apparently we need to watch incoming ships from now on. We need to make sure everyone who is supposed to be here is accounted for, and we need to keep better communication with those we interact with from your home."

"It's not your fault you know."

"It is though. How did we not know we were missing someone? If we would have known, you wouldn't have been held for two months. How the hell didn't I know? You're my mate for fuck's sake. I should have sensed you sooner."

I pulled him to me. He was angry with himself. "Hey, it's not your fault. Now you know those—Klimnu are even sneakier than you thought. Now you know you need to have more warriors guarding the area and up your security. It's not a big deal. I survived."

He shook his head. "No thanks to us. If it weren't for Eliana saving you..."

I kissed him to shut him up. I wouldn't let him beat himself up over a mistake. He didn't judge me for my past stupidity so I could forgive him and his species for not realizing I was supposed to be studying their land. It was a mistake I knew they wouldn't ever let happen again.

He kissed me back slowly at first until I nipped his lip then he added more pressure. I knew my lips would be bruised and swollen but I loved it. He pulled back before we ended up staying in bed all day.

"I want to know more than just your body, Leia."

The words froze me. I pulled back with a dazed expression. I hadn't realized what I was doing until that moment. I was treating him how I did with the other men. I thought I always had to be sexual. That wasn't my life anymore. "It's going to take some getting used to," I whispered and blushed.

He gripped my chin forcing my eyes to his. "It's okay

sweetheart. I'll show you what real love is. You'll never mistake me for any of those other men you were with. And trust me when I tell you, there will be no other men. There will be no drugs, and there will be no abuse. You are my world now. I'll do everything I can to make sure you're happy."

I felt the tears again and groaned before wiping them away and laughing. "You've got to stop being so sweet. I'm an emotional wreck, and I certainly don't deserve someone like you, but I'll do my best to be worthy of you."

He glared at me and his orange eyes flared. This time it wasn't due to arousal. I could feel his anger spread through my body.

"You are worthy and you do deserve me. You deserve happiness just like everyone else."

I would try to believe him, but it wouldn't be as easy as he made it sound. Five years was a long time to erase, but for him I'd try even harder.

"Tell me about you."

He smiled. "I was a punk for a long time. I'm the younger brother, and Pyra was always golden. He was perfect at everything. He is also pretty powerful like our dad. I did a lot of things trying to get him into trouble. Then as adults he slept his way through all of the females. So, I did the same. There isn't one Denynso woman here, that isn't family, that hasn't been with us both. It was like a competition. He always won, and then when Eden came something in him changed. I was jealous, but also not. She's feisty and she has also been turned into a Denynso. Something we never knew was possible. She's carrying my niece or nephew, and I love her to death, but she is one crazy emotional woman. Our females get angry. They don't usually cry. Eden cries all the time. It took us all some time to get used to seeing tears."

I laughed. "Women are emotional period. We like to cry. It helps us let out the emotions we aren't willing or ready to talk about. I never cried a lot, I used other means to express. I have a lot of anger, a lot of grief. I never had a chance to mourn my mom because my dad couldn't bear to look at me. I look just like her, and I was a daily reminder of the woman he lost. But still I was 17 and he should have taken care of me instead of kicking me out."

"Have you seen him at all?"

"I tried when I got clean, but I didn't know if it would set me back, and I had worked too hard. Then I came here and got taken."

"Maybe you'd like to go see him?"

"Not now. I'm too much of a wreck. I want to have my life together before I see him. I want to show him that even though he threw me away that I still ended up okay. Seeing him now—would only disappoint him more."

"Whatever you want."

"I want to meet your family."

He sighed. "I wanted you to myself for the day, but if you want that's fine. Mom is going to be thrilled. She helped with washing you up and stuff. I didn't feel right."

"I know. She seems like a very kind woman. She talked to me the whole time."

"Shit, I keep forgetting you were aware the whole time. That's so strange."

"I know." I smiled and for the first time in a long while it was real. I didn't force it, and it felt good. Maybe this was exactly where I was supposed to be to be healed. I had been taken for a reason. I spent days trapped inside of myself, even then. Those creatures took everything I feared and played my own memories against me. I was in my own personal hell for 57 long days. I still couldn't believe it. This all felt like a sweet dream.

8
<hr>

She was something else. He knew she was damaged from her imprisonment, but it was even worse than that. Her life had been rough. He wasn't sure what 'living on the streets' was like especially not on a place like Earth, but he had a feeling it hardened people. She had walls built higher than anyone he had ever met.

It would take time to get her to fully trust him. Her story hurt him. He wanted to go find her father and beat him to a pulp. But Gyyx believed that everything happened for a reason even if the reasons were terrible. As much as he was beating himself up over not sensing her sooner, he knew there was a reason. Cause and effect.

"Now let's get out of here before you end up ravaging me again," she said and winked before sliding out of bed.

He shook his head and chuckled. She was a strange creature. She went to the bag of things from the girls and sifted through it. He heard gasps and small girly giggles.

She noticed his stare and blushed. "Sorry it's been

awhile since I've had anything so pretty, that isn't also slutty."

He didn't say anything. He froze when she stripped her dress with her back to him. Thin scars lined her perfect skin. He studied her every move as she slid on each article of clothing. The scars must have been recent. They were still angry and healing in some places. Gyyx wasn't sure if they were from the Klimnu or the last man in her life, and at the moment he chose not to ask, but he would find out, and he would find a way to make whoever it was suffer.

She spun and gasped. "I forgot..."

He didn't say a word. Her eyes said it all. She pleaded with him to ignore what he had seen. He stood from the bed and left the room. He couldn't ignore it, and it was on the tip of his tongue to question her. She already reveled a lot and he wouldn't pressure her to tell him more.

He hated that his mate had been abused. Denynso males cherished their females. He didn't understand how anyone could do differently. He paced his living room while she finished getting ready. He looked down and groaned realizing he was walking around naked. She did things to him that made him forget the most basic things in life—like clothing. He went back in the room and saw her in the bathroom brushing her long hair.

She saw him in the mirror and shrugged. He smiled but it was forced as he slid on clean shorts and a shirt. He waited until she came out and then he went into the bathroom and combed his flattened Mohawk. He never liked to spike it. It was too much work and he spent his time out with the warriors.

He brushed it and was done. When he came out she

was sliding on a pair of sandals and when she stood up she was a few inches taller. He looked down. "What the hell are you wearing?"

She laughed. "They're called wedges, they make short people like me taller, and they're sexy."

He nodded. "I can't disagree, but I love how small you are."

"I hate it. Being five feet tall and weighing 80 pounds when you're on the streets isn't a good thing, but I learned to protect myself. People underestimate me, and I guarantee your friends will too. They all will treat me like something delicate."

He stood in front of her and laughed when her head still didn't even meet his shoulders. He looked down. "You are my delicate mate."

She glared and then chuckled. "Right, you haven't gotten to know me well yet."

He doubted she was very strong but he didn't want to hurt her feelings. She was tiny and small everywhere. He didn't see her being able to do much more than maybe kneeing him in the nuts. "Okay sweetheart. I get it you're tough."

She raised a brow. "You doubt my skills?"

He held up his hands and laughed. "Never."

She pursed her lips. "I see how it is. Fine I'll prove it."

"Oh, don't be mad."

She smiled. "I'm not, but you'll still see. One of your friends will make a comment about my size I bet. Hell, they all might."

"Let's go my fierce little mate. Mom and dad will want to suffocate you with love and welcome you to the family."

For a few seconds, she froze. "You won't tell them—"

"No that's your past. I won't tell a soul. You talk about it to whoever you want, or not."

"Thank you." She wrapped her small hand around his forearm, and he led her out of the bedroom. The house felt different. More alive now. It was even brighter with her there. She already changed him. He didn't feel so gloomy anymore. He also knew what Pyra meant when he had said, *"One day you'll know Gyyx and you won't doubt why I've changed. When you meet yours you'd be willing to change anything."*

All it took was meeting his mate. Every ounce of insecurity he felt all but disappeared. He'd never need to over shadow Pyra. He'd never feel like he was less because he was the youngest again.

When he stepped outside with his mate close, he stayed alert. There hadn't been any attacks in a week, but no one knew when they would start again. Every day without an attack was a blessing, but all of the warriors were all tense and on edge waiting for their peace to end.

He led her down the stairs and walked towards his parents. Pyra was the first to stop them.

"Well hello little one! It's great to see you awake." His brother had no idea and he chuckled.

She tensed digging her nails into his arm and then she shocked him.

Her smile widened. "I'll let that go since you're my new brother, but please keep in mind that powerful things come in small packages, and I'd be careful about what you imply about me."

Pyra's eyes went wide. He was tall, even taller than Gyyx and he laughed. "Is she for real?"

"I'd be careful, she's fierce and not at all delicate," Gyyx said with humor.

"Oh well, you're my new sister. I think a nickname is necessary, right? Isn't that what humans do to show affection?" He was seriously trying to be nice.

She relaxed realizing he hadn't meant to offend her. Of course she was small compared to him. Everyone was.

"Oh well okay. I guess I can deal with that. Plus, you're a freakin' giant, and I don't think anyone is bigger than you."

Pyra laughed and yanked her from me lifting her off the ground and hugging her tightly. "Welcome to the family, little one."

She gasped at his strength and he let her go. "My god you're a freakin beast." Then she seemed to remember what he said. "And thank you."

The whole way everyone stopped them and welcomed her to the family. He felt her emotions swell by the time they got to his parents' house she was close to crying again.

"So many nice people. They all accept me because of you? It's strange."

"We are one giant family."

"Apparently."

He led them up the stairs and the door swung open before he'd even had a chance to knock. His father knew everything.

9

I stared at the man who was an older version of my mate. Even Pyra didn't look as much like the king as Gyyx did. It was crazy.

The man smiled and his teeth glistened in the sun. Automatically I felt a calm override my nerves. He pulled me from his son's arms and wrapped his around me. My head came up to right below his pecks, and I found myself burying my head into him taking in his comfort. The comfort of a father. The dam broke and I sobbed against him. I didn't know why, but I wasn't able to stop it.

No one said anything and he patted my hair soothingly and let me cry. After several minutes, I pulled myself together and blushed when I pulled back. "I'm so sorry. You are just very comforting."

The man laughed and shook his head with a light in his bright orange eyes. "Oh, my new daughter. It's a great day for new family members. I am happy both of my sons have found their other halves."

I stepped back, but he grabbed my hand and pulled

me inside leading me through a giant foyer and into a dining room that rivaled anything I had seen during my time with Bill. He was the rich man that liked to have me hanging from his arm. He was older, fat, but incredibly wealthy. He paid well too. But even his giant house and dining room didn't compare to the immaculacy to this place. It wasn't even over decorated and it didn't scream wealthy.

He led me and Gyyx to the table. "Sit, food will be served, Thiea will be here shortly. She is so excited to meet you—"

"Leia."

"Leia, what a pretty name."

"Thank you." The men were all charmers; all three of them. It was strange but you could tell they were the royalty. There was just something about the air that surrounded them.

Thiea came down the stairs wearing a long silk dress and her orange eyes shined brightly. Her white hair was curled and pulled from her face. Her face was long and fierce. Even though she looked sweet, I knew inside she was an independent woman. She could hold her own.

She smiled and floated to me. Yes, I didn't even see her feet touch the ground. She pulled me from Gyyx and hugged me. "Oh my, you're so beautiful my dear. I'm so glad you're awake. My poor boy was a wreck."

"Mom," Gyyx said and I could hear the embarrassment in his tone.

"Oh stop, she knows you were hurting for her, don't you?"

I nodded. "I was aware. So, I got to know you all pretty

much. Well everyone who was around a lot. It's quite strange."

"Oh I imagine. Now we must feed you and put some meat on those bones of yours."

"Mom."

I turned and laid my hand on his arm. "It's fine. She's right. I could gain some weight."

He wasn't happy when his parents carted me off taking over. Every time I looked at him he was pouting. I found it incredibly adorable. I knew he wanted me to himself, but alone with him meant either sex or him digging deeper into my past wanting to get to know me, and for a while I just wanted to forget everything. I knew the time when I was questioned about my time with the monsters would be coming shortly, and I wanted to enjoy his family before they bombarded me, asking me questions. Some of which I wouldn't even know how to answer.

Several hours later Gyyx sat next to me and sighed. "Sorry, they're excited."

"It's okay. I like that your parents want to know me. I've always wanted a big family."

He chuckled. "Well Sweetheart, now you've got one. They won't let you go now."

I smiled. For the first time I felt settled. I didn't feel the urge to get high or find some random man to sleep with. I had everything I needed and my heart would eventually heal.

"Good," I said.

His mother peppered me with questions, and none of them were all that hard to answer. She seemed to know that there were topics that were off limits. I wasn't sure how, but she was very intuitive.

"So, you were supposed to be our first exchange student?"

"Yes, I was on my way here when the ship was attacked. I don't remember much about what or how it happened though."

"And then they kept you?"

"Yes."

She waved her hand at her husband. "Now's not the time. We can figure it out later. Now we just have to thank the Goddesses she made it out alive and in one piece. You're one tough woman."

"Finally, someone sees it," I said and winked at Gyyx. He laughed and shook his head.

His mother smiled at me and patted my hand. The warmth from her reminded me of the one I had lost and never mourned. It was nice to be around a woman like her. I found I liked where I was very much.

LOVED BY THE ALIEN PRINCE

COVER

GRACE KENSINGTON
LOVED BY THE
ALIEN
PRINCE
ALIEN WARRIOR MATES I | BOOK 6

1

———

One week. That's how long it had been since I had woken up and still I hadn't done anything. Gyyx kept trying to pamper me. He wouldn't let anyone question me about the Klimnu, and I was grateful but a day before there was an attack again. The warriors were all on high alert looking for Ullie knowing he was with the enemy now. He knew inside secrets and had access to the compound. It was time to tell them my story even though it wasn't going to be fun. A lot of truth was going to come out, but they deserved to know anything I was able to tell them.

I sighed and ran my hand over his bare chest. He smiled and his eyes cracked opened.

"Good morning, beautiful."

"Morning." I rolled over and kissed him. When he tried deepening the kiss I pulled away shaking my head. "Nope, not today, buddy. I'm going to tell everyone what happened to me. It's time I meet with your family and everyone else. I've been here a week now, and they're all worried especially now that there has been another attack. You know that. You're a warrior too."

He sighed and nodded. "I know it's time, I was thoroughly enjoying not having to worry, but that little prick is going to pay for switching sides. Why the hell would he do that? He's a fucking warrior for god's sake."

"Some people do bad things because they feel like they don't have a choice."

He glared but even though I didn't agree with what Ullie did I got it. I had made a lot of my own bad choices.

"You can't think that the things you did are as bad as what Ullie did?"

"Just because I'm your mate doesn't make my past squeaky clean, Gyyx. What if he was forced?"

He rolled his eyes. "It didn't' seem that way from what Elaina said. She was there when he would have handed them over to the Klimnu. Ero was knocked out. So clearly I'm right."

I laughed. "I'm not saying I think he is innocent. Sometimes things aren't as they appear to be though."

"Okay, okay, let's not fight. You need to get dressed if we are going to have breakfast with everyone."

I nodded and gulped. It was the day they were all going to learn of my captivity. I wasn't even sure if my story would help them, but I was determined to finally do some good in my life. Maybe it would help make up for all the bad I had done so early in my life. I could only hope it would redeem me.

I climbed out of bed and picked the least sexy outfit the girls had given me and cleaned up. When I was done, I brushed my long hair and did a side braid. My bangs needed trimming.

"Hey babe, do you have any sharp scissors?"

He smirked at me. I blushed realizing it was the first time I had called him anything other than his name.

"What for?"

"I need to cut my bangs; they're too long."

He paused as if thinking and nodded. "Yeah, I'll get them."

"Thank you."

No more than two minutes later I held a very sharp pair of shears. Carefully I began to cut some of the length off. My tongue peeked out and pressed on my upper lip as I concentrated to get them even. My hand shook as I trimmed away the long hair.

By the time I was done, I realized I was pretty good. Besides the shaking hand due to the shears being pretty heavy and I had small hands, I did damn good. I was definitely out of practice. Captivity pretty much made me lose a part of myself.

Now it was time to take that part of me back. Erase the past and finally move forward with my mate. Life would be so much brighter. I knew I could really fit in this world.

Gyyx stuck his head in the bathroom. "You ready? I'm starving."

I chuckled. "You're always starving, but yeah I'm done."

"You look beautiful."

Hearing those words from someone who actually meant it took some getting used to. I didn't say anything, but I couldn't hold back the smile. Each day it got easier to hear him compliment me.

I followed him outside. It always seemed to be bright

and sunny. The sky was always clear with no clouds. I was beginning to wonder if there was any different kind of weather. I wondered if it rained or snowed. Were there ever any gloomy days?

I held his hand as he led us to the eating hall. It was the place where they held meetings and had their community dinners, which was often. They were a very close knit species. At least the ones here. Gyyx had told me about the others. They were all segregated to family lines or whatever. His parents and the warriors kept in contact, but once the Klimnu starting attacking the other groups of Denynso locked up their compounds tight and didn't let anyone in and a select few were allowed out to get supplies. Otherwise they lived behind their walls. It was a shame because if they would all work together they would be more powerful than their enemies.

A tall man stood beside me out of nowhere, and I jumped. He was actually shorter than all of the other warriors and not as bulky. He looked more human. He didn't have a Mohawk, and he didn't have white hair. He had dark brown hair and eyes that matched. The dark orbs held such sorrow. And then he spoke. "Damn you're fucking tiny. I bet Gyyx could tear you in two."

My eyes widened. "Wow, you're really going to go there the first time we meet?"

Gyyx slammed into him throwing him to the ground. "Don't fucking talk to her like that, asshole!"

The man groaned and jumped to his feet and rubbed his back. "It was a joke damn." Then he looked at me. "Sorry, I'm Ero and you must be Leia."

I frowned. His smile was fake. Anyone could see this guy was miserable, and I had a feeling I knew why. He didn't resemble any of the Denynso I had seen yet. "Yes, I'm Leia, and for the record Gyyx didn't need to defend my honor." I hated that he felt like he had to run to my defense. I could have easily taken Ero down myself.

Ero smirked and nodded when he moved forward he cringed and tried to cover it up. But I was an artist. I spotted things like discomfort and insecurities a mile away. He was an artist's dream for drawing. His eyes alone were enough to make any one of us want to do a happy dance. Not because we thought it was funny but because no one could fake that kind of emotion.

2

____

As soon as we entered the large room the voices stopped. Every single person in the room stopped to stare at me. I felt like some sort of circus freak. They had all been trying to get Gyyx to let me out of his cabin, but he refused. It was our "honeymoon" he had said. He wanted me to himself for at least a few days. Then there was an attack and now it was time to get back to the real world.

I didn't know what that meant for me anymore. I hadn't done anything artistic since before, and I was itching to draw something—anything. I didn't have any materials or anything though. I hadn't wanted to ask because I thoroughly loved getting to know him. He was an amazing man, and I was madly in love with him—not that I'd said it yet. It was too soon.

Gyyx squeezed my hand. "After we eat she's ready to talk about her captivity. No fucking questions before she eats a decent meal."

Everyone nodded and the insistent chatter picked up

again. Some of the Denynso didn't even realize I had been in the Klimnu hands for 57 long and horrible days. Even though the room felt like a college campus full of people chatting about inconsequential things, I still felt eyes on me.

Everyone wanted to know what I had been through and what I learned. I nodded at a few of the warriors who smiled and tilted their head in a nod, and then I felt arms around me, pulling me away from Gyyx.

"Oh my gosh, I thought you'd never wake up!"

When I gasped, her arms didn't loosen and I felt wet tears on my shoulder. It was Eliana. Instead of freaking out about having a woman hugging the life out of me I hugged her back and whispered, "Thank you."

I felt her nod and then she pulled back. "I wasn't just going to leave you there. Not after I knew you weren't some trick of the mind."

I nodded knowing exactly what she was talking about. The Klimnu were freaking good. They could manipulate their shape. If they could get in their victim's head and steal their memories, they were as good as done. They used the memories as a way to break their prey down.

"I'm so grateful for you. I would have died had you not taken me out of there."

Gyyx growled, and I patted his arm reassuringly. Eliana nodded in understanding. She didn't deny it. She was the only person who knew what I had gone through even if they only had her for a short time.

She grabbed my hand and squeezed it. "We'll talk more later, okay? You better eat before the fire in Gyyx's eyes burns me." She laughed but she glanced at my mate leery. He was glaring daggers at her as if her talking to me was an inconvenience.

"Stop," I whispered.

"I'm starving woman, stop chitchatting."

"Well then go eat, you big baby."

"Not without you."

I rolled my eyes. "Fine, lead the way."

He led us to a table where his brother and another woman sat. I assumed that was Eden. Gyyx told me she had been a victim of the Klimnu too. Only she died and Ciyrs brought her back to life. On Eden's other side another male sat. He tipped his head and smiled at me. His eyes shined. There was something different about him. It was Ciyrs. I knew he tried so hard to help me wake up. It was strange. I actually knew these Denynso. They didn't seem to realize that I was aware when I was out. I was pretty sure Ciyrs was beating himself up over not being able to make me wake up sooner. He was mated to Eliana and she seemed to have this mothering thing towards me.

He sat across from Pyra and I sat next to him and blushed when they stared at me.

"It's good to see you awake." Pyra was a simple man. He went back to stuffing his face, and these men could eat. Their plates were loaded and they devoured food.

"Thank you," I said in a hushed whisper.

Eden smiled and nodded. She rubbed her belly and sighed. She was a lot different than I expected.

I ate in silence lost in my own thoughts. Gyyx left me alone as if he knew I needed this time to deal. I was about to relive the last two months. The whole thing was it was more mental than physical. The Klimnu got more power by getting inside of my head than physically touching me. Humiliation was another way to feed their lust for power. Something about fear and disgrace fed them. I wasn't sure how it worked. I only knew that I dealt with the same two, the whole time. The one Eliana somehow snuffed out. I still had yet to learn exactly what she did, and then the other one. The one who liked me, the one who used illusion to shake me to the core. Otherwise the other Klimnu pretty much stayed away from me.

"They are all so anxious, and I really don't know how much help I'm going to be," I whispered, but of course they all had good hearing and Pyra frowned.

Before Gyyx could respond Pyra said, "Anything you can tell us will be helpful. We need to stop them from getting onto the land, and we only had a week with no attacks. I fucking hate those nasty pricks. I want to know how they manage to get here. What is it they want?"

"The King." I did know that.

Both Gyyx and Pyra growled. "They won't get him. We'd die first."

My heart dropped even though I knew that would be the answer. Gyyx would sacrifice his life for his father.

Eden smiled at me as if she was used to this, and she probably was. "We will all give our lives for Creia."

I nodded. There was such a strong loyalty for their leader.

Finishing my food I sat back and sighed. It was now or never. "So, when am I going to lead story time today?" I felt the sarcasm drip and shook my head. "Sorry being sarcastic helps when I'm nervous."

"You don't even have to talk. See the thing is dad is one powerful male. He only has to touch you and your memories become his. It will be like he is living it, and he can send it to us. It's hard to explain. He is telepathic to all of those who share his blood, and every warrior does. It's part of the ritual. Therefore, he has a link with all the males. Each one of us will have your story fed into our heads from you to him, then to us. That way we all see it. Live it and understand it."

"Whoa, so Eden and Elaina won't?"

"Oh, we will because of our mates and our connection to each other. So yeah we will."

"That is so weird."

"Yep," Eden said with a smile. "It's a lot to get used to being around people who are so gifted. It's intimidating."

I shrugged. "I don't really mind. I'm just an artist." Then I took a deep breath. "Well let's get this over with."

Gyyx nodded and then suddenly the king sat next to me.

"Are you sure you want to open your mind to me. I need your guards down fully."

I hesitated. "Guards down?"

"Yes, everyone has guards. Since you suffered yours will be thicker and harder to break through, it will be painful. That's why I need you to put them down yourself because I don't want that. If you're willing to open up to me, it will be easier and less—invasive."

I nodded still feeling nervous. "Uh—okay so how do I put my guards down?"

The kings took my hand and shut his eyes. At first I didn't feel anything and then wham it was like the Klimnu only it didn't feel evil. It was a gentle caress. Without opening his eyes, he said, "Okay Leia, I need to you relax and take a deep breath."

I closed my eyes and listened. Doing my best I shut everything out around me and let the king invade my most intimate thoughts and all of my memories. A part of me worried what he would think after he knew what I was like before, and I wondered if everyone would see that part of my past or if he could block some things out. I certainly hoped so.

3

———

I felt his mind traveling into mine. It was like tiny pricks of static. He sifted through my memories. It was strange having him in my head, and thankfully it wasn't painful. I was beginning to understand he was a powerful creature. It made sense on why the Klimnu wanted him so badly. He really was the key to getting back their power.

As of now they were nasty creatures. They were grotesques and horrible vile things. I knew what they were in the past. What they were before the toxins. Apparently, the king could cure them, but he refused. Said they changed because of their selfishness. It was their punishment for wanting too much and expecting it.

The Klimnu were chatty things. They loved talking about themselves and then showing me images of what they used to be. It was no surprise they were a little selfish. They were the ultimate beautiful creatures. And what was beauty, was no longer theirs.

I took a deep breath getting out of my own thoughts when I felt a small pain.

I felt Gyyx's hand on mine and I heard complete and utter silence, all except the sound of my heart beating rapidly in my chest.

2 MONTHS *earlier*

"Anna, do you really think I should do it? I mean what if they all think I'm weird or something?"

"Oh honey, they won't. And you aren't weird, you're a woman who is learning to be on her own. Getting away and gaining new life experiences is what it's all about"

I shook my head. "I know that but it's all still so fresh. I haven't been this person for very long."

She cupped my cheeks. "That is who you are Leia. Don't let your past insecurities hold you back."

I nodded. "Okay I'll go. It might be good to get away from all the things from my past. I'm having cravings again."

Her eyes widened. "Fight them sweet heart."

My eyes filled with tears. "I'm trying."

She nodded and led me back into the break room. I sat down and while my hands shook Anna handed me a glass of water. It wasn't what I wanted—what I needed, but having her around to keep me on the right road was helping. If I was alone I would have already cracked.

I closed my eyes and let the coolness from the water ease the ache. I was in control. "Tomorrow I leave," I whispered. Suddenly leaving to another planet seemed like the best idea I had ever had. I would get away and hopefully learn a lot of new things.

Later that night as I dragged myself up the creaky stairs to the room above the shop I realized a few things. I was slowly overcoming my addiction. Every day was a challenge, but it was worth it in the end.

I stripped off my clothes and fell into bed. I didn't even bother getting dressed. I was thoroughly exhausted.

THE NEXT MORNING I woke up feeling both terrified and excited. I was the first from school who signed up for the foreign exchange program. It was a once in a lifetime experience and couldn't have come at a better time. I had been clean for 3 months. My counselor said I would be fighting for years to overcome this and even then it would always haunt me.

I rolled out of bed and went into my tiny hole in the wall bathroom. It had a shower, a toilet, and hot water. That's all I needed. I turned on the water and the pipes groaned and creaked in protest. It was an old building. The water got luke warm at best, but I'd had worse so I couldn't complain.

I scrubbed clean and stepped out into the cool air shivering. It would be nice to be somewhere different. I hoped somewhere warm. This weather was getting ridiculous. I took the folded piece of paper out of my pocket and unfolded it so I could check the directions to the meeting point one more time. I had never traveled by spaceship before and I was afraid that I would somehow take a wrong turn along the way, get lost, miss my trip to

Uoria, and be stuck in the same life with dark memories that haunted me no matter how hard I tried to put them behind me.

The bright green piece of paper led me to one of the university's many outlying study buildings; this one was so far at the other end of the campus that I was afraid my short legs weren't going to get me there in time. For a brief moment, I entertained the idea of waving someone down and asking them for a ride, but just the thought made my stomach turn as I remembered how many times I had done something similar, and the consequences I had suffered because of it.

Forcing myself to think about something beyond those memories distracted me so much that I almost didn't realize I had gotten to the building. It loomed ahead of me in brilliant chrome and black detailing and for a moment I just stood back and admired it. It was extremely impressive for a building that existed purely for the purposes of housing ships and arranging travel for the students and researchers at the university. I stood on the sidewalk outside and looked at it. Somewhere inside there the crew was waiting for me, waiting to bring me aboard a ship that would take me on a journey far from Earth and far from everything I had ever known, and everything I had been trying to outrun.

I took a deep, steeling breath and strode into the building, exuding as much confidence as I could even though there were butterflies swarming in my stomach. No one I knew had ever traveled off of Earth so I had no one to give me advice on what the trip would be like or how I was going to handle it. This was truly an adventure into the unknown and I was nervous, but ready to embrace it. There was no way it could be worse than anything I had already endured.

The woman at a massive, gleaming front desk looked up at me and flashed a smile so big and bright it looked like she had been rehearsing it.

"Hi," I said cautiously, approaching the desk and holding up the green sheet of paper as if it was my pass to the building, "I'm Leia. I'm here for my trip to Uoria."

"The foreign exchange program!" the woman said with excitement, "They are just fueling up the ship and will be ready to go in a few minutes. Go through that door and go to the end of the hall. Type your name into the keypad beside the door and it will let you out into the loading area. Have a fantastic trip!"

"Thank you."

I followed the woman's point to a tall metal double door at the end of the room and it opened as I approached as if it could sense my presence. It led into a long, wide corridor lined with doors with nothing more than numbers to differentiate them. I followed the corridor to the end and found the keypad by the door. My fingers shook slightly as I typed my name into the keys, but I didn't know if they were shaking more from nervousness or excitement.

The door swung open as soon as I finished typing my name and I stepped out into a huge room that swarmed with people. I waited just inside the door until a woman in a short dress and pointed hat came up, took my elbow, and led me toward the ship in the middle of the room without saying anything to me.

A few moments later I was settling into a large plush seat that surrounded me like a pod, securing my seatbelt as tightly as I could, tucking my small bag in behind my feet. It didn't contain much, only the few articles of clothing I had that I felt comfortable wearing in a school setting and my meager art supplies. I closed my eyes and let out a long breath, knowing this moment was the last of life as I knew it and that soon I would be experiencing something incredible, something that would fuel me to another level of my art.

4

———

The top of my pod was still open and a pleasant-looking man appeared above me.

"Hello, Leia. You are my only passenger today."

"Yes," I said, not really knowing what else to say when he paused.

"The flight from Earth to Uoria takes approximately five days when the conditions are good. If you prefer, I can put you to sleep so that you can pass the trip in your pod rather than experiencing all of it. Would you like me to do that for you?"

My mind immediately panicked at the thought of him doing anything that would put me into a state of not being able to control myself or make decisions. It was much too close to what the men had done to me, how they had controlled me for years using drugs and manipulation to keep me as their compliant servant. I shook my head adamantly.

"No. I'll stay awake."

The pilot got a strange look on his face, but nodded.

"That's fine. We have plenty of supplies to sustain you through the trip. If you change your mind, though, just let me know."

"I will. Thank you."

"I'm going to go ahead and close your pod up now. It will open when we get out of orbit and it is safe for you to move around the rest of the ship. Make sure your seatbelt is secure and just relax. The takeoff is the worst part."

He smiled, but I didn't find his words terribly reassuring, and when he closed the pod, the loud clicking sound of the lid clamping into place made my stomach flip. I rested my head back on the seat and gave my seatbelt another tug just to make sure that it was tight around me. A few moments later I felt the pod around me start to shake slightly as the pilot began the lift-off process. The shaking grew more intense and right as I felt like I couldn't take it anymore, the shaking eased and I felt a tremendous surge upwards.

What felt like hours later, there was a click and a hissing sound as the lid to my pod popped open and eased upward a few inches. I released my seatbelt and pushed the lid up the rest of the way so that I could climb out. We were still days away from the planet where I planned to spend the next six months, but I already felt like Earth was a lifetime away. The sense of freedom and possibility surrounded me and for the first time in years I felt all the tension, fear, and worry ease out of my shoulders. It would be less than 24 hours before it all returned and what was supposed to be my salvation became my hell.

I had just eaten a huge lunch and was settling into my

pod for a nap on the second day of the journey when I felt the ship lurch and shudder. It settled only for a moment before shaking even more violently and tilting to the side so harshly I tumbled out of my pod and onto the floor. I heard a scream from the front of the ship where the flight attendant stayed for the majority of the time and then a series of pounding sounds that felt like they were shaking my bones.

The door between the chamber where my pod sat along with a table and cluster of chairs and the small room where the flight attendant stayed dented then split, and my breath caught in my throat as a loathsome-looking creature climbed through the break into my chamber. It looked like a slimy skeleton covered with ghastly white skin and oily strings of hair coming from its comparatively tiny head. Steeply pointed teeth jutted from its mouth and claws several inches long protruded from the ends of its thin fingers.

I scrambled backwards as four more of the creatures climbed into the room, the last one dragging the pilot along with him. They seemed to notice me suddenly, all of them turning their eyes to me at the same time and approaching with long strides that covered the floor space between us in seconds.

"What are you?" I screamed, flattening my back against the far wall of the chamber and starting to work my way around the room toward my pod.

"We are Klimnu," the first creature that had come into the chamber said in a voice that made my skin crawl.

"Run!" the pilot screamed, thrashing against the hands of the creature that held him, "Get into my cockpit and call for help."

The Klimnu that held him pulled the pilot up off the ground and pulled his head back by his hair. The pilot kicked and another of the Klimnu grabbed his legs so that he couldn't move anymore. An instant later the one who held him slashed his throat with his fangs. The blood poured in a thick, glistening curtain down the front of his body and I felt my stomach turn. Pulling his head back further, the Klimnu burrowed his mouth into the pilot's neck until he found his spine, then bit through it with a sickening crunch. The rest of the man's body collapsed to the floor and the Klimnu held up his head like a trophy.

I fought the vomit that rose in my throat, struggling to stay in control and keep my mind clear so that I would have any chance at all to get into the cockpit and call for emergency help.

"What are you?" I asked in a strangled voice, still working my way around the wall.

The first Klimnu took a step toward me and I gasped, pressing myself harder against the wall.

"We are Klimnu," he repeated angrily.

"Why are you here?" I asked, the tears pouring down my cheeks like acid.

"Ynn, our planet, has become a wasteland. There is nothing there and even we are struggling to survive. We are going to Uoria to join our brethren there. There is no famine, especially with the Denynso to sustain us."

"What do you mean?"

The creature gave a horrific sound that might have been a laugh and was suddenly only inches from me, blocking me against the wall with his disgusting, slimy body. Instead of answering my question, he reached up and ran the tips of his sharp claws along my cheek and down my neck. I shuddered at the feeling, but when I tried to wriggle away from him, he tilted his hand so that the points of the claws bit into my skin like needles.

"You are a pretty little thing," he said, his voice lower now like he was trying to cajole me with his words, "I don't think I am going to let my men kill you. I would much rather keep you as my pet."

He looked at me the way that the men who had bought, sold, and traded me did and I felt myself grow dizzy with fear and disgust.

"I would rather die," I hissed and I felt his claws slash across my neck, digging deeply enough to make my blood flow but not enough to comply with my wishes.

I withheld the cry of pain that bubbled up in my throat. I didn't want to give him the satisfaction of making me appear weak and vulnerable in front of him.

"Perhaps you will have the opportunity to experience both," he said and grabbed me by the front of my shirt, dragging me toward the door.

I felt the warmth of the pilot's blood soaking through my clothes as the creature dragged me through it on our way through the ship. No matter how hard I struggled, I couldn't free myself from his grasp. I could see out of the corner of my eye that he was dragging me through the side hatch of the ship and I grabbed onto the sides, desperately trying to stay within the ship, but he pulled me so hard the skin tore from my hands and I couldn't hold on any longer. A moment later I was in a dark hallway and I knew my life was no longer my own.

5

———

In an instant I realized that the dark hallway was a connector between the ship that I had been on and another one. The Klimnu had attached their ship to the university's and torn through the wall, leaving it gaping and vulnerable. The creature dragged me down the hallway and into a large open chamber in the center of the ship. Behind us the rest of the creatures crawled through the doorway. One held a small black contraption in his hands.

"I have the black box," he said.

His voice was not as slimy as that of the creature that still gripped me, but he was no less disgusting as he passed close by me on the way toward an open door on the other end of the chamber. I knew that the black box was stolen from the university's ship and that it contained all the programming for the trip to Uoria. In taking that box they had essentially stolen an auto-pilot flight right to a planet that they wanted to dominate. My stomach sank as I realized that there was no escape now. Without the black box, even if a miracle struck and I was able to get myself free of the Klimnu and back onto the university's ship, the emergency rescue crews would have no way of finding it.

The Klimnu holding me turned me roughly so that I was staring back down the hallway toward the ship. In an instant the ship exploded, becoming a massive ball of orange flame. I screamed as the ship disappeared and the hallway collapsed in on itself, closing the opening in the side of the ship and closing me in with my disgusting, threatening captors. I knew it was my last chance. Maybe if I could free myself from the grip of the creature that held me I would be able to get into the control room of this ship and reach out for help, or at least figure out how to steer the ship onto the closest planet so that I could get away.

Years of martial arts training from when I was younger came back to me in waves. I felt the lessons, the discipline, and the power flowing through my muscles as I channeled the confidence and intensity I once held. This was knowledge from a time before I ended up on the street, before I had to turn to the sickening men to stay alive. I took a breath and lashed out at the creature. My leg lifted and came in contact with the side of his head, making a deep cracking sound that resonated through the chamber. The creature let out a shriek that nearly brought me to my knees, but the feeling of his hands holding me in place released and I took advantage of the sudden freedom by taking off running across the room.

I ran a few steps and then dropped to the floor, using my small frame to my advantage by sliding through the legs of two of the creatures that came at me. Getting past all of the creatures, I scrambled to my feet and took another step toward the open door on the other side of the room. I felt a surge of energy and hope as I reached a hand toward the doorframe, hoping to grab onto it so that I could pull myself through. Before I could, however, I felt a sharp, searing pain in my back.

I fell back, pulled by some unseen force. The intensity of the pain took my breath away and I couldn't withhold the sharp gasp that came from my lips. A moment later the creature who wanted to keep me as his pet appeared by my side. I looked up and realized that the pain came from more than a dozen fine wires that came from the ceiling. The creature walked around me and touched a button on the wall. I screamed as the wires retracted, lifting me a few inches off the floor with the hooks embedded in my back. The weight of my body pulled the hooks through my skin, slicing through my back, but held so that I dangled from the ceiling with my toes barely grazing the floor beneath me.

"Misbehaving will do you no good," the Klimnu hissed at me, "It will only make this far worse for you."

I opened my mouth to speak, but he covered it with his hand and I felt like I was being gagged. My voice would not push through my throat and I could barely breathe. Even when he pulled his hand away from my face I couldn't make a sound and only the smallest amount of air seeped through my mouth and nose into my lungs.

That is where I stayed for the next four days, hanging from the ceiling of the main chamber of the ship unable to make any sound. The Klimnu passed by me throughout the day as they went about their normal business, walking past me as if I was a gruesome decoration. Occasionally one of them would tip a small amount of water down my throat, but they never brought me food and by the time they told me we were preparing to land, I was nearly delirious with hunger.

Four days later.

The shaking of the ship as we lowered toward the ground intensified the pain in my back and I felt fresh tears following the dry, sticky path of those I had already cried over the last few days. I have never been one to cry often, but the excruciating physical pain and emotional despair I was in drew more tears from me than I remembered crying in the last several years.

Even with the pain, however, the shaking was welcome because it meant that we were nearing the surface of Uoria and perhaps they would free me from the hooks that held me in place. It may mean that I was a few steps closer to death, but that relief would be welcome.

When the shaking of the ship calmed, the group of Klimnu came into the chamber and without a word, the one who had held me in place when they first captured me came to my side and wrapped an arm tightly around my hips. He used his long, slimy fingers to pry each of the hooks from my back and as they swung through the air I could see droplets of blood spatter across the floor. He picked me up over his shoulder and I draped over it like a ragdoll, incapable of moving.

He carried me out of the ship and I got my first breath of fresh air. The university had warned me that breathing on the strange planet would be challenging at first, but I didn't care. The warm air smelled sweet and as it washed across my skin I felt a brief moment of relief from the agony. After only a few seconds, however, the creature brought me into a building and darkness engulfed me. He threw me to the ground and I felt pain shoot through my hip as it cracked against a stone floor. My eyes gradually adjusted to the darkness and I could just make out the nearly bare space around me. There was a plate of something that resembled food on the floor and I descended on it, eating ravenously as the metallic sound of the barred door slamming reverberated in my head.

I don't know exactly how long I stayed on that cold stone floor before the Klimnu returned. My captor opened the barred door and stepped into the cell with me. He ran one of his fingers along my leg and then through my hair. I shivered in disgust and turned my face away from him. To my utter surprise, he stepped away.

"Who are you?" he asked.

"Leia."

"Why were you on that ship?"

"I am part of an exchange student program with Uoria. I am here to study the land and the culture and work on my art," I answered shakily.

There was a pause and I could feel tension growing in the cell.

"I don't believe you."

"What do you mean?"

"My brethren say that you must be a scientist. Uoria has only allowed a few humans to visit and they have all been researchers."

"I'm not a researcher."

"You must be," he said, taking a step back toward me, causing me to cower against the wall, "You know something about the Denynso that has brought you here to do more research. Tell me what it is."

"I don't have anything to tell you," I said, my voice sounding slightly more pleading than I would have liked it to.

"We will accomplish our goal, Leia, whether you cooperate with us or not. I do warn you, though, if you choose not to cooperate, I can promise you will not live to see the sun again much less do any studying."

The Klimnu walked out of the cell and locked the door behind him, leaving me alone in the darkness. I curled my knees to my chest and sobbed into them. I had finally made it to Uoria and yet I was back in the torturous, brutal hands of captors who sought to control my every breath.

"Seven days."

They were the first words I had heard since my captor left me in the cell. I had been fed once and given only a bucket of water to drink. I barely had the strength to raise my head to look at the Klimnu who stood on the other side of the bars staring at me like an animal in one of the zoos back on Earth. His mouth curled up in a disgusting, skin-crawling smile and I could see that he was looking at me in much the same way as the one who had captured me and told me he wanted to keep me as a pet.

That creature appeared behind the one at the door and pushed him aside, opening the door and stepping into my cell. He knelt down beside me and I felt him touch me. My body recoiled and his hand wrapped more tightly around me. He leaned forward and ran his tongue along my skin, causing bile to rise in my throat and my chest to constrict painfully.

"Are you sure you don't have anything to tell us about

the Denynso?" he asked, lifting his head away from my arm and bringing it to the other one so he could repeat the lick.

"I told you that I don't know anything about them. I am just an art student. I'm not a scientist or a researcher or anything else. The whole reason I'm here is to learn about them."

I sobbed as his teeth dug down into my skin, drawing fresh blood to join the dry streaks from other bites that covered my body. This had been the greatest torment; him coming into the cell with me to lick and touch me without speaking, then biting or clawing me when I had no information to give him.

"THIRTY DAYS."

My captor stepped into my cell and I raised my head to look at him. The weakness in my muscles made it almost impossible, but anger and bitterness were replacing my fear. They kept me so close to the edge of death, hovering just on this side of life, that I didn't feel that I had anything to fear any longer. It would take only a moment to finish me and then at least I would be free. I refused to cower from him any longer.

The creature came into the cell and sat down beside me. This was strange. He had never sat with me before. After a month, I had become accustomed to him coming into the cell and torturing me, prodding me for information, touching me in ways that made me feel sick. Sometimes he would feed me. More often, however, he didn't.

He reached out and touched my leg and an idea

suddenly occurred to me. Perhaps I could lure him into trusting me. If I could use what I learned from the time with the men, I might be able to lower his guards and find a way to free myself.

I didn't withdraw from his touch like I usually did and he looked at me. His sickening hands tore my shirt away from me, but I continued to fight the revulsion. As if testing me, he leaned forward and bit into my breast savagely. I drew in a pained breath, but still didn't move away. The creature shredded my pants with his claws and suddenly I was in nothing but my bra and panties. I was thankful for the relative warmth of the room, but felt exposed and ashamed as he looked at me. I closed my eyes and brought myself to the distant plane of existence I had trained myself to escape to when I was under the hands of the men who felt they owned me.

When his touch finally left my body, I quickly covered myself and curled against the wall.

"You never told me why you wanted to come here," I said cautiously, trying to start a conversation with him that may both lull him into complacency and give me information I could use to help me if I ever managed to get out of the prison.

The Klimnu hesitated for a moment, and then looked at me.

"We want Creia."

"Who is that?"

"The king of the Denynso."

"Why do you want him?"

"The Klimnu feed off the temper and aggression of the Denynso. The more we provoke them, the greater the benefit. Even more powerful than their temper, however, is their blood. Their blood gives us even greater strength. We are already the far more superior species in terms of intelligence and capability. Their blood gives us the intensity and power of their warriors to make us the ultimate race."

His words were some of the most terrifying I had ever heard and I could sense his growing agitation, so I allowed the conversation to end. He left and a few minutes later another of the group brought me food.

"Forty days."

In the ten days since I had begun to give into the roving tongue and prodding fingers of my captor, I had learned more about the planet where I was now imprisoned and the powerful warriors who lived there. He stepped into the cell again and I immediately started talking.

"You never explained to me why you want Creia," I said, hoping to dissuade him from touching me.

"To get back at him," he said, reaching forward and running his fingers down my shoulder despite my hopes.

"Why?"

"The Klimnu were once beautiful creatures," he said and I withheld an exclamation of surprise that this wretched creature could say that anything like him had ever been beautiful.

He continued to talk and I learned that there was a time when the Klimnu were strong, beautiful, and powerful. Knowing their own planet was on a rapid path toward destruction, the Klimnu decided to take over the lush, healthy, and clean planet of Uoria for themselves. The Denynso, however, had been there since the beginning of their kind and were not willing to let the Klimnu take over. As they tried to take over, the Klimnu came into contact with plants that contained toxins so potent and virulent they immediately began to transform the once lovely creatures into the contorted, disgusting versions.

I listened to my captor talk, horrified yet fascinated at what he was telling me. He told me how they approached the incredible healers of the Denynso and asked that they heal them. These healers agreed to provide the antidote to the toxins if the Klimnu agreed to leave the planet and stop their efforts to take over. They refused and only increased their violent attacks. The more violent they became, the worse their condition became. Finally, they appealed to Creia to command his healers to remove the toxins and return them to their health and strength.

"The king refused," my captor said, his voice seething with anger, "He said we deserved what we got because of our selfishness and cruelty."

"If you wanted so much to be healed, why couldn't you just promise peace and find another planet?"

As soon as the words came out of my mouth, I knew I had gone too far. His eyes flashed with fury and before I even saw his hand moving I felt the vicious tips of his claws slash across my back, opening the still-healing wounds form the hooks that had held me in the ship.

"You are not the only human we have attacked," he told me through gritted teeth, "The other survived because she was mated to the most powerful warrior of the Denynso race. You will not be so lucky."

He fell into a frenzy, biting me all along my body and

slashing at me with his claws. When he finally had his fill and left, I lay on the floor quaking with pain, feeling the life draining from my body. I closed my eyes, welcoming death.

"FIFTY-FIVE DAYS."

Death had not come as I had prayed. My captor had toyed with me, leaving me just at the edge of life so that he could return as my body healed and torture me more. I couldn't remember the last time I had eaten when another of the creatures stepped up to my cell and slid a plate of food toward me. It took all of my strength to eat what had been given to me and the creature seemed to take pleasure in watching my struggle. Suddenly I heard a scream reverberating off the walls on the corridor in front of my cell. It was muffled as if it was coming from a different area of the building, but it was undeniably a woman screaming for her life.

My eyes darted around me and the Klimnu laughed.

"You hear our new guest," he said and my ears pricked up, "She is different than you. She is special."

"What do you mean?" I struggled to ask.

"The Denynso will come for her. She belongs to one of them and he will ensure they find her, which means he will bring the warriors right to us."

As soon as he said that, I knew this was my only opportunity. I was already so tiny and on top of that became grotesquely thin. The next day I pushed myself through the bars of my cell as soon as my captor left and made my way through the halls. I moved as fast and I could and went until I couldn't go any further. When I fell, I was sure that was it. I knew the Klimnu would realize I was gone and come to find me. But then I saw a woman coming down the hall toward me and I used the very last of my strength to ask for help.

7

___

"The next thing I remember is hearing voices around me but not being able to respond to them or wake up. I thought I was dead, but then I felt Gyyx near me and I knew I was alive and going to be safe."

When I was finally finished sharing my memories with Creia, I felt drained but relieved. I sat back and reached out to grab Gyyx's hand. I needed to feel him close to me.

"Burning the prison didn't stop them," my mate said, growling deep in his throat as he processed what he had just heard about my experience with the Klimnu, "They will be back, especially if they can replenish from Ynn."

I watched as the control in the room around me disintegrated. The warriors jumped to their feet and the room filled with the sound of shouts. I squeezed Gyyx's hand, telling him with the pressure that I needed to get out of the room. Creia stood and pounded his hand on the table in front of him, demanding attention and quieting the room around him.

"The Klimnu will return. They are after me and they will not rest until they achieve their goal."

"Unless we wipe them out of existence," Pyra said and I saw Eden reach up to stroke his arm calmingly.

"There is nothing we can do tonight," Creia said, "Gyyx, take your mate home. Let her rest. She has been through even more than I could have imagined. Take care of her and we will move forward tomorrow."

Without replying, Gyyx stood and scooped me into his arms. Usually I didn't want him to carry me, but at that moment I needed the feeling of his heart against me and the sound of his breath surrounding me. I felt tiny cradled in his arms and the strength of his body made me feel safe. As he carried me home I felt my body aching for him, needing his touch to soothe and comfort me. It was his touch that brought me out of the deep, consuming sleep that I had not been able to free myself from, and his love that was helping me overcome the darkness of the days behind me. I needed that touch now.

When we got back home Gyyx carried me directly to the bedroom and laid me down on the bed. Before I could pull him down with me, however, he straightened and began to pace around the room, stalking like a caged animal.

"What's wrong?" I asked.

He shot a withering glare at me and I felt my breath catch in my throat.

"Are you kidding me?" he asked, nearly shouting, "After what I just found out about what those disgusting creatures did to you, you can seriously ask me what's wrong?"

"I'm alright now," I told him, reaching out for him.

He came to the side of the bed and let me run my hand down his chest. I could feel his heart pounding beneath my fingers and the orange of his eyes flashed with anger despite the desire lingering there.

"I hate to think about them touching you," he said softly, "The thought of one of them licking you..." he trailed off and I could see his body shudder.

"Fix it," I whispered, "Replace those memories."

I eased closer to him on the bed and turned his face toward mine so I could rest my lips against his. He kissed me back gently at first, then with greater intensity until I could feel my need reflected in him. I climbed onto my knees and swung one leg over his hips so that I straddled his lap facing him. Not taking my eyes away from his, I pulled my dress off over my head and dropped it to the floor behind me. His only reaction was a soft moan, so I went a step further, releasing the clasp on the back of my bra and peeling it away so that I exposed my bare breasts to him. That was enough to trigger him into action.

Gyyx flattened his hands on my back, the size of them nearly covering the entire expanse, and applied pressure until I arched back, thrusting my breasts up toward him. He dipped his head and ran his tongue around one of my nipples, causing it to harden and the ache between my thighs to increase. Moving with incredible patience, he switched to the other nipple and repeated the motion, nurturing that one to a taut peak as well. His tongue roved across my breasts and then up to my neck before he brought a kiss back to my lips and stood, cradling me against him so that he could turn me and lay me back down on the bed.

I complied with him as I always did, letting him conform my movements to his wishes as he pulled my panties from my hips and dropped them to the floor. He didn't remove any of his clothing and the juxtaposition between him being fully clothed and me being completely naked sent a shiver through my body and directly into my core. Gyyx returned his mouth to my skin, tracing the curves and planes of my body with his tongue as if trying to cover every inch that the Klimnu may have touched or licked. I could feel the disgust of the creature's touch disappearing as my mate nurtured me.

Suddenly the torturously slow, tender movements of Gyyx's mouth stopped and he pushed my legs apart, scooping his hands beneath me to hold my pelvis up. His mouth opened and engulfed my core, sucking lightly as his tongue explored the intricacies of my folds and dipped within me. I cried out loudly, burying my fingers into his long white hair. He moved his mouth up, concentrating his attention so that just the tip of his tongue swirled around the tender, hypersensitive pearl of flesh at my peak and for a moment I thought I was going to dissolve under the intense, glorious sensations he was creating within me.

In the next moment, his finger slid into my body and everything crashed around me. My body clenched around his hand, squeezing it tightly as I screamed his name and dug my nails deeply into his back.

"I love you," I gasped as I collapsed back down onto the bed.

His face lifted and he looked down at me with wide, vibrantly orange eyes.

"What?" he asked.

It was the first time I had said it and perhaps I had not chosen the most opportune moment, but it had spilled out of me with the same purely natural energy of the blistering orgasm he had just given me and there was no reason to pretend it hadn't.

"I love you," I repeated, holding his face between my hands.

"You're not just saying that because I made you come so hard I think the warriors probably heard you?"

"You've done that before," I pointed out to him.

Gyyx rose up over me and lowered down so that his body engulfed mine and captured my mouth in a deep, seeking kiss.

"I love you," he whispered when our kiss broke.

Gyyx spent the rest of the night kissing every inch of me, soothing the scars on my back and making up for every moment of pain and abuse I had ever endured. The next morning I was thoroughly fulfilled and more at peace than I had ever been in my life. I told him I was going to visit Eliana and Eden and left him lying in bed, drained and with a satiated smile on his lips.

I had only gone a few yards from the house when I heard a voice near me.

"You are mine," it hissed.

I looked around, frightened by the sound, but didn't see anyone.

"You are mine," the voice repeated and I recognized it as the slimy sound of the Klimnu that had captured me.

I spun around, trying to see him, but around me the land was quiet and empty.

"I own you. You belong to me," the Klimnu said and I suddenly felt his presence behind me.

I remembered what Gyyx had told me about the Klimnu being able to use illusion to manipulate people, so when I turned and saw Ero close behind me, I didn't hesitate. The anger that had built up inside me for two months in that prison boiled over, fueled by my love and loyalty for Gyyx. Being mated to my powerful Denynso warrior had me feeling stronger both mentally and physically than I had ever felt before. My hand lashed out before the disguised Klimnu had the chance to react. It hit him so hard he stumbled back and I swept my leg forward, taking his out from under him so that he hit the ground. Not giving him the opportunity to recover, I jumped and landed with my elbow in the middle of his throat. There was a satisfying crack and the creature gurgled beneath me, the attack causing his illusion to fade so that I looked at his disgusting face again.

"You do not own me," I told him, enunciating each word carefully to ensure he heard them, "I belong to my mate, and my mate only. You will never touch me again."

I shoved the heel of my hand into his face, crushing his nose. Before I could hit him again, I felt hands pulling me back and spun around to see the real Ero tugging me away from the bleeding and struggling Klimnu.

"Leia!" he shouted, trying to get my attention, shocked he said, "Calm the hell down. Are you okay? We'll take it from here."

"He used an illusion to look like you. He said that I belonged to him. He was trying to take me back."

"Don't worry," he said as two more warriors ran up to us, "He won't be bothering you anymore."

Ero turned me by my shoulders and started guiding me back toward the house.

"We finally heard from the university," he said in a cheerful tone that belied the sounds of screaming behind us, "They are sending a professor for the exchange program."

"Do they know what happened?" I asked.

He shrugged.

"We handled it."

A furious Gyyx stepped out of the house and pulled me into his arms, possessively removing me from Ero's touch.

"When will she be here?" I asked, wrapping my arms around Gyyx.

"A few days."

As he said it, I could swear I saw a flicker of orange in his eyes.

DESIRED BY THE ALIEN WARRIOR

COVER

GRACE KENSINGTON
DESIRED BY THE ALIEN WARRIOR
ALIEN WARRIOR MATES I | BOOK 7

1

Sign up for Grace Kensington's Mailing List

2

———————

There wasn't really anything to look at through the window of the ship, but it was better to stare out into the dark expanse than it was to look ahead of me at the bright, almost iridescent white interior of the pod chamber I had been looking at for the last four days, so I continued to gaze out. I sat in my pod, tucked down so I was reclining in the thick padding that filled the rounded egg-like pod with a notebook open in my lap. The top of the pod was as wide open as I could get it and I hadn't closed it since the moment the pilot announced we were out of Earth's atmosphere and I was able to open the pod and move freely around the chamber. I hate being confined in any way. It makes me feel out of control, which was something that I never handled well.

"How are you doing in here?" a flight attendant asked, leaning against the side of my pod and looking down onto the notebook in my lap.

I sighed and smiled up at the frail, rather plain-looking but pleasant girl who had been rotating shifts with a young man during the voyage. The trip from Earth to Uoria was long, but I had been unwilling to undergo the sedating process that would have allowed me to sleep throughout the entire five-day sailing. It might be tedious to stay within the same area for such a long time, but giving up five days of my life was not something I was going to do, especially not when I still felt like I had so much to do to prepare for my teaching position on the new planet.

"I'm doing alright. I'm definitely ready to get out of this ship, though."

The flight attendant gave a short laugh and nodded.

"I can totally understand that. These voyages can get stressful. At least you decided to stay awake though. Sitting around here during voyages that are more than a day with passengers that go to sleep can really wear on the nerves."

"I'm sure. I bet there is only so much you have to talk about with your coworker over there."

We both glanced across the chamber at the other flight attendant. He was sitting in one of the long chairs beside the tall windows opposite of my pod, plugged into a game that he held in his lap with the same level of interest and consideration that I held for my work. We laughed and the flight attendant shook her head.

"Yeah. He's an exhilarating conversationalist."

"Do you always travel with him when you're working?"

As a teacher, I am naturally curious and constantly found myself feeling like I was doing little research projects throughout my days, trying to find out more about any situation or person that I encountered. I didn't know much about space travel, considering this was my first excursion away from Earth, and it fascinated me to find out about the intricacies of the travel companies and their staff. This curiosity sometimes got me in trouble, but I figured that there wasn't much that could happen just by asking about how they planned their shifts.

"Yes. The university charters teams and we essentially stay together throughout our careers."

"I guess they want to foster closer bonds and trust between the members of the teams so that you can cooperate on a higher level and manage crises more effectively."

The flight attendant stared down at me with a slightly blank look in her eyes.

"That sounded like it came directly out of the training manual."

I laughed. That was not the first time that I had had someone accuse me of sounding like a textbook.

"I guess it's like my grandmother always said, 'You can take the professor out of academia, but you can't take academia out of the professor.'"

The flight attendant giggled.

"I love old-fashioned sayings like that. I haven't heard that one since I was a little girl." She gave a sigh and peered over her shoulder briefly, "It looks like it's just about lunchtime. Can I get you something?"

I nodded.

"Yes. I'm starving. Thank you."

I had packed snacks in the luggage I kept with me at my pod, but I hadn't anticipated the somewhat small portions they served me on the ship and had already eaten almost all of them so I was rationing them carefully so that they lasted throughout the rest of the voyage. When the flight attendant walked away, the pod chamber fell still and quiet again. Even the other attendant had turned off his game and was somewhere else in the ship helping prepare the meal. I let my mind wander to Uoria again and what could be waiting for me there.

I thought about Leia and what the university had told me about the first student who had made the journey to the new planet. It had been two months since the brilliant but troubled young art student had made the courageous decision to the be the very first Earth student to join in the exchange program with the Denynso and make the trip to Uoria to study the culture and the land. Since she left, the university hadn't heard anything about her, and while many of the other professors and even the organizers of the program felt that there was nothing to be concerned about considering how intensive the level of study would be, suddenly arriving on another planet where there had been no previously established school or connection, I had felt a twinge of nervousness every time I thought about her.

I didn't know Leia extremely well. Our relationship had not gone far beyond the level of educator and student, but I had always felt a personal interest in her. Though Leia didn't talk about it, I could tell that this was a young woman who was constantly struggling with her own set of demons from her past and was constantly running. She ran by choosing to go to the university. She ran in the type of art that she created. And she ran by being eager to be the first student to sign up for the exchange program even though it was completely uncharted territory and no one had any idea how the engagement with the Denynso was going to go. It seemed strange, even, to call the program an "exchange" program considering no students from the other planet had made the decision to go to Earth to study. Instead, they had requested a professor be sent to the planet in order to instruct them about the history, culture, and environment of Earth.

The lack of news from Leia and the seemingly evasive response of the Denynso when they asked questions about what they wanted to know about Earth and why they didn't want to send their own students or representatives to Earth to learn instead had made it more difficult for the university to find a professor willing to take on the challenge. Even those who didn't think it was strange at all for a young girl on a study abroad program to not check in with the university or send any type of update were reluctant to involve themselves in a program that didn't seem thoroughly planned, especially considering it was designed to foster cooperation and involvement between Earth and a culture known for being fearsome and ruthless warriors.

Though scientists and journalists had had successful excursions to Uoria over the years and had brought back a tremendous amount of information that helped to illuminate the culture and facilitated in laying the foundation of greater cooperation and involvement between the two species, they also brought back stories of aggressive, violent men who towered over seven feet tall, a vicious other species that roamed the planet and engaged in bloody warfare with the Denynso, and laws that governed visiting humans under the threat of severe punishment.

This veil of mystery had made the other professors too afraid to leave their positions on Earth and embark on the journey. Despite my own nervousness, however, I had been intrigued by the stories and eager to find out more. After the Denynso representatives had finally gotten back to the university to tell them that Leia had been on a personal retreat during her time on Uoria gaining inspiration for her art but had recently emerged and had gained special permission from the king and queen to extend her original six month stay into the indefinite future, I decided that if the young, embattled girl could dive into the experience so completely and so quickly, and gain such incredible meaning from it that she decided to leave her home planet and live on Uoria, maybe I should be courageous as well.

With no husband, children, or anything else concrete tying me in place at the university, I finally stepped forward and volunteered. That had been only a day before the scheduled flight, not enough time for me to put together a real lesson plan for the classes or even really narrow down what I wanted to teach. The program had given me fairly loose guidelines about how they wanted the instructing structured, leaving most of the planning and management completely up to me. Without really knowing what age group I would be teaching, what they wanted to learn, or what type of environment and resources I would have access to, I had brought with me as much teaching material as I could and spent the journey putting together my ideas. It was yet to be seen what would really happen once I arrived and got started.

3

The ground furled away behind Ero like a ribbon as he ran through the forest, his feet pounding into the soft undergrowth with an intensity like fire. Gnarled roots rose up to trip him and branches brushed at his skin, but he was moving too fast to really notice either or for them to impede his speed or his progress. He ran like he had never run before, with a speed that far surpassed any of the other Denynso. A skill that he had learned about when he was still young, his ability to run faster and harder than anyone else was something that he rarely shared with anyone else. He used it instead as his way of escaping when his mind was filled with too much thought or emotion. Even if he didn't have anywhere to go, he would run. His feet brought him wherever they wanted to go, through the dark forest, over the rocky ledges, or through the wide fields behind the village. He ran until he had no energy left inside him, then he would collapse to the ground and let the darkness of sleep make everything go away.

He ran now to escape the confusing, overwhelming feelings he had been experiencing for the last few days. They started after he rescued Leia from the Klimnu attack. At first, he thought the aggression and anger had been related to finding the mate of one of his friends terrified and in danger only a short time after she had escaped from nearly two months of imprisonment under the hands of the slimy, vicious creatures. Though he was not as large or powerful as the other warriors of the Denynso, he still had within him the ability to grow fierce and angry when something or someone that he cared about was threated, and even though he and Leia had not gotten off to a great start, she belonged to Gyyx, which meant he had loyalty toward her.

When the aggression and intensity were still there the next day, however, Ero began to wonder if that was really the source of these feelings. He was not accustomed to this level of emotion within him, especially when he couldn't identify a clear source, and he didn't like how it made him feel. He felt confused, on guard, and violent to the point that he had gotten into several scuffles with the other men after he heard them teasing him. He was accustomed to their bullying. At a foot shorter than the other warriors and nowhere near as well-built, he had been the butt of nearly endless ridicule and teasing since he was orphaned as a child and left to be raised by the community. In a way it was his form of interacting with them. However, over the last few days, he had not reacted the same way as he usually did, laughing off the jokes and keeping the negative feelings he experienced toward the other men concealed. Instead, he had lashed out and fought.

After one particularly intense encounter with one of the other warriors, Pyra had pulled him aside to ask what was happening to him. That is when Ero broke away and started to run. He had been running for hours now and was so far from the village that he wasn't sure he would be able to get back before the families came together for dinner. Not that many of the people there would notice. Pyra and Eden, Ciyrs and Elianna, and Leia and Gyyx, the mated couples, were so wrapped up in each other that they didn't really care what happened around them most of the time. The other warriors were still filled with adrenaline and anger after the battle with the Klimnu days before that had ended with them burning the building where they had brought Elianna after capturing her and where she found Leia after they had kept her prisoner and tortured her for 57 days.

Ero turned back and started running the way he came, pushing himself harder and faster until he could barely see what was going past him. He was nearly back to the village when he heard someone call his name. He slowed and jogged back toward the voice, finding Pyra standing at the edge of the forest.

"Running again?" Pyra asked.

Ero put his hands on his hips and glared back at the tremendous warrior, feeling the anger spiking in him again as he saw the teasing flicker in his orange eyes. The orbs that used to be blue were vibrant, nearly glowing orange now that he was mated to Eden and something about them made Ero feel uncomfortable when he looked at them.

"What are you doing here?" he asked accusingly, and immediately felt bad for the tone in his voice.

He didn't understand what the hell was happening to him. He had never been like this and now suddenly he felt like he could tear anyone who got near him limb from limb just for looking at him in a strange way or saying something that he thought might have a negative meaning. Fortunately, Pyra didn't seem to notice his aggressive tone, or was choosing to ignore it, because if he had been offended by it and decided to engage Ero in a fight, there was no way the smaller warrior could have overpowered him.

"I have been sent out into the forest to get some sort of fruit that Eden wants."

"You are all the way the hell out here to get some fruit?" Ero asked incredulously.

Pyra nodded and sighed.

"Yeah. Apparently she is having cravings and says that she absolutely has to have this particular fruit and she won't settle for the cooked kind that we already have. She needs it right off the bush and she needs it right this second."

Pyra said the words in a tone of resignation that said he thought the venture was ridiculous and wasn't thrilled about having to do it, but that he loved Eden so much he would literally go to the ends of the planet for her no matter what it was she asked of him. This was especially true now that Eden was carrying his child. The pregnancy was still not common knowledge among all of the Denynso and those that knew were approaching the situation with caution. Not only was this first birth among the children of the king and queen, but Eden had been a human when she first came to Uoria. She had nearly died at the claws of the Klimnu and the tribe's healer had brought her back to life. In doing so, however, Ciyrs had somehow changed her into a Denynso. The pregnancy was completely unprecedented and no one, not even the elders, had any idea what to expect.

"That sounds like you are having so much fun with this whole experience."

Laughing softly, Pyra shrugged and nodded.

"What am I going to do? You know how women can be."

Ero shook his head, feeling the tingling in his legs and the pent-up energy and emotion in his belly that had fueled his hours of running over the last few days. If there was one thing that he definitely didn't know about, it was women. He wasn't mated and no female had ever caught his eye.

"Actually, no. I have no idea how women can be."

He saw Pyra take a step back and give him a once-over that made him feel scrutinized and uncomfortable. A strange growl rumbled in his throat and he had to hold back the compulsion to lunge at Pyra. The larger warrior, the biggest and most fearsome of the species, gave a knowing smile and rubbing his own face with one hand.

"You might not know yet, but from the looks of things I think you will be finding out pretty damn soon."

For a moment Ero didn't understand what Pyra was talking about, then he saw his eyes give a brief glance to the front of his pants. Ero rolled his eyes and reached down to the try to rearrange the raging erection he had been sporting most of the time since the day of the Klimnu attack. It was an uncomfortable reminder of the strange, unfamiliar feelings he had been experiencing and he was embarrassed to have Pyra point it out to him.

"Shut up," he said, managing to tuck his hard-on in a way that made it not look so obvious.

"Don't worry about it, buddy. You should have seen me when I was first around Eden. It was not a pretty sight. Well," he got a mischievous glint in his eyes, "I guess it was for her."

"Thanks for that image," Ero said, "It doesn't make sense, though. I haven't met any new women since Leia, and I know all this is not about her. I don't understand what the hell is going on."

"Don't stress about it," Pyra told him, starting toward the path leading into the forest, "With the attitude you've been throwing around and that situation you've got going on there, you're going to figure it plenty soon enough."

With the other warrior's words bouncing around in his head and somehow making him feel even angrier, Ero started running again.

4

———

"What's going on?" I asked, staring out the window again, "We landed forty minutes ago. Why am I still in here?"

The flight attendant paced back and forth in front of her, wringing her hands and throwing occasional glances over her shoulder toward the pilot's cabin. She obviously felt the tension and frustration that I was feeling. I didn't like to be kept waiting, especially when I was waiting to be let out of a tiny space ship chamber I had been in for the last five days.

"I'm not sure," the flight attendant said, barely braving a look in her direction, "The pilot just said that there has been a delay. Apparently, your escort hasn't arrived at the landing point yet."

"Why does that matter?" I asked, reorganizing my notebooks and papers in my bag again just to give my hands something to do, "I'm sure I'm smart enough to make my way from a space ship to a meeting hall. This planet can't be so primal that they don't have roads, right?"

The flight attendant looked over at her with a touch of desperation in her eyes.

"Actually, I've never gotten off the ship during one of these flights. I just stay inside and use the sleeping quarters on the top floor to take a shower, sleep, and change between legs."

"You've never gotten off the ship on another planet?"

"No."

"Your job is to travel around the universe carrying passengers in between planets and you have never once had the curiosity to step outside and see one of them for yourself? You don't wonder what they might look like or what the people living there are like?"

The flight attendant shook her head, suddenly looking even younger and less remarkable as her eyes welled up in tears.

"I'm too afraid."

"Of what?"

"Of what the other species might be like," she said, dropping her tone slightly, "My grandmother always said that we should stick to our own kind and that humans don't have any business running all over other planets intermingling with other species. She says if we were supposed to be interacting with them, that they would already be on our planet and we wouldn't have to travel to find them."

"How incredibly closed minded of her."

The statement should have offended her, but instead the flight attendant just nodded.

"I haven't even told her that this is what I do for a living. She just knows that I work for the university."

I sighed. I will never understand the level of intolerance and ignorance that was still so pervasive. It was as if people got over one hang up that they had and decide that it was awful to have that viewpoint, only to move on to the next one with the same level of intensity and stubbornness. I rubbed my temples, trying to release some of the tension that was building there.

"Regardless, why am I stuck here until some escort comes? That wasn't part of the itinerary the program gave me."

The flight attendant shrugged again.

"Apparently it's against the law for humans who have just arrived on Uoria to travel from their ship unaccompanied. Everyone who visits has to be escorted to the meeting hall where they will meet the king and queen before they are allowed to stay."

I sighed again.

"So, who are these escorts?" I asked, "Other academics? Law enforcement?"

"I think they are warriors."

"Fantastic. So, between the leading university research department for interplanetary exploration and cooperation and a group of warriors, they couldn't coordinate one meeting. That bodes terrifically for the future of the success of this program."

I was usually calmer and more pleasant than this, but it seemed space travel was pulling the worst out of me. Always described by everyone who met me as headstrong and fiercely independent, I have a very low tolerance for anything that I saw as incompetence, which this level of disorganization and improper handling of a situation definitely was in my mind.

Finally, the pilot's voice came over the speaker in the chamber, announcing that the escort had arrived and I was welcome to come to the exit door. The flight attendant looked even more relieved than I felt.

"Oh, good. I was getting worried we were going to have to stay here for even longer. Is there anything I can help you with before I go upstairs for my break?"

I shook my head, reaching out to squeeze the girl's hand comfortingly. No matter what the origins of the fears she was experiencing, they were obviously very real and I suddenly felt bad for her. I hated to see a person feel so limited by their own minds that they were unable to face any changes in their normal situation or confront anything that may alter their point of view because it was too uncomfortable for them.

"No, I'm fine. You go on ahead. Maybe I'll see you on my trip back in a few months."

The attendant smiled and returned the squeeze with her hand.

"Thanks. I'd like that. They'll have your bags for you at the door."

Without saying another word, the flight attendant scurried across the room and disappeared through the hatch that led to the small chamber where the attendants spent much of their time during the flight and where, I presumed, there was a set of stairs or an elevator that would bring her up into the staff sleeping quarters overhead. Taking a final glance around the chamber, I walked toward the front of the chamber and through a sliding door to the exit hatch.

The other flight attendant stood at the door, holding my bags in each hand and looking like he was still seeing the images from his beloved game flashing on the backs of his eyes. I reached for the bags and took firm hold of them by their handles.

"I can get these. Thanks," I said.

The attendant relinquished the bags, but I had only taken one step down from the ship onto the landing platform when I felt hands grab at them again.

"I'll help you," a male voice said and I looked down at the platform to see a man reaching up to hold onto my luggage.

He was certainly attractive, but if this was one of the famed warriors of the Denynso people, I found myself a touch disappointed and a bit confused. I had heard tales of enormous, powerful men so breathtakingly beautiful that women couldn't control themselves around them, which, I will have to admit, is one of the influencing factors for signing up for the program. The man in front of me was lovely, but at only around six feet tall and quite slender, he was decidedly not enormous and looked less fearsome than many of the professors who walked the halls of the university back on Earth. I pulled the bags back toward me.

"No, thank you, I can do it myself."

"I'm happy to help."

I gave a final tug, yanking the bags out of his hands.

"I have them."

I stepped down from the platform and when I straightened in front of him I saw the escort's eyes travel over my body in a way that I didn't really like. His gaze stayed on me for just a bit too long and I couldn't quite interpret the look on his face. It was somewhere between shock and an emotion that I couldn't define. Finally, he lifted his eyes to mine.

"You definitely don't look like the other human women that have come here," he said.

I shot him a scathing look.

"What is that supposed to mean?"

The man stammered for a minute, obviously trying to come up with an explanation.

"I just mean your hair. The other women have dark hair, except for Eden, but her hair is more red. Yours is...golden."

I wasn't convinced that that was actually what he was thinking. Leaving him still muttering, I pushed past and started down the steps of the landing platform.

"What's your name?" he called after me and I heard his footsteps follow me down the stairs.

"Zuri Hase. Didn't they tell you?"

"No. I'm not the original escort you were supposed to have."

"Oh," I said, some of the bitterness leaving my voice.

Maybe something bad happened and that's what caused the delay. I didn't want to be mean to him if his schedule for the day was thrown off just as much as mine was.

"I'm Ero," he told her as he caught up to her, "It's nice to meet you."

5

____

hat the hell was wrong with him?

The one time in his entire life when he had actually been trusted to do something important, and he was already screwing it up. Pyra was supposed to escort the new professor from the ship just like he had with the other women, but at the last minute he asked Ero to step in for him. Ero didn't know if there was something wrong with Eden and the baby requiring his attention, or if something else happened that took him away from his responsibilities, but he hadn't really cared in the moment. He had just been excited to have been the one that the older and more respected warrior had chosen to take his place.

Not only had he managed to be almost an hour late for the set time that he was supposed to meet her because he tore the lacing on his pants and had to go all the way back to his house to change them so that he didn't greet her with the intense erection that he was still sporting everywhere he went, but he had also offended the woman almost as soon as she stepped out of the ship. He couldn't really help it, though. He was expecting the same type of woman as Eden, Elianna, or Leia. However, what stepped out of the ship was a shock. Instead of tiny and fragile-looking, Zuri rivaled some of the females of his species in size. She was only a few inches shorter than him and had a body that was lush, full, and curvy. The effect was bewildering. He had become accustomed to the small human women and was startled by someone who looked so different, but at the same time, he was drawn to all of the soft curves and swells. They seemed to have a powerful effect on his body as well, making him twitch and harden even further as the intense, almost animal feelings built in his chest.

As she took long strides to pull out in front of him so that she walked ahead of him by several feet, Ero got an even fuller view of her body. Wide hips shifted beneath her long, loose skirt, accentuating the deep curve of her waist beneath her tight shirt. Something about her size made him uncomfortable, reminding him of his own size concerns and how small he felt compared to the other warriors. He jogged forward again to catch up with her.

"Tell me about your program," he said.

It came out more as an aggressive, almost violent, demand than an actual request inviting conversation and he saw her look sideways at him.

"What do you want to know about it? Are you going to be a student?"

It sounded like she was teasing him and he didn't like how that taunting made him feel. It was worse than when it came from the warriors. Hearing this woman making fun of him, even as subtle as it was, made a sharp pain go through his chest and he felt defensiveness building through him. *Who did she think she was making fun of him?*

"No," he said, "I'm a warrior. I have no reason to go to school."

"Oh, really? So, you know everything that you need to know and never need to learn anything else?"

Well, shit. This conversation was just going downhill as fast as he could get the words out of his mouth. What was it about this woman that made him completely out of control? She was cute, but definitely not so beautiful that he should be stumbling over his words and humiliating himself every time he opened his mouth. So why was he getting harder every time she talked to him, and why did he want to keep talking to her no matter what came out?

"That's not what I said," he said, "I just...I don't really need to know about Earth."

"So, you know about the program. Why did you ask?"

"I know that you're here to teach about Earth. I don't know any more than that."

He was getting more and more frustrated, while also feeling worse every time he spoke and he saw the darkening across her wide blue eyes. It was a confusing feeling that he was really starting to hate.

"Well, to be completely honest, I don't really know a whole lot more than that, either. I just signed up to be the professor for the exchange program one day before my flight. I didn't really get much of a chance to figure out what I was going to teach."

There was laughter in her voice and he felt some of the tension ease out of his body. She glanced over at him and he noticed that her soft, rounded face really was pretty. Her skin was pale and smooth, not sprinkled with freckles the way that Eden's was, and her golden blond hair framed it as it flowed around her shoulders. Her mouth was wide, with full, soft lips slicked with lipstick that made them shine in a way that was undeniably alluring.

"Why did you want to come?"

He was honestly curious about why she decided to come to the planet to teach. If she had only signed up right before she left to be a part of the program, she obviously hadn't spent much time planning and getting herself invested in the concept of teaching on Uoria. There was a period of silence and Ero was worried for a minute that he had made her angry again and broken the brief moment of pleasantness between them. Finally, she sighed, but it wasn't a sigh of exasperation. Instead, it sounded like she was trying to figure it out herself.

"I'm a professor at home, obviously, and I love teaching, so that's the main appeal. I'm excited about getting the chance to teach Earth customs, and I think I'm even more excited about getting to experience some new things."

"Is Uoria very different from Earth?"

She gave a short laugh.

"I've only been out here for about five minutes. I'm not really sure. So far, it doesn't look too far off. Not as many buildings."

They fell silent as they walked. They reached the center of the village and Zuri hesitated, no longer knowing where to go now that she had more options than just going straight ahead. He subtly stepped around her so that she could see him and guided her through the village and to the meeting hall.

"We'll go inside and meet the king and queen, and then I can show you around more if you'd like."

Zuri stopped right before the door to the meeting hall and looked at him.

"Thanks, Ero, but now that I have been successfully escorted from the ship, I think I can take it from here. I appreciate your help."

His stomach dropped and a sick feeling rolled through him. She had already grabbed onto the latch of the door and was pulling it open when he started toward her.

"No. I actually have to come with you. My job isn't finished until I get you to the king and queen. That means I have to bring you all the way to them."

Zuri sighed as if it was the biggest burden in the world for her to deal with him any longer.

"Fine."

She wrenched the door open and stepped inside, not bothering to hold the door open for him but letting it swing shut behind her so that he had to slam his hand against it to stop it from actually hitting him. She paused just inside to let him walk past her and guide her to the reception room. He stormed through the hall, his fingers tingling with anger. He was sure that if it had been Pyra or even Gyyx who had met her at the ship, she would be more than happy to go along with them for anything that they wanted her to do. She was only being so resistant because it was him. He was just too small and slim to be appealing to her. He didn't have enough muscles and wasn't tall enough to keep her attention. She was just like everyone else.

6

———

"We're so glad that you came."

I was still a bit startled by the woman talking to me and it took a moment for me to be able to respond to her.

"Thank you. I'm glad to be here."

The woman, who I was taken to meet was the queen, she was so large she even made me feel small, which is quite a feat most of the time. I was not used to having women be taller than me, and her shoulders were broad and strong. She was beautiful in a dignified way that I had always admired about the older professors at home and she looked at me with tenderness in her eyes that made me feel like it was my mother looking at me. She strode forward toward me and reached for my hand with both of hers.

"I'm Theia, Queen of Uoria. This is my husband, Creia."

Her hands nearly engulfed mine and she held them warmly as a massive man came up behind her, smiling at me kindly. I wasn't sure what to expect from the royal couple, but this certainly wasn't it. As I stood there in the huge meeting hall with Theia's hands grasping mine and a row of warriors standing behind me, I started feeling like I should have done more research about the planet before I made the decision to suddenly come here for six months to teach. I felt even less like I understood the culture now that I had seen Ero, compared him to the truly huge warriors who joined us in the meeting hall, and met the monarchs.

"It's very nice to meet you," I said, really meaning it.

Being near the king and queen made me feel somewhat more at home and I was starting to feel much more confident about my role, even as I wondered how much studying I was going to be able to shove in the brief amount of time I had before I started teaching. I wanted to have a little bit of a grasp of the culture before I tried to interact with them on a regular basis.

"We have loved having Leia here with us, and we are very excited to do more with the exchange program."

The statement struck me as strange. Leia had only been here for two months and from my understanding, she had been alone on an artist's retreat for most of that time. I supposed she just meant that they loved the idea that she was there and that the idea of the people of Uoria and Earth interacting and cooperating.

"I hope that I can be a positive influence on the program. I'm excited for the opportunity to share our customs and history with you."

I heard snickering from behind me and I glanced over my shoulder. A couple of the warriors were trying to maintain straight faces and I looked back at the king and queen.

"Did I say something funny?" I asked.

The royals looked faintly uncomfortable and the king shot a glare at the warriors, who immediately fell silent.

"You'll have to forgive our warriors. They aren't accustomed to such formality."

"It's quite alright," I said, looking back toward the warriors, "I don't think of it as formality so much as intelligence."

At the end of the row of warriors I could see a dark look roll over Ero's face. There was something about him that both drew me to him and repelled me. I could see the hint of disdain in his eyes when he looked at me, and I knew it was because I am not like the more delicate women who had already come. I was accustomed to that look, but somehow it coming from him made me angry.

"Well, it has been a long trip. We would love for you to join us for dinner if you're hungry."

Theia had released my hand, only to loop her arm through mine and start leading me gently through the room toward a large arched door at the far end. As we passed by the row of warriors, I heard Ero's voice.

"I'm sure she's hungry."

I stopped and looked at him.

"Excuse me?"

He looked back at me with an expression that said he didn't think I was going to hear him.

"Like she said, it was a long trip and I've heard that the food on the ships isn't very good. I just meant that it's time for dinner and I'm sure you'd like to join us."

I didn't bother responding. Instead, I let Theia lead me the rest of the way across the room and through the doorway into a large banquet room. The space glowed with firelight and was filled with delicious smells coming from platters of food lined down the long tables positioned in a squared U-shape around the edge of the room. Most of the chairs were filled and I noticed the distinct difference between the Denynso and the three human women sitting close to me.

"Everyone," Theia said and immediately everyone in the room quieted and turned to me, "This is Zuri Hase. She has joined us from the university to be a part of our exchange program. We are thrilled to have her here to help us understand the people of Earth more and hopefully get us closer to our goals of cooperation and eventual integration. Please make her feel welcome."

I saw several of the warriors tense when the queen mentioned integration, but most of the people in the room smiled welcomingly at me. I saw a very thin woman coming toward me, her arms open as if to hug me. It took me until she was almost at me to realize that it was Leia. I gathered her into a hug, disturbed by how fragile and bony she felt in my arms. She had never been a large girl, but she seemed even thinner now than I had seen her.

"It's so good to see you!" Leia exclaimed and I smiled down at her.

"It's wonderful to see you, too. Are you well?"

Leia laughed and nodded. I'm sure she knew what I was thinking, but she wasn't volunteering any information.

"I'm better than I've ever been. Come meet the other women."

Theia smiled at me and released my arm, allowing

Leia to pull me toward the table where I saw two other human women sitting beside each other. She introduced me to Eden, who had her hands rested over her belly in the nurturing, protective way of an expectant mother even though it was only a slight swell, and Elianna who was tiny and delicate looking with dark hair that hung around her face and brought out her piercing green eyes. I was happy to have other human women with me and immediately felt a connection with them. We had been talking and eating for several minutes when I heard Ero's voice come over the rumble of the other voices around me.

"We'll have to keep a special eye on her and make sure she doesn't get hurt. I don't know if Ciyrs has enough healing power to take care of everything she's got going on."

Humiliation, hurt, and anger flowed through me and made my face burn. The three women shot furious looks at the warriors but I held up my hand to quiet them before they said anything. I climbed backwards over the bench beside the table and rushed out of the banquet hall, bursting out of the building before I let the tears stinging in the corners of my eyes spill down my cheeks. *What the hell was wrong with him?*

I was so tired of that attitude. I couldn't stand men trying to make me feel like I was worth less because I wasn't frail and dainty. Even worse was how much I wanted Ero specifically not to think of me that way. I hated the way that he made me feel. It was a confusing, uncomfortable mixture of wanting absolutely nothing to do with him and wanting everything to do with him. I had butterflies in my stomach when I looked at him, but in that moment, those butterflies were replaced by a wave of sickness. Behind me I heard Ero calling my name, but I didn't slow down. I didn't know where I was going, but I kept going. I just needed to get away from the banquet hall and the sound of Ero's voice.

The darkness around me got deeper and more intense as I ran, but I still didn't stop. I told myself I would eventually find my way, that I would come upon a house or other building and be able to ask directions to wherever I was supposed to live for the six months I planned to stay on the planet. Unfortunately, that didn't happen. Within a few minutes of leaving the banquet hall, I was lost. Within a few minutes after that, I was hopelessly lost. And by the time I felt the long, slimy fingers stroke the back of my neck and saw the gleaming fangs coming down at me, I knew I was gone forever.

7

———

"What the fuck is wrong with you?"

Ero's head snapped back as Pyra grabbed him by the back of the shirt and yanked him backwards so that he and the other men could surround him. The three much larger men glared at him, their jaws twitching angrily and bright orange eyes searing into him almost painfully. Ero didn't know what to say to them. His stomach was twisted in knots and he felt like he was going to shatter at any second. *What had he done?*

"How could you say something like that about her?" Gyyx demanded, stepping up close enough to Ero that he felt like he needed to step back, only to find himself within inches of Ciyrs's chest.

Though Ciyrs was a healer and not a warrior, he was still powerful and larger than Ero.

"I don't know," Ero said honestly, "I don't know what the hell is going on in my head. Ever since the Klimnu attack on Leia, I've been out of my mind. I can't think straight, I'm angry all the time. It only got worse when Zuri showed up."

The three other men looked at each other knowingly and some of the anger exuding off of them eased. Pyra stepped forward and clapped him on the back, then wrapped a massive hand comfortingly around the back of his neck.

"You've always been the scrawny one of the group, so I guess it makes sense that you haven't figured out yet that all of this has absolutely nothing to do with the Klimnu attack and everything to do with Zuri."

"What are you talking about? And don't call me scrawny. I'm so sick of everyone making fun of me and treating me differently because of my size."

Suddenly realization hit him and it felt like a rock fell into his gut.

"Holy shit, that's exactly the same thing that I've been doing to Zuri, isn't it? I've spent my whole life pissed off because the people around me bullied me for being smaller than what they thought I should be and the second I meet a woman – an adorable woman, by the way – who just happens to be bigger than I would think she was going to be, I treat her in the exact same way. That's just great. I just don't get why I'm suddenly so aggressive and angry."

He looked up into Pyra's eyes, then at Gyyx's, then at Ciyrs's. He let out a long, ragged breath.

"Yeah, you just figured it all out, didn't you?" Pyra asked.

Ero nodded, covering his eyes with one hand.

Before he could open his mouth to reply, he heard a scream. All four men turned toward the sound and another scream tore through the air. Without speaking, they all ran in the direction of the sound, pulling weapons from the sheaths on their waistbands as they went. Within moments they saw the source of the screaming.

Klimnu swarmed the center of the compound, standing off against the other warriors who had come out of the meeting hall. The scream was pouring from Elianna as she fought against the tight hold that one of the men had around her waist, trying to keep her from running into the cluster of slimy, skeletal creatures. She had an incredible gift, given to her by Ciyrs after she became his mate, that would allow her to kill any of the creatures she touched. Running into such a large group of them, however, would mean almost certain death. She was tiny and could only kill two creatures at a time, opening her to the threat of death by the others surrounding her.

"Get in the meeting hall!" Pyra shouted, his voice so loud that it made even Ero shake with intimidation.

Pyra's mate, Eden, looked up at the sound of his voice and Ero saw her hands protectively covering the slight swell of her pregnant belly. She had fear in her eyes, but she didn't move.

"Go!" Pyra shouted again, and finally Eden complied.

She grabbed Leia's hand beside her and yanked her back into the hall, slamming the door to the building just as one of the Klimnu broke free of the rest of the group and started toward the hall, wanting to get inside to the small human women. They had both been injured by the Klimnu before, and this was a species that did not respond kindly to their efforts being thwarted. When they went after someone, they went after them with the pure and unadulterated intent to kill, which meant that when someone escaped that fate, especially a fragile human woman, it only infuriated them more intensely and fueled their hatred toward the Denynso who protected them.

The four men surged forward and Ero immediately felt himself pulling ahead of the others and running into the group of Klimnu so fast that they didn't even have time to react. He balled his fists and spread his arms to the sides, tightening his muscles so that he caught the creatures by their necks as he passed, bringing them to the ground. The chaos that ensued shattered the control and organization that the Klimnu had had, and suddenly the compound filled with the sounds of battle.

Out of the corner of his eye, Ero saw the warrior release Elianna. She ran forward toward one of the Klimnu that Ero had brought down and reached toward him to grab him around the neck before he was able to stand all the way again. His strangled cries filled the air along with the acrid smell of burning flesh as she reduced the creature to ash. He saw Ciyrs look at her with affection and desire in his eyes, and pull her against him for an intense, almost violent kiss before they parted and went after more of the Klimnu. Larger warriors followed behind them to guard their backs as they burned as many creatures as they could get their hands on, the warriors slashing with lethally pointed daggers at any of the other creatures who attempted to intervene.

Pyra grabbed one of the creatures and lifted him into the air, taking him by his head and his waist and snapping him in half in one sharp movement. Ero heard the breaking bones and saw the life leave the Klimnu's eyes before Pyra dropped his limp body to the ground and moved on toward another of the creatures. Knowing he was not large or strong enough to do anything like that, and didn't have the burning gift that Ciyrs and Elianna shared, Ero used his own skills to contribute to the battle. He ran around the edge of the fray, taking down creatures that were getting the upper hand on warriors using his incredible speed and the fighting skills he had taught himself when he was younger by watching the other warriors train. Suddenly his ability to run so fast felt like more than just something he could use to escape.

The clash continued on for several long minutes, and then Ero noticed Pyra stepping out of the middle of the battle, dragging a man behind him. Ero looked closer and realized that it was Ullie, the Denynso warrior who had betrayed his people by giving up the secrets of the warriors and the ability to infiltrate the compound to the Klimnu. He had escaped the last battle between the species, but now he was at the mercy of the larger, stronger warrior who had him by his long white hair and was pulling him up onto the stone steps of the meeting hall.

Ullie struggled hard against Pyra's grip, but blood was streaming down his body from several wounds already sustained during the battle and since he was already at a disadvantage to Pyra, there was truly nothing he could do. It was time that he met his fate.

Once at the top of the steps, Pyra tilted his head back and let out a battle cry that trembled through the compound and brought stillness to the battle as everyone, both Denynso and Klimnu, turned in his direction.

Without hesitation, Pyra forced Ullie to his knees, used his hair to pull his head back, and stared directly into his eyes as he drew his dagger across the traitor's throat. There was a strange gurgling sound and then Pyra dropped Ullie, allowing his body to crumple to the steps and slide down toward the men.

Pyra looked out over the cluster of opposing species, his hand still wrapped around the dripping dagger.

"This ends now," he growled, then kicked Ullie's body so that it fell the rest of the way to the dirt, "Take him with you."

The Klimnu complied, moving as quickly as they could to gather their dead and wounded and leave the compound, the battle having been lost without a single Denynso warrior's death.

Panting, Ero watched as some of the other warriors followed the Klimnu away from the meeting hall to ensure they left the compound. Suddenly panic gripped him. They still hadn't found Zuri. He ran toward Pyra.

"I have to find Zuri," he said.

Pyra looked down at him and nodded.

"She's yours. Go get her."

Ero didn't respond, but took off running, pushing himself harder and faster than he had ever run before, allowing the tight feeling in his chest and the quiet voice in his mind, the voice that sounded like Zuri, guide him toward her.

8

I have never run so fast in my life. To be honest, running is not something that I have ever enjoyed and have gone to great lengths to avoid having to do it for any considerable period. At that moment, though, running was the only thing I could focus on. I didn't know what the creature was that had reached down from the tree to take hold of me, but I fought it off as best I could and managed to knock it out of its place with a large branch I picked up from the ground. I hoped it was unconscious. I didn't wait to find out.

I ran deeper and deeper into the forest, knowing I was getting further and further away from the meeting hall. The terror gripped me so hard I felt sick and suddenly my mind drifted to Ero. I was still infuriated at him, but somehow, I felt like if I thought about him hard enough, I might be able to find my way back to him. I didn't understand, but I had no other recourse and focused in on him. I thought about the curve of his shoulders and the flat plane of his belly. I thought about the beautiful dark brown hair and the intense eyes that seemed to vacillate between dark brown and almost glowing orange. I had noticed a few of the other warriors had orange eyes, and I wondered what that meant.

As I thought of him, my steps slowed. I was breathing so hard I could barely get each breath all the way in before my lungs forced it back out. My back hit one of the trees and I slid to the ground, leaning my head back and closing my eyes to try to regain control of myself. I continued to think about Ero, imagining him there with me. It was as if I could see him there, ready to guide me back toward the compound and away from the terror that held me so firmly.

Suddenly I heard crashing in the trees ahead of me. I thought the slimy, skeletal creature that had reached for me had somehow found me and I tried to scramble to my feet to ready myself for another encounter. Instead, I saw Ero. He stopped running the instant he saw me. He stood a few feet away, his shoulders rising and falling with his labored breath and the sliver of his chest revealed by his shirt shimmering with sweat. He was beautiful and in that moment, I had never wanted something so much.

Without saying a word, Ero lunged toward me and dropped to his knees in front of me, forcing my legs apart so he could position himself between them and lean forward to crush his mouth against mine in an intense, almost animalistic kiss. A primal need for him over-whelmed me and I tore at his shirt, pushing away the thin fabric until I could throw it aside, revealing his slender but gorgeous body. He reciprocated, yanking my shirt over my head and tossing it over to join his. I hadn't worn a bra under the shirt and my breasts bounced free, giving him full access to grab one in his hand and bring his mouth down to the nipple to suckle me. I cried out at the feeling of his mouth and spread my thighs further to encourage him to come closer.

He took the invitation eagerly, grabbing me and lifting me up so that he could reach under my skirt and peel away my panties. His hands moved so quickly I could barely keep up as he released the ties at the front of his pants and pushed the garment down to release an erection that made my mouth water. Sitting down on his knees, Ero grabbed my hips and pulled me forward so that I had to brace myself with my hands on the ground behind me to keep myself from falling. He pulled me until I positioned my legs on either side of him and my hips in his lap.

A second later he was inside me and I gasped at the sudden feeling of him filling me. He pushed my skirt up higher so that it bunched around my waist and wrapped one arm around my hips, using the other hand to grip one of my breasts as he pounded into me at a fevered pace. I let my head drop back and moans poured from lips. I felt him pull me forward and I complied, lifting my hands off the ground so that he could sit me up in his lap. My feet were planted on either side of him, giving me stability as he bounced me harder and faster, capturing my mouth in an almost painful kiss just as my muscles clenched around him and I dissolved into a shattering climax that pushed him over the edge. He groaned into my mouth and forced me down hard into his lap so I could feel his cock pulsing against my walls, spilling his hot streams into me.

As our bodies slowly relaxed, Ero gently eased me

back until I was lying on the ground with him on top of me, his head nestled into the curve of my neck.

"I thought I lost you," he murmured.

His hand stroked the curve of my waist and the swell of my hip and I felt him fill his palm with my flesh and give a gentle squeeze. I closed my eyes and felt a tear slip down my cheek.

The next morning the sun had barely risen when I was standing in the meeting hall before the king and queen. My bags were stacked behind me and I gripped my notebook in my hand.

"Please, I can't do this. Send me home."

CHARMED BY THE ALIEN WARRIOR

COVER

GRACE KENSINGTON
CHARMED BY THE
ALIEN
WARRIOR
ALIEN WARRIOR MATES I | BOOK 8

Sign up for Grace Kensington's Mailing List

2

—————

"Please, I can't do this. Send me home."

I watched as Theia and Creia exchanged worried glances and eased closer to the edges of their seats so that they could stare down at me. They leaned closer, not enough that I felt like they were trying to intimidate me, but enough that I felt them closing the space between us as if they were trying to make our conversation more private. The row of warriors standing on the far side of the room were not looking at us, but I would see them turning their ears subtly toward us as if they were trying to listen in on the conversation without us noticing them.

I mirrored the action of the king and queen, leaning slightly towards them and meeting their eyes so that they could see that I was very serious about my request.

"Please. I've been here for less than 24 hours. I'm sure that the university shuttle is still here. I would like to be on it when they leave to return to Earth."

Theia looked at her husband again and then back to me.

"Like you said, Dear, you have only been on Uoria for less than a day. How could you possibly know already that you want to go home? I know that our planet is different from yours, but if you give yourself time to get accustomed to it, I'm sure that you could learn to love it as much as the other human women who have come here."

I shook my head adamantly.

"I'm sorry. I know that I made a commitment to be a part of the exchange program between the university and the Denynso, but I've realized in my time here that I'm not cut out for this type of environment. I'm sure that the university can find another professor who will be willing to take my place."

Creia rubbed his face with his hand, looking distressed. I knew that the program meant a lot to the king and queen, but they seemed far more upset about me wanting to leave than I thought they would be. After all, I had just gotten there the day before and I hadn't even figure out who I was teaching yet, much less actually started teaching, so I didn't understand why they seemed to have so much emotionally invested in my staying on as the foreign exchange professor to teach the Denynso about Earth customs and traditions.

"You did make a commitment to us in regards to the exchange program, but I feel that there may be more that should be keeping you here."

"What do you mean?" I asked, even though I felt sure that I already knew exactly what he was talking about and didn't want to think about it anymore.

"I thought that you may have felt more of a connection with..." he hesitated and Theia looked at him with a meaningful glance that said *be quiet before you make this situation worse,* "the people of Uoria than you expected to and would want to spend more time getting acclimated to the new weather and culture."

The words came out flatly and it was obvious that that wasn't what he had originally intended to say.

"Is this about the Klimnu attack last night?" Theia asked.

My body shuddered as I thought about the horrible experience that I had had the night before. I had only been on the planet for a few hours when I heard Ero, my escort from the ship, making fun of me to the other warriors. His comments about my size had been cruel even though he said them like they were a joke, and they brought up memories that I would rather have left behind me. When I left the banquet hall it was so dark that I managed to get myself lost and ended up in the thick forest that surrounds the Denynso compound, putting me right in the grip of slimy, disgusting, skeletal creatures that tried to capture me.

"Yes," I replied.

Even though the experience with the Klimnu in the forest had been terrifying, I knew that that was not actually the reason that I wanted to leave. Those creatures were awful, but the truth was I could have handled the situation and gotten over it. That is, if Ero hadn't found me hiding in the forest. I had been feeling an intense and confusing attraction to him since I met him, which is part of why the comments he had made were so painful, and when he found me sitting up against the tree, it was like we couldn't keep our hands off each other. We didn't even talk. We were just suddenly ripping each other's clothes off and fucking with such intensity I could still feel him inside me as I stood there in front of the royal company pleading my case.

"I hope you know that that is not a common experience and that our warriors are the best in the galaxy. You are safe here. I'm sure that Ero will protect you. We have already assigned him as your personal guard and he will make sure that you are well taken care of while you are with us."

I shook my head again, closing my eyes against the tears that were building up in them. I didn't want Ero taking care of me. He had already broken me. It had been so long since any man had touched me, and after Ero did I felt disgusted by myself. I had allowed this man, this close-minded, arrogant man who thought I was less than the other women on the planet because I was tall and curvy, overtake me because I was feeling a moment of terror and weakness. I hated that he had been able to do that to me, and even more that I couldn't stop thinking about him even after he escorted me to the quarters chosen for me for my time staying on the planet during the program and left.

"I just don't think that I have it in me to do this. Please, allow me to take the shuttle back to the university. I will personally help find a replacement for my position."

Creia and Theia looked at me sadly, but nodded. I knew that part of the agreement for the exchange program was that they were not allowed to keep me on their planet against my will. Technically I didn't even have to ask them to let me leave. I did out of respect for them and desire to maintain the communications and cooperation that were gradually building between the Denynso and the humans. I didn't want my own personal issues to get in the way of the relationship the species had been working so hard to develop.

"Shall we call Ero to escort you back to the ship?"

"No," I answered quickly. The last thing I wanted was to see him again. I wanted to be off the planet as soon as possible and get the thoughts of him behind me, "I can make it back myself."

"We can't let you do that. We will send Pyra with you." Theia stood from her throne and stepped down to me, reaching out to take my hand in hers like she did when we first met, "I have to say that I am very sad to see you go so soon. I was hoping that you would find the same type of comfort and happiness here that your fellow human women have."

"Thank you. I'm sad, as well. I'm sorry that this didn't work out the way that we hoped, but I'm sure that the next professor that comes here will be an amazing part of your program."

Theia grasped my hand more tightly for a second and I saw a look of true sadness in her eyes. I wondered how much she knew about my time with Ero. Creia came up and patted me comfortingly on the back.

"You are always welcome to return if you change your mind. We will make sure that the university knows that any time you want to come back, you have a place here."

"Thank you," I said, still startled by how deeply they seemed to be feeling my decision to leave.

Theia gestured over my shoulder and the massive warrior called Pyra came to my side. He didn't look at me, but nodded at the king and queen and agreed to be my escort back to the ship. We walked back in silence, Pyra occasionally glancing my way. When we got to the ship, he turned to look at me.

"Are you leaving because of Ero?"

His question startled me and I stared at him.

"What do you mean?"

"Exactly what I asked."

I stiffened at his attitude.

"I'm leaving because of the Klimnu attack," I said, deciding I might as well keep up with the story I told the king and queen.

He looked at me, scrutinizing my face, and then shook his head.

"No, you aren't."

I grabbed my bags and climbed up onto the ship platform without another word. I wasn't going to let some warrior I didn't even know try to judge me for my decisions. I wanted to go home and that is exactly what I was going to do.

3

Ero was still smiling when we made his way back from his patrol. He had been thinking about Zuri since he woke up, still hard from the dreams he had had about her, and was excited to get showered and changed so that he could meet with Eden, Eliana, and Leia. Before he started his patrol that morning he had sent them messages asking that they meet with him in his house that afternoon so that they could help him with a very special project. They had no idea what he had in mind, but he knew that they would come. As the mates of his fellow warriors, they had loyalty to him and they want to make him happy. When they found out what he was thinking about, he knew they would be even happier.

He had just stepped out of the shower and finished drying off when he heard the women knocking at his door.

"Come on in. The door's unlocked!" he yelled out of his bathroom into the house.

He heard the door open and the excited voices of the three women filled the house as they came in and settled in in the living room. Ero laughed as he heard Eden's distinct voice criticizing how stark his house looked. Everything he had heard about human women, as little as that was, was right. As soon as they mated and "settled down" they suddenly turned into creatures of nesting and decorating. They may have been just fine with a plain, basic home before, but as soon as there was a mate to take care of, the home had to be perfect and suddenly there was a need for things like curtains and extra pillows. Of course, things like that were not a priority on Uoria to say the least. In fact, Ero had never even seen a throw pillow and the only curtains that he had ever heard of were the thick, unadorned ones that covered the windows during the annual week of solid sunlight.

Eden, however, was changing that. She had started taking old clothing and blankets and turning them into all kinds of decorative items that she put up around her mate Pyra's house. The other women had followed suit, learning to sew these items for their mates, another warrior and the healer of the tribe. Ero had heard both of them telling somewhat awe-filled and confused stories of waking up or coming home from their patrol to find new decorative items had just appeared in their homes. As much as they grumbled about it, Ero knew that they secretly liked it. It made them feel special to have their mates taking care of them, and, like any Denynso men, they were completely and fully dedicated to making their women happy.

"Can you believe the condition of this couch?" Eden

said in a tone that Ero knew she thought was subtle, but was actually loud enough for him to hear.

She had gotten worse with her nesting in the last several weeks after finding out that she was pregnant with her and Pyra's first child. This pregnancy was extremely special. It was the first of the new generation, and because Eden had been changed from a human to a Denynso, no one was entirely positive whether it was going to be more like a Denynso pregnancy or a human pregnancy. Either way, she was filled with hormones and suddenly totally obsessed with making sure that everyone was living in a beautiful place. It was adorable in kind of a frightening way. Maybe one day Zuri would be like that.

The thought startled Ero and he glanced up at himself in the mirror. There were streaks of orange across his eyes and as he thought more about her and the idea that one day she may carry his child, he watched the usual brown of his eyes turn to bright, vibrant orange. He shook his head, forcing his mind to go to different thoughts. The last thing he needed was to walk out into the living room and have his eyes do all of his talking for him. He needed the opportunity to talk to the women about what was on his mind before they already knew just by looking at him.

"I think that my couch is just fine," he said, walking out into the living room.

Eden turned sharply to look at him and made a face like she couldn't believe he would even say that. There was no hint of apology in her expression, but he wasn't upset with her. He admired the fire in her and knew that she was the perfect match for the massive and intense Pyra.

"Well, that makes it even more upsetting," she said.

The women giggled and Ero smiled at them as he dropped down onto the large armchair across from the couch where all three of them sat. Eden was gently rubbing the small swell of her belly, Eliana was looking around in her sharp, scrutinizing way, and Leia was staring at him softly, still looking so small compared even to the others, neither of which were big. He winced as soon as that thought went through his mind. It was that kind of thinking that had gotten him into trouble with Zuri in the first place. He really needed to get himself to stop thinking that way. Especially since he had realized just how wrong that thinking was.

It had definitely startled him when she first stepped out of the space ship and he saw that she was only a few inches shorter than him and was full, soft, and curvy, unlike the other three women that were all nearly two feet shorter than their mates and thin. The more he looked at her, though, the more he realized how cute she really was, and the sexiness of each of those inches. This was made especially obvious when each of those inches were wrapped around him and he had the chance to bury his face in her breasts, grab her lush hips, and satiate the aggressive hard-on he'd had since before she even arrived on the planet. Now all he wanted was to make it up to her for the cruel jokes he had made and show her just how much he cared about her.

He just needed the human women to help him.

"So, what do you girls think of Zuri?" he asked, trying to introduce the conversation as casually as possible.

All six eyes snapped to him and there were a few seconds of tense silence.

"Zuri?" Eden asked.

"Zuri Hase?" Eliana followed.

"As in Zuri, the foreign exchange professor?" Leia said.

"Yes. To all of those."

The three women exchanged glances and Ero watched as they seemed to communicate without speaking. Finally, they all turned back to him.

"We think she's wonderful," Eden said slowly, "What do you think of her?"

Ero smiled and the women squealed and clapped in a way that made them all seem like little girls, but filled him with even more excitement. He almost caught himself clapping right along, but there was no way he was going to let that get back to their mates. He certainly didn't need the warriors having any more to make fun of him about. They already teased him relentlessly about being smaller and less muscular than them. There was no need to add girly celebrating to the mix.

"Here's the thing," he said after letting them get out their excitement, "I didn't get our relationship started on the best note."

"Yeah, we noticed," Leia said.

"What the hell is wrong with you, by the way?" Eliana said.

"Yeah, why would you ever say something like that about a woman? Especially a woman that you apparently care about?"

"It's just that..." Ero started to try to defend himself, but the girls weren't going to give him any slack.

"It's just that you are an insensitive jerk," Eliana said as if it was a fact that he just needed to accept so he could move on with his life.

Ero sighed.

"Probably. I don't know why I would say something like that. The point is, though, that I want to make it up to her. I want to plan something amazing for her to show her how much I care about her and I figured since she is human and you are human that maybe you would be able to help me out."

The women looked at him for another uncomfortable second like they were evaluating his worthiness to receive their help, and then they broke into smiles.

"We'd love to help," Leia said.

Of the three, Leia knew Zuri the best. She had been a student at the university before coming to Uoria, and in fact, it was the same exchange program that brought Zuri to the planet that brought Leia. This gave the two women a special bond and Ero hoped he could use that to his advantage when coming up with ideas for the special date he wanted to have with Zuri.

"Did you have anything in mind?" Eden asked.

Ero shook his head. He had never dated anyone before. Dating wasn't the same type of practice on Uoria as it was on Earth, but even the Denynso customs weren't something that he had experience with. The desire to spend time with one specific woman just to be near and make her happy was something that was completely foreign to him and he didn't know where to start coming up with something that they could do together that she might enjoy.

"Well, on Earth, a lot of people go out to eat on dates,

but considering there are no restaurants on this planet and everyone eats together in the banquet hall basically every night, I guess that's not really an option," Eden said with a hint of disdain in her voice.

She was still working on getting used to all the differences between Earth and Uoria, and some of the strangest ones seemed to bother her immensely.

"They could have a picnic, though," Eliana offered, "We could help you put together something and instead of coming to the banquet hall, you could bring her out onto the cliffs and eat together, just the two of you."

"That sounds nice," Ero said, "Is that it, though? I want to do something really spectacular for her, something that will really show her how much I care about her and how sorry I am for hurting her feelings."

Suddenly Eden looked at him more closely. She took her hand away from her belly and leaned closer so that she could look him fully in the face.

"Oh my god. You slept with her."

"What?" Leia shrieked.

Ero knew his eyes were bright orange now and there was nothing he could do about it. Just thinking about her filled him with such intense desire and need to be near her that he felt like he couldn't catch his breath. This must be the same feeling that Pyra had when he met Eden that reduced the usually fearsome warrior to an incoherent, broken shell because he thought she was dead, or made Ciyrs stronger and more powerful than he could ever have imagined when he met Eliana and she had to be rescued from the Klimnu, or gave Gyyx the power to bring Leia back from the brink of death after her weeks in captivity. It was something that he had never experienced before, and he wanted more than anything to explore it further.

"It just kind of happened," he admitted, "That's another reason I want to do this for her. I want her to know that it wasn't just something that I did because she was there and vulnerable. I really think that she's my mate."

It was the first time that he had put that thought into words and it sent a little bit of a shiver through him. He couldn't wait to get this date planned, find her, and tell her everything he'd been thinking about, and just hoped that she felt the same way.

4

I wanted to stay awake for the trip back from Uoria like I did when I first left Earth, but two days into the trip, I couldn't take the thoughts rolling through my mind anymore. Every time I stopped reading one of the books in my luggage or glanced out of the window at the stars beyond my pod chamber, all I could think about was Ero. I hated that I was still thinking about him and the feelings it brought up when I did. He was so beautiful and had made me feel things that I hadn't experienced in my entire life. I wanted to think that having sex with him in the forest had been just a one-time fluke, a momentary loss of clarity and judgment, but my heart felt like it was something so much more, which made the pain even worse.

It didn't matter how I felt when I thought about him. What mattered was how he had spoken about me and how he looked at me. I had been through enough years of being mistreated and made fun of for my size. I had dealt with enough of the taunting and teasing, the hurtful jokes and the backhanded comments, from the person in my life who was supposed to care about me the most. I had gotten rid of him two years before and I wasn't about to put myself back into the same situation just because Ero made me feel breathless and all I wanted was to be back on Uoria with him.

Finally, I called the flight attendant over and asked her to let me go to sleep. She gazed down at me with wide, sad-looking eyes.

"Are you sure?" she asked.

Since I had spent less than 24 hours on the planet after stepping off the university shuttle, the staff was the same from the trip there. There was generally a 24 to 36-hour break between the two legs of any journey that long to allow the pilot to rest and give the staff some time off from their sometimes grueling responsibilities on board. I had managed to get back on the ship just before they were to take off again and the flight attendant looked extremely surprised to see me. I hadn't gone into detail about what had happened, but it was almost like she could see the hurt in me and knew that there was something going on in my mind that I didn't necessarily want to share.

"Yes," I said.

I had been resistant to sleeping through the five-day journey on the way to the planet, not wanting to give up that much time or control, and wanting to use the time to start preparing my lesson plans. Now that I had no lessons to plan, I wanted nothing more than to miss some of the time that was just tormenting me. Maybe when I woke up back at home, I would feel better. Though I was nervous, I figured nothing worse could happen to me while I slept for the next three days than was already happening to me.

Once I was ready, I settled into my pod, attached the straps that would hold me in place in the event of turbulence, and closed my eyes. I heard the flight attendant's voice telling me to relax and just let the process take effect. I had read through the brochure about the flight carefully so I knew the basic concept behind the sedating process. As a teacher, I am accustomed to taking information presented to me very seriously and accept facts as the truth that makes the world make sense. Repeating this concept through my mind and reviewing the steps of the process as they happened helped me to relax as I felt the seat beneath me soften to cradle my body more closely.

I opened my eyes and watched the glass portion of my pod darken gradually, creating a soothing feeling around me. Everything went absolutely silent for a moment as the pod closed itself off to prevent more sounds from coming through to me, and then a small speaker opened on the wall beside me to stream soft white noise into the space. It was one of those sounds that sounds obtrusive and almost uncomfortable at first, and then becomes such a comforting element of the environment you don't want it to go away.

After a few moments of the sound, I became aware of a faint, almost powdery scent. The fragrance increased and I started to feel deeply relaxed and sleepy. I let go of the tension and control within my body and my eyes drifted closed again. For a brief moment, I could see Ero smiling at me behind my eyelids, and then everything went black.

When I woke again it was three days later and the ship was settling into place on the landing platform in the university bay. Beneath me I felt my seat growing harder and the white noise gradually stopped as the automated system started easing me out of the sedated state. The pod's sound defenses ended and I could hear the loud scraping sound of the retractable metal ceiling of the landing bay sliding back into place above the ship.

The glass at the front of my pod became clear again and I heard the soft hiss and pop of the locks releasing. I released the straps over my chest and used one hand to push the lid of my pod out of the way. The light inside the chamber was blinding for a second, so I sat still until the effect dissipated and I was able to see again.

The flight attendant was standing beside my pod, smiling broadly and offering me a cup. I took it and swallowed the strong coffee it held, then handed it back to her.

"You look happy," I said groggily, pulling myself out of the pod.

"I love it when we get back home," she said brightly."

"You really should consider changing your job," I said, and then immediately felt bad for it.

She had opened up to me about how her grandmother felt about her traveling away from Earth and why she took the job. I sighed and gathered her in a hug.

"Thank you for helping me during my trip – both times."

I tried to laugh, but she continued to look at me with the sadness in her eyes.

"It was my pleasure," she said.

I walked through the ship to the exit door and

picked up my luggage. It was just like when I arrived on Uoria, except that where there was so much hope and excitement when I arrived on that planet, there was only sadness and disappointment here. I felt like a failure and all I wanted to do was go home and start trying to put it all behind me. As soon as I got there, however, I found out that getting a few days of relaxation to myself before heading back to the university and hoping they would let me take over my usual classes again wasn't going to be nearly as easy as I had hoped it would be.

It seemed like it took hours to get from the landing platform through the university back to my house. All around me I could hear whispers speculating why I had made such a sudden return, changing what was anticipated to be nearly a seven-month absence into one that lasted less than eleven days. The people who were brave, or discourteous depending on the perception, enough to actually stop and talk to me about the situation shared the gossip of the department.

Wild rumors and explanations ranged from I was too scared to even get out of the ship in the first place, to I had gotten to Uoria only to find it a desolate wasteland destroyed by some recent war that Earth had not been informed of, to my personal favorite which was that there had actually never been an opening for a professor in the exchange program but that was used as a cover-up because I was pregnant by the department head and needed to disappear until the baby was born, but it turned out to be a false alarm which is why I had suddenly came back. No one seemed interested in my explanation that I simply decided that the experience wasn't for me and wanted to come home. Apparently, that wasn't salacious enough.

Of course, I wasn't about to give them the honest, and legitimately salacious, explanation.

I finally made it home in the middle of the evening when the sun had already gone most of the way down and the first thing I noticed was that my living room light was on. I had all of the lights throughout the house on a timer to turn on and off throughout the day so it looked like I was home to anyone who didn't know for sure that I wasn't, but this was one of the times when it should have been off and my bedroom light should have been on.

I approached the back door carefully, putting myself on the opposite side of the house from the light, and eased inside. Traveling with any form of personal defense tool wasn't exactly my style, but I knew that the dictionary in my bag would pack a hell of a wallop and that once they were disoriented, I was pretty capable of taking someone down if necessary. I reached for the dictionary as I walked toward the living room, moving toward the sound of the television and faint munching.

"What are you doing back so soon?"

A sudden, familiar voice startled me and I nearly dropped everything I was carrying. A figure appeared in the doorway to the living room carrying a bowl of popcorn and looking at me like I should have expected her to be there.

"Samira!" I gasped, tossing my bag onto the kitchen table as she turned on the light with the switch on the wall beside her, "You scared the hell out of me. What are you doing here?"

I looked back up at her wide brown eyes and saw a

flicker of hurt move across them. Looking closer at her face I realized she didn't look nearly as casual and relaxed as I thought she had. Instead, she looked drawn and there appeared to be streaks of tears down her cheeks. The bowl she gripped was still overflowing with popcorn, but there wasn't a lingering smell of fresh popcorn in the air, meaning she had probably made it long before now but just hadn't eaten it.

"You said I could come here whenever I needed a place to go," she said, her voice cracking slightly with emotion.

At just 18, my favorite student was still so young, but her genius well out-weighed her years. In that moment, though, she just looked like a terrified little girl. I crossed the room to her and gathered her into my arms. She shook against my chest, crying.

"Of course you can. You can always be here. I'm sorry if I snapped at you. I was just surprised."

"You surprised me, too. I didn't think you were going to be back anytime soon. I just didn't have anywhere else to go and so I thought I would stay here for a few days until I could figure things out."

Samira was nearly as tall as me, but her curviness came across as more soft and feminine than just sturdy. As I draped my arm around her and led her into the living room to sit on the sofa, however, she felt small and fragile.

"What happened?"

She looked up at me with tear-filled eyes and I knew exactly what had happened. I had been teaching Samira since she had entered the university at the age of 15, a stunningly remarkable student that had brilliance I had never seen, but just needed to learn to rein it in. Since then I had gradually worked past a strong shell to get to know her and learn about her painful childhood and continued horrific relationship with her stepfather. She was stuck in a tormented world of having a mind that far exceeded the intelligence, logic, and abilities of any of the adults in her life, but an age that made it so that she had no escape. Efforts to protect her were made from various teachers and neighbors, including me, went completely unheard, constantly forcing her to stay in a place of darkness and trauma.

Now she was finally 18 and was not just allowed to leave, it seemed she had been forced to, given one less horrible session with her stepfather and then turned out onto the street where she would be forced to fend for herself. I had told her two years before that she was always welcome at my house and given her a key. It seemed she finally had the chance, and the courage, to do it.

5

———————

"It's going to be perfect," Leia said, patting Ero on the back as she and the other women made their way out of the house.

"I hope so," he smiled, feeling a little nervous now that the planning was over and he was actually going to get to go through with the night he had arranged for Zuri.

"The bond's already there," Eden assured him, stepped past him onto the porch, "You just have to make sure now that she understands what that means. Remember that she isn't a Denynso. Ask these ladies. It takes a little more than just a good lay to get a human girl to stay with you forever."

She meant it as a tease, but her words made Ero feel even more nervous. He nodded and watched the women start toward the road, but all three stopped when they saw Creia approaching. The king rarely left the hall unless there was a specific event, which meant that whatever he had to say was very serious.

"Hello, girls," he said affectionately to the women as

he passed them, towering over them but smiling gently at them, "Ero, I need to have a word with you."

"Alright."

He made no move to go inside and the women started to turn away, but Creia held up his hand to stop them.

"No, you should stay. Your mates will need to know about this, too."

"Is there something wrong?" Ero asked, the intense look on the monarch's face making his stomach turn.

Maybe there had been another attack or capture. But if there was, why would the king come to him instead of Pyra or Gyyx?

"It's Zuri," the king started and Ero already felt his heart start to pound.

"What happened?" Ero demanded.

He could feel the aggression he had been trying to fight building back up inside him and the anger making his muscles tighten and twitch. Lashing out at the king could have dire side effects so he had to keep himself under control, but he was starting to feel again like he could rip anyone near him limb from limb if he found out that she was hurt in any way.

"She left," the king said bluntly, "She went home."

Ero felt something inside him break and his vision blurred.

"...What?"

"She went home, Ero. She decided she couldn't stay here and continue with the program. I felt like you should hear it from me. I've noticed your behavior recently and I thought that perhaps you saw her as a potential mate."

The king was speaking softly, trying to comfort Ero,

but he only felt rage and a type of emptiness he could never have imagined. He heard the women gasp and whisper to each other, but he couldn't make out their words.

"When did she go?" he asked when he had control over his voice again.

"This morning. She got back on the shuttle back to the university."

"Did you know about this?" Ero demanded, turning fiercely toward the women.

"What the hell do you mean did we know?" Eden responded, stepping toward him without fear, "Would we have just sat in your house with you for the last three hours trying to put together this big date for you if we had known that she was gone?"

"I'm sorry," Ero relented, and turned back to the king.

"Did she say why?"

"Just that the program wasn't for her and that the Klimnu attack had frightened her so she wanted to go home. She says she will find a replacement for her position in the program."

"It had nothing to do with the Klimnu," he muttered and saw the king nod.

"I know, Ero."

He couldn't take it anymore. He felt like fire was rushing through his veins and that he was inhaling liquefied stone so that it solidified in his lungs with every breath. Without another word, he started to run.

His feet pounded into the ground harshly, carrying him at the fastest speed he could achieve away from the houses and into the forest. He ran like he had before he understood what was going on with Zuri, ran like he would eventually be able to outrun the pain and the disgust at himself. He was just like the warriors. He had bullied Zuri for her size and then just expected her to be fine with it if he explained he was joking. Instead of being there to forgive him, though, she had left him behind.

Ero paused in the middle of the forest, close to where he and Zuri had spent their few minutes together, and put his hands on his hips, looking up through the branches of the trees at the setting sun. Suddenly from behind him he felt a harsh push and hit the ground.

"Do you feel better now?" Pyra demanded from above him and Ero scrambled to turn around.

"What the hell, Pyra?"

"Do you feel better now that you chased her away?" the huge warrior shouted, shoving Ero further away from him with his boot, "Does it make you feel big and powerful to know that you hurt her feelings enough that she didn't even want to stay here anymore?"

Ero jumped up and squared his chest at Pyra.

"No, you ass, it doesn't make me feel better. I feel like shit. I just sat in my house for the last three hours trying to plan a date for her so that I could tell her that I love her, and instead I find out that because of my own fucking mouth she's gone back to Earth and I'll probably never see her again."

"So, you're just giving up? Just like that?"

"What?"

"You're just going to give up. She left, so you are going to do the same thing you always do and take the weak route. Instead of manning up and doing something about it, you are going to run around and whine."

"What do you suggest I do about it? She's on a space

ship right now heading back to another planet. It's not like I can just walk up to her and tell her I'm sorry."

"Why not? Is there a rule that says that if you want to say you're sorry it has to be on Uoria?"

Realization hit Ero and determination took the place of the anger and devastation. He took off in the direction of the hall, hoping that Creia had returned so that he could request a special audience with him. He wasn't going to give up. For the first time in his life he felt strong and powerful, and he knew that was because he had discovered his mate. He wasn't going to give up on her just because he did something stupid and made her leave. This was his last chance to do something that really mattered and show his mate that there wasn't anything that was going to keep her away from him, even if she tried to put an entire galaxy between them.

When he finally stood in front of the king, Ero felt more courageous and sure than he ever had in his life. It no longer mattered to him that he had always been seen as the orphan of the planet or that he was so much smaller than the other warriors. What mattered to him was getting to Zuri, and that meant requesting something that no Denynso had ever done.

6

The sun burned into my eyes as it came through my bedroom window, searing into me as if teaming up with my alarm clock to try to get me out of bed. It was the second morning I had woken up in my own bed, but I still didn't feel like I was really at home. There was something missing that made me feel like I was visiting my own life, and I knew exactly what it was.

"How are you doing this morning?" I asked Samira as I padded into the kitchen.

I picked up a mug and poured a cup of coffee from the machine set in the corner of the counter. The first sip brought the same thought that it always did: *thank the universe for automatic brewing.*

"I'm feeling a little better," she said, looking up from the book in her lap.

"That's good. Did you have anything that you would like to do today? I still have... well, technically like six months off, but I'm planning on giving myself about another week before I go back to the university and try to blend back in."

"I can't really think of anything." She sighed and I saw a look of nervousness flood over her face, "I know at some point I'm going to have to go back to my mom's house and get my stuff. They said I needed to be completely moved out by the end of the week."

Her voice sounded so defeated it made me angry, but I didn't show it. This was a girl who had seen enough anger and aggression in her life, turned toward her, when she didn't deserve it. She deserved gentleness and compassion now.

"I'll go with you," I offered, pouring another cup of coffee now that I was starting to feel a bit more awake.

"Thank you," she let out a tremulous-sounding breath, "I'm way too scared to go by myself."

"Is your stepfather going to be there?"

She nodded.

"He's not working anymore. He doesn't have anything to do but sit around the house and terrorize whoever gets in his way."

"He won't terrorize me."

The mug slipped out of my hands and shattered on the floor at my feet, sending a wave of coffee splattering across my legs. I gasped and jumped out of the way before I looked up to make sure that my eyes weren't deceiving me. Ero was standing in my kitchen.

Samira looked shell-shocked and didn't move from her seat, but stared at him, wide-eyed.

"Ero!" I managed to gasp.

"Who is she talking about?" he demanded, pointing at Samira.

I blinked at him, not sure what I was supposed to be thinking in that moment. Was he seriously standing there, in my kitchen, on Earth, asking me about Samira?

"Ero?" I repeated, "What are you doing here?"

Finally, it seemed that his attention returned to me and he crossed the room toward me in two long strides.

"I came for you. I left two days after you did," he said, then looked down at my coffee-soaked legs, "Oh. I'm sorry."

That's when it hit me that I was still in pajamas, no makeup, and hadn't even brushed my hair yet. Embarrassment flooded over me and I pushed past him to rush toward my bedroom. I heard him following me and I tried to shut the door so that he couldn't get inside, but he was too fast and too strong for me to hold him back.

"What are you doing?" I asked, spinning around to face him.

Ero grabbed me, wrapping his arms around my waist and pulling me to him for a kiss that took my breath away. When his mouth lifted off mine, I looked up into his eyes and saw that there was no longer a hint of brown, only intense orange.

"Your eyes," I said, not letting go of my grip on his shoulders, "They changed."

"They changed because of you. That's why I'm here. I haven't been able to get you out of my mind. You are my mate."

I pushed out of his arms and stepped away, combing my fingers back through my hair.

"I heard what you said about me, Ero."

"I know, and I am so, so sorry. I don't know what I can say to you to make you understand that, but please, tell me and I will say it. I will do anything you need me to do to convince you that I didn't mean to hurt you and that I would never, ever do it again."

"I have spent too much of my life feeling bad about myself and being told that that's how I should feel because of the way I look."

"I don't want you to feel that way," he said, closing the space between us and pulling me into his arms again, "I want to spend every day of the rest of my life making you feel as beautiful as I see you. I know that you don't trust me yet, but please, just give me the chance to show you. Come back with me. Everyone on Uoria misses you so much already."

"I was only there for a day."

Ero laughed softly.

"They must just realize how wonderful you are." He nuzzled me with his nose and kissed me gently, "I'm sorry it took so long for me to get here. No one from Uoria has ever travelled off of it before, especially to Earth, and it took a couple of days for us to arrange transport."

"At least you're here."

"Does that mean you're willing to come back with me? Give me another chance?"

"I will come back, but only on a trial basis. Like you said, I don't trust you yet. I can't just let myself get swept away by you."

"Thank you," he said, sounding so relieved and happy it made my lips finally curve up in a smile, "And definitely don't forget your books. I've only been here for a day and what I went through trying to find you and navigating this ridiculous planet tells me that there is a lot more to learn about Earth than we ever expected."

I laughed and he met the sound with another kiss, pressing his body to mine so that I could feel him getting hard beneath his clothes. My knees weakened a bit, but I forced myself to resist the aching of my body and gently eased him away from me.

"Not so fast. I told you I'll go back with you. That's all you get for now."

He gave a sigh, but nodded.

"I'll accept that. Now... tell me who is terrorizing that woman in the kitchen."

7

———

Ero flexed his fists as he stood on the outside of a white wooden door, waiting for whoever was inside to respond to the doorbell he had just rung. He waited for a few seconds and then rung the doorbell again, following it up with a few pounds with his fist on the door. Out of the corner of his eye he could see Zuri standing at the bottom of the front steps of the house, her arm wrapped protectively around Samira. The teenager had her head buried in the older woman's shoulder and appeared to be shaking with fear. The sight made him even angrier and he pounded on the door again.

"What the fuck do you want?" an obviously drunk man said as he wrenched the door open.

Ero pushed into the house as soon as the door was open enough and immediately turned to the man. This was the first human man he had ever encountered, and he was struck by his size. On Uoria, Ero was tiny compared to the other warriors. Here, though, he towered by several inches over the man, who stumbled back, his red-rimmed eyes fixed on Ero's orange gaze.

"I'm here for Samira's belongings," Ero said, keeping his voice low, but ensuring there was enough intensity in it that the man understood he was not to be challenged.

"Who are you?" the man stammered.

"I'm the mate of a very dear friend of Samira's, which means that she matters to me and I don't like to see her cry or be scared because some full of himself asshole has been using her as a punching bag since she was 10, not to mention other things that I can't even get myself to say or I will pick you right now, snap you in half, and bring you home with me to use you as Klimnu bait."

The man took a swing at Ero, who immediately caught his fist in his palm and squeezed until he felt the bones shattering into pieces beneath the man's skin, causing an agonized scream to echo through the house. When Ero released him, the man cowered back against the wall, cradling his hand to his chest.

"Never try something like that again. Not against me, not against your stepdaughter, not against your wife. Not against anyone. I've traveled once. I can do it again, and if Zuri doesn't decide to stay with me on Uoria, I will be doing it again, which means I will be here all the time. Do you understand me?"

His voice had lowered to a fierce growl and he could see the terror in the man's eyes. Behind him he heard the women climbing up the stairs and he extended one hand toward the door, gesturing for them to come in, but not taking his eyes away from Samira's stepfather. They stayed locked in that position for several minutes while Samira and Zuri rushed through the house packing everything that she could fit into her luggage. When she was finished, Ero took another step toward the man. He met his eyes and stared intensely at him for several long seconds before turning and walking out of the house, slamming the door so hard behind him that the glass in the window shattered.

The three were silent until they were back at Zuri's house sitting in the living room. Samira finally looked calm, relaxed as if she had been vindicated.

"Thank you," she said, turning to Ero, "I can't tell you how much that means to me."

"It means a lot to me, too," Zuri said.

Ero turned to her and smiled, reaching up to stroke her face.

"You mean everything to me," Ero said, "I'm so glad you're coming back with me."

"You're going away again?" Samira asked.

Zuri nodded and Ero noticed the sad look in her eyes suddenly disappear.

"Come with us," she said, leaning toward Samira and grasping her hands.

"What do you mean?"

"Come with us. Come to Uoria with us." Samira started to protest and Zuri shook her head, leaning closer, "No, no, listen. It could be perfect. It would get you away from everything and give you a break. Ciyrs and Eliana have been working on creating healing ointments for the warriors to bring with them into battle, and you could help them. No one understands chemistry and biology like you do. This is a real way that you can use it. It doesn't have to be forever. It doesn't even have to be for long. I don't even know how long I'm going to be there.

Just come. Please. It will make it even better for me there with you."

Samira looked back and forth between Ero and Zuri and Ero saw a change come over her. He smiled at her, reaching to take Zuri's hand and join in the encouragement for Samira to join them on their trip home. Through his bond with Zuri he had built an affection for the young girl, and more than anything he wanted to make Zuri happy.

He knew that back home the women were putting together the surprise they had planned for Zuri, getting it ready in the hopes that he would be able to convince her to come back with him. It had been a major risk to ask them to do that for him and to climb into a spaceship as the first ever Denynso to travel through the galaxy, but she was worth every single risk, every single moment of fear, and every single moment of doubting himself and his ability to be the mate that she deserved.

8

———

For the third time in less than a month, I climbed out of my pod and stretched. I didn't feel as stiff as I had the first two times and I couldn't decide if it was a good thing or not that my body seemed to be getting used to compressing into the pod and going through five days of space travel.

I wanted to get out of the ship as quickly as I could. Ero had had to return in a separate ship because of the short notice of our travel and I found myself missing him intensely during the five days of the voyage. It was a strange feeling. I still didn't trust him completely, and there was doubt in the back of my mind of whether I was going to stay on Uoria for more than a few days, but when I was away from him, I wanted to be near him. It was like I was connected to him in a way that I had never been to anyone else. Sometimes I found myself thinking about him and it was almost as though I could hear his voice in my head.

Samira followed me timidly out of the ship, looking

around as if she was waiting for something to happen. Unlike my first time arriving at Uoria, no warrior stood at the base of the platform.

"I guess they figured that you didn't need an escort."

I heard Ero's voice from the other side of the platform and my heart lit up. I turned to him and he came toward me slowly, reaching out to intertwine my fingers with his.

"I think I have my own," I said softly.

"I hope so," he replied, "Leave your bags here. I'll have Pyra take care of them."

"Did you let anybody know that I brought Samira along with me?"

Ero nodded.

"I told them when I arranged my transport back home. They have everything arranged."

"Will we be sharing a house?"

He looked at me with an expression I couldn't quite decipher and shook his head.

"No, Samira will have her own quarters while she's here."

Before I could ask anything else, I saw the three women coming toward me with their mates and a man I didn't recognize. They were all smiling and I felt a surge of happiness to see them again. Leia looked at Samira strangely for a moment, then seemed to realize that she recognized her.

"Samira?" she said, "Do you remember me? I helped you with a research project about a year ago."

Samira leaned closer and her face lit up.

"Leia? I heard that you signed up for the exchange program," she climbed down off the platform and stepped into Leia's open arms, "It's good to see you."

The sentiment sounded so genuine I felt a twinge of emotion in my throat. These were women who had been through so much. Seeing them coming together for a moment of empathy and strength was truly beautiful. On the other side of the two women I noticed a man who I didn't recognize. He was tremendous, nearly as big as Pyra, but there was something soft about him that made me question if he was a warrior. His eyes were focused on Samira and I thought I saw a flicker of fire in his eyes.

"Eden," Ero said, looking at Eden.

I glanced over and saw the pretty redhead holding her mate's arm and leaning her head lovingly against him.

"Everything's ready, Ero. This is Ty," she looked over her shoulder at the man and I noticed he was wearing an apron slung low over his hips, "He's going to keep an eye on Samira."

I watched Ty meet Samira's eyes and it was obvious that he thought she was as gorgeous as everyone else did. With long dark hair, eyes to match, and olive skin, she stood out anywhere she went.

"Keep an eye on me?" Samira said, but didn't take her eyes away from Ty.

"It's kind of an Uoria thing," I told her, "Human visitors get babysitters."

"Guards," Ero corrected.

"He'll bring you to your quarters and I'll go find mine and we'll meet up later with the other women, ok?"

"Actually," Ero said, giving me a gentle pull on my hand, "you have other plans this evening."

"I do?" I asked.

Ero nodded and I saw Eden introduce herself to Samira and then hand her gently off to Ty. Pyra scooped up all of my luggage in one arm and Samira's in the other and followed them. She turned around just before they disappeared into the darkness away from the lights of the ship.

"Ero, when you get to the chocolate, thank Ty. He made it."

They walked away and I felt Ero turn me so that I faced him.

"Chocolate?" I asked.

I was confused, but the sparkle in Ero's eyes intrigued me. He guided me down the steps of the platform and we walked slowly away from the ship. There was a brief moment after we stepped away from the lights of the ship where the darkness around us was almost impenetrable, then my eyes adjusted and I felt the moonlight washing over me. The light pooled at our feet as Ero continued to guide me away from the compound toward an area of the planet I hadn't had the opportunity to see during my short first visit.

"Are you going to tell me where you're taking me?" I asked, something about the situation causing me to nearly whisper rather than using my full voice.

"No," he said.

"Why?"

"Because then it wouldn't be a surprise."

I fell silent and allowed him to guide me along until we reached what looked like a small, still lake of purple water. The surface glittered with tiny candles tucked into large blue flowers that floated on top of the water. It created an almost mesmerizing effect and I barely noticed him leading me toward a blanket stretched across the ground.

"A picnic?" I asked.

"You don't like it?"

I turned to him, feeling the beginnings of tears in my eyes.

"It's perfect."

We settled onto the blanket and Ero opened the square basket positioned on the edge. He started pulling out containers containing a variety of foods that I didn't recognize.

"Do you know what any of that is?" I laughed.

"Most of it," Ero said, tilting one of the containers to look through the bottom at whatever was inside.

He pulled another container out and I immediately knew what it was. I took it from his hand and opened it, pulling out a piece of brownie.

"Do you know what this is?" I asked, not knowing how familiar the Denynso were with Earth foods.

"Chocolate?" he said, sounding like he was making a complete guess.

I nodded and pulled onto my knees so I could lean toward him.

"Have you ever tasted chocolate?"

He shook his head and I crawled slightly forward so I was close enough to him to hold the piece of brownie to his lips. Without taking his gaze from mine, he opened his mouth and let me place the brownie on his tongue. I watched as his eyes widened and then darkened slightly as the taste flooded through his mouth. His lips closed over my fingers and I withdrew them slowly.

"Thank you, Ty," he muttered and I laughed softly.

Ero reached into the container and took out another small piece of brownie. I parted my lips so he could feed me, letting my tongue slip across his finger as I closed my mouth. He drew in a breath and his face came close to mine. His lips brushed mine softly and he paused, keeping them hovering close enough that I could feel his breath on my face. He waited until I leaned closer to him, offering my mouth to him, to kiss me again. This kiss was deep, passionate, and tasted rich like chocolate. When he pulled back, we were both breathless.

"Are you hungry?" he asked quietly and I shook my head.

"No."

"Come with me."

He helped me to my feet and led me around the edge of the lake. I watched the candles floating on the surface of the water as we walked, and it seemed like their glow was guiding me away from everything in the past and toward something incredible that I hadn't even begun to imagine. When we reached the opposite side of the lake, he paused and gestured toward a steep path cut into a rock face.

"Are you serious?" I asked.

"Trust me."

"Is this your way of trying to get me to lose weight?"

I was joking, but I felt his hand come to my lower back and apply pressure to my hip until I turned around to face him. He stepped toward me so that I stepped back and pressed to the rock wall. My breath caught as I felt his body brush against mine.

"I never want to hear you say that again, do you understand?" I nodded breathlessly, overwhelmed by his sudden exertion of power. "Because I love you," he dipped his head down to kiss the curve of my neck and shoulder, his hands coming to my hips, "Every inch of you," his touch traveled to my waist and up to my ribs, "Every single beautiful inch," his thumbs brushed across my nipples and I gasped, "I haven't seen enough of you. I want to see more."

I nudged forward with my hips, needing more of his touch. He turned me around again and patted me on my butt.

"Go on," he encouraged.

I complied, climbing my way up the steep path with the motivation of him directly behind me, his hands occasionally reaching up to stroke my back or touch my hip. When I reached the top of the path, I stopped and felt my mouth fall slightly open. I had stepped out onto a wide plateau strewn thickly with flower petals and dotted with candles. The effect was dizzying in the most wonderful way imaginable.

"This is..." I started, but couldn't find the words to finish.

"I wanted to give you the most romantic human date I could," he said, coming up beside me, "The women said flowers and candles were always romantic."

"You came up with this?" I asked.

Ero nodded and took my hand again, drawing me further onto the plateau until we reached another blanket stretched out across the ground. This one was so perfectly matched to the colors of the flower petals that I hadn't even noticed it was there until he brought me to the edge of it and pulled me into his arms.

"I am so sorry," he whispered, and I felt my heart constrict.

"Ero, stop." He looked at me with pain in his eyes and I brought one hand up to brush the hair away from his face, "Don't tell me how sorry you are." I ran my hand down the front of his shirt, "Show me."

Without another word, Ero ducked his head and caught my mouth with his. He kissed me with greater meaning than any words could have ever expressed, and I felt myself melting under his touch. I remembered what he said in my bedroom, that I was his mate, and suddenly I could feel it with such clarity and depth it was as though I had always carried him with me, but I had to discover him.

Ero's hands moved slowly and gently over me, removing each article of clothing and caressing the newly exposed skin with his mouth, kissing and licking his way across my shoulders, down my chest, and onto my belly. He knelt down in front of me and unbuttoned my pants, then eased the zipper down. The movements were careful, reverent, and I could feel myself getting hotter and wetter with each touch. I was shaking with need for him by the time he eased my panties down off my hips and guided me to step out of them, leaving me finally bare in front of him.

He hadn't removed any of his clothing, but standing naked as he knelt at my feet and ran his lips across my belly made me feel worshipped and beautiful. My hand came to the back of his head, tangling in his long dark hair, as he moved his mouth further down my body until it teased at the valley between my hipbones. He paused there, nipping his teeth at the soft swell of my belly before easing down and drawing his tongue through the wet heat between my thighs.

I cried out, reaching for something to grab onto but finding nothing so I settled for digging my nails into his back. This seemed to only fuel him further and he used one hand to ease my thighs apart so he had better access to my core. His tongue continued its skilled movements until I felt the pressure building through me and I pushed him back.

"Get undressed," I said, my voice smoky with desire.

As Ero complied with my request, I eased myself onto my knees so that when he was completely bare I could touch my body to his and finally feel all of his skin against mine. We both drew in breaths as our skin touched and our bodies became still, both trying to preserve the moment for what it was. Finally, he rested his forehead against mine and his eyes drifted closed. He kissed me gently and rested his hands on my hips.

"Please let me make love to you," he whispered.

My body clench and any reservations I had crumbled around me as I wrapped my hands around his neck and carefully lowered myself onto my back and let him part my thighs so he could settle in between them. The tip of his erection settled at my opening and he moaned when he felt how ready I was for him. I bent my knees so my legs drew up beside his waist, causing him to slip inside me slightly. I gasped. He had been inside me before, but I hadn't had the opportunity to really cherish feeling him enter me, and now I was welcoming him, allowing him to gradually move deeper into me until finally I enveloped all of his hard, thick length.

Ero withdrew slowly and then sank in again, eliciting

a deep groan from his chest that made a new wave of desire roll through me. I lifted my hips slightly and he plunged into me harder. He maintained his control for several minutes, rolling his hips so that he thrust in long, slow strokes that seemed to massage me and nurture me toward the edge. I reached up and touched his face, and Ero turned to kiss the inside of my wrist.

I could feel the tension building through my body and I ached for release. I gripped his head and pulled his down so that he kissed me, catching himself with his hands on either side of him. Lifting my hips higher in the air, I nudged him and bit his bottom lip.

"Please, Ero," I whimpered.

He understood my plea and started pounding into me with such intensity that I cried out with each thrust and within seconds, my body was contracting around him in a series of hard, blissful tremors. He gave a deep grunt and I felt him pulse inside me as his streams met each of my spasms.

Ero fell forward onto me and we were suddenly back in the same position we had been in the forest. He kissed my neck softly and I ran my hand down his sweaty back. This time I had no compulsion to get up and run away from him. I wanted to lie there with him forever.

"I don't want to go to my house tonight," I whispered to him.

He nuzzled closer to me.

"I'll be there," he whispered back.

"You will?"

"Samira took the house that had been set aside for you."

"She did?"

Ero pulled himself up so that he could look at me and I smiled at him, fulfilled and enthralled by the orange of his eyes and the rise and fall of his chest.

"I thought it only appropriate considering you don't need it anymore."

"I don't?"

"No. We're bonded for life now and if I can help it, you won't be out of arms reach except when I'm on patrol, which means you will be coming home with me."

I smiled and lifted my head to kiss him. I knew that I was never going to live on Earth again. I would keep my house there, just in case Ero and I wanted to go on an interplanetary honeymoon. Maybe I would take my Denynso students, whoever they turned out to be, on field trips now that my mate had proven that their kind could successfully travel through space. I was his now, completely and fully his, and wherever he was, I knew that that's where I would be.

SMITTEN BY THE ALIEN

COVER

GRACE KENSINGTON
SMITTEN BY THE ALIEN
ALIEN WARRIOR MATES I | BOOK 9

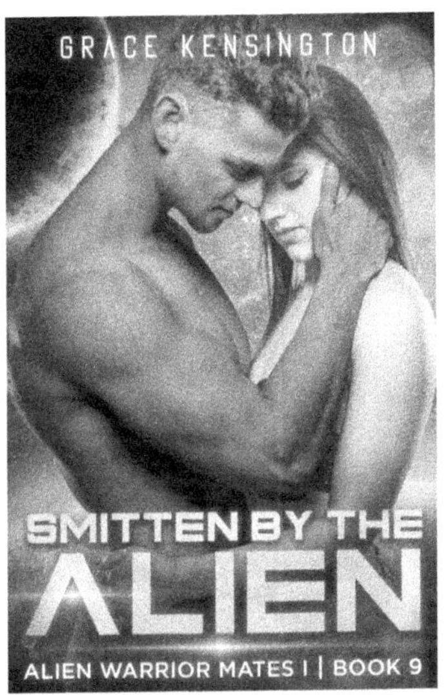

1

Sign up for Grace Kensington's Mailing List

2

---

*D*ear Diary,

    I still can't believe this is actually happening. One minute I was hiding at Zuri's house trying to decide what I was going to do next and being terrified that at any minute my evil son of a bitch of a stepfather was going to show up and kill me, and the next minute I was following Zuri and some warrior who is apparently in love with her to the university space shuttle to head to Uoria. I still can't believe how easily Ero made him go away.

    I just re-read that sentence. I can't believe I am still not brave enough to even write his name. I am literally on another planet, nowhere near anywhere where he would be able to get near me, and I still can't bring myself to write it. Maybe one day I will get over everything that he has put me through since my idiot of a mother decided to marry him. I will never understand that.

    What am I doing here? It seemed like a fantastic idea at the time when Zuri and Ero suggested that I come along with them when they returned to Uoria. Anything to get out of his line of fire for when he finally got over the shock of Ero scaring the living hell out of him. That and I really didn't have anywhere else to go and wasn't sure where I was going to live or what I was going to do for those little life details like food. Coming here was a way for me to stay with Zuri, who is the only person in the entire world that I trust, know that I will have somewhere to live and stay safe while I figure out what the hell I am going to do with my future, and use some of my chemistry and biology knowledge to actually do something good rather than just filling out tests.

I have only been on Uoria for a couple of hours and I am still so overwhelmed by everything that is going on. I thought that I would be spending time with Zuri, maybe getting a chance to talk to her about everything that had been going on with me in the last few weeks. As soon as we got here, though, Ero whisked her away somewhere and I got handed over to the human women and to a man named Ty. I was happy to see Leia, even though we don't know each other terribly well. To be honest, though, I was happier to see Ty. I wouldn't say this to anybody but you, but he is the most beautiful man I have ever seen in my entire life. He is huge beyond description and so gorgeous I couldn't even talk to him for the first few minutes. From what I understand, he is my own personal protector for while I'm here. That could make this experience much more pleasant.

I'm going to try to get some sleep. They gave me my own house to live in while I'm here, which is a major change from what I'm used to. There won't be anyone to bother me or to tell me what to do. Or to do anything else to me. Maybe I'll get lonely at some point, but for now this is all just too incredible for me to get my mind around. I might only have six months here before our exchange period ends and we have to go back to Earth, but I'm not going to think about that. I am going to take advantage of every moment that I have and deal with whatever is ahead of me when it comes.

Samira

I FINISHED my diary entry and tucked the notebook under my pillow. I know it is a completely outdated form of recordkeeping, but I had always found comfort in being able to actually write down my thoughts. I never read back through the stacks of notebooks I had accumulated throughout my eighteen years, but I figured that if I ever wanted to relive any of those moments, at least they would be there. On my darker days I figured that if my stepfather ever got his hands on me and I wasn't able to get away, at least the people who found me would have my journals to follow what had happened to me in the last several years of my life.

The house that the Denynso had put aside for me was small but comfortable and I settled back on the bed. It had taken some convincing for the human women to actually leave me alone in the house rather than staying with me and helping me get settled in. I didn't want to be rude to them, but the last thing I wanted that night was to sit around and regale them with the stories of what led up to coming with Zuri. For now, I was more than happy to let them believe that I was just another exchange student who had joined the program for people of Earth to come to Uoria and exchange knowledge, ideas, and cultural traditions. Unless I had the chance to spend time with Zuri, I would rather be alone. Well, Zuri or Ty.

As soon as I saw Ty, I knew that I wanted to spend

more time with him. He didn't have the gruff, aggressive feeling that the other men did and I found myself wondering if he was a warrior like Pyra and Gyyx, the Denynso mates of Eden and Leia, or if he was something else like Ciyrs, the mate of Eliana. The three human women seemed so happy with their Denynso men, and I found myself curious about the quiet, calm man entrusted with guiding me to my house and who said he would be my guide and protector while I was on Uoria. I wanted to know more about him, to find out what lurked behind those eyes and gave him an energy and presence that made me feel almost safe and comfortable near him.

3

───────

"What the hell is wrong with me?" Ty asked, pouring a few more ingredients into the huge bowl in front of him and going at it with a spoon with such intensity Pyra took a step back.

"What do you mean?" the enormous warrior asked.

Ty paused his assault of the cake batter and looked at Pyra.

"If you haven't noticed, my apron has a bit of a tent situation going on here and I haven't been able to think straight since last night."

Pyra glanced down at the front of Ty's apron and saw exactly what he was talking about. Though better concealed with the thick white apron hanging over him than it would have been if he was just standing there in the soft tie-front pants that were the usual wardrobe of the Denynso men, it was still pretty obvious that he had a raging hard-on. The baker shifted slightly and Pyra looked up at him with a knowing grin.

"Yeah, I've noticed. Why are you even asking? You

watched me go through it months ago, then Ciyrs, then Gyyx, and now Ero. It seems that the efforts to communicate and cooperate more effectively with Earth have had a much different impact than we originally anticipated. These human women get here and the Denynso men start dropping like flies. It looks like you are the one that came under the line of fire this time."

He reached out and dipped a finger in the bowl of batter and Ty pulled it away from him roughly. Even though he was baking a cake specifically for Pyra to bring to his mate Eden, who happened to be a couple of months into her first pregnancy and constantly in the throes of either a dramatic emotional situation or a craving, Ty didn't like when Pyra stuck his fingers in the batter. Not only did it just seem pretty unsanitary, his perfectionist ways made Ty feel like it threw off the entire balance and measurement of the batter so the cake wouldn't turn out exactly as he had wanted it to when he first started baking it. In the back of his mind he knew that that was being a little bit ridiculous, but he couldn't help it. Just like the warriors couldn't shake off their compulsion to fight and protect, Ty couldn't fight off his compulsion to create and perfect.

"That can't possibly be it," Ty said, adding a few drops of dark brown liquid from a bottle he kept on the top shelf of his spice cabinet.

"Why not? I was there when Zuri got back with that new girl. Anyone with eyes can see that she's beautiful."

"Samira."

"What?" Pyra asked, running the tip of one of his fingers through a mound of sweet powder on the counter and licking it off.

"The new girl. Her name is Samira."

"Uh-huh. I guess your big old orange eyes definitely noticed that she's beautiful."

"My eyes aren't orange!" Ty protested, then picked up a cookie sheet so he could see his reflection. Sure enough, there were streaks of orange through the usual brown of his eyes. "Shit."

"Yep. They might not have made their complete changeover yet, but those eyes cannot deceive. They know that your mate has shown up, and unless you are preparing yourself to fight Ero for Zuri or you are going to break into the space shuttle and try to pry out that little flight attendant who always runs and hides the minute that the ship lands, that means that your mate is Samira."

"She can't be."

"I don't get it. Why are you so pissed about your mate showing up? You have the whole nurturing and taking care of someone thing down pat. You've been taking care of all of us warriors for as long as I can remember. And you are plenty old enough to get mated."

Ty groaned and started distributing the batter into three hexagonal pans he had placed in a row in the middle of the counter.

"That's the problem right there. I am plenty old enough, but is she? Did you see her? She looks barely old enough to be out of her mother's house much less in somebody's bed. I just don't feel right looking at her the way that I obviously look at her when she is so young."

"She's old enough to be Zuri's student, which means that she is old enough to be in college. I don't think that Zuri would have brought her here if she wasn't an adult, but if it makes you feel any better, I can ask Eden how old she is exactly."

"How would she know that?"

"They are human women. They tell each other everything. It's a little disturbing actually. I think that she had told the other girls far more than I would ever want any of them to know about me because last time I was in the room with all of them, they all seemed to be far too focused on the front of my pants. And since I am no longer in the fun pre-mating phase that you are currently finding yourself enjoying, there would be nothing to draw their attention there unless they were trying to confirm a story that they heard."

Ty laughed, feeling better now that he at least had Pyra to commiserate with him a little bit. It wasn't exactly the same thing, but they had both found themselves at the mercy of the confounding and sometimes irresistible human women who had started infiltrating their planet.

As he slipped the cakes into the oven, Ty found his mind wandering back to Samira. The second she stepped off the shuttle from the university the night before, he was enraptured. This was something he had never felt before. While some of the warriors were known for having as many female conquests as they did battle victories, Ty had never been that kind of man. He had thought he had feelings for a couple of the females of the tribe a few times before, but even when they had sex no bonding ever occurred. Now that he had seen Samira, he realized that those feelings were nothing and that he was truly screwed. If Pyra was right, and truth be told, Pyra was almost always right, especially when it came to things that he had experienced himself, there was nothing that

Ty could do about his newfound attraction to Samira. If the constant erection wasn't enough to tell him, the hint of orange in his eyes was unmistakable.

Samira was his mate and would be the only one for him for the rest of his life. He would just have to decide if he could deal with it or if he was going to let her age keep him from pursuing her and risk living the rest of his existence alone and longing for her. It was not a decision that he wanted to make.

4

———

When I woke up the morning after arriving on Uoria, I had a few disorienting moments when I had no idea where I was. In the first few seconds after I woke up but before I opened my eyes I thought that I might still be at Zuri's house, and then I had a moment of panic thinking that I was back at my mother's house and that the pounding I heard was my stepfather knocking on the door trying to get into my bedroom. My eyes snapped open and I saw the unfamiliar room around me and I was briefly terrified. Finally, I regained my senses and remembered that I was in Uoria in my own little house, and that I was, for once, safe.

After just a few seconds of feeling calm and in control again, however, I heard the loud pounding and again became afraid. I sat up in the bed and pulled the covers up around me, pulling my knees to my chest like I always did when I felt scared. It was a protective position that made me feel like I was retracting into my shell. Too many memories of nights spent just like that in my bed at home, or in the corner of my bedroom, or even, on particularly horrible nights, curled in the closet just like that so that I could try to guard myself as much as I could.

"Samira?"

I heard my name added to the pounding and instantly recognized the voice as belonging to Ty. He was standing at the front door to my house, knocking insistently on the door and calling me. When I listened to his voice, however, I realized that it was not anger or frustration, but genuine concern and worry for me that was causing him to call out to me so loudly. I gathered my blankets close around me and hurried across the house to the door.

"Yes?" I said, pulling the door open and stepping behind it as much as I could to conceal myself while still being able to look at him.

I could see Ty's eyes scanning what of my body he could see and then snap up to mine, a look that somehow combined intrigue and shame crossing his face. He was even more gorgeous now that I was looking at him in daylight. Rather than the Mohawk style I had seen among most of the other men, Ty wore his stark white hair down and loose except for a braid down the center of his head that reached to the base of his neck. I am not a small woman, yet he towered over me, making me feel small and delicate. This was something I had never felt, and I loved it. I wanted to explore more of it, to see just how powerful he was and how well he knew how to use that power.

"Ty?" I said, realizing that he hadn't said anything since I opened the door.

He shook his head hard like he was trying to bring his thoughts back into reality and gestured behind him.

"The king and queen want you to come to meet them and to have breakfast in the meeting hall. Usually human visitors have to report to them first, but since you were a bit of a surprise, they weren't in the hall last night when you arrived and said that it was fine to have your greeting this morning."

I was confused by the formality of it, and by being described as a "surprise".

"I thought that Zuri told everyone that I was coming."

"She did, but we didn't get the communication until right before your arrival. Ero sent the message when he arranged transport back here, but the transportation officials didn't let us know until the day before you got here. "

"I don't understand. If they didn't tell everybody that I was coming, how did they have a house ready for me and how did they choose you as my guard?"

A bit of panic was starting to build in my chest. It was that feeling of being out of place and unwanted. I didn't want to be an imposition to anyone and my mind was suddenly reeling with plans for how I was going to get myself back to Earth now that the shuttle was already preparing to leave and there was no way I would be able to get back on it before take-off.

"You aren't an imposition," Ty said and then suddenly looked shocked.

I looked at him, stunned. He had just responded to what I was thinking, using my exact words to comfort me.

"How did you know that I was thinking that?"

He stuttered for a few seconds like he was trying to come up with words to explain what had just happened, and then I noticed his eyes had dropped again. Without realizing it, I had stepped out from behind the door and was standing fully in front of him. My blankets had slipped down slightly and he could plainly see that I sleep naked with the top of the blanket barely covering my nipples and the two sides wrapped around me closed just beneath the apex of my thighs. His eyes lifted to mine and felt my breath deepen slightly. I had known this man for just a few hours, but in that moment, all I wanted was for him to touch me. The feeling was overwhelming, deep and intense like it was something that had always been in me but that I was just discovering.

Instead of fulfilling that wish, however, Ty turned his eyes away from me and cleared his throat softly. I gathered my blankets closer around me reluctantly and stepped backwards into the house.

"Do you want to come in while I get dressed?"

He shook his head.

"I'll just wait here."

Feeling slightly hurt, I closed the door and went back to my bedroom to get dressed. I wasn't sure what to wear. He had mentioned the king and queen, but I knew from Zuri that they weren't like the kings and queens you hear about from history classes at Earth. She described them as kind and approachable, people who associated with the rest of the tribe that they ruled with compassion, affection, and respect. Still, they were the monarchs and I didn't want to offend them with my clothing. I wished Zuri were there to help me.

Suddenly I felt like I heard Ty's voice in my head telling me that I would look beautiful in anything. It sent a shiver down my spine and brought a flutter to my belly. Smiling to myself for reasons that I didn't fully understand at the time, I draped my blankets back over my bed and dressed.

5
______

Dammit, dammit, dammit, dammit, dammit.

Ty sighed and sagged back against the door to Samira's house. How could he be so stupid? Tuning into the thoughts of another person was extremely intimate, which is why it was something that only mates, with a few very specific exceptions, shared. It was part of the bond that occurred between the men of his kind and their women, and it allowed them to stay fully connected. This could be very helpful when they needed to find each other, when one needed the help of the other, or they wanted to express something private to each other without anyone else hearing it.

The fact that he could already connect with Samira was startling to say the least, considering they had never even touched each other much less bonded. Now he had been dumb enough to not only listen to her thoughts, but reply to her both speaking to her and sending his own thoughts to her. He knew he was probably scaring the hell out of her, or at the very least making her think that she was crazy. He hadn't even decided yet what he was going to do about these intense feelings he was experiencing for the stunning but so young woman that was now dressing in the house behind him. This was not a good time to start toying with her by listening to her thoughts and sending her his without her understanding what was going on.

He had been chastising himself for a few minutes when he felt the door give way behind him and fell back. Samira let out a scream and he turned as he fell so that he came down on his hands rather than on his back. His fall had caused her to fall and land on her back, which meant that he landed over her, his hands on either side of her and his face level with hers. They lay there for a few tense seconds, staring at each other. Their breaths came out ragged, mingling between them and surrounding them with a sound that only partially concealed the pounding of their heartbeats.

Ty could see something flicker in her eyes. It looked like desire and when she licked her lips, he almost lost the control he had been struggling so hard to maintain around her. She was even more startlingly beautiful when he was this close to her, but she still looked so young. He felt like he would be taking advantage of her if he gave into his craving for her at that moment, and if he did that he would never be able to forgive himself.

She was not tiny like Eden, Eliana, or Leia, but taller like Zuri. The extra inches made it so that their bodies lined up perfectly and he had to move extremely carefully to get out of the position hovering over her so that she didn't feel his raging cock pressing down on her. It was like it had a mind of its own, straining against his pants as it tried to get to her, just knowing that hers was the body it was made for.

"I'm sorry," he muttered, climbing backwards and standing up.

He wanted to reach down to help her up, but he worried about being able to maintain his self-control if he touched her in that moment. It was already taking everything that he had not to sweep her off her feet and carry her back into the bedroom where he could spend the rest of the day bonding with her. He didn't want to test his capacity to withhold himself if he touched her skin, even just her hand, in that second.

"It's alright," she said, standing up and brushing herself off, "I'm sorry I didn't realize you were leaning against the door."

He looked at her fully and saw that she had put on a pair of tight black pants and a black shirt that hugged her curves and dipped low over her breasts, creating an enticing swell of cleavage. His mouth watered and he felt his heart start to pound. They needed to get out of her house as soon as possible.

A few minutes later they were walking through the compound toward the meeting hall. Ty noticed that she was able to keep up with him without struggle thanks to her long legs and a fast pace that made her breasts bounce and her long, thick hair sway across her back. Suddenly she turned to him.

"You never answered me when I asked how the house was ready for me if nobody knew I was coming until right before I got here."

"That house was originally intended for Zuri. It was the one chosen for her when she came here the first time for her teaching position, and when she left so suddenly it was just left there without anybody living in it. We assumed that whoever took her place as the new exchange program professor would end up moving into that house, but then we found out that Ero had gone after her and that she would be returning with him."

"So, if that is the house that was supposed to be hers, where is she living now that she's back?"

Ty glanced at her strangely. He assumed the human girls would have filled her in on all of the gossip from the planet, especially the mating between Zuri and Ero considering she was Zuri's friend.

"She's with Ero. She's his mate, that's why he went after her."

"His mate?" she asked, sounding surprised.

"They didn't tell you any of this?"

"Everything was kind of a whirlwind. I wasn't even expecting to see Zuri again for months. I had no idea that she had come home so quickly after leaving. I was staying in her house after an issue with my stepfather and she showed back up, and then the next morning Ero got there and it was all very fast after that. I didn't ask any questions."

He could see the hurt and fear in her eyes and felt the need to comfort her. Ty lifted an arm and rested it gently around her shoulders. He worried that she would pull away from him or be intimidated, but she didn't. Instead, she seemed to relax a bit at his touch. She stepped a little bit closer to him so that her hip brushed his as they walked.

"May I ask what happened with your stepfather?"

He wasn't even sure what the term meant, but from

the way she said it he could tell that whoever that man was, he had done something terrible to her. Samira must have noticed the hint of uncertainty in his voice because she glanced up at him with a smile.

"You don't know what a stepfather is, do you?"

Part of him wanted to pretend that he did so that he didn't look dumb in front of her, but at the same time, he knew that the goal of the exchange program with Earth was to bring humans over so that they could educate the Denynso about the cultures, customs, and history of the planet and its people so she was probably not surprised that he was unsure of some of what she said. Finally, he shook his head.

"My mother and my father got divorced when I was pretty young, then she married...," she hesitated as if she couldn't bring herself to say the word that was right at the tip of her tongue. She closed her eyes and let out a breath, "she married her second husband, which is what a stepfather is. Does that make sense?"

She didn't say it like she was mocking him and Ty realized that he really enjoyed learning more about the other planet, even if it was something that broke his heart even to think about.

"I guess. I mean, I get what you are saying, but I have to admit I don't really understand it. We don't have divorce among the Denynso."

She looked surprised.

"You don't? Everybody just stays married no matter what?"

"Well, no. We don't get married. We bond. There is only one other person in the entire existence that can create a bond with each of us, and once we have found that mate and complete the bond, it is for life. There is no such thing as two mated people just deciding that they no longer want to be mates and then finding new mates. They are with their mates, or they are alone. That's just the way it is."

She got a soft, almost sad look in her eyes and Ty stopped walking so that he could turn her to face him. He wanted to be closer to her, just to look at her. The feelings building inside him were threatening to overwhelm him, and even though he felt guilty for even thinking about her that way, he needed to feel her near him.

"And they're happy?" she asked, looking up at him.

Ty nodded, reaching up to brush a strand of her dark hair away from her face. He traced the curve of her jawline with one fingertip. She was so beautiful. He had never seen any woman that looked like her, that was so breathtaking he literally couldn't stop looking at her.

"I have never seen Pyra, Gyyx, Ciyrs, or Ero as happy as they are now. Finding our mate is something that we look forward to our entire lives. We know that once we find her, we will be complete. The bond is something that can't be broken and I have never known a mated pair to ever be unhappy together."

"Never?"

"I mean, they argue, of course. There's always going to be bickering and disagreements between people who truly love each other. They don't last, though. Nothing keeps them from wanting to be together."

As they spoke their bodies had drawn closer to each other and Ty could see her trembling slightly. He touched her face again, bringing his fingers beneath her chin so he could tilt her face up to look at him again. He wondered if she could feel it too; if she understood what was happening between them and what it meant. She tilted her face so that her cheek pressed further into his palm and Ty started to ask her what she was feeling when he heard someone shouting his name from behind them.

6

———

The sound of the deep, gruff voice calling Ty's name jolted me out of the peaceful calm that he had created between us and I stepped back away from him. His hand fell away from my face and I immediately missed his touch. He was so incredibly sweet, so caring and attentive in a way that I had never experienced. When he talked about the mated couples and how happy they were together, I felt my heart reaching out to him, seeming to melt with each of his words. There was something in the way he was saying them that made it feel like he was telling me much more than just about how they created partnerships in his culture.

What really stood out to me about what he had said was the concept of bonding as opposed to marriage. He hadn't explained what the bonding was or how they went about knowing that they both wanted to bond, and I was desperate to find out. The way he talked about it was so reverent and mysterious, but at the same time, when he said it I could feel a primal heat and energy come off of him. My body responded instantly and again I felt the need for him to touch me. It was unlike anything I had ever felt about another guy. The teenage boys that flocked around me and even the older students at the university had been a bore and even though I dated, I never felt a strong connection to anyone. Now all I could think about was Ty and the way I craved him.

"Tyant!"

The booming voice sounded intense and demanding, almost like whoever was yelling was trying to be forceful and intimidating to whoever was around to listen, but particularly to Ty. I saw Ty's eyes close briefly before he turned around to face the man walking toward us. He had the Mohawk of the other men and the long stride of a warrior. I immediately tensed. Pyra, Gyyx, and Ero seemed nice in the very brief time that I had had to interact with them, but I was quickly finding that I didn't like the other warriors very much. Their aggressive, almost violent personalities made me feel the same type of crushing oppression that I had become accustomed to feeling from my stepfather and I was not about to let myself feel that again when I had just so narrowly escaped him. I came here to get away from the things that frightened me and held me back, if only for a little while, and the thought of them putting me right back into that feeling was something I couldn't tolerate.

"The king and queen want you now," the man said as he approached.

He wasn't looking at Ty, but at me. I saw his eyes scour over my body and lock on my mouth. He licked his lips and I felt my body stiffen uncomfortably. There was none of the gentleness, the connection in his eyes that was in Ty's, and I noticed that his eyes remained a dark purple color rather than shifting occasionally to orange as I noticed that Ty's did.

Ty stepped up closer to me and I felt myself leaning toward him.

"We're on our way," Ty said.

"Maybe I should take over from here," the man said, "After all, shouldn't our lovely new guest have a warrior to protect her like the other human women have?"

"Ciyrs isn't a warrior," Ty said.

"Ciyrs didn't escort Eliana when she first came here. Pyra did. But as we know, Pyra is extremely mated and has a little more on his plate than the rest of us do, so there seems to be a position open that requires a warrior to step in and take over. You did a fine job getting her to her house, but I'll take it from here. Why don't you go on back home and bake something?"

The words were so vicious that even I felt the venom coming off of them and I shifted uncomfortably. I didn't feel like a person in that moment, but more like a toy that these two men were batting around between them, trying to gain dominance over the other.

"She was given to me," Ty protested.

"Excuse me?" I said, taken aback by the words coming out of Ty, "Given to you? Is that what you men do on this planet? Just gather up the women as they step off the shuttles from Earth and hand them out like party favors?"

Tears were stinging in my eyes and I felt like I couldn't be near either of the men anymore. While I was furious with the warrior for his arrogance, I was heart-broken by Ty. He had been so sweet and suddenly he seemed just like all of the other men who had come my way.

I took off running, not entirely sure where I was going but confident that I would be able to find my way to the meeting hall on my own. Going on my understanding of patterns and grids, I used my instincts to weave my way through the compound until it opened out into a large space with a towering building at its center. I saw Zuri standing on the steps leading up to the front door with Ero standing a few steps beneath her, his head rested on her stomach as he held her around her hips.

I ran toward her, part of me feeling horrible for breaking up the beautiful moment between the couple. She looked up and noticed me. Gently easing Ero away from her, she came to meet me, gathering me in her arms even before she spoke.

"What's wrong?" she asked.

I shook my head and tried to explain what had just happened. I could feel the eyes of the other men on me and I found myself longing for Ty even though I was still upset with him. At least with him nearby I felt like I was protected.

"Where is he?" the enormous warrior I remembered from the night before as Pyra stalked toward me.

"I left him near my house," I answered.

"And you said he was with a warrior?" I nodded, "And he insulted you?"

"Not me, really. More Ty, I guess. He told him that he would take over from there and that he should be the one that was guarding me."

"Oh, shit."

Without any more warning than that, Pyra shot off in

the direction of my house, Ero following even faster after him.

"What was that all about?" I asked Zuri.

She stroked my hair and smiled at me. I could see something different about her, but I wasn't sure what.

"Can I ask you a question, Samira?"

"Of course."

"What color are Ty's eyes when he looks at you?"

"Sometimes they're brown and sometimes they're orange."

Her smile grew slightly and she nodded, looping her arm through mine and guiding me toward the door to the meeting hall.

"Let's get you inside to meet with the king and queen and then get some breakfast. I think we have a few things to talk about."

"Look what you did," Dillyn said tauntingly, "You made the pretty little thing run away. Well, maybe not so little. Young, though. Fresh and tender just like..."

Before he could get another word out, Ty's fist connected with his cheek and Dillyn went sprawling across the ground. The impact sent a surge of adrenaline through Ty and he launched at the prone warrior, tackling him down into the dirt before Dillyn could even get his wits about him again. He could barely believe what he was doing, but Ty couldn't stop his attack. The anger and protectiveness that filled him was unlike anything he had ever felt. Usually calm and docile, he had always been a nurturer, not a fighter. Suddenly, though, he had discovered the beast inside him. As soon as Dillyn started talking about Samira that way, he had felt like something inside him had unfurled like a tightly wound metal spring that someone suddenly released.

He continued to wail on Dillyn, pounding him into

the ground with all of the fury that boiled within him. After a few moments, he felt a tug on his shoulder and his name coming through the loud ringing in his ears.

"Damn, Ty, get off of him!"

He felt another hand on his other shoulder and the combination of the two finally pulled him away from Dillyn. The warrior writhed on the ground, blood pouring from his face and streaked across his chest. It felt like his constantly present erection had gotten even harder and now Ty was so filled with energy and adrenaline all he wanted to do was find Samira, toss her over his shoulder, and bring her back to his house. In the back of his mind, though, he could still hear Dillyn talking about how young she was. The conflict made him feel sick and he needed to get away from the situation.

He pushed past Pyra and Ero, heading for his shop. It was the one place where he felt completely comfortable and could get out his stress in a way other than beating the shit out of a warrior for upsetting Samira and then talking about her in such a disrespectful way. He heard the two warriors fall into step behind him, but that was fine. He didn't mind them coming along. In fact, he thought it might be nice to have them to talk to. Since they were both recently mated they might be able to help him navigate all of his confusion. He thought that maybe they would be able to talk him out of his compulsive need for Samira.

"She's 18, Ty," Pyra said as soon as they stepped into the shop behind Ty.

"Holy shit," Ty said, resting his elbows on the counter and burying his head in his hands, "She's only 18."

"That's an adult," Pyra reminded me, "and she is far

smarter than other women her age. You really are not that much older than she is. I don't understand why this is stressing you out so much."

Ty raised his head and looked at the two warriors standing in front of them. These were men he had been taking care of for years, using his unusual talents and strengths to nurture them and make sure that they had what they needed. He was like Ciyrs in a way, but whereas Ciyrs healed them if they were sick or injured, Ty took care of them while they were well and helped to make sure they stayed that way. It was not what people expected of a Denynso of his size, but it suited him. Now he was feeling more like one of the aggressive, violent warriors and it was all because he was struggling between knowing he had found his mate and not knowing if it was right to pursue her.

"What if I hurt her? What if she isn't ready to handle all of this and she ends up going back to Earth?"

"I just went through that exact situation," Ero reminded him.

"I know, but you went after her and she came back. Zuri is a grown woman. She knows who she is and what she wants out of life. She made the decision to leave you, but she also made the decision to come back to you. What if Samira leaves and is too afraid to come back? I don't think I could stand knowing that I had hurt her or taken advantage of her in some way while trying to bond with her, and then having to be alone for the rest of my life."

"Here's the thing, Ty," Ero said, "I didn't know if Zuri was actually going to come back with me, but I had to try. You already know that Samira is your mate. Whether you bond with her now or 5 years from now when she's your age, she will still be your mate and she will still be linked to you forever. Remember, though, that 5 years from now, she will be older, but so will you. When is it going to be right? And are you willing to possibly lose her forever because you were too afraid?"

Ty didn't have a chance to respond before he saw a figure appear in the doorway.

"We're going to head out of here," Pyra said, taking Ero by the arm and dragging him out of the room.

"Hi, Samira," Ero said as he struggled to keep up with Pyra.

"Hi, Ero," she replied, and then turned to Ty, "Hi, Ty."

"Hi," he said, turning the bread dough he had been working on out onto the counter.

"What are you doing?" she asked, taking a few steps toward him.

"Making bread," he answered shortly, still not looking up at her.

Suddenly he felt her come up beside him and rest a hand on his upper arm.

"Can I help?" she asked softly.

8

I watched Ty's hands kneading into the dough on the counter and felt the flutter in my belly grow more intense. His powerful hands worked over the dough masterfully, and I wanted them on my body. The conversation I'd had with Zuri resonated through my mind, and as I looked at him, I knew my dear friend and professor was right. This big, beautiful man was my mate, and after Zuri had given me a careful explanation of exactly what it entailed, I knew that I wanted more than anything to bond with him.

I touched his arm, feeling the muscles tense and shift beneath his skin as he continued to press into the dough. His rhythm seemed to increase a little and I lifted his arm so that I could slip beneath it. He cleared his throat, but lowered his arms around me so that his hands rested over mine. Lifting them up, he brought them down onto the dough and guided me in kneading it. The dough felt soft and warm beneath my hands, and Ty's hands felt strong and comforting over them. I could feel the heat from his body radiating toward mine, and with each long press down into the dough, his erection brushed against me.

The feeling of it made me moan softly and I arched my back to press my hips back toward him so that I returned the touch with more intensity and intention. His hands pushed mine deeper into the dough, kneading harder as his breath dropped and I could hear him struggling to control it behind me. I leaned back so that my back touched his chest, subtly rolling my hips against him. His breath caught in his throat and his hands stopped moving.

"Samira," he said imploringly.

"Yes, Ty?"

"Stop."

"Why?"

I rolled my hips a little harder and heard him groan.

"This isn't right."

"Why?"

I was going to force him to tell me exactly what he was thinking so that I could prove how wrong he was. I knew exactly why he thought it was wrong. Zuri had learned from Pyra that he was upset about my age. I didn't care what he thought, though. I had fallen for Ty as soon as I saw him and there was no way that I was going to let a few years of difference between us keep from having him as my mate. I would just have to prove how much of a woman I really was.

"You're too young," he finally whispered.

I pressed back into him and tilted my head so I could kiss his neck.

"Am I? Do I feel too young to you?"

Ty gave a soft grunt and I withdrew my hands from the dough, brushing the flour off of them.

"No," he said gruffly.

I turned around to face him. The orange streaks in his eyes were covering more of the brown now and I felt a surge in my heart as I remembered that Zuri told me the Denynso men's eyes changed to orange when they mated. I knew I was getting to him. I just had to press further. I touched his face gently, easing it forward with my fingertips against his cheek until I could touch my mouth to his. My lips parted and I touched the tip of my tongue to his bottom lip, tempting him to open his mouth. When he did, I flicked my tongue across his, deepening the kiss briefly before pulling back, catching his bottom lip between my teeth as I went.

"Do I kiss like I'm too young?" I asked, my voice dropping the more I spoke.

He shook his head and I smiled, leaning in to kiss him again. He returned the kiss, but only slightly as if still struggling to control himself.

"Please, Samira," he said, his eyes closed.

"Look at me, Ty," I said and he opened his eyes, "Do I look like I'm too young?"

His eyes grew sad and he nodded.

"Yes."

"Do I?" I asked, taking the hem of my shirt and pulling it off over my head.

"We're in my shop, Samira," he said, "Anybody could walk in at any second and see you."

"I want you to see me."

"I can see you."

His defenses were dropping and I was eager to keep going.

"Your house is connected to the shop, isn't it?" I asked, referencing what Zuri had told me.

"Yes."

I walked across the shop to the door on the back wall. I knew it led directly into his house and that he rarely locked it. That afternoon was the same as usual and the door opened easily beneath my hand. I glanced over my shoulder at him as I stepped into his house.

"Where is your bedroom, Ty?"

He didn't answer and I stepped all the way into the house, deciding I would just figure out where the room was on my own. After a few seconds, he hadn't followed me. I unbuttoned and unzipped my pants and pulled them off, tossing them back through the door into the shop. They hit the ground and I heard Ty groan. The door swung open further and I saw his broad form fill the doorway. I had undressed myself down to nothing but a black lace bra and matching panties, and when he looked at me, his eyes went completely orange.

"Do I look too young now?"

He still didn't answer and I turned away from him, giving him a full view of all of my curves in the barely-there panties, and walked further into the house. I glanced around and saw a stairwell in the far corner. I crossed to it and climbed the stairs slowly, letting my hips sway with each step. I could feel him following me, his eyes on my body as I put myself on display for him. I wanted him to want me with the same fire and intensity that I wanted him, and when I was finished with him, I wanted him to have no question left in his mind whether I was old enough to be his mate.

I made it up the stairs and found that almost the entire upper floor was his bedroom. A massive bed sat in the middle of a huge room, making it look like a pedestal where I was more than ready to worship. I turned to face him as Ty stepped into the room.

"Come closer," I told him.

He seemed reluctant, but he complied, closing the space between us with a few long, slow steps. I kissed him, drawing his tongue into my mouth and sucking on it suggestively as I pressed the front of my body to his. I could feel his erection pushing into my belly and I nudged against him.

"Undress me," I said.

I felt his hands shaking slightly as he brought them to my back to release the hooks on my bra. He peeled it away from my body and dropped it to the floor at our feet, and then hooked his fingers in the waistband of my panties to ease them off of my hips. I wriggled them off of my legs and stepped out of them, now completely bare in front of him.

Walking backwards, I made my way to the bed. When I felt the edge of the mattress on the backs of my legs, I turned around and crawled onto the bed, arching my back as I went. I reached the pillows and turned so I reclined back on them.

"Take off your shirt."

He complied and I felt my body clench at the sight of his chiseled chest and rippled stomach. I wanted to get my hands on him so badly, but I was determined that it was going to be him that took me. I might be seducing him, but when we finally did bond, he was going to be the one that made it happen.

"Everything else," I said, fighting to keep my voice steady.

His eyes glowed back at me and I could see the struggle continuing behind them as he at once fought his desire for me and gave in to my seduction. My mouth watered when I finally saw his fully naked body, his muscles beautifully formed under smooth skin, and his perfect, powerful-looking erection standing out from his hips in a way that made me almost lose control. I licked my lips and I saw Ty's cock twitch.

"Oh," I said, "Is that what you want?"

I beckoned him forward with one finger, encouraging him to climb onto the bed with me. He laid down beside me and I got on my knees between his legs, reaching forward to finally wrap my hand around his gorgeous erection. My fingers couldn't touch as I encircled his thick shaft and the tingle between my thighs spiked. I leaned down and drew my tongue along the underside of him from the base to the tip, then licked again to gather the drop of crystalline fluid that had gathered there. He groaned and I met the sound with the slide of my mouth over the head.

I slipped down further, moving slowly to savor every vein and ridge against my lips and tongue. Holding the base in one hand, I picked up a smooth, steady rhythm that brought him further and further into my mouth with each glide. My attention wrenched groans from his chest and soon Ty was gripping the comforter on either side of him, his eyes squeezed closed as he concentrated on the sensations I was sending through him. I could feel him getting harder in my mouth and I released him, giving him a few seconds to cool to bring him back from the brink.

Moving forward, I straddled his hips, settling myself so my pelvis touched his and my core cradled his erection. I rested his cock against my palm and rocked my hips, causing me to slide up and down him. The hot wetness from my body transferred to his, making my movements silky and easy. With each rock, I brought my core further up his shaft, eventually getting to a point where the tip teased my clit with each stroke. The breath caught in my throat at that feeling and I repeated it, pressing up slightly with my palm to increase the pressure between our bodies.

"Do I feel too young?" I asked. He didn't answer and I pressed harder, burrowing him in my folds without letting him enter me, "Do I, Ty?"

Suddenly he grabbed me by my hips and flipped me onto my back. I gasped at the movement and felt my body get even wetter as he hovered over me, staring down into my face with intensity that took my breath away.

"No," he growled and I felt the tip of his erection tease at my opening.

"Are you my mate, Ty?" I whispered.

He moved his hips forward slightly, massaging me and building pressure low in my belly.

"I am your mate."

"Do you want me?"

"More than anything I have ever wanted in my life."

I took a long, shuddering breath.

"Show me."

He pushed forward and filed me, taking his time to let

me stretch around him. I whimpered at the intense feeling and clutched at his back. Just when I thought I couldn't accommodate any more, Ty gave a hard thrust, sinking all the way into me and eliciting a sharp cry at the blissful combination of pain and pleasure. We paused there for a moment, letting our bodies learn each other. He kissed me languidly, his mouth moving across my familiarly.

Finally, his hips relaxed and I felt him start to move within me. My walls held him firmly and he groaned deeply as he built his rhythm. Each long, deep thrust coaxed sounds from my lips and I gave myself over to him, allowing him to bond me to him completely and irrevocably. Slow sex had never done much for me, but this was a transcendent experience and when I came, suddenly and with blinding intensity, I felt like I was drawing him into my body and my soul. He responded to the scream I let out at my climax with a growl and he gave one more hard thrust and released into me. My body milked him and I clung to him, emotion starting to over-whelm me.

He finally opened his eyes and I saw that they were completely orange.

"My mate," he whispered, leaning down to nuzzle my neck and touch a kiss to my shoulder.

"Always," I whispered back, licking the front of his neck.

9

———

Ty and Samira stayed in bed for the rest of the afternoon, exploring each other as she proved to him again and again that she was everything that he needed, and he showed her over and over that he was everything she could handle. They finally drifted to sleep, completely spent, in each other's arms, but were awaken less than an hour later by frantic pounding on Ty's door.

"This seems awfully familiar," Samira joked as Ty rolled away from her and climbed out of bed, pulling on his pants.

He shot her a smile and walked out into the corridor and then down the stairs. The pounding continued, and Ty was aggravated by the time he reached the door. He didn't want to talk to anybody. He wanted to shuck off his pants and crawl back into bed with Samira.

"What do you want?"

Ero stood on the other side of the door, his expression strained.

"You need to come with me," he said.

"I'm busy right now," Ty said, not really caring what was going on.

Ero shook his head.

"I'm sorry. I know you have Samira here and that's wonderful and I'm sure I'm going to be really happy for you pretty soon, but you need to come with me."

"What's going on?"

Both men turned in the direction of the stairs and Samira's voice. She was walking toward them, buttoning one of Ty's shirts on over her pants. Ty's heart lit up. The shirt engulfed her, but it made her look adorably sexy and completely his. She came to his side and looked at Ero intensely.

"What's going on, Ero?" she repeated.

"The warriors just got back from their patrol. They said that they have really important information and that they need all of us in the meeting hall immediately."

Without hesitation, Ty ran back up the stairs to put on his shoes and shirt. When he got back down, they left the house and hurried toward the meeting hall. Ero was an impossibly fast runner, a skill that had become a tremendous benefit in their last battle against the Klimnu, and he seemed to be struggling to keep himself slow enough that Ty and Samira could keep up with him. Ty knew this meant that something extremely serious was going on with the warriors.

They entered the hall and saw it was crowded with Denynso. Several warriors stood on a low stage at one end of the room and Ty saw that Pyra was in the middle, his face stern and concerned. As soon as Ty and Samira settled onto the bench with the other human women, he began to speak.

"We have just returned from our normal patrol, but this time we found something we have never seen before. At the far end of the compound there is a cave in the cliff. Until now we didn't think anything of it. Today, however, we decided to investigate further and found that it is not a cave, but a rock tunnel that dips far into the ground. It was extremely difficult to find and impossible for any of us to navigate because of our size. We believe that this is the way that the Klimnu are getting into the compound. The Traitor told them about the cave and has been providing them with information and resources for quite some time."

A shocked whisper rippled through the crowd and Ty cuddled Samira a little closer to him, part of him terrified that she was going to hear all of this and be afraid and compelled to leave. Instead, she looked fascinated.

"We need to build our defense and devise our plan of attack," Pyra said and sounds of affirmation rose up through the tribe. "It is time we settled this conflict with the Klimnu once and for all."

Ty felt Samira stand up suddenly, causing his arms to drop away from her.

"I'll help," she called out.

There were a few gasps throughout the room and I reached up to pull her back down, but she stayed strong.

"Who is that?" Pyra asked.

"It's me, Samira. I want to help."

RESCUED BY THE ALIEN

COVER

GRACE KENSINGTON
RESCUED BY THE ALIEN
ALIEN WARRIOR MATES I | BOOK 10

1

S ign up for Grace Kensington's Mailing List

2

"I want to help."

The whispers in the room around me grew louder and I could feel the eyes of all of the Denynso burning into me. The ones who didn't know who I was tried to figure out why there was a new human girl offering her help to the clan, and those who did know who I was expressed their surprise that I was so willing to just throw myself into what I was quickly realizing to be an extremely dangerous situation. The massive, intense-looking warrior Pyra stared at me from the platform at the other end of the banquet hall, evaluating me silently.

It felt like we were stuck in some kind of standoff. Beside me I felt Ty, my brand-new mate, gently pull on my hand as if he was trying to tug me back down to sit on the bench beside him. I resisted the tug and continued to stare at Pyra, my shoulders squared and my jaw set. I know that to them I was small and weak, but on Earth, I was not. Slightly taller than average with broad shoulders, round hips, and a sturdy build, most people considered me a very strong and capable-looking woman. Add to that the fact that I am far more intelligent and resourceful than nearly anyone I have ever met, and have a stubborn streak that can rarely be broken.

The fact that my body was still humming from a day of intense, all-consuming bonding with my mate only worked to make me more determined and give me greater strength and energy than I had felt in a long time. In an instant I had changed from just a human foreign exchange student that had come to Uoria with my favorite professor in order to escape the torment of my stepfather back on Earth to a member of the clan who was fully committed not just to loving and protecting my mate, but to doing whatever I could to defend the entirety of the clan and my future in it. For the first time in my life I felt truly and completely part of something, and from the look on Pyra's face and the intensity in his voice, I knew that was being severely threatened. I was not going to stand by and allow that to happen. I knew that I came to this planet for a reason, and it seemed to be showing itself.

"I want to help, Pyra," I repeated, taking a step forward so that he could see me more clearly.

I had only encountered Pyra briefly, but I knew him to be the most powerful and aggressive of all of the planet's warriors; known throughout the galaxy for his skill in battle. If I could convince him to accept my help and allow me to utilize some of my own skill and knowledge, the rest of the warriors would truly have no choice but to follow along with it.

"Are you sure, Samira?" Pyra finally asked.

His voice rumbled through the banquet hall, seeming to quiet the whispers as it rippled through the crowd to me.

"Yes."

"What can you do?"

It wasn't a challenge or meant to be mocking. He was genuinely asking me how I could contribute. There was a war coming, and though I wasn't sure about all of the details, I could tell that it was something that had been building up for quite some time. This was not going to be a simple fight. It was going to require more than just the size and strength of the warriors. I stared up at him for a moment, and then an idea suddenly shot through my mind. I turned and rushed toward the bench where the other human women sat.

I crouched down in front of them and looked at each directly in the eyes.

"We were planned for our mates since birth, right?" The women nodded, "And we are the only human women who have ever been mated to Denynso men in the history of the clan, right?" They nodded again and I started to feel even more courageous, "So don't you think it is a little bit strange that in a clan that has never had a human woman mate, five are chosen in less than a year?"

They glanced at each other and I saw their expressions grow nervous. Eden's hand drifted to the swell of her belly as if protecting the child that grew inside.

"We don't know that there weren't other human women that were supposed to be mates. They just never came onto the planet, so their Denynso men didn't find them. Each of us had a specific reason for being here.

Maybe there would have been more bonds if there was a more open visiting policy."

"No," Zuri said, meeting my eyes with an expression that said she was following my thought process, "It doesn't work that way. Samira's right. There is a reason that we all came here at the same time."

"What are you thinking?" Eliana asked.

"There are five of us. We each have our own skills and abilities. If war is coming, the enemies won't expect women to be a part of it, which means that we can band together and help our mates, and the rest of the warriors, finish this."

The rest of the women nodded and I stood back up, turning to Pyra.

"Bring us to the cave."

The whispers started through the room again and I felt Ty come to my side.

"What are you doing?" he said to me telepathically.

I was still getting used to the ability for him to read my thoughts and for me to read his, but in that moment it seemed like he didn't want the others to hear him questioning me. I drew closer to his side and leaned in to him even though I knew I didn't actually have to be close to him to communicate through my mind.

"Zuri suggested that I come here so that I could use my chemistry and biology knowledge to help with some healing potions. Maybe that's not all I can do, though."

"The Klimnu are dangerous, Samira. They nearly killed Eden, Eliana, and Leia, and they attacked Zuri. They won't hesitate to hurt you just because you are a woman. In fact, you might be in even more danger because you are a woman. The Klimnu are known for their hunger for women and for not really caring if those women want anything to do with them."

"Are you sure that you want to go?"

Pyra's voice interrupted our conversation and I stepped away from Ty to address him.

"Absolutely."

3

———

Ty stared at Samira, trying to keep his mouth from hanging open as he processed what was going on. He was still coming down from the elation of finally bonding with her and had been taken off guard by Pyra's announcement that it was time to declare war on the Klimnu and eliminate the threat that had been plaguing the Denynso. Now he was watching as his beautiful mate offered herself as a tool for them to use in battle. It was all so overwhelming and he didn't know what he was supposed to think. He wasn't a warrior and had never been involved in any of the battles or the raids. The thought of Samira handing herself over to the violent and aggressive warriors so that she could be a part of whatever battle plan they devised was terrifying.

"We need to go now. Tonight we plan how we are going to handle these creatures once and for all."

He looked around the room, meeting eyes with the warriors. They started to walk forward toward him, gathering at the base of the stage. Ty watched Samira turn back toward the other women.

"Eliana, Zuri told me that you are working on healing ointments."

"Yeah. Ciyrs, Eden, and I have been working on some potions we hope will help make the healing process much faster when people are injured. Right now it is a pretty involved process that can have some rather...unintentional effects, and we are hoping that we might be able to come up with some ointments that will allow us to treat some of the problems that way rather than having to always use our hands."

Ty knew exactly what Eliana meant with her delicate wording. It was well-known that the healing procedures used by the clan healer Ciyrs and his mate Eliana often resulted in extreme arousal, and sometimes even a link that rivaled the connection between mates. This is what had happened between Eden and Ciyrs, creating some tension between Ciyrs and Pyra even though the connection between the Eden and the healer would never go any further than just a very close friendship.

"Ciyrs and Eliana can't always do the healing," Eden explained, "It takes so much energy that it can put them at risk if they try to heal too serious of an injury, or too many people at once. We've been trying to find a way to help that."

"If there is a war coming, there will be injuries, potentially a lot of them. And that means that Ciyrs and Eliana are not going to be able to handle the healing completely by themselves. We need that potion finalized as soon as possible. Can the three of you go work on it now?"

Eliana and Eden nodded and stood. Ty watched Samira turn her attention to Zuri and Leia.

"If the two of you can come with me, we can go to the cave and get an idea of where it goes. That is going to be at the center of all of the planning."

"Samira," Ty started, reaching out a hand to place on her shoulder, "The warriors can plan their battles. They do not need you to do it for them."

"Don't question your mate, Ty."

Pyra's intense voice right behind him made Ty jump slightly and he turned to face the warriors who had gathered close to them.

"We are coming with you to the cave," Samira told Pyra.

"She's smart and she's brave," Pyra said, "Be proud of her."

"You can't bring the women into battle, Pyra," Ty insisted.

"We aren't going into battle tonight," Samira said, "We are finding out where the cave leads and coming up with strategies. If I can help with that, why shouldn't I?"

Ty knew that he had no argument against her. There was nothing that he was going to be able to say that was going to stop her from doing exactly what she wanted to do. Just like she had been able to convince him that she was not too young to be his mate despite his mind telling him that she was and him trying his hardest to resist her, if she was set on being a part of the preparations for the battle with the warriors, he was not going to be able to convince her to do anything else. The thought was frustrating, but at the same time it made him even more proud to be her mate. Like Pyra had said, she was smart and she was brave. These human women were proving that the Denynso had known nothing about Earth and its inhabitants.

"We're leaving now," Pyra said, starting toward the door.

"Are you coming with me?" Samira asked.

Ty felt a surge of protectiveness and knew that there was no way he was going to be able to let her go off into some unknown area of the planet where there very well could be direct connection point between the compound and the Klimnu without him. He nodded and she returned the gesture, extending her hand to him. Ty took her hand and intertwined their fingers, immediately feeling calmer when his palm pressed against hers and he could feel her soft skin touching his.

They filed out of the meeting hall and Ty watched as Eliana, Eden, and Ciyrs took a sharp turn and headed off toward Ciyrs' shop. Those three had been working tirelessly on the ointments for weeks and he was hoping that they were going to find the right formula soon. The war was not going to wait, which meant they were running out of time.

Ty and Samira followed the warriors as they made their way across the compound, walking so quickly that she had to jog to keep up. Leia and Zuri caught up with them so that they all walked together, moving across the compound toward an area that Ty had never seen. Though he had spent his entire life in the compound, because he was not a warrior, he had not had reason to spend much time roaming around and exploring the borders. It was only the warriors who had to go on patrol who had the opportunity to really learn the entirety of the land that surrounded the compound. Now it seemed that part of that land had been breached, allowing the Klimnu access to their compound and to them. They would need to not only find that breach and learn everything that they could about it, but find a way that they could use it effectively to fight off the Klimnu and keep them from ever returning.

4

———

I still wasn't sure exactly what I was doing even as I followed the warriors through the compound. Holding Ty's hand gave me strength and I squeezed it slightly the further we got away from the meeting hall so that feeling it in mind would make me feel braver as the distance between the brightly lit hall and us became greater and we got closer to the dark, unknown areas of the compound. I had only been on Uoria for two days and I had not had much opportunity to explore it during that time so I didn't know where we were headed or what we might encounter along the way. The thought was unnerving, but at the same time exciting. I knew now that I was a part of these people for the rest of my life and that I was going to do everything I could to ensure that they were safe and that we could all continue living our lives comfortably and happily in the compound.

The thought suddenly struck me and I felt my hand tighten on Ty's. He looked down at me with concern on his face. That was one of the strangest things that I had encountered during my time on the planet, but one that I was learning to love. While I was on Earth, I was not accustomed to men being considerably larger than me. Not only am I taller than most women, but I happened to spend the vast majority of my time at a university involved in a department that seemed to be dominated by men who were smaller than average. The result was me being taller than, just as tall, or only an inch or two shorter than all of the men who I encountered. This was most certainly not the case when it came to being on Uoria, and especially not being near Ty. My mate was tremendous beyond description and just standing beside him made me feel small, delicate, and protected.

I needed that feeling now as the realization hit me that choosing him meant choosing to leave Earth forever. I could not be with him and live on my own planet, which meant that I was going to have to leave everything that I knew and the people I cared about behind. It was a sudden and frightening realization, but one that I came to without hesitation. Now that I was bonded to Ty, I couldn't imagine a single moment of my life not devoted to him. It didn't even cross my mind to be sad about leaving Earth, or even bitter at the thought that I was going to be the one who was expected to make such a complete and life-changing alteration. I would never for a second entertain the thought of asking him to leave Uoria to be with me on Earth. Though just 48 hours ago, I knew nothing about this man or what it meant to bond to him, the second that I did, I understood that meant I now, and forever, belonged to this planet and these people.

I had been so lost in my thoughts that I didn't realize we had left behind all of the buildings of the compound and were now walking past a lake filled with purple water. It was quiet and beautiful, but something inside me felt the tightness of apprehension in my chest when we started to walk along its edge. I had never been completely comfortable around water when I was living on Earth, and the purple of the water combined with the knowledge that I was on a totally different planet made me wonder what could possibly lurk beneath that surface. I took a step further away from the edge and Ty smiled down at me. The fact that he didn't say anything about the water or what was living in there seemed to confirm to me that I should be nervous.

When we got the rest of the way around the lake I saw that we had approached a large bank of cliffs. I noticed Ero stiffen where he stood in front of us and heard Zuri gasp. They grabbed hands and looked at each other.

"What is it?" I asked.

Zuri turned to look at me.

"This is where Ero and I came the night that we arrived back here. We had a picnic right by the lake and then went up on top of that cliff."

She pointed to a cliff nearby.

"I don't understand."

"The cave is at the base of that cliff," Pyra said from the front of the group, "If the Klimnu are using that tunnel to connect with the compound as we suspect that they are, that means that they could have been within just a few feet of Ero and Zuri when they were up there and the two of them didn't even know it. Everything that has been said near these cliffs might have been overheard by the Klimnu, and they could be using that passage to get in and out of the compound unnoticed. We think that the Traitor has known about the tunnel for quite a while and has been using it not only to bring the Klimnu information and supplies, but also to get to them and back into the compound quickly without anyone realizing that he was gone. That's how he was able to betray us so completely and for so long."

"Who is he talking about?"

"There was a warrior named Ullie," there was a hiss from a few of the warriors and Ty turned to them sharply, his hand coming up as if to quiet them, "Refusing to say his name is just giving his memory power. Don't let the sound of that one word be what is going to weaken you when you face battle with the Klimnu. If you let it be your defeat, it will be, but if you use it to enrage and empower you, it will only make you more effective when it comes time to fight."

"Ty's right," Pyra said and Ty felt a surge of pride go through him, "We aren't going to revere Ullie. We are going to remember what he did to us and ensure it never happens again." He turned to Samira, "Ullie fashioned himself as a warrior. He came to battle with us and fought beside us. Then he made an alliance with the Klimnu and enabled them to breach our compound and discover our defense plans. He is why they were able to injure Eden, capture Leia, hold her prisoner, and nearly kill her, and try to do the same to Eliana. We found out about his betrayal while we were in battle with the Klimnu but it was not enough to prevent another battle and to completely eliminate them."

The group started walking toward the cliffs again and Samira hurried to keep step with them.

"What happened to Ullie?" she asked.

Ty glanced down at her with a stern face.

"Pyra killed him."

Samira stopped short. She had always heard about the Denynso and their reputation for being fierce and fearsome warriors. She knew that they had fought wars with other species attempting to take over their section of Uoria and protected the planet from many threats. Hearing Ty describe Ullie's death so matter-of-factly, though, was a shocking, harsh hit of reality that made her truly come to the realization that they were not just talking about a distant and abstract threat, or going to see something that could be dangerous in theory. They were marching into war.

Suddenly something strange occurred to her and she ran forward to talk to Pyra.

5

———

Ty followed after Samira, he wanted to be near her to hear what she had to say to Pyra as much as he wanted to protect her. He was quickly learning that the unexpected followed her, and that he was probably never going to feel completely confident that he knew what was going to happen next. That was something that he truly loved about her.

That realization hit Ty hard. He knew that he was drawn to her and incredibly turned on by her. He had even come to terms with the fact that even though she seemed so young, she was a grown woman who was more than enough mate for him. He had not had time, however, to wrap his mind around the emotions that all of that entailed, and he certainly hadn't thought, until that very second, that he loved her. His mind reeled at the thought and he longed to grab her, spin her around in his arms, and tell her not just that he loved her, but that he wanted to spend every moment of the rest of his life loving her.

Now was not the time, though. He wanted that moment just with Samira, not with most of the warriors of the clan, Leia, and Zuri. That was something that he needed to express to her when they were alone; when he could whisper it to her as he slowly undressed her, laid her down on his bed, and made love to her over and over again. The thought buoyed him as he caught up with Samira and heard her talking animatedly to Pyra.

"Don't you get what I'm telling you? You said that Ullie was a warrior. That means that he was most likely around your size, right? At least around the size of the other warriors."

"Yes," Pyra replied.

"Well, if you can't get anywhere near the tunnel to find out what is on the other side, why do you think that Ullie could?"

They had made it to the foot of the cliff and were making their way over the rocky terrain to a section several feet off the ground where Ty could see the wide mouth of a cave. He had heard the warriors talking about that cave before. Several had even brought some of the women there when they wanted to be alone. None had ever thought anything strange about it. Now, however, it seemed to stare down at them ominously, gaping in the reddish-brown stone of the cliff as if tempting them to come in and meet their fate.

Pyra paused and turned to look at Samira. Ty could see the look on his face changing gradually as if he was processing what Samira had said to him.

"I guess he couldn't."

"No, he couldn't. Which means that either he was

using another part of the cave to interact with the Klimnu..."

"Or there was someone else helping him."

"Exactly. Now what we have to do is figure out which one of those is the case. If it is just that there is another section of the tunnel that you couldn't find that is big enough for all of you to fit in, or there is some way that that tunnel is bigger than you thought it was, that is not that big of a deal. In fact, it would just make it that much easier to get to the Klimnu. If it is that there was someone else helping Ullie, though, we are dealing with much bigger problems."

Ty's chest constricted painfully as a surge of anger and protectiveness rolled through him. He wasn't even a warrior and he had been infuriated when he found out that Ullie had betrayed all of them and was essentially funneling them into the hands of the Klimnu. Now that he had found and bonded with Samira, this anger and was even greater. She was bringing out the beast in him, and for the first time he had no interest in waiting at the compound putting together packs of supplies for the warriors and being ready to take care of them when they came back. He could leave that to the women. He wanted to be a part of the fighting.

"How do we find out?" he asked.

"We have to go into the cave," Samira told him.

She looked over at Leia and Zuri, who stepped forward toward her, nodding as if they understood exactly what Samira needed even though she hadn't said it. Ty reached toward Samira but she shook her head at him.

"The warriors and you are too big to get inside, Pyra

already said that. We have to start under the assumption that the tunnel truly is as small as they thought it was when they found it and then go from there. That means that we have to go in. It's the only way."

Samira got on her toes and lifted her mouth to Ty's. He kissed her gently, wanting to draw as much of the feeling of her as possible into him so that he could feel less afraid while she was out of his sight. As their lips parted he could see that Ero and Zuri, and Leia and Gyyx were kissing as well, two more pairs of mates drawing strength and confidence from one another. The other warriors waited patiently for the expressions of their bonds to be over. Even those who were not bonded understood the importance and solemnity of the bond and would not try to interfere with a moment between mates.

Samira turned to Pyra when she stepped back from Ty.

"Show us where to go."

Pyra started climbing up the side of the cliff and the women followed. The path was steep, but they all held their own as they traversed the uneven ground and climbed over rocks and jutting sections of the wall. Ty followed close behind them, wanting to be there to catch her just in case Samira happened to lose her footing and fall down the side of the cliff. Gyyx and Ero scrambled up behind him, their eyes locked on their own mates as they went. Beneath them were the rest of the warriors, watching them with expressions on their faces that said they very much hoped none of them were going to go tumbling down the cliff.

Fortunately, they all made it to the plateau in front of

the mouth of the cave safely and formed a line so that they all could stare into the cave. The darkness inside was so intense Ty felt like he could reach out and touch it.

"How did you find out about the tunnel?" Samira asked.

"We were doing our patrol and we heard a sound from inside the cave so we decided to see if there was anyone in there. We thought everyone was accounted for in the compound, so we wanted to make sure that no one was hurt in there. You go just a few yards into the cave and then the ground suddenly drops off into the tunnel. I could only make it down the tunnel a couple of feet before it got so tight that I almost couldn't get myself back out."

"If I had known that I was going to be spelunking today, I probably would have chosen a little bit better of an outfit," Samira said, adjusting her shirt down over her waistband, "Alright, ladies. Are you ready?"

The other two women voiced their affirmation and stepped forward so that the three stood separate from their mates and Pyra. Ty saw Gyyx reach into the bag he wore around his hip and pull out a torch. He handed it to Samira, reached back into his bag, and pulled out a flint. He lit the torch and stroked Leia's face one more time before stepping away.

"Go straight in, go as far as you can, and then come back," Pyra said. He reached into the bag on his own hip and pulled out his dagger, handing it to Samira by the handle, "If you find any Klimnu or anything else that scares you, don't hesitate. Kill it and run."

Samira nodded, took a breath, and started into the cave.

6

All of the fear I had been trying to suppress as I followed the warriors to the cliffs suddenly hit me as I stood there looking into the cave. The torch in one hand, the dagger in the other, and the lingering feeling of Ty's lips against mine, however, gave me confidence as I squared my shoulders and started forward into the darkness. Zuri and Leia followed me, coming close to my sides but staying just a step behind as if allowing me to take the lead.

We walked carefully, none of us knowing what to expect as we stepped past the opening to the cave. None of us had ever been inside it before and if I didn't miss my guess none of us were familiar enough with the topography and composition of Uoria to know if the caves on this planet were anything like the ones on Earth. I had only gotten the chance to read up a little bit on the planet and all I had learned was that there were many different areas of the planet and a huge enough variety of climates and features that I could safely guess it did not maintain the same rules as Earth. While that was an exciting thought if I had the opportunity to just roam around and explore, it made venturing into the darkness of the cave even more frightening because I had no idea what I was going to encounter with each step.

I could hear my own breath as we walked through the wide first chamber of the cave. The torch splashed orange and yellow light through the chamber, cutting through the darkness and illuminating the sandy ground at our feet. The floor of the cave was studded with sharp stalagmites, the tips sparkling like ice in the light of the torch even though it wasn't cold enough in the cave for them to actually be frozen. As we walked deeper into the cave I noticed that the walls that had been far enough apart that I hadn't even been able to see them in the light of the torch were starting to close in. We took a few more steps and I saw the entrance to the tunnel that Pyra had talked about. It would have been easy to miss if we hadn't been looking specifically for it. As it was, I almost didn't notice it.

The walls seemed to close in completely, giving the impression that the first chamber was the entirety of the cave. Behind a particularly massive stalagmite that disappeared up into the darkness, however, was a narrow, low opening. The edges of the opening were uneven, but smooth, so it was difficult to tell if the wall had formed like that, or if someone, or something, had broken through the wall many years before and the edges had weathered over time.

"Yeah, there's no way that the warriors could get in

there far," Leia said as I held the torch a little higher so that more light shined on it.

"I'm surprised that Pyra was able to even get in it at all, much less go a few feet into it," I replied in agreement.

"I don't even know if Ero could make it very far in there," Zuri said. Leia and I both looked at her and she shrugged, "I love my mate dearly, but he is tiny compared to the others. I've embraced it."

We laughed, thankful for the moment of levity that broke the fearful tension that was building in the cave. I let out a breath and handed Zuri the torch.

"Hold this up so that as much light as possible gets in there. I don't know how tight it is past this entry so I don't want to be in there with an open flame." She nodded and help up the torch. Leia stepped up and stood to her side so that her body would block some of the light and prevent it from dissipating throughout the cave, "Alright," I said, "Here I go."

I ducked my head and stepped through the opening. I probably could have walked through it without ducking, but I thought I would be cautious until I made it into the tunnel. As soon as I stepped in, I reached above me and found that the ceiling was higher than the top of the entry, but still only a few inches from my head. I opened my arms as far as I could get them and found that the walls were so close my elbows were still bent when I flattened my palms on either wall.

"Are you OK?" Zuri asked from the outer chamber of the cave.

"I'm fine," I replied, taking a few more cautious steps, "It is really tight in here. There is definitely no way the guys could have gotten a whole lot further than I am right now." I paused for a second, "Even Ero."

Both of the other women laughed and I started forward again. The light from the torch illuminated several feet ahead of me, but all I saw was the darkness. I held the dagger tightly in my hand, occasionally adjusting my grip so that I felt I had absolute control over the blade just in case I came upon another visitor of the tunnel who was less than pleased to see me.

The tunnel got no wider as I walked, but I could feel the ground beneath my feet start to dip so that I knew it was leading me down through the cliff and into the ground. It was a strange feeling, knowing that I had started many feet above the heads of the warriors and in a few moments, I would be beneath them. Orienting had never been my strong point, but I was struggling with every ounce of processing ability that I had to keep track of the direction that I was moving and figure out where I was headed so that I could tell Pyra when I made it back. I couldn't let myself think "if".

"Zuri, it's tight in here, but I'm running out of light, do you think that you'd be OK bringing the torch in?" I called back over my shoulder.

The path ahead of me had gotten so dark that I wasn't able to see more than a few inches and I wasn't comfortable continuing on without light if I didn't absolutely have to.

"Do I think I would be OK like you think I might get stuck in there, or do I think I would be OK like you think I might catch us on fire if I go in there?" she called back.

"Well...both...maybe...just a little bit," I said cautiously, trying not the offend her.

Zuri was beautiful, but the truth was she was a little bigger even than me, and I wasn't entirely convinced that she would be able to navigate the tighter curves of the tunnel, especially if it got any smaller.

"Well, damn. That's comforting," she said.

I could hear in her voice that she wasn't upset. Ero had done amazing things for her in even the small amount of time that they had spent together and I would have to remember to thank him for the love, comfort, and confidence that he had given this woman who had meant so much to me during some of the most difficult times in my life.

"Sorry."

"It's alright. I'm on my way. Leia can bring up the rear and at least her tiny self will be able to get out in case all goes to hell and we burst into flames in here."

"Geez, Zuri, you sure do know how to make a girl feel better when she's creeping through the darkness holding a dagger."

"The things we do for our men."

I heard Zuri's voice close behind me and felt the warmth of the flame from the torch glowing on my back. I glanced over my shoulder at her and smiled.

"Don't I know it," I joked back, "But with the things that Ty is capable of, I am just fine with this little contribution."

Zuri let out a sound like she knew exactly what I was talking about.

"I am fine with just about anything as long as Ero keeps doing the same things to me that he was doing when we were on top of this cliff."

I laughed, but as soon as the sound made it all the

way out of my throat, I felt the tension build inside me again. We were trying so hard to talk casually and joke about our men to distract us from walking down the tunnel, but it didn't have as much of an effect as we were hoping. Instead, as soon as I stopped talking, I felt even more nervous than I had before.

7

————

"**W**here are they?" Ty growled as he paced in front of the cave.

"Calm down, Ty," Pyra said, "They have only been in there for a few minutes. Everything is fine."

"That's really easy for you to say, Pyra. Your mate is safely in a healer's shop playing around with herbs and leaves and shit trying to come up with healing potions. Mine is wandering around in a rock tunnel that none of us have any idea what might be in it, where it leads, or if it is being used to bring our enemies into our compound. I'm a little stressed out right now."

"So, I take it you got over your whole 'she's too young' thing and finally bonded with her?" Pyra asked.

Ty stopped pacing long enough to glare at him briefly, and then went back to pacing.

"Yes."

"And?"

"And what? It was the most incredible experience of

my life, I'm hopelessly in love with her, and now I'm terrified that I've just watched her walk into her death. How is it that a group of warriors and a nurturer just sent three women into a potentially extremely dangerous tunnel with nothing more than a torch and a dagger?"

"They're going to be fine, Ty. You need to learn to have some faith in your mate. I know they seem small, but if Eden has taught me anything in my time with her, it is that human women are far more capable than we give them credit for. Zuri tells me that Samira is incredibly smart and resourceful. I wouldn't have let them go in if I didn't think that they would be safe."

"And what happens if they aren't? What happens if they get into the tunnel and it turns out that the Klimnu are using it, and they are in there? What then? Do you really think that they will be able to fight them off with a single dagger? We have no idea how many of them there are, and reserves could have arrived since the last battle. If we can't get in to them, it would be hopeless."

"So, talk to her. Connect with her and make sure that she's OK. She might be able to tell you what she's seeing."

Pyra walked away, leaving Ty alone near the mouth of the cave. Ty stared into the darkness, straining to hear even the smallest hint that the women had made it into the tunnel or were headed back toward him. When only silence greeted him, he closed his eyes, took a breath, and concentrated on connecting directly to Samira.

"Are you alright?" he asked.

He waited a few tense moments.

"We're fine," he finally heard and felt his body relax slightly, "Pyra was right. This tunnel is extremely small. I didn't see anything that indicated that there might be a larger section or some kind of false wall that might open it up more. This is definitely it."

"How far have you gone?"

"Pretty far. The ground is getting steeper. I think we are probably all the way underground now. It's cold and feels kind of clammy down here."

"That's what the Klimnu feel like," he thought absently.

"I've never seen them."

"Zuri and Leia have. They'll tell you."

"I know. Wait..."

The connection went silent and Ty felt panic building inside him again.

"What? Samira? What's going on?"

"I feel air moving."

"What does that mean?"

"Air doesn't move inside a closed space. If I can feel air moving, it means that we are getting close to an opening in the tunnel. Get near Pyra. I want to be able to talk to him."

Ty called out to Pyra and gestured for him to come closer.

"Samira says that she can feel moving air," he told the massive warrior, "She wanted to be able to talk to you."

"Ask her if she can tell where the air is coming from."

Ty did as Pyra asked. It felt strange standing beside Pyra and having a silent conversation with his mate. He felt like the ability to communicate this way was such a private thing and it almost seemed inappropriate to be sharing it with Pyra. Of course, he knew that the way Ciyrs had healed Eden when she first came to the planet had created such a strong link between them that they were actually able to communicate telepathically, so Ty knew that it could be much worse. He didn't know how he would cope with knowing that another man was able to roam freely through Samira's thoughts or talk with her without anyone knowing what he was saying.

"Tell Pyra that I don't know yet. We can feel it on our faces and on our sides, so either it is one big opening, or there are two."

"Is the torch holding up?"

"The air in here is getting damper. It's fine for now, but I'm a little worried that it is going to go out soon. What do we do if it does?"

"Run the blade of the knife against the wall. Hopefully it will generate enough of a spark that you will be able to relight the torch."

"And if not?"

Ty hesitated. He didn't really know what to tell her. The thought of her being stuck inside the tunnel far underground without even so much as a light source made him feel sick.

"It'll work, Baby. Just keep going. I'm right here. Just know that I'm right here."

8

———

Ty's words gave me strength as I continued walking toward the feeling of the moving air. It was cold and thin, not what I expected coming from deep underground. Then I remembered my few visits to the caverns on Earth when I was younger and the way the air felt thinner once we got deep inside them. As I thought that I started to wonder if I was always going to be trying to draw parallels between the world I left behind and the one that I chose for my future. I wanted to embrace Uoria for all it had to offer, which meant that I would need to find a way to stop thinking about it as something to compare to Earth and start realizing all of its potential and beauty.

I took a calming breath and asked Zuri to bring the torch a little closer. The warmth from the flame seemed to dry the air around me just enough so that it no longer felt like it was crawling across my skin and I glanced down to realize that the ground at my feet had become wet and muddy. The terrain had definitely changed and I had the strange feeling that we had entered an area far from the cliffs where we had started. It felt like we had done more than just walk through a tunnel, that we were much further away than we should have been.

"Ty?" I called out to him in my mind.

"Yes? I'm here."

"Can you go into the cave?"

"Pyra said we won't fit in the tunnel."

"No, no, that's OK. You definitely won't fit. I just need you to find the entrance to the tunnel and yell into it for me."

"Did your torch go out? Are you lost?"

Ty's thoughts were starting to sound frantic and I tried to send him calming vibes. I didn't know if it worked that way, but I was hoping that I could send him soothing feelings through my thoughts that would work the same way holding his hand would.

"I'm not lost and the torch is still just fine. Don't worry about that. I just need you to go into the cave, walk all the way to the back, and find the entrance to the tunnel. Pyra can probably show it to you. When you get there, just shout in to me."

"Alright."

Ty didn't sound convinced. I kept walking as I waited to hear his voice, but it never came.

"Did you shout?" I asked, hoping that he would say that he hadn't.

"Yeah. I screamed your name a few times."

"As loud as you could?"

"Yeah."

I took a breath.

"OK. Is Pyra there with you?"

"Yes."

"Have him try."

I waited for a few seconds but still didn't hear anything.

"Did either of you hear the guys shouting?" I asked Zuri and Leia.

I could barely make out Leia's face behind Zuri, but I could see that both women were shaking their heads. I closed my eyes briefly, trying to orient myself and figure out what this meant.

"How far do you think that we walked?" I asked.

"What do you mean?" Zuri asked.

"Do you think that we've come so far that if the guys were shouting into the tunnel we wouldn't be able to hear them?"

"No. Those men are loud; besides, the tunnel would only amplify the sound. We haven't gone far enough that the sound couldn't travel to us. Why?"

"I had them shout into the entrance to the tunnel."

Zuri and Leia both got nervous expressions on their faces that told me they understood exactly what I was saying.

"How did we get that far away?" Leia asked.

"I don't know," I replied, "but do we go back or do we keep going and try to find out where this tunnel leads?"

There was a moment of heavy silence. Even Ty wasn't talking to me through his thoughts.

"We came in here because Pyra and the other warriors believe that this tunnel has something to do with the Klimnu being able to get into the compound and attack and we are the only ones who could get inside," Zuri said slowly and carefully, "If we don't keep going, there'll be no way for any of us to find out what's going on, and it could leave the entire clan at even greater risk."

"You're right," I said, nodding, "We have to keep going. Turning back now isn't going to help anything."

"We're going to keep going," I told Ty through my thoughts.

"Do you want me to keep shouting?" he asked.

"No," I replied, "Just stay close to the entrance and as soon as you hear us coming, let me know. It might be a little while, but just listen for me. When you hear my voice, shout in to me."

"I will. Samira?"

"Yes?"

"I love you."

I felt my breath catch in my throat and my grip loosen on the knife. I had to regain my composure quickly to prevent myself from dropping it.

"I love you, too."

If I had been vacillating at all in my determination to continue forward, that had sealed it. I had never seen the Klimnu and I didn't know exactly what they were capable of, but in that moment, there was absolutely nothing that could have frightened me enough to stop me from fighting to protect Ty, his people, and our future together. I tightened my grip on the knife even further, set my jaw, and surged forward. I picked up speed until I almost left the other women behind. The faster I walked, the less nervous I felt, and suddenly I realized that I was excited to find out what was at the end of the tunnel. I knew for certain now that if this was in fact the path by which Ullie had been interacting with the Klimnu to remain undetected, he had not been acting alone. Unless the creatures had always come to him through that tunnel, which was highly unlikely considering the amount of vigilance the warriors used to protect the compound, there was someone else, someone small, who was acting as a go-between for the Traitor and the Klimnu.

I was determined I was going to find out who that was.

T y sat on the floor of the cave beside the entrance to the tunnel, leaned back against the cold stone wall so that he could listen for any sound coming from the tunnel. It felt like he had been sitting there for hours and he wanted to connect with Samira and talk to her the entire time she was away, but he knew that she needed to be able to concentrate if she was going to gather all of the information that they needed about the tunnel and wherever it led and then get back to them safely. Pyra had gone back outside of the cave to talk to the other warriors and the silence surrounding Ty was becoming overwhelming. He closed his eyes and went back over the events of the last few days in his mind.

He never expected this. From the time he was a little child he knew that he was not going to be a warrior. The destiny of each Denynso man is set from the time of birth and it is evident early on what a man is going to do with his life, whether that is to join up forces as one of the clan's fearsome warriors so that he can march into battle and help the others defend the clan and the planet, or take on another role within the group. As a very young child it was already evident that being a warrior was not what he was made to do. While he was nearly as massive as Pyra, his spirit was gentle and nurturing, not aggressive. He had never been prone to fighting or lashing out. Instead, he was drawn to cooking and baking. He used his skills to prepare food for the warriors to take with them while they were in battle and to strengthen them when they came back.

It wasn't until Samira came along that he ever felt the intensity of what the warriors felt. She sparked something in him that was so powerful he was almost afraid of it himself. Suddenly he was ready to use his tremendous size and strength for more than he had ever used it for, and was ready to step forward and be a part of defending the planet from the Klimnu in what they hoped would be their final showdown. He always knew that he would change when he met his mate, but he never expected that the change would be so drastic and powerful. It brought to mind elements of his inner self that he had hidden for so long he didn't even know if he could still use them, elements that he had always feared and tried to forget that he had, but now knew may be the key to him helping the warriors.

"Can you hear me?"

The sound of Samira's voice suddenly coming through the tunnel broke Ty out of his thoughts and brought him to his feet. For a moment, he thought that he may be hearing her talking to him through her mind, but her voice sounded too loud for that to be what was happening. He leaned into the mouth of the tunnel.

"Samira?" he shouted.

"Ty! Is that the first time you heard me calling for you?"

"Yes. Just now. Are you OK?"

"We're fine. We're coming your way, but the torch finally went out so it's dark. Just keep talking to me."

Ty nearly sagged with relief. He felt a smile break across his face as he crouched down so that it was easier to call into the tunnel.

"I'm here, Baby. I'm right here. Just keep coming toward me. Listen to my voice. I'm right here waiting for you."

Ty kept talking, repeating himself over and over because he couldn't think of anything else to say that he would want the other two women listening to as they walked through the tunnel. Finally, he heard footsteps coming toward him and a few moments later he could feel Samira's presence near him. He reached out and his hands touched her. Even in the intense darkness he knew he was touching his mate. She curled into his arms and he pulled her back away from the mouth of the tunnel so that the other two women could step out into the main chamber of the cave.

"Pyra!" Ty shouted, "Bring us a new torch."

Heavy footsteps sounded in the front part of the chamber and Ty saw the bright glow of a new torch flame cutting through the darkness toward them. They rushed toward it, using the illumination to guide them around the stalagmites that jutted up from the floor of the cave. As soon as they stepped out onto the plateau, he saw

Samira take a deep breath and lean over to rest her hands on her knees. She continued to draw in long breaths as if she were trying to replace all of the air from the tunnel in her body with fresh air. He stroked her back gently, trying to calm her, as Gyyx and Ero rushed forward to scoop Leia and Zuri into their arms. Everyone stayed silent for a few seconds as the men comforted and cuddled their mates. Finally, Pyra stepped forward.

"What did you find?" he asked.

Samira straightened and curled close to Ty's side before she spoke. He wrapped his arm around her waist, giving over as much of his strength to her as she needed.

"I don't know if we'd be able to describe it to you effectively," Samira said.

"But I can draw it for you," Leia said, "I just need some paper and a pencil and I can sketch everything we saw out for you."

"Let's get back to the compound, then. The sooner we can find out what you saw, the sooner we can start building our defense plan."

Leia, Zuri, Gyyx, Ero, and Pyra started back down the side of the cliff to where the rest of the warriors were waiting for them. Ty held Samira back, waiting until the last of Pyra's Mohawk disappeared beneath the edge of the cliff to turn to her. He curled her up into his arms so that her chest pressed against his and her arms looped tightly around his waist. She rested her head against his chest for a brief moment and then looked at him, leaning back slightly so that he could see her entire face gazing up at his.

"I love you, Samira," he said softly.

A smile broke across her lips and he thought he saw

the glimmer of tears in her dark eyes. She cuddled him a little closer, bringing her body forward so that as much of her pressed against him as possible.

"I love you, too, Ty."

His heart swelled and he felt his body getting hot again. The heat radiating off of his skin told him even more that he had definitely found his mate in Samira. That searing, glowing heat told all other females to stay away from him and gave both him and his mate even more reason to take off their clothes. She took her arms from around his waist and trailed her fingers down his arms, tracing the curves of his muscles with her fingertips. He could see her eyes getting smoky as she touched his skin, feeling the warmth on hers.

"I wish we didn't have to go with the warriors," he murmured to her.

She nodded, her long eyelashes dipping down over her eyes as she continued to touch him tenderly.

"I do, too. How long do you think that the meeting will be?" she purred back.

"I don't know. However long it takes for you three to tell us what you saw and for them to decide how we should move forward with the war."

The mention of war seemed to dampen the smoldering building inside her and she got a solemn look on her face.

"What's going to happen, Ty?"

Ty put his hands on her arms, gently squeezing her.

"Everything's going to be fine. I promise. The Denynso are the best warriors in the galaxy. Once we figure out how the Klimnu have been learning about us and getting into the compound so easily, the warriors will be able to defeat them."

"Why aren't you a warrior?"

The question stung him a little, but he had to remind himself that she wasn't familiar with their kind and didn't know how things worked with them. She wouldn't understand that it wasn't his choice what role he was going to play within the clan, or what skills he would have. From the little bit that he knew of Earth, he knew that each person had a choice of what they were going to do with their lives and what types of skills and abilities they were going to use throughout their lives. He figured that as strange as that seemed to him, it must seem strange to Samira that each of the Denynso were born to fulfill a certain role and meet their specific responsibilities so that the entire clan operated effectively.

"I wasn't meant to be," he answered.

He expected her to pry, to try to figure out more, or to criticize him for not being one of the powerful, fierce men who had a reputation throughout the galaxy. Instead, she smiled at him and got up on the tips of her toes to touch a kiss to his lips.

"We should probably catch up with everyone else before the think that we've been kidnapped. I don't think that they need any more stress in their battle planning."

10

———

I pondered what Ty had told me as we hurried across the plateau and down the side of the cliff. The rest of the group was already considerably ahead of us and we took off at a run to catch up with them. Even at my height, though, Ty's long legs created a stride with a length that far outdid mine, putting him several steps ahead of me within just a few seconds. I called up to him and he turned back to me. As soon as I caught up to him, he reached down and scooped me off of my feet, draping me over his shoulder so that he could carry me as he ran. I let out a scream, but it quickly turned into a laugh as I bounced along with my head at his waist level.

I was dizzy by the time we caught up to the rest of the group and he finally lowered me back to my feet. He held me stable for a few seconds so that I could get my wits about me again and then we started back toward the compound. Everyone was silent as we walked, each person lost in his own thoughts and absorbed in his own worries. I fought off the ominous feelings that fell over the group, trying to remain positive as we walked. I knew that what we found at the end of that tunnel was going to change everything, and I needed to find as much strength as I could in my positivity before we had to tell them about it.

When we made it back to the meeting hall, I noticed that everyone who had been in the main room was now gone. The long tables and benches were empty and there was a strange sense of tension in the air like the walls and floor themselves knew that something was about to happen and they were bracing themselves for it. One of the warriors rushed out of the room and came back a few moments later carrying several large sheets of parchment and a dark pencil. Leia sat at one of the tables and spread the materials out in front of her. She took a breath like she was preparing herself and stretched and wriggled her fingers. She had the look of an artist who had not drawn in quite a length of time and was trying to get herself back into that flow that allowed her to create.

She picked up the pencil and let the tip hover above the parchment.

"The tunnel was long and narrow," she described, starting the sketch, "It was only a couple of inches taller than Zuri and Samira, and tight enough that we had to walk single file."

"That means that Ullie was not the only one helping the Klimnu," Pyra said, leaning on his palms on the table so that he could watch as Leia drew.

I nodded and picked up where Leia had left off.

"What's strange about the tunnel is that we noticed we seemed to have gone much further than we should have. I called out to Ty, but he couldn't hear me. There's no reason why he shouldn't have been able to hear my voice when I was calling to him from what I thought was just a few dozen yards away. Especially with my voice coming through a tunnel like that, he should have been able to hear me for much longer. The same goes for when we were heading back. He wasn't able to hear me until we were almost at the mouth of the tunnel."

"What do you think that means?" Gyyx asked.

"We aren't sure. What we know is that we walked for a while and then everything seemed to feel different. The tunnel got cold and wet, and then we started feeling moving air."

Leia took the page where she had drawn the tunnel and set it aside, pulling a fresh sheet closer to her.

"Samira had us wait in the tunnel while she went ahead. After a few seconds, we heard her calling for us. The tunnel took a sudden turn and when we came around it, the tunnel opened out into what looked like a jungle."

Leia started sketching, her hand moving feverishly across the paper as what we had seen in the subterranean jungle developed under the tip of her pencil. She drew out what had looked like massive trees hung heavily with thick, rope-like vines. The light produced by the torch seemed small once we were out of the tight tunnel and it only illuminated enough of the area to show that the tops of the trees seemed to connect with each other to create one thick, dark ceiling that overhung the entire area.

"How do the trees grow underground?" Pyra asked as we described the forest.

I shrugged.

"We don't know."

I kept describing the underground forest, letting Leia bring my words into visual reality on the page as she sketched the thick roots of the trees that spread through small sections of undergrowth. All around the trees was calm, deep-looking water. Though I couldn't see much of it, I knew that these surroundings didn't have the expansive feeling of being outside. We hadn't managed to go through a tunnel into an outdoor area of the planet. Instead, we were definitely in an underground chamber of the cave, contained within an area of indeterminate size.

"What else did you find?" Ty asked.

His voice sounded strained, like what we were telling him frightened him.

"We couldn't see much, but it looked like there were sections of the tree ceiling that were broken and there was a strange slime dripping from those areas. That's what started the torch going out; a big glob of it fell right on the flame. I got a little on my arm, too."

I held out my arm to show them where the goo had hit, and noticed that the skin was starting to redden. I touched it and it stung. Ty grabbed my arm and looked at the area.

"What's happening?"

I stared at my reddening skin and a memory suddenly popped into my mind. I turned to Zuri and held my arm out to her.

"Zuri, do you remember when you first got home and you had that section of your back that you said had been hurting? I looked at it and it was red and you said it stung when I touched it?"

Zuri nodded, reaching out toward my arm. I pulled it back sharply, shaking my head.

"What's wrong?" she asked.

"Is that where the Klimnu touched you while you were in the forest?"

I remembered what she had told me about the night that she ran from the meeting hall and ended up lost in the forest at the edge of the compound. A Klimnu had hung from one of the trees, dangling down to grab at her as she ran past. The experience had terrified her, but it had also apparently left a reaction on her skin.

"The Klimnu touched me more than I care to discuss while I was with them, though," Leia said, looking up from where she was sketching a droplet of the clear slime coming down from the trees, "And I never had a reaction like that."

"Maybe it is like an allergy. Some people react to it, and some people don't. I've never been near the Klimnu, so I don't know what they feel like, but you described them as slimy."

"Yeah, they're disgusting. They're like pale, slimy skeletons with long fingers and really disturbing eyes."

"Could this slime have something to do with that? Could some people be vulnerable to the slime and react really strongly to it, and other people be resistant to it?"

My mind was spinning as my research projects came pouring back to me and ideas started to form in my mind.

"What are you thinking, Samira?" Zuri asked.

She could recognize the look on my face as the one I always wore when things started to make sense to me. She had always been the one to nurture my curiosity and help me use my intelligence to work out solutions, form ideas, and discover new things through my research.

"I'm thinking that I need to get to Eden, Eliana, and Ciyrs."

11

———

Ty paced through the living room of his house, pausing every few steps to listen closely to see if he heard the door to his shop opening. It had been several hours since Samira and Zuri had run off with Pyra to Ciyrs's shop to tell them whatever it was that she had figured out. He had wanted to go along, but she told him that he should go home and get some rest, that it could be a while before she was finished. He knew that there wasn't really anything that he would be able to do to help, but he hated being away from her and not even knowing what was happening. A few times he thought about checking in with her telepathically, but he didn't know what she was doing and didn't want to risk distracting her at a critical moment and possibly ruining her work.

He took a deep breath to calm himself. Pacing around the house and worrying about her wasn't going to do anyone any good. If he was going to be a part of this war, he was going to have to start with being courageous enough to face the demons inside him and take control of the part of his destiny he had run from for so long.

Ty glanced toward the door one last time, and then looked around the room. He would have to start with something small, just to make sure that he could even do it anymore before he tried anything more impactful. His eyes fell on a small plant that sat on the table across the room. It was a bioluminescent fern he often used as illumination at night when he didn't want to access the solar energy collected from the panel on his roof and stored in a small cell that would allow him to do things throughout the home like turn on lights and heat water for a shower. It was nearly morning, but it was still dark enough that the vibrant blue glow of the plant stood out against the shadowy room.

He concentrated on the plant, allowing his thoughts to etch it in his mind. The longer he looked at it, the stronger the outline against his thoughts became until it seemed that everything else in his brain had gone completely black and all he could see was the glowing plant. When he had isolated it enough, he imagined his thoughts sending invisible ropes out of his mind and encircling the plant. He pulled with his mind and the plant trembled. Suddenly a scream in the back of his mind made the plant stop moving and he fell to his knees.

Ty gasped for breath, trying to stop the shaking of his body and to hold back the sharp tears that stung his eyes. The scream had been a memory, an echo that he would never be able to forget. He had heard it so many times in the years since it had actually happened and each time it had pushed him further and further away from the power contained within him. So far that now it seemed he may no longer be able to harness it.

"Ty?"

He had been so shaken by the scream that he didn't even realize the door to his shop had opened and Samira stepped into the living room. He lifted his head and looked at her. She ran forward toward him and dropped to her knees on the floor at his side, wrapping an arm around his back and tilting her head down to look him in the face.

"Hi," he managed weakly.

"What's wrong? What happened?"

Ty sat back on his heels and shook his head.

"I was trying to do something I haven't done in a long time. I was hoping that it might help the clan during the war, but I don't think that I can do it anymore."

"Why?"

He looked at her for a long second. He had never told anyone about this before. No one knew what had happened or how it had impacted him as he grew up. Telling the story would be painful and make him more vulnerable than he had ever been, but if there was anyone in the world who he could be that vulnerable in front of and not feel afraid, it was his mate. As safe as he made her feel, she made him feel the same way and he was finally ready, for the first time in his life, to be completely honest.

"My father killed my mother," he said cautiously, gauging her reaction carefully.

"Intentionally?" she asked softly.

"No. He loved her with everything in him. He would never hurt her on purpose."

"What happened?"

Ty drew in a deep breath, held it for a moment, and then let it out. This was a moment that could define his entire future, something that could truly end everything he had built for himself as he grew up and after his parents died. Samira looked back at him with wide, innocent eyes veiled with worry and genuine, deep love.

"My father had a skill that other Denynso don't. It is extremely rare. In fact, since his death, there has only been one other who has had it. One day he was using it and he lost control. My mother happened to be in the path and it killed her. He died less than a year later. Everyone thinks that he got sick, but I know that it was the heartbreak of being without her and the guilt of feeling like he caused her death that eventually just stole his will to live."

"I'm so sorry, Ty." Samira paused and brought her hand to his back to rub it gently, "Will you tell me something?"

Ty nodded.

"Are you the other Denynso with that skill? Is that what you were saying that you don't think you can do anymore?"

Ty nodded again, feeling the tears building in his eyes again.

"I haven't used it since my father died. Almost 20 years."

"Use it now," she said.

"What?"

"Use it now," she repeated matter-of-factly, "Show me."

She said it with such confidence, such absolute faith that he would be able to overcome this massive challenge; it gave him a surge of determination. Ty stood up again and brushed the tears away from his cheeks. Forcing the sound of the reverberating scream out of his mind, he turned his focus back to the plant. The sun was coming up now and the glow was not as strong, but he let his mind etch it against his thoughts again. The ropes of concentration shot out of his mind and coiled around the plant. He forced his focus to sharpen and in an instant the plant rose up off of the table and flew across the room into his outstretched hand.

12

―――――

I gasped as I saw Ty's hand close around the pot that held a strange looking plant. His eyes snapped to me and I saw his lips twitch before a smile curved them. He let out a short laugh as if he was completely shocked that it had actually worked. I smiled back at him.

"That was incredible!"

He laughed again and looked around the room. A moment later a cushion lifted off the couch and sailed through the air at him. He tossed it at me and I batted it away. Suddenly he took off and ran up the stairs toward his bedroom. I was so startled by his sudden movement that I didn't have a chance to react before I felt a tug in my belly. I looked up at him standing at the top of the stairs and met his eyes. He gave me a mischievous smile and the ground disappeared from under feet. I squealed at the realization that he was carrying me toward him telekinetically, but I barely had time to be frightened before he opened his arms and caught me.

I felt his heart pounding against my chest and his

erection pushing into my belly. Wrapping my legs around his waist, I leaned in and nipped at his neck, letting my teeth sink playfully into his skin. I followed the bite with a long draw of my tongue. Ty growled and grabbed my butt in both hands, digging his fingertips into me. He started toward the bed, but I pulled my head back to look at him.

"I am so gross from that tunnel."

He made a moaning sound in his throat and turned, carrying me down a short hallway toward a room I hadn't gone in the night before.

"I guess I'm just going to have to fix that for you," he said.

He lowered me to my feet and I saw that we were in a large bathroom. There was a sunken tub in the middle of the room and a series of marble shelves that looked like a small staircase along the wall beside the tub. Several bottles lined the shelves and I noticed what looked like a soft sponge on the edge closest to the tub.

Ty went to work undressing me, carefully and slowly removing each article of clothing and showering the newly exposed skin with gentle kisses. When I was completely naked, he turned on the faucet and took a bottle from the shelf. He drizzled some of the liquid from the bottle under the faucet and the tub filled with bubbles. They shimmered with an array of iridescent colors and a sweet, sultry smell rose to me. I inhaled deeply and felt his hand come to mine. He led me gently down into the tub and held my hand until I settled onto the seat along one side. I moaned as the warm water came up over my breasts and I closed my eyes, allowing my head to drop back against the side of the tub.

I could hear Ty undressing behind me and a moment later he stepped down into the tub with me. He bathed me silently, using the soft sponge to tenderly remove all of the grime I felt clinging to my skin from my time in the tunnel and then the hours I had spent in the shop with Ciyrs, Eden, and Eliana. When he was finished, he placed the sponge on the side of the tub and I felt him settle back so that he sat on the seat beside me. His hand touched my hip and I let the feeling guide me over to him and then up into his lap so that I faced him, straddling his hips.

My breasts brushed against his chest and I felt my breath deepen. The water made our bodies slick against each other, and the concealment of the bubbles increased my excitement as I moved my body against his to compensate for not being able to see it. Ty held me close to him, his head tucked into the curve of my neck and shoulder as one arm encircled my waist and the other hand explored my back and shoulders. His breath was labored as I felt the tip of his tongue touch my collarbone.

"Can I bring you into the bedroom now?" he whispered.

I shook my head.

"No."

"No?"

"Here."

I rolled my hips against him and felt him twitch. He lifted me enough to touch the tip of his erection to my opening and then eased me down until I settled into his lap, cradling him deep inside me. I clutched at his shoulders, whimpering at the intense, full feeling. When I opened my eyes again, he was staring at me, the glowing orange of his eyes seeming to burn into me.

"Tell me again," he said and I knew exactly what he wanted.

"I love you."

He lifted me slightly and thrust hard up into me.

"Tell me again," he growled.

"I love you," I gasped.

"Again."

"I love you."

Ty suddenly stood and lifted me off of his lap. In an instant I was on my hands and knees beside the tub. I cried out as Ty's tongue slid across me, slipping between my folds and concentrating on the throbbing swollen bud at my core. He repeated the action and I arched my back, sobbing at the incredible waves of pleasure he sent through me. Suddenly he knelt behind me and entered me again, pushing all the way inside me in one hard thrust. He buried his hand in my hair and I felt the other hand go to my hip to stabilize me as he pounded into me. I whimpered and moaned with each deep stroke, the intensity of the feelings making it difficult for me to hold myself up.

His hand left my hip and slipped around so that his fingers dipped between my thighs and almost instantly the sensations overwhelmed me. I screamed his name and pressed back against him, accepting one final hard thrust as I felt his cock throb and spill into me. He bent forward, his arm coming up around my waist to support me as he kissed the back of my shoulder and along my spine.

"I love you," he murmured into my skin, "I love you, I love you, I love you."

When we could move again, we got up and walked slowly into the bedroom, drying off with plush towels before slipping under the covers of the bed to sleep off the long, exhausting night. I lay on my side so that he could curl around me, fully enveloping me with his warm, soft skin. I held his hand and rested it over my heart, reveling in the synchronicity of our breath as we fell asleep.

13

"Are you sure you have to go so soon?" Ty groaned from the bed.

"Yes," Samira called to him from the bathroom where she was collecting her clothes from the floor, "I have to go back to my house and change before people catch onto the fact that I've been wearing the same thing since the morning after I got here."

Ty chuckled.

"You aren't going to stay there tonight are you?" he asked.

She stepped into the room and smiled at him.

"If I have my way, I'll never stay there again."

Ty crawled to the end of the bed and rested his hands on her hips so he could pull her close and kiss her.

"I'll tell the king and queen that they can consider that house vacant."

She grinned and kissed him again, lingering on his lips for a few moments before pushing him away as his hands started to travel to her breasts.

"Not now, Big Boy. We have things to do."

The statement was meant playfully, but it fell hard in Ty's gut. They had only slept for a few hours because they knew that the rest of the clan would be making their preparations and that every moment mattered. Suddenly he realized he hadn't even gotten a chance to ask her about what had happened in Ciyrs' office the night before.

"Did you figure out the healing potion?" he asked, climbing out of bed and heading for his bureau.

Her face lit up.

"I think we are really close. I suggested that we integrate some of the slime into the potion kind of like on Earth when doctors use small amounts of germs and viruses to create vaccinations. It gives the body the opportunity to learn to fight off that particular infection. I thought that maybe if we put the slime into the potion, it could counteract injuries and trigger the warriors' bodies to fight harder, speeding up their healing and protecting them from further injuries and reactions."

"Wow. You really are incredibly brilliant."

She flashed him a huge smile.

"That's what they tell me. Get dressed while I run to my house and change. I'll meet you at Ciyrs' shop."

An hour later Ty was walking up to the shop when he heard shouting. He started running, fear flooding him. When he burst into the shop, however, he saw that everyone was grinning and hugging each other.

"What's going on?" he asked.

"We think we figured out the healing potion," Ciyrs told him, "Thanks to your amazing mate, we are really ready for this showdown."

Ty crossed to Samira and kissed her.

"You are amazing," he agreed.

"What do we do now?" Pyra asked from where he stood against one wall, his hand rested protectively over Eden's belly.

The room fell quiet for a moment.

"We need to figure out who was helping Ullie," Samira said, "And I think that means going back to the tunnel."

"No," Ty said, "It was too dangerous the first time. You can't go again."

"We have to, Ty. There's no other way. I have been thinking about this a lot, and I am convinced that there is something about that tunnel that we don't know. It still doesn't make any sense that we only walked for what seemed like such a short time and then got so far away."

"Do you think there is some kind of portal or transporter in the tunnel?" Zuri asked.

"There might be. You said that the Klimnu have incredibly advanced technology on their original planet. What if they brought some of it here and put it in the tunnel so that they and whoever has been helping them can use it to get them to different areas of the planet more quickly?"

"If that underground forest that you found is some kind of Klimnu bunker, but they aren't the ones using the tunnel, how are they getting into it?"

Ty saw Samira's face get tense again like she was thinking through something complicated.

"I have a theory. It is outlandish, but it's all I have right now."

"Tell us."

Samira turned to Ty.

"Last night I had the warriors tell me everything about the Klimnu. What they are, where they come from, what they do, everything. Something that stood out to me was that they have the ability to look like something else when they want to confuse or manipulate people."

"That's right," Eliana said, "They did that to me."

"Me, too," said Leia.

"Me, too," said Eden.

Samira nodded at them.

"Zuri, I need you to show me exactly where you encountered that Klimnu. I can explain the rest once we get there."

The group left the shop and hurried toward the woods at the edge of the compound. When they got there, Samira looked around.

"Is this how you got to the prison that you burned down?" she asked.

The warriors confirmed that it was and Ty saw a smile starting to form on her lips.

"Look, Zuri. Look around you."

Zuri looked around for a few seconds and when her eyes dropped to the floor, Ty saw them grow wide.

"It's an inverse," she muttered.

Samira nodded.

"A reflection." She turned to Leia, "Leia, do you see it?"

Leia followed the same path with her eyes that Zuri did and suddenly a hand flew to her mouth.

"I don't understand," Ty said.

"Neither do I," Pyra added.

Samira gestured at the trees.

"These are the trees from the underground forest."

She pointed to branches overhead and the patchy leaves, "Those are what we saw as roots with bits of undergrowth around them. What we thought was water was the sky. And this," she leaned down and touched the thick moss and undergrowth that covered that section of the forest floor, "This is what we saw as the leaves that created the ceiling."

"It's a reflection," Pyra repeated what the women had said and Samira nodded, "What you thought you were seeing was wrong, but you were seeing something that was really there."

"Yes."

"That means," Zuri said, crouching down to touch some of the moss. She ran her hand across it for a moment, and then suddenly pulled it back, "Ero, could you pull this up for me?"

"Pull up the moss?" Ero asked.

"It shouldn't be difficult. Grab this edge and pull."

Ero did as he was asked and as soon as he pulled on the edge of the moss, it peeled away from the ground, revealing a narrow gouge in the ground shining around the edges with thick, clear slime.

14

I gave a mirthless laugh as the deep hole in the ground came into view. It was all coming together in my mind and I was watching it unfold in front of me. The warriors tensed around me as they all started to understand what was going on.

"There will be holes like this all the way through the forest right up to where the prison was. That's how so many of them survived the fire. All they had to do was find one of these holes and drop down into the chamber."

"What about the tunnel, though?" Ty asked, "You were so wrapped up in feeling like it took you further than you thought. Did you feel like you walked this far?"

"Definitely not. The Klimnu definitely put a transporter in that tunnel that brought us from there all the way to here in between steps. But I don't think that it was meant to be used for getting the Klimnu from there to here or the other way around. If it was, you would have noticed them coming from that side of the compound."

"Why did they put it there?"

"I think it was for whoever was helping them along with Ullie. It had to be someone small enough to get through the tunnel easily and someone who would have access to another transporter that wouldn't be noticeable. Someone that no one would notice and no one would miss."

Suddenly Zuri's eyes widened.

"I know exactly who it was," she said, her voice sounding gravelly with fury, "Does anyone know what time it is?"

"Mid-afternoon," Ero told her.

"We don't have much time. Ero, I need you to get to the launch platform now. Don't let the shuttle leave."

Ero took off with such intensity that he was invisible within seconds.

"Do we all need to go?" Pyra asked.

"Two of you come with me to the launch platform. Some of you start finding as many of these holes as you can. The rest of you, find every warrior in the compound and get them to the meeting hall. Leia and Samira will meet you there and fill you in."

I watched as everyone dissipated to follow Zuri's instructions. Ty held my hand for a few lingering seconds and then gave it a squeeze.

"I'm going to help them find the holes," he said.

"No, we need you in the meeting hall."

"Why?"

"You said you wanted to fight. This is your chance."

We met eyes and without saying anything else, we started running toward the meeting hall. Soon I was stumbling over my own feet trying to keep up with him, and he swept me up to put me on his back so that he could carry me the rest of the way. I didn't know if I was ever going to get used to being carried around like a rag doll, but part of me loved feeling so small and having him take control like that.

By the time we got to the meeting hall, the main room was loud with the voices of all of the warriors of the clan except for those who were back in the woods finding all of the holes that led down into the forest chamber. Pyra hadn't bothered to go the stage on the other side of the room. Instead, he was standing in the middle of one of the long tables, staring down at the warriors.

"Listen to her!" he shouted, "All of you be quiet and listen to her!"

Finally, the warriors quieted down and started to settle onto the benches. I saw Leia sitting at one of the tables, her illustration of the underground forest in front of her. She was adding labels to it, pointing out what we had realized each of the elements was.

"Ty?" Pyra said when he noticed him standing there beside me.

"I want to fight," Ty said.

"You aren't a warrior, Ty. You don't have to do this."

"I want to. I think that I could make a difference."

"Show him," I said to Ty.

"Show me what?" Pyra asked.

"I'm not sure," Ty said to me.

"This is your chance, Ty. You were born to do this. You have a gift unlike anyone else on this planet and you owe it to your father to embrace it."

"What is she talking about, Ty?" Pyra asked.

I saw Ty turn back to the warrior and then look over his shoulder. His eyes narrowed as I had seen them do earlier. An instant later a massive sword fell from the hooks holding it on the stone wall and shot forward, narrowly missing hitting Pyra. Ty snatched it out of the air and lowered it slowly to his side. The warrior's erupted in shouts and Pyra struggled to get control of them again.

Before he could respond, the doors to the meeting room swung open and I heard the scuffle of people entering. I turned around and felt my heart constrict painfully.

15

———

Ty turned toward the doors to the meeting hall and saw two warriors dragging a thrashing woman between them. Zuri came up behind them and he saw blood trickling down her chest from a large gash across the front of her shoulder. Ero walked beside her, his jaw twitching and his eyes wild with fury. The woman gripped between the warriors was small and plain. She wasn't pretty or interesting-looking like the human women who had come to call his planet home, and suddenly it struck him... she was unnoticeable.

Samira looked stricken beside him like she knew who the woman was.

"Who is that?" Ty asked.

"She was the flight attendant on our voyage from Earth. She mans all of the trips on the university shuttle."

"So, she would have been the attendant when Eden, Eliana, and Leia came here, too?"

Samira nodded.

"This is who had been helping Ullie and the Klimnu," Zuri said with acid in her voice.

Pyra glared down at the woman, who stared defiantly back at him.

"I don't understand," he said, "Who is this woman?"

"She has been posing as a flight attendant on all of the shuttles from Earth. She was getting information from us and bringing it back to Ullie and the Klimnu. That's how they knew that Leia was coming and were able to intercept the flight and kidnap her. The transporter in the middle of the tunnel wasn't to get her from the cliffs to the underground chamber. It was to get her from the ship to the tunnel. That's why she disappeared into her quarters as soon as the ship landed, and why she told us that she never got off in between voyages. She has a transporter in her quarters that brought her directly into the tunnel so that she was never seen moving in or out. That meant she could meet Ullie at the mouth of the tunnel and collect materials to bring to the Klimnu and go through the transporter again to the get to the chamber, or she could go directly to the chamber."

"Why would you help them?" Leia shouted at her, "How could you help such vile creatures?"

The flight attendant scoffed.

"You consider the Klimnu the vile creatures? My grandmother came here when she was young. She was one of the first human visitors to ever step foot on this planet. I bet if you asked the king and queen, though, they wouldn't even admit that she was ever here."

"Your grandmother?" Zuri spat, stepping around to look at the attendant, "You told me that she said humans should never leave Earth and that you should always keep to your own kind; that she didn't even know what you were doing for a living."

"She doesn't know what I do, and she does believe that humans should keep to their own kind. That belief comes from her brief time here. When I was younger she told me stories about how vicious and violent the Denynso men were. She told me that they were all cruel and insatiable. They would just as soon slit your throat as they would bed you. She fell in love with one of the warriors who was here at the time, but as soon as he was finished with her, he had the king and queen rescind her permissions to be here and sent her back. She has never recovered and we all watched her suffer and were limited for our entire lives because of it."

"You can't blame our entire species on the fact that your grandmother fell in love with a warrior who wasn't her mate. There are very clear warnings before any humans come to Uoria," Pyra told her, "There have been since the very first visitor. One of the reasons we limit how long humans can stay here, especially human women, is because of situations like that. We are a warrior race. It is who we are. Your grandmother knew that before she ever stepped foot here, and if she let a warrior bed her knowing that he wasn't her mate, she can only hold herself responsible."

"Bring her back to the shuttle and lock her in the pod. Make it very clear that she is never to come near this planet again and that if she does, we cannot be held responsible for our actions."

The warriors turned and dragged the woman out of the meeting hall. As soon as they were gone, Samira ran from Ty's side over to Zuri.

"Are you alright?" she asked, touching the gash on her chest.

"You left Pyra's knife in the tunnel," she said, "Guess who found it?"

"Oh, god. I am so sorry, Zuri."

"It's alright. The warriors were a little resistant to taking her into custody until they saw her swinging at me with it. A little blood is worth getting her off the planet and away from us."

"We need to get you to Ciyrs."

"What are we going to do about the Klimnu?"

Everyone turned to look at Pyra. His shoulders were square and his Mohawk seemed to have gotten taller and sharper. Ty knew his body was preparing for war.

16

───────

"I'm not staying here, Ty," I said, following Ty to the door to the meeting hall.

"Yes, you are. You and the other women are going to stay here where you'll be safe while we go take care of the Klimnu."

"If it wasn't for us you would have no idea how they were getting into the compound."

"And we appreciate that, Samira, but the Klimnu are vicious, horrible creatures. I am not letting my mate be in harm's way. I'll be back soon enough and we'll go home, together, and start our life."

I loved the way that sounded, but I hated that after everything we did to help them, the warriors were just going to leave us women behind so that we could sit around and be worried about them, feeling useless.

"Ty," I started to protest again, but he shook his head.

"No, Samira. You aren't coming with me. You have to stay here and look after Zuri and Eden. We know what we're doing."

He kissed me a final time and joined the warriors standing at the door. They all looked so powerful standing there. Their bodies had changed with the coming war, giving off even more of the intense, animalistic impression that already made them so intimidating. Pyra opened the door and they marched out, slamming the door behind them. The meeting hall fell silent. All of the other women were sitting along one of the benches, but I couldn't sit. I paced around in front of them for a few minutes, tormented by the thought of Ty and the other men marching off into such incredible danger and us just sitting here.

I knew that they had planned out their attack carefully. It was designed perfectly, but I was still terrified for them. It was not enough for me to sit and wait and hope that what they had come up with would actually work. Finally, I stalked across the room to one of the wall sconces that held torches and pulled one down.

"What are you doing?" Zuri asked, standing up.

She had a bandage covering the wound on her chest, the sweet smell of the healing potion Ciyrs had finally perfected seeping through it toward me.

"I can't just sit here. That's my mate out there, and my new home. We started this for them, and I'm not going to let them finish it alone."

I started toward the door and heard footsteps coming after me.

"I'm coming with you."

I turned around and saw Eliana close behind me. I knew of the incredible power that she shared with her mate and that it could be an intense force against the Klimnu. I nodded and looked back at the other women.

"Zuri and Eden, neither of you can come in your conditions. Leia, I'm trusting you to take care of them and make sure that the potion is ready for when the warriors come back. Eden can help you apply it. Stay connected with your mates as much as possible, but don't let them know you're worried. You don't want to distract them. If anything happens, Eliana will connect with Eden."

Eliana grabbed another torch and we rushed out of the meeting hall in the direction of the cliffs. She knew the land better than I did and I let her lead. The darkness had built around the planet and the feeling of impending battle hung heavy over the compound. I ducked my head and continued to run. The fear dissipated as we reached the cliff. I knew that I had faced my own share of battles before and I had come out alive even though then I had little to live for. Now I had everything to live for and I was either going to save it, or die trying.

We climbed the cliff carefully and headed through the chamber into the tunnel. Now that we knew that the transporter was somewhere in the middle, we stayed as close to each other as possible. We didn't want to risk one of us transporting and the other one not. The steepness of the tunnel and the haste in my motivation made my steps fast and for a moment I felt like I was falling. I regained my control and we pushed our way through the tight passage, me guiding her since she had not been with us during the first trip down to the chamber.

"When you start to feel moving air," I whispered to her, "blow out your torch. We don't want to call attention to ourselves."

"Are you sure that the way they planned it out is going to work?" she asked.

"I have to be," I said.

A few more steps and I felt the movement of air against my cheek. We simultaneously blew out our torches, reaching down to hold hands so that we could stay together in the darkness.

"Be very careful where you step," I told her, "Remember that what looks like water is actually the sky. You don't want to fall into it. Stay on the branches."

We continued forward and suddenly saw flickers of light ahead of us. I pressed myself to the wall of the tunnel and glanced around the corner at the underground forest. Just as Pyra had expected, the entire chamber crawled with slimy, skeletal creatures. Some climbed on the trees, others dangled from the vines, and still others lounged between the branches that looked like roots traversing the ground. One stood on a particularly large branch, releasing small illuminated balls onto the ground so that they floated through the space and filled it with a soft light.

"How much longer?" Eliana whispered.

I brought a finger to my lips to quiet her. There was a slight cracking sound and a few of the Klimnu looked up toward the ceiling. There was another slight sound, and then another. Suddenly the entire space filled with loud, soul-shaking screams as the Denynso warriors dropped down through the holes they had found and enlarged earlier in the day.

The Klimnu scrambled, caught completely off guard by the warriors using their own tactic against them. Following Pyra's instructions, they clung to the trees, wrapping their muscled arms through the hanging vines to keep them from falling into the reflection of the sky.

None of us knew what would happen if someone was to fall. It seemed that it would be like shooting directly up into the sky, and none of the warriors wanted to test the theory.

Chaos ensued quickly. I watched the Klimnu thrash at the warriors, biting and clawing at them, and crawling up onto each other so that they could better access the men staying close to the trees. I watched as three of the warriors wrapped both arms in the vines and used their powerful upper bodies to pull themselves up so that they were suspended between two trees, enabling them to kick at the Klimnu that approached. The hard hits sent the creatures flying backwards. One skidded across the branches and slipped into the sky, disappearing completely. I heard nothing and there was a moment of intense realization among to warriors.

Suddenly Eliana surged forward. I saw her run toward a Klimnu climbing up the side of a tree toward Pyra and grab it by its neck. The disgusting creature's scream reverberated through the space and I nearly gagged on the scent of burning flesh and ash. In only a few seconds, the Klimnu she held disintegrated into a pile of ash. Inspired by her courage, I left my place in the tunnel and started forward. Before I could even step off of the small section of land in front of the tunnel and onto one of the branches, though, one of the Klimnu dropped down in front of me.

His eyes rolled as he licked his lips and clicked his long claws together. I saw his fangs dripping with saliva and felt my stomach flip. He reached for me, and I let out a scream. I knew that Ty would recognize it immediately.

"Samira!" I heard him yell.

"Ty," I screamed back, "Get me."

I felt the tug in my belly and let go of my control of my body. My feet left the ground and as I rose above the creature who had been threatening me, I planted a kick in the middle of his face, tossing him back into the sky. I continued to kick as I flew toward Ty, managing to knock a few more of the creatures out of their paths toward the warriors. When I reached Ty, he pulled me against him and instructed me to hold onto one of the hanging vines. He pointed out a branch that started just a couple of feet beneath us.

"Jump onto that branch. Keep holding onto the vine for stability, and just swing onto it. Stay there."

I did as he asked, closing my eyes as I held tightly to the vine and jumped. I hit the branch and immediately tangled a vine around my legs to hold me more securely in place. The smell of burning flesh had gotten nearly overwhelming and all around me I could hear the screams of the Klimnu and the men as they clashed. Ty used his mind to lift the creatures and toss them out of the way, Ero ran with such incredible speed that he was able to run from branch to branch across the sky without sinking, Pyra literally snapped and tore the creatures to pieces with his bare hands.

"Jem, no!"

Ty's sudden, tormented scream brought a lull to the battle. I looked around and realized that there were only a few Klimnu left. A warrior stood far out on one of the branches, locked in a struggle with one of the larger of the creatures. Two more had abandoned their previous goals and were now creeping toward the warrior, determined to take a Denynso life. Jem turned to land a solid punch in the middle of one of the creature's faces and knock him off balance. He started to fall, and then grabbed onto Jem's shirt to regain his balance. I looked up and could see Ty struggling to pick him up.

Jem rose a few feet off of the branch, but the Klimnu tugged at him. Pyra rushed down the tree toward them, but Jem held up a hand.

"Stop, Pyra. Don't come out here. You're what they want. Remember, they are trying to get to Creia. If they kill our leader, they weaken our defenses and they can get to the king. There's only one way to stop them, and that is to eliminate them."

Jem thrashed for a few moments, nearly working his way back down to the branch. The creatures tugged him.

"Let me pick you up!" Ty screamed.

"No! Put me down. I'll be fine. These are the last of their kind here and there is something about me that they don't know."

One of the creatures scoffed and reached out a hand to claw Jem's face.

"And what is that?" he asked mockingly.

Jem smiled up at all of the warriors.

"I've always wanted to fly."

The warrior wrapped his arms around the three Klimnu and launched himself backwards off of the branch, disappearing into the darkness of the sky. Eliana screamed and I heard Ty cry out the warrior's name. He disentangled himself from the vine and started down the tree toward where Jem had fallen. I reached out and grabbed him by his shirt.

"Stop, Ty."

"I let him die! He was right there."

"Stop. He did what he wanted to do. It's alright. He's among the stars now."

Ty leaned down and pulled Samira out of the hole in the forest floor. Around them the rest of the warriors were emerging from the moss and taking deep, long breaths of the night air. It was the first night in as long as any of them could remember where no one had to be afraid.

"If that sky was a reflection," he asked, looking up into the sky above them, "That means it was just as much an illusion as the Klimnu were able to make themselves."

"Yes."

"Then where is Jem? If that wasn't the real sky, where did he go?"

Samira wrapped an arm around Ty's waist and hugged him close, knowing that it was him that needed her strength now.

"I don't know, baby. Wherever he is, though, he saved Uoria."

They walked slowly back to the meeting hall, many nursing wounds, but all alive. Jem was the only one they had lost. When they got inside the hall, Ciyrs, Eliana, Leia, and Eden immediately went to work patching up injuries with the healing potions they had created. Samira had instructed them on how to create several different types of ointments so that they could handle a variety of injuries quickly and effectively without having to go through the challenging and emotionally charged process of healing.

Samira and Ty stepped back and watched everything happening, the entire scene surreal and overwhelming. They watched the moments unfolding in front of her as if they were a series of postcards flashing past her eyes, or individual cells from a movie suddenly coming to life, each contained within its own crystalline second of existence.

Gyyx and Leia kissed in a corner, the tremendous warrior holding his tiny mate off of the ground so that he didn't have to lean down to her.

Eliana and Ciyrs exchanged meaningful glances as they worked with the warriors, occasionally pausing between patients to touch each other's cheeks or nuzzle noses.

Ero and Zuri sat on one of the benches facing each other, his legs straddling the bench and hers wrapped around his hips as they rested their foreheads against each other's and murmured unheard sentiments.

Pyra was on his knees in front of Eden, his arms wrapped tightly around her hips and his mouth pressing to her belly over and over again as she stroked the back of his head and wiped tears from under her eyes.

Each moment was singular and perfect. The couples existed only for each other right then and it didn't matter what else was going on around them. Ty felt a surge of nearly overwhelming love for Samira and turned to face her.

"I don't know how to do this," he said and she looked at him with worry in her eyes.

"Do what?" she asked.

Ty reached up to tuck a strand of her long, dark hair behind her ear and brush his fingertips across her cheekbone.

"Marry me, Samira."

She looked startled and then a veil of confusion fell over her eyes.

"What?"

"Marry me."

"You said that Denynso don't get married."

"We don't, but humans also don't live on Uoria, and as you might have noticed, that tradition hasn't held up well in the last few months either."

"Do you even understand what marriage is?"

"Not entirely, but you can teach me. I know that it is to humans what our bonding is to us."

"Well, as close as it comes. It's about making promises to each other and standing up in front of everyone that you care about and making public vows committing yourselves to each other."

"We can do that."

"You don't have to do this, Ty. I know that we are mated. That's enough for me."

"I know I don't have to, I want to. I want to give you the experience that you would have had if you had ended up with a human man. I want to know that your commitment to me means the same to you."

"It means more to me, Ty. I love you with everything I have and I am fully and completely committed to spending my life here with you."

"Do you have friends on Earth? A family?"

"A few, I suppose. My mother is there. Though I rarely see her. She hides from my stepfather even more than I do."

"Wouldn't you want them to see you get married? We don't celebrate bonding here. It is a very personal experience, as you know." She smiled and glanced away briefly, "But I think that there is nothing in this galaxy worth celebrating more than what I found with you. I waited for you for my entire life and I know that I resisted you at first, but that only makes me love you all the more because I was so close to pushing you away. I could have lost you forever and I would have spent the rest of my life alone and longing for you rather than spending each moment treasuring you. So, please, Samira. Bring me back to Earth and marry me."

"Then we'll come back to Uoria?"

"Of course."

Ty watched her eyes and saw them sparkle. A smile broke across her lips and she jumped forward into his arms.

"Yes. Yes, I will marry you." She pulled back and looked him in the face again, "Thank you, Ty."

The moment between them broke as a hush fell over the meeting hall. They turned their attention to the opposite side of the room where the king and queen were entering. Creia climbed onto the stage and reached down to help Theia up, leaning forward to touch a kiss to her fingers that he held as she settled into place beside him.

He looked out over the crowd and one by one the warriors approached, standing three deep and several across in front of him. They lowered to their knees and bowed their heads to the king, who reached over them with one hand. Ty left Samira's side and joined them, taking his place at the back of the group, now both a warrior and a nurturer.

"I have never been more proud than I am tonight to be the king of this great tribe," Creia said, his voice low with emotion. "Tonight, these men," he turned to look directly at Samira, "and women, put their lives at risk to protect our compound, our people, and our future. We lost one of our warriors. Though he was just one of our great numbers, his life was not inconsequential. We will miss him in everything that we do, and remember his sacrifice for generations to come. Even he, though, would not want this night to be about sadness. We will mourn for our Jem tomorrow. Tonight is a night of celebration."

A cheer rose up from the crowd and the warriors climbed to their feet. Ty rushed forward to the king and queen, calling to Samira in his mind for her to join him. As soon as she was by his side, he stepped close to the edge of the stage.

"Sir," he said, and the king turned to face him.

His face lit up and he reached out to touch Ty's hand, crouching down at the edge of the stage.

"I heard magnificent things about you, Ty. I am so proud of you, and your father would be, too."

Ty felt emotion burning in his throat and nodded his acknowledgment.

"Thank you. I come to you with an official request."

"What can I do for you?"

"I need permission to travel to Earth along with a few of the warriors and the human women."

"Is everything alright?"

Ty turned and smiled at Samira.

"We're getting married."

There was a high-pitched scream behind them and Ty whirled around to see Eden standing just a few feet away, one hand clutching her belly and the other covering her mouth. Pyra ran to her side and wrapped his arm around her.

"Eden? What's wrong? Is it the baby?"

Eden shook her head rapidly and pointed at Ty and Samira.

"They're getting married!"

A ripple of whispers and exclamations rolled back through the room and Ty could pinpoint when each of the human women heard the news. While most of the Denynso didn't even know what the word "married" meant and were questioning the entire concept, each of the human women let out a delighted scream.

"You want to get married?" the king asked.

"I am the only one of my kind to have my power, I might as well be the first of my kind to get married." He chuckled, but then his face grew serious, "With everything that Samira has done for me, there will never be enough ways that I can show her how much I love her. This is just one more way that I can try. You want to promote understanding and cooperation with the humans. Since so many of them have found their way to us, don't you think it's time that we learn about their customs as well?"

"I do," Eliana said and the other human women laughed.

"You have my absolute permission and admiration," Creia said and stood so that he could go back to his wife.

Ty turned and kissed Samira. Behind him he could hear the other human women talking to their mates. He laughed against Samira's mouth. He had a feeling his was not going to be the only wedding the Denynso saw. He turned and saw Pyra nod, then reach down and rub Eden's belly again. Ty smiled. There was so much waiting for them in the future. Now with Samira's hand in his, the threat of the Klimnu gone, and the demons from his past no longer tormenting him, Ty finally felt ready to face each moment and discover what lay just ahead.